Book 2

HER
DAUGHTER'S
DREAM

HER DAUGHTER'S DREAM

FRANCINE RIVERS

Tyndale House Publishers, Inc., Carol Stream, Illinois

Visit Tyndale's exciting Web site at www.tyndale.com.

Check out the latest about Francine Rivers at www.francinerivers.com.

TYNDALE and Tyndale's quill logo are registered trademarks of Tyndale House Publishers, Inc.

Her Daughter's Dream

Designed by Beth Sparkman

Edited by Kathryn S. Olson

Published in association with the literacy agency of Browne and Miller Literary Associates, LLC, 410 Michigan Avenue, Suite 460, Chicago, IL 60605.

Unless otherwise indicated, Scripture quotations are taken from the New American Standard Bible,® copyright © 1960, 1962, 1963, 1968, 1971, 1972, 1973, 1975, 1977, 1995 by The Lockman Foundation. Used by permission.

Scripture quotations in chapter 41 are taken from the *Holy Bible*, New Living Translation, copyright © 1996, 2004, 2007 by Tyndale House Foundation. Used by permission of Tyndale House Publishers, Inc., Carol Stream, Illinois 60188. All rights reserved.

Library of Congress Cataloging-in-Publication Data

Rivers, Francine, date.
  Her daughter's dream / Francine Rivers.
    p. cm. — (Marta's legacy ; 2)
  ISBN 978-1-4143-3409-7
  1. Mothers and daughters—Fiction. 2. Self-actualization (Psychology) in women—Fiction.
3. Domestic fiction. I. Title.
  PS3568.I83165H46 2010
  813'.54—dc22   2010020821

ISBN 978-1-4143-3684-8 (International Trade Paper Edition)

Printed in the United States of America

16 15 14 13 12 11 10
7 6 5 4 3 2 1

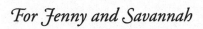

For Jenny and Savannah

Acknowledgments

Most of the novel you are about to read is purely fictional, though there are bits and pieces of personal family history woven throughout. The manuscript has taken various forms over the last two years, and in the end morphed into a saga. Many people have helped me in the process of writing the stories of Marta and Hildemara in the first volume and Carolyn and May Flower Dawn in the second. I want to thank each and every one of them.

First of all my husband, Rick, has ridden the storm through this one, listening to every variation of the stories as the characters took form in my imagination and acting as my first editor.

Every family needs a historian, and my brother, Everett, has played that role to perfection. He sent me hundreds of family pictures that helped flesh out the story. I also received invaluable help from my cousin Maureen Rosiere, who described in detail our grandparents' almond and wine-grape ranch, a pattern I used in this novel. Both my husband and my brother shared their Vietnam experiences with me.

Kitty Briggs, Shannon Coibion (our daughter), and Holly Harder shared their experiences as military wives. Holly has been a constant help to me. I know of no other person on the planet who can find information on the Internet faster! Whenever I ran into a wall, Holly tore it down. Thanks, Holly!

Holly's son, U.S. Army Lieutenant Daniel Harder, gave me information on the engineering and ROTC programs at Cal Poly. He is now on active duty. Our prayers are with him.

Ila Vorderbrueggen, a nurse and personal friend of my mother's, helped me fill in information about long-term patient care in the Arroyo del Valle Sanatorium. I've enjoyed our correspondence.

Kurt Thiel and Robert Schwinn answered questions about Inter-Varsity Christian Fellowship. Keep up the good work, gentlemen!

Globus tour guide Joppy Wissink rerouted a bus so that Rick and I had the opportunity to walk around my grandmother's hometown of Steffisburg, Switzerland.

All along the course of this project, I have had brainstorming partners when I needed them. Colleen Phillips raised questions and encouraged me from the beginning. Robin Lee Hatcher and Sunni Jeffers jumped in with ideas and questions when I didn't know which way to go. My agent, Danielle Egan-Miller, and her associate, Joanna MacKenzie, helped me see how to restructure the novel to show the story I wanted to tell.

I would also like to thank Karen Watson of Tyndale House Publishers for her insights and encouraging support. She helped me see my characters more clearly. And, of course, every writer needs a good editor. I am blessed with one of the best, Kathy Olson. She makes revision work exciting and challenging rather than painful.

Finally, I thank the Lord for my mother and grandmother. Their lives and Mom's journals first inspired the idea of writing about mother-daughter relationships. They were both hardworking women of faith. They both passed on some years ago, but I cling to the promise that they are still very much alive and undoubtedly enjoying one another's company. One day I will see them again.

January 1951

Dear Rosie,

Trip called. Hildemara is back in the hospital. She had been there for nearly two months before they got around to telling me about it. But now they want my help. My sweet Hildemara Rose, the smallest, the weakest, the most dependent of my children. She has struggled from the beginning. And now, somehow, I must find a way to give her the courage for one more struggle.

I didn't always see it, but recently the Lord has reminded me of all the times Hildemara's courage and spunk have served her well. She chose her own path in life and pursued it against all odds (and against my advice, I might add!). She followed that husband of hers from one military base to another, finding apartments in strange cities, making new friends. She crossed the country by herself and came home to help Bernhard and Elizabeth hold on to the Musashis' land, despite threats and fire and bricks through their windows.

And I needn't remind you of her response when faced with the same kind of abuse that our dear Elise succumbed to so many years ago. She was smart enough to run. My daughter has courage!

I have been forced to admit that I have always favored Hildemara a little above the others. (Is any of this news to you, my dear friend? I suspect you know me better than I know myself.) From the moment my first daughter came into the world, she has held a special place in my heart. Niclas always said she looked like me, and I'm afraid it's true. And we both know how little regard my father had for my plain looks. And like Elise, she was frail.

How could a mother's heart fail to respond to such a combination? I did what I felt I had to do. From the start I determined that I would not cripple Hildemara Rose the way Mama crippled Elise. But now I wonder if I did the right thing. Did I push her too hard and, in so doing, push her away? She wouldn't even let her husband call me for help until they both thought she was past the point of no return. I wish now I'd been more like my mother, with her gracious and loving spirit, and less like my father. Yes, that's right. I see clearly that I inherited some of his selfish and cruel ways. Don't try to convince me otherwise, Rosie. We both know it's true.

Now my hope and prayer is that I can bring Hildemara close again. I am praying for more time. I want Hildemara to know how much I love her, how proud I am of her and her accomplishments. I want to mend my relationship with her. I want to learn how to serve my daughter. I, who have rebelled all my life at the very thought of servanthood.

I started thinking about Lady Daisy and our afternoons at Kew and tea in the conservatory. I think it's about time I shared some of these experiences with Hildemara Rose. . . . I will make all the wonderful sweets and savories for Hildemara Rose that I once served to Lady Daisy. I will pour India tea and lace it with cream and conversation.

God willing, I will win back my daughter.

Your loving friend,
Marta

Hildemara Rose

HILDEMARA LAY IN the darkness, her nightgown damp with perspiration. Night sweats again—she should be used to them by now. Her roommate, Lydia, snored softly. Lydia had been steadily improving since she arrived six weeks ago, which only served to depress Hildemara more. Lydia had gained two pounds; Hildie lost the same amount.

Two months and still no improvement, hospital bills mounting daily, crushing Trip's dreams beneath their weight. Her husband came each afternoon. He'd looked so tired yesterday, and no wonder when he had to work full-time and then go home and take care of all her duties: laundry, cooking, seeing to Charlie's and Carolyn's needs. Hildie grieved over her children—Charlie on his own so much of the time, Carolyn being raised by an indifferent babysitter. She hadn't touched or seen her children since Trip brought her to the hospital. She missed them so much, she felt physical pain most of the time. Or was that just the *mycobacterium tuberculosis* consuming her lungs and decimating her body?

Pushing the covers back, Hildie went to the bathroom to rinse her face with cool water. Who was that gaunt, pale ghost staring back at her in the mirror? She studied the sharp angles, the pallor, the shadows beneath her hazel eyes, the lackluster brown color of the hair around her shoulders.

I'm dying, Lord, aren't I? I haven't enough strength to fight this disease. And now I have to face Mama's disappointment in me. She called me a coward last time. Maybe I am giving up. She cupped water in her hands and pressed her face into it. *Oh, God, I love Trip so much. And Charlie and sweet little Carolyn. But I'm tired, Lord, so very tired. I'd rather die now, than linger and leave a legacy of debt.*

She'd told Trip as much last week. She only wished she could die at home, rather than in a sterile hospital room twenty miles away. His face had twisted in anguish. "Don't say that. You're not going to die. You have to stop worrying about the bills. If your mother came, I could bring you home. Maybe then . . ."

She'd argued. Mama wouldn't come. She'd never helped before. Mama hated the very idea of being a servant. And that's exactly what she'd be—a full-time maid and washerwoman, babysitter and cook, without pay. Hildie said she couldn't ask such a thing of Mama.

Trip called Mama anyway, and then he went down on Saturday with Charlie and Carolyn so he and Mama could talk things over. He'd come out this morning. "Your mother said yes. I'm taking a couple of days off to get things ready for her." He wanted to repaint Carolyn's room, buy a nice, comfortable bed, a new dresser and mirror, maybe a rocking chair. "Charlie and Carolyn will have the small bedroom. You and I'll be together. . . ."

"I can't sleep with you, Trip. I need to be quarantined." She could barely absorb the news that Mama had agreed to help. "I can't be near the children." At least, she could hear them; she could see them. Mama said she'd come. Mama was moving in. Hildie trembled, taking it all in. She felt a little sick to her stomach. "I'll need a hospital bed." She gave Trip instructions about her room. No rug. A window shade rather than curtains. The simpler the room, the easier to keep sanitized. Trip looked so hopeful, it broke her heart. He leaned down to kiss her forehead before he left. "You'll be home soon."

Now, she couldn't sleep. Rather than get back into bed, Hildie sat in a chair by the window and looked out at the stars. What was it going to be like, having Mama living under her roof, taking care of her, taking care of her children, taking care of all the chores that needed to be done so Trip didn't have to do everything? Would Mama despise her for not fighting harder? Her eyes burned; her throat ached just thinking about having to lie in bed sick and helpless while Mama took over her family. She wiped tears away. Of course, Mama would do it all better than she ever could. That realization hurt even more. Mama had always managed everything. Even without Papa, the ranch ran like a well-oiled machine. Mama would fix Trip wonderful meals. Mama would be the one to give Charlie wings. Mama would probably have Carolyn reading before she turned four.

I should be grateful. She cares enough to come and help. I didn't think she did.

When the night air had cooled her, Hildie slipped beneath the covers again.

She wanted to be grateful. She would say thank you, even as she had to watch the life she loved slip away from her. She had fought hard to be free of Mama's expectations, to claim her own life and not live out her mother's impossible dreams. Even the one thing at which she'd excelled would be stripped from her before she closed her eyes for the last time.

Mama would be the nurse. Mama would carry the lantern.

Carolyn

CAROLYN WAS HAPPY that Daddy let her stay with Oma Marta in Murietta until Oma was ready to move to their house. If she had gone home with him and Charlie, she would have had to go to Mrs. Haversal's across the street every day while Charlie was at school and Daddy went to work. It had been like that for a long time, ever since Mommy went away. But now, Mommy was coming home and Oma was coming to stay. It would be wonderful!

Carolyn played with the rag doll Oma had given her, while Oma packed her suitcase with clothing and a trunk with sheets, crochet-trimmed and embroidered pillowcases, two blankets, and a pink rose tea set with tiny silver spoons. Oma put the suitcase and trunk in the back of her new gray Plymouth, and then she stacked two cushions in the front seat so Carolyn could sit high up and see out the window on the long drive home. Oma even let her roll her window down so she could put her hand out and feel the air.

They pulled into the driveway just when Charlie got off the school bus. "Oma!" He came running. Oma took the front door key out from under the flowerpot on the front porch.

Everything had changed inside the house. Carolyn found her bed and dresser in Charlie's room.

A small table stood between Charlie's bed and hers. She went back to her old room and watched Oma swing her suitcase onto a new, bigger bed. The pink walls were now bright yellow, and new lacy white curtains hung over the windows. There was a big dresser with a mirror on top, a little table and lamp, and a rocking chair with flowered cushions.

"I'm going to be very comfortable here." Oma unpacked her clothes and put them away.

Oma stepped to the window and drew the white lacy curtains aside. "I'm going to have to get used to having neighbors this close." She shook her head and turned away. "I'd better get dinner started. Your daddy will be coming home soon."

"Is Mommy coming home?"

"In another day or two." Oma opened the door into the spare bedroom. "This is where she'll be." Leaving Carolyn in the bedroom doorway, Oma headed for the kitchen. Carolyn didn't like the room. It felt cold and strange without a rug on the floor and no curtains on the window, just a shade pulled down to block out the sunlight.

Carolyn came into the kitchen. "Mommy isn't going to like her room."

"It's exactly the way she wants it. Easy to keep clean."

"Mommy likes plants on the windowsill. She likes flowers in a vase." Mommy always had pictures in frames on her dresser.

"Mommy doesn't like germs." Oma peeled potatoes.

"What are germs?"

Oma chuckled. "You'll have to ask your mother."

Oma had dinner ready before Daddy came home from work. They all sat around the kitchen table. "When do you pick her up?" Oma set a pitcher of milk on the table and sat in Mommy's chair.

"Day after tomorrow."

"Plenty to be thankful for, haven't we?" When Oma stretched out her hands, Charlie took one and Carolyn the other. Daddy took their hands too so they made a circle. He hadn't said grace since Mommy went away. He spoke quietly now, calmly, said *amen* and sighed, a smile tugging at his lips. Oma asked questions about his work, and Daddy talked for a long time. When everyone had finished dinner, Daddy stacked the dishes, but Oma shooed him away. "You and the kids go visit or play or whatever you normally do. I'll take care of cleaning up."

Daddy took Charlie outside to play catch. Carolyn sat on the front steps and watched.

Oma handled the baths that night, Charlie first so he could do his homework. She sat on the closed toilet while Carolyn played in the bubble bath. Oma gave Daddy a book to read to them, with Carolyn on one side and Charlie on the other. When he finished, he kissed them both and sent them to bed. Oma tucked them in with prayers.

In the middle of the night, Carolyn awakened. She'd gotten used to sleeping with Oma. Charlie didn't have monsters in his room, but Carolyn worried about Oma. Crawling out of bed, she crept down the hall to her old bedroom and opened the door. Oma snored so loudly, she'd probably scared all the monsters out of the house with the noise she made. Scampering back to Charlie's room, Carolyn dove into bed. Snuggling down into the covers, she looked at Charlie sleeping on the other side of the room, thought of Mommy coming home, and went to sleep smiling.

Daddy left for work right after a breakfast of scrambled eggs, bacon, and fresh-baked biscuits. As soon as Charlie left for school, Oma tipped Carolyn's chin. "Let's go brush your hair and put it in a ponytail. What do you say?" She took Carolyn by the hand and led her into her bedroom. She patted the bed and Carolyn climbed up onto it. While Oma brushed her hair, Carolyn watched her grandmother in the mirror. She liked her white hair and tanned, wrinkled cheeks. She had warm green-brown eyes like Mommy's.

Oma smiled back at her. She brushed Carolyn's long, curly blonde hair into her hand. "You look like Elise. She was my little sister, and she was very, very pretty, just like you." When all the tangles had been worked out, Oma wound a rubber band around Carolyn's hair. "There. That looks better. Don't you think?"

Carolyn looked up. "Is Mommy dying?"

Oma smiled at Carolyn. "No. Your mother is *not* dying." She ran her hand over Carolyn's hair. "She needs rest. That's all. Now that I'm here, she can come home and rest. You'll see your mother every day."

Carolyn didn't see the mixture of emotions in Oma's face that she had seen in Daddy's. Oma didn't look uncertain or sad. She didn't look afraid. Oma wore glasses, but behind them Carolyn saw clear, warm eyes filled with confidence.

Oma told Carolyn they were going for a ride. "I need to get to know the area, find out where things are."

"What things?"

"Grocery store, for one. You and I are going to explore!" She made it sound like a great adventure. "We're going to find a library, where we can check out enough books to last a week. And I want to stop by the church, meet the pastor. Your daddy said you haven't gone for a while, but that's going to change."

"Will Mommy go, too?"

"No. Not for a while."

Oma drove fast, pointing this way and that, while Carolyn perched on pillows, taking in the sights. "Look over there. What do you know! A cheese factory! We'll pick up some good Swiss or Gouda cheese while we're in town. And there's a bank."

Oma took her to lunch at a small café on Main Street. Carolyn ate a hot dog and drank Coke. Before heading home, Oma wanted to wander through a department store. She looked through all the kitchen gadgets and bought a few. Then they went to the grocery store, and Oma filled the big basket. "Time to head home. We want to be there when Charlie gets off the bus."

Oma pulled into the driveway just as the school bus disgorged boys and girls. "Perfect timing!" Charlie ran up the street, whooping. Oma laughed and told him he sounded like a wild Indian. She handed him a bag of groceries. "You can help unload." She gave a smaller bag to Carolyn and carried in another bag and the package from the department store.

Charlie sniffed out the package of Fig Newtons like a bloodhound, opened it, grabbed a handful, and headed out the door to find his friends. Amused, Oma shook her head. "He's like one of my Summer Bedlam boys." Oma tore brown paper from the package and opened a big white box. "Look what I found when we were out shopping." She laid out a small embroidered tablecloth and matching napkins. "You and I and Mommy are going to make high tea every afternoon. It's been years since I've done it, but I have all the recipes right here." She took a worn leather book from her purse and set it on the table. She got a dreamy look on her face. "We're going to make this a special homecoming." She glanced at her watch and suggested they sit on the porch and enjoy the sunshine.

❅ ❅ ❅

When Daddy brought Mommy home, Oma stood, holding Carolyn's hand. Mommy climbed out of the car, waved hello, and went straight into the house. Carolyn called out to her and followed them inside, but her father blocked her. "Leave your mother alone. She's going to bed." Mommy went down the hall into the cold room with the strange bed and closed the door. When Carolyn tried to go around Daddy, he caught hold of her and turned Carolyn around. "Go play outside for a while so Oma and I can talk. Go on now." He gave her a push.

Confused, Carolyn sat on the front steps until Daddy came out. He went right past her, got back into his car, and drove away.

Oma came out onto the front porch. "Your daddy had to go back to work. You'll see him this afternoon."

"Can I see Mommy?"

"No, *Liebling*." She shook her head and ran her hand over

Carolyn's head. "Do you want to stay out here or come inside and help me make lunch?" Carolyn followed Oma back inside.

Her mother didn't come out of her room at all that day, except to use the bathroom. And every day after that was the same way. If she saw Carolyn in the hallway, she waved her away. Mommy didn't sit at the kitchen table for dinner or with the family in the living room when they listened to *Lux Radio Theater*. No one except Daddy and Oma could go into Mommy's room. Daddy often spent all evening behind the closed door while Oma took a book from the pile she'd checked out of the library and read stories to Carolyn and Charlie.

Carolyn often went outside after Charlie went to school. One day she picked daffodils that had sprouted up from bulbs Mommy had planted a long time ago. Mommy loved flowers. They made her happy. When Carolyn had a fistful, she went inside, crept along the corridor to Mommy's room, and opened the door. Mommy lay on her side, sleeping. Carolyn tiptoed to the bed. She stood chin level with the top of the mattress.

"Mommy?" Reaching up, Carolyn touched her mother's hand. Her mother's eyes flickered open. A smile curved her mouth. Carolyn held up the daffodils. "I brought you flowers, Mommy, to make you feel better."

Mommy's expression changed. Pulling up the sheet, she covered her mouth. "You're not supposed to come in here, Carolyn. Go! Now!"

Her lip trembled. "I want to be with you."

"You can't be with me." Her mother's eyes filled with tears. "Get out of here, Carolyn. Do what you're told."

"Mommy . . ." Carolyn reached out to give her the flowers.

Her mother reared back. "Mama!" Mommy started to cough. "Get away from me!" she choked out between coughs. When Oma appeared in the doorway, Mommy waved frantically. "Mama! Get her out of here! Get her away from me!" Sobbing now, still coughing, Mommy bunched the sheet over her mouth and hunched over. "Keep her out!"

Oma hustled Carolyn out of the room and closed the door firmly. Frightened, confused, Carolyn wailed. Oma picked her up and carried her into the living room. "Hush now! You didn't do anything wrong. Listen to me." She sat in the rocker. "Mommy's sick. You can't go in that room. If you do, she'll go away again. You don't want that, do you?"

"No." Why couldn't she go in? Oma did. Daddy did. Charlie stood in the doorway and talked to Mommy. Why did she have to stay away?

"Shhhh . . ." Oma lifted Carolyn into her lap and rocked her. Carolyn stuck her thumb in her mouth and leaned against her grandmother. "Everything is going to be fine, *Liebling*. Your mother is going to get better. You'll have plenty of time with her then."

Carolyn never went into Mommy's room after that. The closest she came was standing against the wall outside the door when Oma took in a tray of food. She could catch a glimpse of Mommy then. When the weather warmed, her mother came out of her room wearing a pair of slacks and a sweater. She sat on the front porch, where Oma served tea, egg salad and dill sandwiches, and pecan cookies. Carolyn waited inside until Oma told her she could come out, too. She sat in the chair on the farthest end of the porch as far away from her mother as she could get. Her mother drew the blue sweater more tightly around her thin body. "It's cold."

Oma poured tea. "It's seventy-three degrees, Hildemara Rose. You need fresh air."

"It's hard to keep warm even with the sun shining, Mama."

"I'll get you a blanket." Oma put another sandwich on Mommy's plate.

"No blanket, Mama. It's better if we try to look as normal as possible."

"Normal? The neighborhood already knows, Hildemara Rose. Why do you think they all stay away?" Oma gave a tight laugh. "Cowards! The lot of them."

Mommy nibbled at the small sandwich. "You're a wonderful cook, Mama."

"I learned from the best." Oma set her teacup in its saucer. "I learned from Rosie's mother. They had a hotel. I've told you that, haven't I? Chef Brennholtz tutored me at the *Hotel Germania*. He returned to Germany and got caught up in the war. Last I heard, he was chef to one of the ranking Nazis. After Warner Brennholtz, I worked for the Fourniers in Montreaux. Solange shared her French recipes. Lady Daisy's cook, Enid, taught me how to make these tea cakes." Oma talked about Lady Daisy's love of Kew Gardens. Oma pushed her in a wheelchair, and they visited the park every day. "It was hard work, but I never minded. I love English gardens. Of course, it's too hot in Murietta. . . ."

Oma and Mommy talked about Carolyn, too. "She needs a playmate."

"Well, the mothers won't want their children having anything to do with her."

"I've been thinking. It might be good to get a puppy."

"A puppy?"

"For Carolyn."

"I don't know, Mama. A dog is a big responsibility."

"It wouldn't hurt her to learn a little. It might make her less dependent." Oma smiled at Carolyn. "She's become my little shadow."

Mommy leaned her head back and closed her eyes. "I'll talk to Trip." She sounded so tired.

That night at the dinner table, Daddy, Oma, and Charlie talked about getting a puppy. Daddy suggested buying a cocker spaniel. "Small enough to live inside the house and big enough that it couldn't squeeze through the fence."

"You don't have to *buy* a dog." Oma gave a short laugh. "People are always trying to give pups away. Any mutt will do."

Charlie groaned loudly. "Not a mutt. Can't we get a German shepherd, Dad?" He'd stayed overnight with a friend whose family had a new television set. "Roy Rogers has a German shepherd. Bullet runs so fast, he's like a streak of lightning."

Oma looked unconvinced. "And where's he going to run? A big dog like that needs space."

Charlie wasn't about to give up. "We've got a yard in front and a yard in back."

Dad kept eating. "I wouldn't have to worry as much with a police dog around. He'd have to be trained, though. I know someone who can give me pointers."

A few days later, Dad lifted a ball of fur with drooping ears and bright brown eyes out of his car. He handed the pup to Carolyn, who snuggled it against her chest. "Hang on. He wiggles a lot. Don't drop him." He laughed as the pup licked Carolyn's face. "I think he likes you."

After that, Carolyn spent most of the day outside with the puppy, which they named Bullet. When she went inside, he sat by the front door and whined until she came back out. Mommy would come out and sit on the porch while Oma worked in the kitchen, and Carolyn ran around the yard, Bullet on her heels, leaping, yipping.

❆ ❆ ❆

Whenever Oma went anywhere, Carolyn went with her. Sometimes they drove as far as the strawberry fields in Niles, where Oma talked with the Japanese farmers and bought flats of fruit to make jam. Other times they went to the cheese factory by the bridge over the creek that ran through Paxtown. Oma would take her into the storage room with the old Greek gentleman, who bored samples from big wheels of cheese while he and Oma talked of their old countries. Oma ran all the errands for the family: she shopped at Hagstrom's grocery store, picked up supplies for repairs at Kohln's Hardware, and bought clothes for Charlie and Carolyn from Doughtery's department store. Sometimes Mommy argued with her about that.

Every Sunday, Oma took Carolyn to the Presbyterian church while Daddy and Mommy and Charlie stayed home. Daddy always said he had work to do, and Charlie stayed home because Daddy did. Once a month, Oma took Carolyn with her to the farm in

Murietta. While Oma talked with the Martins, Carolyn climbed into the tree house or fed carrots to the white rabbit or watched the chickens. Carolyn slept with Oma when they visited the farm.

Carolyn didn't suck her thumb when she slept in Oma's big bed. She curled up against Oma and felt warm and secure. She dreamed about tea parties with the white rabbit that ate carrots from her hand. He stood on his back legs, tapped his foot, and told her he wanted ice cream tomorrow. She giggled in her sleep.

Everything felt good and safe and comfortable.

3

1952

It took almost a year, but Mommy got better, just like Oma said she would. She spent more time out of her room than in it. She sat at the kitchen table with the family, and she spent time in the living room, though she didn't encourage Carolyn to sit beside her or get too close. "Just play on the rug where I can watch you." Charlie built forts with Lincoln Logs; Carolyn colored in her coloring books or sat plastered to Oma's side, listening to another story.

Often at night, Carolyn would hear Mommy and Oma talking. Sometimes they raised their voices.

"I can do the dishes, Hildemara."

"I'm not an invalid anymore."

"Calm down—"

"I don't want to be calm. I don't want to sit by and see you do everything for Trip and my children. I'm strong enough now to do some of the work around here."

"I'm trying to help!"

"You've helped enough, Mama. Sometimes I think you help too much."

Once Carolyn overheard Daddy. "That's between you and your mother. Stop complaining! She saved us, Hildie. We'd be further in debt than we are now if she hadn't come and helped us out."

"That doesn't mean it can go on like this forever, Trip. This is *my* family. Mine!"

"You're being ridiculous."

"You don't see what I see. I'm losing—"

"It isn't a contest."

"You don't understand!"

Carolyn became frightened when her parents fought. She stuck closer to Oma, hoping she'd never leave.

Mommy moved back into Daddy's big bedroom. A truck came and took away the hospital bed and rolling tray table. Mommy scrubbed the floors and walls and painted the room pink. Daddy moved Carolyn's furniture in. Oma found a round braided rug and trunk for her toys, and she bought fabric with flowers all over it and made curtains.

Bullet jumped the fence and chased the mailman. The poor dog had to be on a chain after that. Daddy built a house big enough for him and Carolyn to sit inside.

Oma said having a room all your own was a luxury, but Carolyn didn't like being in a room by herself. She was afraid the monsters would move in under her bed again.

When Oma packed her suitcase, Carolyn watched, confused. "Where are you going?"

"Murietta."

Carolyn went back to her room and packed her little suitcase, too, just like she always did when Oma took her down to Murietta for a weekend at the farm.

"You're not going with me, Carolyn." Oma sat on her bed and lifted Carolyn to her knee. "You're going to stay here with your mommy."

"I want to go with you."

"You belong here."

"No, I don't."

Oma hugged her and kissed the top of her head. "I hope I haven't stayed too long." She set Carolyn on her feet. "You be a good girl for your mother."

"I love *you*."

Oma cupped her face and kissed each of her cheeks. "I love you, too, *Liebling*. Don't you ever forget that." She stood and took Carolyn's hand. "Come on, now."

Everyone stood outside on the porch. Oma said good-bye, giving each of them a hug and kisses on both cheeks, all except Mommy, who wouldn't let her. "Have it your way, Hildemara Rose." Oma shook her head as she went down the front steps. Carolyn tried to follow. Mommy clamped hold of her shoulders and pulled her back.

"No!" Carolyn struggled, but Mommy's hands tightened, her fingers digging in painfully. Carolyn screamed. "Oma! *Oma!*"

Oma turned her head away, backed out of the driveway, and started down the street. Thrashing, sobbing, Carolyn tried to break free. "Stop it," Mommy said in a broken voice.

Daddy caught Carolyn by the arm and slung her around. He shoved her inside the front door. When she tried to run out, he lifted her under his arm and carried her kicking and screaming down the hall. "*Stop it!* You upset your mother!" Cursing, he flipped Carolyn over his knees and whacked her twice, hard. The pain shocked and frightened her into silence. Daddy flung her onto the bed. Face red, eyes black, he bent over her, a finger pointing at the middle of her face. "You move and I'll give you the spanking of your life!"

Daddy's hand trembled. "I don't want to hear you cry again. Do you understand me? No more tears! You think you have it tough? I saw kids half your age in bombed-out buildings, scrambling for something to eat. They didn't have mothers who loved them or took care of them. Their mothers had been blown to bits! Oma's gone home. Life goes on. You make your mother cry and I swear I'll . . ." He made a fist.

Daddy's face changed. He ran a hand over his face and left the room.

❄ ❄ ❄

The door opened, awakening Carolyn. She stuck her thumb in her mouth, her heart beating wildly. She hadn't budged from where Daddy had put her. Not even when she needed to go to the bathroom.

Mommy stood in the doorway. She grimaced. "You had an accident, didn't you?"

Carolyn scooted back on the fouled bed, shaking violently.

"It's all right." Mommy pushed the door wider. "Everything's going to be all right." Her mother didn't come into the room. "No one's mad at you." She spoke at a distance. "Trip!" Her mother's voice broke.

When she heard her father's footsteps, Carolyn scrambled back farther, all the way to the wall. Tears ran down her cheeks. Mommy was upset again, and Daddy would be mad. Carolyn remembered Daddy's face, his fist, and his promise. When Daddy appeared in the doorway, she took little gulping breaths.

"She needs a bath." Mommy wiped tears from her cheeks. "A warm bath, Trip, and talk quietly. She looks like she's in shock." Mommy spoke in a choked voice. "I'll strip the bed and wash everything."

Carolyn didn't remember how she got from the bed to the bath. Daddy showered her first and then put a capful of bubble bath in the tub and filled it with warm water. He talked in a happy voice, but he didn't look happy. His hands shook as he washed her. Despite the warm water, Carolyn shivered all over. When he lifted her out, she stood still while he toweled her dry and dressed her in pajamas.

"You're going to use a sleeping bag tonight. Won't that be fun? You'll be snug as a bug in a rug."

She wanted Oma, but she didn't dare say so. She wanted Bullet, but she didn't think Daddy would let her sleep in the dog's cozy little house. She wanted Charlie.

The radio played in the living room. Daddy tried to untangle her hair. "Mommy is making a nice dinner for us. You tell her how good it is. You say thank you." He gave up on her hair and tossed the brush into the sink. The sound made Carolyn jump. Turning her, he lifted her to his knee and pressed her head against his shoulder. "I know you're going to miss Oma, Carolyn, but you're our little girl." She sat limp, hands like dead spiders in her lap. If she moved, would Daddy hit her again? He set her on her feet. "Go on in the living room." He spoke gruffly. She went quickly. Before going through the doorway, she looked back.

Daddy sat on the closed toilet lid, his head in his hands.

Carolyn did everything Mommy and Daddy told her. She didn't question; she didn't argue. Sometimes, after everyone had gone to bed, she would open her bedroom door and creep down the hallway to Charlie's room and sleep curled up in a blanket by his bed. On cold nights, he let her snuggle with him. Sometimes she awakened early enough to go back to her own bed so Mommy wouldn't know she slept in Charlie's room.

The family went to church every Sunday. Carolyn liked Sunday school. The nice teachers read the same stories Oma had. She liked to hear the singing coming through the wall from the sanctuary and wished she could sit in there with its long red carpet and high ceiling and steps leading up to the cross with gold candlesticks and white candles flickering on the table.

One day after church, Daddy turned the car in the opposite direction from home. "I think I've found the place." Daddy smiled at Mommy. Charlie sat tall, peering out the window. Carolyn couldn't see anything.

Daddy turned off the road. The car bounced and jostled. "This is it."

"Look at that tree!" Charlie rolled his window down. "Can I climb it?"

Daddy stopped the car. "Go ahead."

Mommy protested. "It's too tall."

"He'll be fine, Hildie."

"Be careful!" Mommy called after Charlie.

Daddy laughed. "Relax. He's a monkey."

Mommy looked back as Daddy drove on. "An English walnut tree. We could probably get enough nuts off that one tree to pay part of the property taxes."

Daddy grinned. "Just like you to be so practical." He stopped and got out of the car. "Come on. Let's walk the property. See what you think of it."

Carolyn got out after they walked away. She looked for a big tree and spotted her brother high among the branches. Walking back, she stood near the trunk and looked up. Charlie straddled a high branch. She wandered back and heard Mommy and Daddy talking.

"Can we do this, Trip? I mean, neither of us knows anything about building a house."

"We can learn. I've already ordered books from the library. The bank will loan us enough to buy the property. We haven't the money to hire an architect or contractor. We'll have to do it ourselves, Hildie."

"You really want this, don't you, Trip?"

"Don't you? You're the one who says she misses having space around. You talk about the farm all the time."

"Do I?"

Daddy took her hand and kissed it. Drawing it through his arm, they walked together. Carolyn followed far enough behind not to be noticed, close enough to hear. "Just think about it, Hildie. We could stake out the house wherever we want it, hire someone to dig a well. We'd build a shed first to hold whatever tools I'd need to get started. Having a shed would save time in hauling everything back and forth. We could come out a couple times a week after I get off work, get started on the foundations, work weekends. Nothing fancy, just a simple house; one big room to start, add the kitchen next and a bathroom. As soon as we move in, we can add on two more bedrooms."

"You're talking about an awful lot of work, Trip."

"I know, but we'd be building something for ourselves. How else are we going to have our dream home in the country unless we do it?"

"It's a long way from town and schools."

"Only two miles, and there's a school bus. I already checked about that. All Charlie has to do is walk to the end of the driveway. He'll be picked up and dropped off every day."

Mommy looked around again, frowning this time. "I don't know, Trip."

Daddy turned her to face him. "Breathe the air, Hildemara." He slid his hands up and down her arms. "Aren't you tired of living in a house closed in on all sides by other houses? and gossiping neighbors who avoid you like the plague? Wouldn't you like our children to grow up the way you did? in the country with space around them? They'd be safe and free to roam out here. No more living in the shadow of a federal prison."

Stepping away, Mommy bent down and picked up a handful of soil. She smelled it and crumbled the dirt in her hand, letting it sift through her fingers. "Smells good." She brushed off her hands. "We could build a tent-house to start, use a Coleman stove, keep supplies in the trunk of the car, dig a hole, and build an outhouse."

Daddy grinned. "Now you're talking!"

"We could put an orchard of walnut trees up front, plant fruit trees, a few grapevines, and a vegetable garden over there. We could have chickens . . ."

Daddy pulled her into his arms and kissed her. When he drew back, Mommy's face looked pink. Daddy smiled and took her hand. "Let's figure out where to put the house."

Carolyn watched them walk away. She wandered back to the walnut tree and watched her brother climb from one branch to another.

Mommy and Daddy called out. "Charlie! Carolyn! Come on, you two. Time to go home and have lunch." Carolyn climbed into the backseat. Charlie sounded winded from his fast climb down and run to the car. Daddy started the car. "We're going to build a house here, kids. What do you think about that?"

"We're going to live out here?" Charlie sounded worried.

"Yes."

"But what about my friends? If we move, I'll never see them."

"You'd see them in school." Daddy turned onto the road. "And Happy Valley Road has plenty of kids. I saw one riding a bicycle and another one riding a horse."

"A horse?" Charlie's eyes brightened. "Can we get a horse?"

Daddy laughed and glanced at Mommy. "Maybe. But not right away."

No one asked Carolyn what she thought about moving away from the only house she had ever known. Carolyn had no friends or playmates. Only one thing worried her. "Will Oma know how to find me?"

Mommy and Daddy exchanged a look. "Of course." Daddy nodded. Mommy stared out the window.

❋ ❋ ❋

Every Friday after work, Carolyn's father drove the family out to "the property." They went through Paxtown with its Old West buildings, through meadows, and over a hill with a cemetery. Happy Valley Road was the first left on the other side of the hill. Dad had set up a tent-house. Charlie would take off to climb the big walnut tree; Mom laid out sleeping bags on the platforms, set up the Coleman stove, and started dinner. Dad's first project was to dig a deep hole and build an outhouse. Next, he built a shed for his tools and put a heavy padlock on the door.

Left on her own, Carolyn wandered with Bullet. When he scared a man's sheep, Dad drove a steel stake deep into the ground and attached a chain to it. After that, Bullet could only walk in circles. He'd run until he wound himself tight, and Carolyn would walk him in circles the other way until he had more freedom.

Charlie knew everyone on the road within a few weeks. He took Carolyn over to meet their next-door neighbor. Lee Dockery had beehives behind his house. "Call me Dock." He leaned down, smiling at her. "'Hickory, dickory, dock, the mouse ran up the clock.'" His fingers walked from her stomach up her chest and tickled her under the chin. She giggled. He said she could come over anytime and gave them each a honeycomb dripping with sweetness.

Her father told her to stay out of the way. Her mother told her to try not to get so dirty. With Charlie gone most of the time, Carolyn had no one. She often went over to the barbed-wire fence and watched Dock work among his hives. Bees swarmed around him when he lifted wooden frames filled with honeycombs. "Don't they sting you?" she called.

"Bees are my friends. I never take more than they're willing to share."

Dock invited her inside his house and let her spin honey from the combs. He let her dip her finger into the thick, rich, sweet-smelling mass dripping down a tube into glass jars. He called her "honeybee" and petted her head the same way she petted Bullet. Often, he lifted her onto his lap and talked about his wife who had died and how much they had wanted to have children and couldn't. "You look sleepy." He let her rest her head against his chest. He smelled of tobacco and sweat. He stroked her legs under her dress. "Your mother is calling for you." Dock lifted her and set her on her feet. "You have to go home now, honeybee." He kissed her on the mouth and looked so sad. "Come back real soon, and we'll play some games together."

Carolyn ducked under barbed wire stretched between fence posts and ran through the mustard flowers.

"Why didn't you answer me?" Her mother shook her. "Where were you?"

"At Dock's."

"Dock?"

"Mr. Dockery, Mom." Charlie answered for her. "The bee man. He gives us honeycombs." He sat at the makeshift table where the family ate their meals. "He's really nice."

Frowning, her mother let go of her and straightened, looking toward the house next door. "Well, you leave Mr. Dockery alone. I'm sure he has work to do and doesn't need you underfoot."

Carolyn didn't tell her that Dock liked her more than Daddy or Mommy. He said he wanted her to come back and play real soon.

ALL THAT SUMMER, the family still lived in the rental house near the penitentiary during the week and spent weekends on their new property. Neither Daddy nor Mommy read stories or played games anymore. Her father read big books that came in the mail. He made notes and drawings on yellow legal pads. He rolled out white paper and used a ruler to make bigger drawings with numbers all over. Her mother had housework and laundry and the garden. Charlie had friends. Carolyn played alone. She always had the first bath while Charlie listened to a radio program. She was always first in bed, first with the lights out.

Curling on her side, the rag doll tucked tight against her, Carolyn remembered riding around with Oma in the gray Plymouth. She missed opening a package of Wonder bread and eating fresh slices on the way home from the grocery store. She missed having stories read to her and working puzzles on a board Oma kept under her bed. She missed helping in the kitchen and having tea parties in the afternoon. Most of all, she missed Oma's hugs and kisses. Her mother didn't hug or kiss anyone except Daddy.

Charlie went off with his friends every morning, and Mommy did chores inside the house. "Go on outside and play, Carolyn." Carolyn made mud cookies alongside the house, baked them on a board, and pretended to feed her rag doll while Bullet sat beside her, head high, ears perked, panting. Anytime anyone came near the gate, he growled and barked. Sometimes he licked Carolyn's face, but Mommy didn't like him to kiss her. When he did, she always made Carolyn come in and wash with soap that got in her eyes and burned like fire.

She looked forward to Friday night, when Daddy drove them all to the property. Saturday, while her parents poured and smoothed concrete foundations and framed walls, Carolyn went over to Dock's house. When she got sticky, he gave her a bath. He didn't just throw a washcloth to her and tell her to wash herself. He used his hands.

He said he loved her. He said he'd never hurt her.

And she believed him.

❊   ❊   ❊

At the end of the summer, her father finished the big room and the family moved to the property. While Mommy plastered the walls and painted, Daddy started work on the kitchen and bathroom and two bedrooms. Carolyn was glad she would get to share a room with Charlie again. She didn't like sleeping in a room all by herself.

Dock waved Carolyn over when Mommy wasn't looking and invited Carolyn to play when her mother went to work in her garden. He had Chinese checkers and pick-up sticks. He gave her honey and crackers and milk. "Don't tell your mother or father. They'll think you're bothering me and tell you never to visit me again. You want to come back, don't you? You like spending time with old Dock, don't you?"

Wrapping her arms around his neck, Carolyn said she loved him. And she meant it. He always made her go back when

Mommy called. And she knew better than to talk about Dock to anyone.

As soon as Daddy got home, he went to work on the house. The power saw screamed, filling the air with the scent of sawdust, until Mom said dinner was ready.

"You'll be starting school in September, Carolyn," her mother told her. "We're going to orientation day. You'll meet your teacher, Miss Talbot, and learn where to go to catch the school bus home."

Carolyn told Dock she was afraid to go to school. What if nobody liked her? What if the bus left without her? What if . . . ? He lifted her onto his lap and told her everything would be fine. He said he wished she were his little girl. He'd take her away, and she'd never have to go to school. They'd go to Knott's Berry Farm or the San Diego Zoo. He'd take her to the beach and let her play in the sand as long as she wanted. "Would you like to live with me, honeybee?"

"I'd miss Charlie and Oma."

"Charlie has his own friends, and your *oma* hardly ever comes and sees you."

Dock got tired of playing board games. He showed her other games—secret games, he called them, because she was very special. He tied a red silk ribbon around her neck and made a big bow. The first few times, she felt uncomfortable in the pit of her stomach, but he was so nice to her. Gradually, she got over those feelings and did whatever he told her. She didn't want him to stop liking her. Who would be her friend then?

Then one day while they played their secret games, he hurt her. She cried out and Dock clamped his strong, rough hand over her mouth. She tasted blood. Frightened, she struggled, but he held her more firmly. He told her to calm down, to be quiet; everything would be all right; hush now, *hush*!

Then Dock started to cry. "I'm sorry, honeybee. I'm so sorry!" He cried so hard, Carolyn was scared. "I'm sorry. I'm sorry." He washed the blood off her bare legs and put her underwear back on.

He held her between his knees, his face wet and scared. "I can't be your friend anymore, honeybee. And you can't say anything about coming over here. Not to anyone. Not ever. Your mother told you not to come. She'd spank you for disobeying. Your father would shoot me or take me to jail. You don't want that to happen, do you? It'd be your fault." His eyes darted around. "Promise you won't say anything! We'll both get into a lot of trouble if you tell anyone we're friends."

She lay in bed that night, curling on her side, sucking her thumb, still hurting deep inside. Charlie slept like a rock in the other bed. Dock came to her window and tapped softly. Heart pounding, she pretended to be asleep.

The next day, when Dock waved at her, she ducked her head and pretended she didn't see.

He came back again that night and talked softly through the window while Charlie slept. She didn't want to go to Knott's Berry Farm or the San Diego Zoo. She didn't want to go to Mexico. "I'll come back, honeybee. I love you, baby." Shivering, she kept her eyes shut until he went away. She didn't want to play games with him anymore. When all was quiet, she pulled her blanket off the bed, grabbed her pillow, and hid in the closet.

When Charlie slid the door open in the morning, she screamed. He jumped back and screamed, too. Her mother came running in. "What's the matter with you two?"

"Carolyn's in the closet!"

"What are you doing in the closet?"

"I was scared."

"Scared of what?"

She shook her head. She didn't dare tell.

She had nightmares every night. Mommy and Daddy started talking about her in low voices.

"Something's happened to her, Trip. I don't know what, but something's wrong. I feel it. Miss Talbot called this afternoon. She said Carolyn has been falling asleep in the playhouse. Apparently she's sucking her thumb again."

"She hasn't done that in two years."

"Some of the children tease her about it. Miss Talbot tried to talk to her, but she said Carolyn is like a little clam. She hardly talks at all."

Her parents kept looking at her all through dinner. Her father asked if someone was bullying her at school. Her mother said she didn't have to be afraid to tell them anything, but Dock had told her what would happen to her if she did. When she didn't say anything, they asked Charlie. "Have you seen anything going on at school?"

"We're not in the same playground as the little kids."

"What about the school bus?" Dad wanted to know. "Anyone bothering her?"

"I don't know, Dad."

"Well, make it your business to find out." Dad raised his voice. "She's your sister! Watch out for her!"

Tucked in bed for the night and bedroom door closed, Charlie talked to her in the dark. "Tell me who's picking on you, Carolyn. I'll beat 'em up. I'll make them leave you alone." Carolyn thought about how big Dock was, how easily he could hurt her brother. She pulled the blanket over her head and hid under the covers.

When she went to school, Miss Talbot talked with her. "Your mommy says you're having nightmares. Can you tell me about your dreams, sweetheart?" Carolyn shrugged her shoulders and pretended not to remember. Everyone would be mad at her if she said anything about Dock—Mommy, Daddy, Charlie. She had made Dock cry, hadn't she? She had done something terribly wrong.

When Mommy and Daddy started talking about their next-door neighbor, Mr. Dockery, Carolyn felt the terror rise up inside her, catching her by the throat. Her stomach clenched as though Dock were touching her again. She remembered the pain. She remembered the blood. She remembered every word he said. Little yellow and black bees swarmed around her face. She felt cold sensations like insects landing on her and walking around on her skin with little prickly feet.

"I went over this morning, and there are newspapers all over his driveway. He hasn't picked them up in days."

Daddy said something must be wrong, and he'd go over and check on him. Carolyn broke out in a cold sweat while he was gone. He came back and said the mail had piled up by his door, too. He couldn't see anything through the windows. The drapes had been pulled. He made a phone call. Mommy told her to go outside and play when the police came.

Carolyn wanted to run away, but didn't know where to go. She climbed the walnut tree and watched when her father and the other police officer opened the front door of Lee Dockery's house. They came out without him.

Mommy and Daddy talked about Lee Dockery in the living room that evening, after Charlie and Carolyn had been sent to bed. Carolyn got up and sat by the open door, listening.

"We talked with neighbors. No one's seen him in weeks. His truck's gone. So are the beehives. It's like he packed up and took off in a hurry. No one has any idea where he'd go or if he's coming back. They all said he's a strange old bird."

"No one would just walk away from a house and property. Maybe he went to visit relatives."

"No relatives that anyone knows about. I never saw anyone visit. Did you?"

"Charlie and Carolyn went over a few times, but I told them to stay away from him."

"Why?"

"Something about him. I don't know. He gave me the creeps. Trip, you don't suppose . . ." Mommy sounded worried.

"What?"

"Oh, I'm probably overreacting. I just wondered if Carolyn's behavior could have anything to do with him. I did tell her to stay away from him, but what if she didn't?"

Carolyn held her breath. Had they figured out her secret? Would Daddy go after Dock and shoot him, like Dock had said he would?

"Carolyn?" Daddy laughed. "She's much too timid to go visit a strange neighbor without one of us dragging her over there."

Mommy was quiet for a minute. Then she said, "I guess you're right. I just wish I knew what was wrong with her. Trip, she hardly says two words to me. I just don't know what to do anymore."

Then Mommy was crying. Carolyn crept back to bed before she could get into any more trouble than she was already in.

1953

Carolyn's nightmares continued through the winter months but began to lessen as daylight lasted longer. She didn't see as many shadows at night, didn't hear footsteps outside the bedroom window, and didn't have to hide in the closet anymore. She could slip into Charlie's bed. He slept so deeply, he didn't notice until morning.

Dad took time off from building the house to put up a swing. "Might give her something to do. . . ." Carolyn spent hours sitting in the tire seat, turning the ropes until they grew taut, and then lifting her feet off the ground so she'd spin until she felt light-headed and dizzy. Her mother pushed her sometimes. Once, she even sat on the swing herself and showed Carolyn how to pump her legs so she could go higher.

Every few months, Carolyn and Charlie had to go to a hospital for "skin tests." Mom checked their arms every day for a week before taking them back for the doctor to see. When the doctor said, "Negative," Mom smiled and relaxed.

Carolyn made a friend in first grade. New to Paxtown and new to school, Suzie clung to her mother like a limpet and had to be pried off by their teacher, Miss Davenport. Miss Davenport called Carolyn over and asked her to sit with Suzie and "make her feel at home" while she went to greet other children. Carolyn understood Suzie. They became inseparable at school. Every recess, they played hopscotch or climbed the monkey bars or took turns pushing each other on the swings. They ate together in the cafeteria. Suzie told Carolyn she lived in Kottinger Village and her daddy was a soldier in the Army. She had two younger brothers and her mother was "expecting." Carolyn asked what she was expecting, and Suzie said a baby brother or sister.

At the end of the year, Suzie said her father had received a "transfer," and that meant she had to move away. Carolyn's nightmares returned. Only this time, Dock didn't take her away. He took Suzie.

"Carolyn." She came abruptly awake and found her mother sitting on the edge of the bed. She brushed the hair back from Carolyn's forehead. "You're having nightmares again?" When Carolyn started to cry, her mother patted her leg. Carolyn thought of Dock and moved away. Mom frowned and folded her hands in her lap. "I don't know what started them, but you're safe. Everything is fine. Mommy and Daddy are close by."

"Suzie's gone."

"You'll make another friend. You'll see. It won't be as hard next time."

Carolyn thought it better not to try. First Oma had gone away. Then Dock. And now Suzie was gone, too.

❄ ❄ ❄

1954

"I'm doing my best, Hildie." Carolyn's father sounded angry and tired.

"I'm not saying you aren't. Just let me go back to work for a little while so we can save money for the master bedroom."

"What about the kids?"

"It's partly because of the kids! They can't sleep in the same room forever, Trip. Besides that, Carolyn was invited to a birthday party last week, and I couldn't let her go because we couldn't afford to buy a present. Her first birthday party invitation and I had to say no."

"It won't kill her."

"Trip . . ."

"You can't just leave them on their own to fend for themselves."

"I can work night shifts. I'd be home by seven in the morning. They wouldn't even know I was gone."

"Remember what happened the last time you took on too much work and didn't get enough rest."

"Yes, Trip." Mommy's voice sharpened. "We still have the hospital bill. It reminds me—*every single month*."

They lowered their voices, and Carolyn fell asleep again. They argued every night about the same thing until Daddy gave in.

1955

Mom's hours changed to "swing shift," and a key was placed under the flowerpot by the front door. "Be sure to put the key back after you unlock the door. Otherwise, it won't be there tomorrow and you'll have to sit outside until Daddy gets home from work. Charlie, if you go anywhere, you be sure to leave a note as to where you're going. Be home by five at the latest. Carolyn, you stay in the house. Play with your doll or read books, but don't go wandering off."

Dad bought a television set. Mom complained about the money. Dad said everyone else in the neighborhood had a television; why shouldn't they?

Carolyn turned it on every day when she came home from school. She felt better hearing voices in the house. She didn't feel as lonely.

"I think it's time you quit working, Hildie. Carolyn needs you."

"She's doing better."

"Better how? Watching TV? Never getting to play outside the house except on weekends? A little girl shouldn't be alone so much. Things could happen."

What things? Carolyn was afraid to ask.

"School lets out in two weeks, Hildemara. What're you going to do then? leave the kids alone *all* day *every* day?"

"I put in for night shift."

"And you think that's going to solve our problems?"

"I don't know, Trip. What will?"

He muttered something and Mom got mad. "I'm trying to help you, and you can't even say a civil word to me! What happened to the man I fell in love with, the one who wanted us to be a *team* and build something *together*? What happened to *him*?"

"The war happened!" Daddy didn't sound mad this time. He said more, but Carolyn couldn't hear. "I've been thinking there might be another way to work this out."

"What way?"

"Take them down to Murietta. . . ."

Carolyn sighed. She fell asleep in her own bed for the first time in months.

5

THE DAY AFTER school let out, Dad put two suitcases in the trunk of the car and drove Carolyn and Charlie down to Oma's farm outside Murietta. Mom cried the night before they left.

Oma had a casserole waiting on the stove and Daddy's favorite angel food cake on a big blue and white willow dish in the middle of the cottage kitchen table. After lunch, Oma told Carolyn and Charlie to play outside while she and Daddy talked. On the way out the door, Carolyn heard Oma say, "They can stay all summer if they want, but I have another proposition to make."

Dad looked less sad when he said he had to leave late in the afternoon. Stooping, he hugged and kissed them both and said things would be better soon. Carolyn couldn't think of anything better than staying with her grandmother.

❄ ❄ ❄

For the next three weeks, Carolyn and Charlie took turns feeding the chickens and rabbits. Neither Charlie nor Carolyn wanted to

weed the garden, but Oma said they needed to learn how to "pay for
their keep." The quicker they got chores done, the quicker they'd be
free to do whatever they wanted. Charlie always found fun things to
do. They climbed the chinaberry tree and pelted one another with
"bombs." They dug for treasure in the garbage pit, made friends with
the feral cats living in the barn. They weren't quick enough to catch
the mice in the hay, but Charlie managed to capture horned toads,
which he kept in a box until Oma found them and made him turn
them loose. When it got too hot outside, Carolyn sat in the cottage
with Oma, watching *Truth or Consequences*, *You Bet Your Life* with
Groucho Marx, or *Queen for a Day*.

Mom and Dad came for a Saturday visit. They looked relaxed
and happy. Charlie showed Dad the tree house. He asked Daddy
if they could build one just like it in the walnut tree back home.
Oma gave Carolyn carrots and told her to go feed the rabbits.
Carolyn loved the warm, fuzzy white animals and dawdled while
Mom and Oma sat in the shade of the bay tree. Both rocked in the
aluminum chairs. Oma got up after a while and put her hand on
Mom's shoulder and went inside the cottage. Mom put her head
back and stayed outside. She didn't look happy.

Carolyn went into the small washhouse, where she could hear
Oma and Mommy talking.

"Charlie looks so brown, Mama."

"He's outside as soon as the sun comes up."

"Carolyn is happier than I've seen her in months."

"There are lots of things for her to do here."

"Chores, you mean."

"Chores aren't meant to be punishment, Hildemara. They're
meant to teach responsibility. Chores make you part of the family
enterprise."

Oma and Daddy talked over supper.

"How long do you think it'd take, Trip?"

"Not long if I hired help."

"Could you manage it by the end of summer?"

"No, but no later than Thanksgiving, I think."

When Dad said they had to leave after supper, Charlie asked if he could go home with them. He missed his friends. Dad ruffled his hair. "Not yet, buddy." Charlie missed Mom and Dad more than Carolyn did.

Oma never left them alone. She didn't allow Charlie to "mope around." She took them to the library and checked out adventure stories and picture books. She put out a puzzle of Switzerland and told them stories about her faraway friends Rosie and Solange. When they finished that puzzle, she bought another of an English countryside and told them stories of Daisy Stockhard and fancy afternoon tea parties and daily outings to the royal Kew Gardens. When Carolyn asked if they could have tea parties, too, Oma said of course they could, and they would have one every afternoon if she liked.

Sometimes Oma drove them all the way to Lake Yosemite, where she taught them how to swim. By the middle of summer, Charlie could swim all the way out to the raft, but Carolyn never ventured far from shore. Oma sat under an umbrella and read one of the big books she checked out of the library. On the way home, Oma took them to Wheeler's Truck Stop to have dinner. She told them Mom worked there as a girl and earned tips for being a good waitress to the truckers who carried produce up and down Central Valley Highway 99.

"Your mom is a good, hard worker. You should be very proud of her."

Carolyn could see Oma was.

❄ ❄ ❄

At the end of the summer, Oma drove Carolyn and Charlie home. Something new had been added to the property. A slab of concrete had been poured and walls and roof framed. "I wonder if it's another shed."

Oma laughed. "I hope not!" She parked between the house and the new structure being built.

Neither parent had come home from work yet. Oma took the key from under the flowerpot and unlocked the front door. She pushed it open, but didn't go inside. "You two go unpack. I'm going to take a look at the new project."

Carolyn hurriedly put her playclothes in drawers and her toothpaste, toothbrush, and comb back in the bathroom and raced out to join Oma. Her grandmother stood in the middle of the concrete foundation, between the open two-by-four framed walls. Carolyn came through the open space that would be the front door. Oma pointed. "There's going to be a picture window there and a fireplace over here. Over here is the kitchen with two windows, one looking toward your place and one up the hill." She took Carolyn by the hand. "Accordion doors will cover the washer and dryer, and back here is the bedroom with a nice bathroom, tub, and shower." She smiled as she looked around. "Your daddy does good work."

"Who's going to live here?"

Oma smiled broadly. "Well, who do you think?" She hugged Carolyn against her.

Carolyn felt a surge of relief. "It's like your cottage!"

"Like it, but better. Solid foundation, for one thing. We didn't have the money for one when my cottage was put up. And it's a hundred square feet bigger. There'll be a modern built-in stove and refrigerator in the kitchen, room for a table and three chairs."

A police squad car pulled into the driveway. Charlie came running out of the house and threw himself at Daddy when he got out of the car. Daddy laughed and hugged him, holding him tight and rubbing his knuckles against his hair. "It's about time you came home!" He strode toward the framed cottage. He bent to give Carolyn a quick hug and kiss and then straightened, facing Oma. "So? What do you think?"

"It won't be ready by Thanksgiving." She smiled. "But it takes time to do things right." She looked around again. "And it looks very right to me."

Oma went home to Murietta after breakfast the next morning. She wanted to be home for church the next day. Carolyn climbed an old plum tree near the new cottage. Her folks came out and walked around inside the open structure.

"It won't be like the last time, Hildie. She won't be living under our roof. She'll have her own place."

"I'm just a little uneasy, that's all."

"Uneasy about what?" Daddy sounded annoyed. "I thought everything was settled."

"It is. It's just that Carolyn loves her so much."

"Oh." Daddy stepped closer and put his arms on Mommy's shoulders. "You'll always be her mother, Hildie. Nothing's ever going to change that."

She leaned her head against his shoulder. "If I were a better mother, I'd worry more about her being alone so much than where I'm going to fit in with all the changes we're making. I just want to know there'll be room for me in her life."

"Make room."

"It might already be too late."

❄ ❄ ❄

1956

Carolyn stopped dreaming about Dock when Oma moved into the cottage. No more going into an empty house. She flew off the school bus and raced Charlie up the driveway to Oma's cottage. Her brother always won. Charlie dumped his books by the door, gobbled his cookies, gulped his milk, and rode off on his bike with his redheaded buddy, Mitch Hastings. Carolyn stayed to enjoy "afternoon tea" with Oma. She sipped cream-laced tea and ate triangle-cut egg sandwiches while Oma asked about school. After tea, they went outside together and worked in the garden, weeding the flowers in front and thinning the seedlings in the vegetable garden in back.

When Mom came home, Oma stood on the front steps and called out to her. "Why don't you come over for tea, Hildemara? Rest awhile."

And Mom called back. "Can't today, Mama. I have to get out of this uniform, shower, and change. I'd better get supper started. Maybe tomorrow."

"Tomorrow then. Save some time."

Tomorrow never came, and after a few weeks, Oma stopped asking. She would send Carolyn home when Mom drove in. "Better go do your homework, *Liebling*. And don't forget to help your mother."

But whenever Carolyn offered to help in the kitchen, Mommy would say, "I don't need you, Carolyn. Go and play. Enjoy the sunshine while you can."

After a lonely half hour on the swing, Carolyn went back to Oma's cottage and stayed there until Daddy and Charlie came home.

Oma came over. Carolyn came into the house a minute later and heard her and Mommy arguing. "Why do you chase her outside all the time?"

"I'm not chasing her out."

"What would you call it?"

"I spent most of my childhood inside a house, doing chores. I never had the chance to go out and do whatever I wanted. When she comes to the cottage, you could tell her to play instead of keeping her there."

"I send her home to spend time with her mother, and you just send her right back outside again. . . ."

Carolyn ducked out the door again and ran out to her swing. She saw Oma walking back to the cottage. She looked so sad. Carolyn stayed on the swing until Daddy came home and said she should go in the house and help her mother.

❄ ❄ ❄

Mom took extra shifts at the VA hospital so they could buy more lumber and supplies for building. Daddy finally finished the master bedroom and added a step-down utility porch off the back of the house, with hookups for a washing machine and dryer. He bought Mom a mangle for Christmas so she could iron the table-cloths, sheets, and pillowcases like his mother had. She also ironed Daddy's shirts, slacks, and boxer shorts and her nurse's uniforms. The only clothes she didn't iron were the brown polyester pants and flower-print blouses she wore after work every day.

As soon as Daddy finished the utility porch, he started work on a larger addition at the front of the house.

Oma came over to take a look around. Daddy proudly laid out the living room plans: fourteen by twenty feet, twelve-foot wood-beamed ceiling, skylights, stone fireplace, wall-to-wall carpeting, and picture windows looking out on the orchard in front. He showed her the plans he had drawn. "We'll put in a pool with a patio all around and terrace that back hill, plant a garden, have a waterfall over there in the corner."

Oma looked as though she had swallowed something that didn't taste good. "Your own private paradise."

"Something like that."

"Well, it's better than building a bomb shelter like most of the people in the neighborhood."

"Actually, I was thinking about renting a backhoe to dig one in the hill. . . ."

The next time Oma invited Mommy over for afternoon tea, she wouldn't take "Sorry, maybe another time" for an answer.

"I can't stay long. I have to start dinner soon."

"Things won't fall apart if it's not on the table at six on the dot, Hildemara." Oma sounded irritated. She poured tea in a pretty pink rose china cup and offered cream and sugar.

Mommy looked at the platter of spicy chicken sandwiches and egg salad sandwiches with dill and the apple streusel cake. "What is all this? I didn't forget my birthday, did I?"

"I wanted to treat my daughter to an English afternoon tea, the kind I used to prepare for Lady Daisy in London."

Mommy gave her an odd smile. "It's lovely. Thank you."

Oma took one seat, Carolyn the other. "If you'd like, we can do this every afternoon when you get home from work. It would be nice, wouldn't it, the three of us sipping tea and taking time to sit and talk awhile?"

"I can't stay more than half an hour."

"If you had a Dutch oven, you could start dinner in the morning before you left for work." Oma sipped her tea. "You'd have an hour to relax when you got home. All you'd have to do is steam some vegetables and set the table. Carolyn could help."

"You always made a four-course dinner, Mama, and dessert, even after you'd worked all day in town. And you walked there and back."

"Until I drove." Oma chuckled as she lifted her teacup. "Papa didn't think much of that idea at first, did he?"

Mom smiled. "We all thought you'd kill yourself in that Model T. You drove like a maniac."

"Probably still do. I felt free. And no one was going to take that away from me." She cut slices of apple streusel and gave Mom a sly smile. "You know, there's no sin in taking advantage of the conveniences available: a car to drive to work, a washer and dryer in the house, an old-fashioned Dutch oven. It buys you time for other things."

"There's always too much to do, Mama. I wish there were more hours in a day."

"And if there were, what would you and Trip do with them?"

Mommy gave a bleak laugh. "Finish building the house."

Carolyn finished a last bite of streusel. Oma cleared away her teacup and saucer and plate. "Why don't you play outside for a while, Carolyn?"

She didn't want to go outside. She wanted to stay inside and listen. "Can I finish the puzzle?"

"I finished it this morning. There's a new one on the coffee table. You can bring it out here and start sorting the pieces, if you like."

Carolyn ran to get the box, dumped the pieces on the table, and began turning them over, sorting colors and searching for edge pieces and corners the way Oma had showed her. Oma and Mommy kept talking.

"You and Trip and the kids ought to take a family vacation."

"There's no money for a vacation."

"There's money for a bomb shelter."

"With the way the world is going right now, a bomb shelter would be more practical than wasting money on a vacation."

"Waste? Let's talk about being practical, shall we? How long would you have to stay inside a bomb shelter before you could come out into the open again, assuming radiation lasts as long as they say it does? I'd rather die in a split second out here in the open and be in heaven in the twinkling of an eye than live underground like a gopher. No sunlight. No garden. Nothing to do. How do you even get fresh air to breathe without letting in the radiation?"

"Everybody's building them."

"People are like lemmings, Hildemara Rose. Yell 'Fire!' and they'll run." They talked about how everyone these days seemed to be worried about spies lurking everywhere, like moles burrowing into the government and science labs, all looking for a way to bring America down. Koreans could brainwash captives and turn them into Manchurian candidates. Russians were spreading Communism all over Eastern Europe. "Everyone is going a little crazy." Oma shook her head in disgust.

"The bomb shelter is Trip's idea, Mama, not mine."

"Plant another idea in his head. I know; I know! The man's only happy when he's working on a project. But I've heard him talk about how he used to hike and camp and fish back in Colorado. Think of the fun you could have with a tent, sleeping bags, and a couple of fishing poles." Oma sipped her tea. "Charlie is thirteen already. He's always off somewhere with his friends. In another six years, he'll go away to college. And Carolyn's going to be nine soon." Oma lowered her voice. "She needs her mother."

"Like I needed you, Mama?" A quiet edge of bitterness crept into her mother's voice.

"Yes. And where was I? Working, always working. If anyone

has a right to talk about this, I do!" Oma turned the teacup in its saucer. "Just so you know, I came up here to tear down walls, not help you build them."

Mom fidgeted. "I don't know what to make of this."

"Make of what?"

"Sitting in your kitchen, having tea."

Oma scowled at her. "I've invited you over every day for weeks. You wouldn't come!"

"I've spent most of my life trying to live up to your standards and failing."

"So you're going to punish me in my old age. Is that it?"

"I still don't come up to your standards, do I? I'm not a good mother. Trip's too busy to be a father. There's no pleasing you."

"Now, you listen to me, Hildemara Rose. And you listen good. You never failed me, not once. Nor did I fail you, if it comes to that. You were small and sickly when you were born. Was that your fault? You had the most to overcome. I was afraid you wouldn't even survive that first winter out there in the frozen wheat fields. I almost lost you again when you had pneumonia. Do you remember? And I could still lose you if you keep on as you are. Yes! I was harder on you than the others. I wanted you to grow up strong so no one would be able to hold you down. So I pushed you. I pushed hard. And, thank God, you pushed back. Now look at you."

"You sound proud." Mom sounded surprised.

"I am." She raised her teacup and smiled. "I'm proud of both of us."

6

AFTER SEVERAL HEATED discussions muffled by the master bedroom door, Dad threw away his plans for the bomb shelter and bought an Airstream trailer instead. One weekend a month, Mom and Dad packed the trailer and took off with Carolyn and Charlie in the backseat of the sedan. Carolyn found herself looking forward to the weekends away, even though Oma never went along. "Someone has to feed Bullet and pick up the mail." She would wave as they drove away. "Bring me back a souvenir!"

Pigeon Point was Carolyn's favorite place. Dad parked the trailer on the strip of land north of the lighthouse. They set up camp and ate Chef Boyardee spaghetti, sweet corn, and white bread with butter and jam off paper plates. After dinner, they played Chinese checkers, Scrabble, or hearts. When it was bedtime, Mom folded the table down, and the booth seats made a double bed for Carolyn and Charlie. Carolyn liked having Charlie, Mom, and Dad close by. She loved the sound of the foghorn going off every few minutes and surf crashing against the rocks within a few hundred feet of the trailer.

While Charlie and Dad caught Capistrano, blue moon, and shiner perch in the churning white foam pools, Mom and Carolyn climbed down the steep path to the cove beach on the other side of the lighthouse. They combed the beach for seashells and pretty, curling, polished bits of driftwood. Sometimes Carolyn put her arms out, wishing she could ride the wind like the seagulls overhead. She followed the waves down and ran back as they rolled toward her while Mom lounged in the sunshine.

Once they drove north across the Golden Gate and headed west for Dillon Beach near Tomales Bay. All four went out at low tide to dig gooey-neck clams. Carolyn's arms weren't long enough to reach down into the holes she dug, but Charlie managed with his gangling limbs to bring one up in triumph. When the feast was laid on the table, Carolyn fled out the door and threw up in the bushes.

Another time, Dad drove for hours until he found Salt Point. The next morning, Mom, Charlie, and Carolyn watched Dad plod around in the deep tidal pools wearing chest-high rubber waders, prying abalone off the rocks. It was up to Mom to cut the sea snails from their shells and use a mallet to soften the muscle. Dad laughed and said it was a good way for Mom to vent her frustrations. Abalone tasted better than tough, sand-gritty gooey-neck clams. And Carolyn loved the lustrous, iridescent shells. Dad hung them around the front entry of the house. Oma used one as a soap dish.

Mom and Dad decided to take the summer off from building. Instead, they packed for a trip and hooked up the trailer. After three long days of travel over deserts and mountains, Carolyn finally met Grandpa Otis and Grandma Marg in Colorado Springs.

Grandpa Otis lifted her onto his lap. "Look at this pretty little honeybee."

When Carolyn struggled to get away from him, Dad grabbed her by the arm and hauled her out into the backyard. He shook her hard and asked what in the blazes was the matter with her. How could she hurt her grandfather like that? He told her she'd better be nice or she'd be sorry. Mom came out, too, and told him to stop it.

Grandpa didn't touch her again. Neither did Dad. They sat in the small living room talking in low voices. Grandma gave her two cookies and a glass of milk, but she wasn't hungry or thirsty. Grandma and Mom sat at the table with her, talking like nothing had happened. Charlie went outside to play.

It took three days for Carolyn to feel comfortable enough to sit beside Grandpa on the sofa. He read Bible stories to her. After a while, she relaxed against him. He didn't smell anything like Dock. His heart didn't beat as fast. His breathing was easy and relaxed. She liked the sound of his deep voice. She closed her eyes for a while and heard a click. She opened her eyes to see Mom smile and set a camera on the side table.

The next morning they left, heading south this time to Mesa Verde, with its steep, narrow paths and cliff ruins, and on to Monument Valley, with its familiar buttes. Charlie recognized scenes from Westerns and talked about marauding Indians who scalped people and tied them down on top of red ant hills. Mom looked back at Carolyn and told Charlie to talk about cavalry rescues instead.

They spent one whole day at the Grand Canyon. They drove to Bryce the next, taking a hike through the hoodoos before settling into the trailer for dinner and a good night's sleep. "We'll only have time to drive through Zion," Dad told Mom while they lay in bed a few feet away. "Then we'll have to head for Death Valley."

They spent the last night at Furnace Creek, sleeping in pools of their own sweat. Up at dawn, they made the long drive over the Sierras to the Central Valley, where the scents of sandy soil, almond orchards, and alfalfa fields reminded Carolyn of Oma's farm.

As soon as they pulled into the driveway, Carolyn wanted to jump out and run to the cottage. Dad told her to help unpack the trailer. Mom told her to dump her dirty clothes in the laundry room. Then, finally, "Okay, you can go." Unleashed, Carolyn ran.

Oma met her on the front porch, arms open, and hugged her tight. "It's about time you got home. It's been lonely around here." Oma lifted Carolyn's face and kissed her on both cheeks. All the

postcards Carolyn had sent were taped to the front of Oma's refrigerator. Seeing how much Oma had missed her, Carolyn offered to
stay home with Oma next time.

"Oh no, you won't. There's a whole world out there to see, and
your mother and father are showing you a corner of it. Where
would I be right now if I stayed home because I was afraid my
mother might miss me?" She waved Carolyn to a seat at the
kitchen table and turned the burner on under her teakettle. "So
how was it? Did you like your other grandparents?"

"They were nice." Carolyn didn't tell her how she'd hurt
Grandpa Otis's feelings or made Daddy mad, how she'd run away
and hidden for hours, worrying everyone. And she didn't tell her
how Mom complained when Dad would only stop for gas or a
quick lunch before driving again. Oma didn't like complaining.

Oma folded her hands on the table. "Tell me what you saw."

"It's all there on your refrigerator."

"Well, you must have seen other things along the way," Oma
pressed.

Not really. Dad had driven from dawn to dusk, hour after hour,
while she and Charlie half dozed in the backseat. They'd both seen
places they wanted to stop, but Dad said they didn't have time. He
told them they could play when they got to the campground, but
then when they did, it was near dusk, time to eat, time to shower,
time to get ready for bed. Dad was "dog-tired" and didn't feel like
playing games. He'd been driving all day. Carolyn shrugged. What
did Oma want her to say?

"Well. Now that you're all home, I can make a trip to the farm
and see Hitch and Donna Martin about business."

"Can I come with you?"

"I thought you didn't like traveling!"

Traveling with Oma wasn't the same as traveling with Dad and
Mom. "Please?"

"You'll have to ask your parents."

They didn't see any reason why she shouldn't. Charlie would
be off all day on his bicycle or at the high school pool. Dad had to

work. Mom did, too. It seemed no one would miss her. In fact, it would be easier for everyone if she went with Oma. Mom washed Carolyn's clothes and repacked some in a small duffel bag. They walked over together in the morning.

"How long will you be gone, Mama?"

"I was thinking it might be time to see Bernhard and Elizabeth. Carolyn hardly knows her cousin Eddie. And I haven't been down to Clotilde's in two years. She has an apartment in Hollywood. That would take a couple of days' driving time. A week, ten days? If that's all right with you."

Mom bit her lip and looked down at Carolyn. "I guess it's okay."

"We'll call you, Hildemara."

"Take good care of her."

"You know I will." Carolyn and Oma answered at the same time.

Mom looked sort of sad. "Well, you two have a good time together." Turning away, she lifted her hand in good-bye and headed back to the house.

❄ ❄ ❄

Traveling with Oma turned out to be even more fun than Carolyn expected. Oma drove fast with the windows all rolled down. She stopped twice before they even reached the outskirts of Tracy. "I've got to stretch these old legs."

When they arrived at Uncle Bernhard's nursery south of Sacramento, he took them on a tour through the rows of fruit trees in five-gallon buckets, Cousin Eddie trailing along behind. He stood a foot taller than Carolyn and had more muscle than Charlie. Aunt Elizabeth made fried chicken, mashed potatoes, and steamed corn for dinner. They had an extra bedroom for Oma and Carolyn to share.

The next morning, Oma said it was time to be off to Murietta. Everyone hugged and kissed. "Don't make it so long between visits,

Mama. Any chance you could get Hildie and Trip over here? We haven't seen them in a couple of years. Charlie's probably half-grown by now."

"They're building."

Uncle Bernie laughed. "Well, we know all about that."

❄ ❄ ❄

After a couple of days at the farm, where Oma talked business with Hitch and Donna Martin, they drove to Hollywood to visit Aunt Clotilde. She was tall and thin and dressed in narrow black pants and a bulky white sweater. She talked fast and laughed a lot. She took Carolyn and Oma to the movie studio where she worked in the costume department. Garments lined the walls, and sewing machines whirred as half a dozen people sat bent over pieces of fabric. Clotilde gaily called for everyone's attention and introduced Oma and Carolyn. "Okay, folks. Back to work." She laughed. "You have to see the back lot, Mama. It's fantastic!" She led Oma and Carolyn out. She knew everyone: makeup artists, set designers, directors, gaffers and grips, and even a few movie stars who, out of makeup and costume, looked like ordinary people.

One man looked Carolyn over with interest. "I didn't know you had such a pretty niece, Cloe."

"I didn't either!" Aunt Clotilde grinned and draped her arm around Carolyn's shoulders. "She's grown up since the last time I saw her. I've been asking my mother how my plain-Jane sister could come by such a pretty, willowy, blue-eyed little blonde."

Oma grunted. "Hildemara is pretty enough."

"Oh, Mama. I didn't mean anything by it. You know how much I love Hildie, but look at Carolyn. She's pretty enough to be in the movies."

Oma and Clotilde talked far into the night, quiet murmurs. In the morning, the three of them shared yogurt and fresh fruit for breakfast. Clotilde hugged and kissed Oma good-bye. "Come back again soon, Mama." Oma promised she would. Aunt Clotilde brushed Carolyn's cheek with her fingers and smiled. Leaning down, she kissed her on the cheek. "Give your mother my love. She's very special. Just like you." Pulling her robe more fully around herself, she crossed her arms and stood at the door as they left.

Oma didn't head north. "Since we've come all the way down here to Hollywood, we might as well go a little farther and see Disneyland."

Carolyn couldn't believe her good luck. "Charlie is going to be so mad he didn't come along."

"We're not going to say anything about it. It's not like I planned it. We don't want him feeling left out."

They checked into a hotel next to an orange grove and arrived at the gates of Disneyland as they opened the next morning. "We're going to beat the crowd to the train ride."

After they'd taken the grand circle tour, her grandmother took her hand and pulled her along, another destination already set in her mind. When Carolyn saw what it was, she gulped. "A rocket!"

"We're going. It's the closest we'll ever get to the moon." Caught up in Oma's excitement, Carolyn lost her fear and began to enjoy herself. Later, Oma took her on the riverboat ride, then to a race-track, and even a stagecoach. They saw a movie called *A Tour of the West* at the Circarama theater and an exhibit based on one of Oma's favorite books, *20,000 Leagues Under the Sea*.

That night, Oma gave her fair warning before calling Mom and Dad. "Not a word about Disneyland. We don't want to hurt anyone's feelings." But Mom didn't even ask to talk to Carolyn. Oma talked about Aunt Clotilde and the costume workroom and the back lot. "We're on our way home. I'm driving up the coast. The Central Valley is too hot. Two days, I think, maybe three."

On the drive north, Oma talked about the author John Steinbeck and the story he'd written about the Okies who had left the dust bowl and come west to California's Central Valley. "Good, hard-working people like the Martins. I'm blessed to have them. You should read *The Grapes of Wrath* when you're older. Find out what times were like when your mother was growing up in Murietta."

❋ ❋ ❋

They arrived home in time for dinner. Charlie bragged about spending every day of the last week at the Alameda County Fair with his best friend, Mitch Hastings. Oma winked at Carolyn and talked about Uncle Bernie, Aunt Elizabeth, and Aunt Clotilde.

Charlie tapped on Carolyn's bedroom door after Mom and Dad went to bed. "I didn't mean to rub it in about the fair." He flopped down beside her and explained how Mom had given him money for admission and meals. "She dropped me off every morning on her way to work." He stayed until Dad or Mitch's father picked them up just before closing. "It got pretty boring after the first couple days." He gave her a sly grin. "Can you keep a secret?"

Carolyn knew all about keeping secrets.

"Mitch and I snuck into the grandstands and watched the horse races." They'd made friends with a jockey while hanging around the stables. "He broke the rules and let Mitch ride his horse. I didn't have the guts." Charlie and Mitch had shared a pilfered beer and gone on the carnival rides with a couple of girls they picked up. "So, what'd you and Oma do?"

"Went to Uncle Bernie and Aunt Elizabeth's."

"How's Eddie?"

"Bigger."

"I thought you were going to the farm."

"We did. Then we went down to see Aunt Clotilde."

"See any movie stars?"

Nobody she recognized. She didn't mention that Aunt Clotilde said she was pretty enough to be in movies, or Disneyland, or any of the other stops up the coast of California.

"Boy, am I glad I stayed home." Charlie stretched. "I'm sorry you missed the fair."

Carolyn couldn't imagine anything worse than being dropped off in the morning and spending twelve to fourteen hours wandering alone among crowds of strangers.

1961

The summer before Carolyn entered high school brought back nightmares she never thought to have again. Mom and Dad focused on Charlie, who had only one year left before he'd launch into the wild blue yonder of college, hopefully on an academic or football scholarship. Oma mounted her own campaign for Carolyn to think about college, too. Why shouldn't a girl have the same opportunities her brother did? Her mother had gone to nurses' training, hadn't she?

Carolyn spent the summer alone. Sometimes Mitch Hastings came by to ask her brother if he wanted to do something. She hardly saw Charlie. He had a summer job at Kohl's Furniture Store. Even when he was home, they hardly talked. He'd eat and take off with Mitch. They'd go to the movies or the Gay 90s. At the end of the summer, Mitch came over on a motorcycle and took Charlie for a ride. Charlie talked about the motorcycle at dinner that night. He wanted one, too, and figured he could afford to buy one with what he'd saved from his summer job. Dad told him to hold off and think a little more about it. Mom said Charlie would need that money for school.

A week later, Dad tossed Charlie keys to a 1959 red Chevy Impala. "You get a ticket and that little baby will be parked for a month."

Charlie whooped. "No more riding the bus!"

Charlie gave Carolyn a ride on her first day of high school. He told her to stay clear of the upperclass lawn. "They're looking for fresh meat, and you're cute. Mitch thinks so, too." He grinned.

Carolyn felt a fluttering sensation in the pit of her stomach. "Does he?"

When they pulled into the student lot, boys swarmed the car. "Whoa, Charlie! Where'd you get this baby? She's a beaut." One boy opened the hood.

Another opened Carolyn's door. "Hey, Charlie! Who's this?"

Charlie got out of the car. "This is my little sister, Carolyn, and keep your grubby hands off. Carolyn, meet the zoo." He rattled off a dozen names. Some she had seen at the house. Most were complete strangers. Charlie came around the car. "She's shy. Okay? Come on, Sis. They don't bite."

One of the bigger boys grinned broadly. "I'd like to."

"Shut up, Brady."

Even close to Charlie, Carolyn felt hemmed in, trapped. Were all high school boys this big and bold?

A motorcycle roared into the lot and pulled in a few feet away. Mitch took off his helmet, swung his leg over the bike, and watched the gathering. "Hey, Mitch!" Charlie headed for his best friend. Carolyn's heart jumped. When Mitch said hi to her, she couldn't speak, her mouth went so dry. She looked down when her face heated up. When they all headed for the main building, she followed. Carolyn noticed Charlie couldn't walk more than a few feet without someone saying hi and asking how was his summer vacation, what'd he do. She felt conspicuous and uncomfortable. She wished she'd taken the bus.

When two girls came over to Charlie, he forgot about her. Mitch stepped into the main office and came out with a school map. He pointed out where they were on the map. Checking her class list, he gave her directions. Map and class schedule in hand, Carolyn found her way around. At lunch break, she sat at a table with other nervous freshman girls. When Charlie and Mitch came over, the girls gawked and fell silent. Mitch ignored them, but Charlie grinned at them all before turning to Carolyn. "I've got football practice after school. You'll have to take the bus home."

The girls whispered as they watched Charlie and Mitch walk away. Carolyn knew before lunch hour ended which girls wanted to be friends with her because Charlie was tall and handsome and he played football.

To please Oma, Carolyn focused on getting good grades right from the beginning of freshman year. She met other studious girls who didn't socialize with the in-crowd. A few of Charlie's friends tried to make conversation with her in the school corridors. She didn't encourage them, and they moved on to others who liked to flirt. Carolyn watched boys and girls pair up. Charlie put out the word his sister was off-limits, which was fine with her. She felt uncomfortable in her own skin when a boy looked at her, especially one she admired, like Mitch Hastings.

1962

By the time spring rolled around, Carolyn got her wish. No one noticed her. She felt invisible as she moved through the thronged corridors. The only boy who said hi every time he saw her was Mitch. Midterm he transferred into her study hall and sat in the front row. A linebacker, Mitch was taller and broader than Charlie, certainly too big for the student desks. He moved to the back row the next day, taking an empty desk across from her.

Sometimes, she felt him staring at her, but when she glanced his way, he'd be scribbling notes and flipping through his textbook.

She knew from Charlie he didn't date many girls, especially ones who "went after him."

Mom and Dad spent most of Carolyn's freshman year asking Charlie what he planned to do after he graduated. Charlie didn't know. Mom and Dad became increasingly frustrated. "You're a senior! You can't put off sending out applications for college!" The tension mounted. It got so Carolyn wished she could live with Oma. The more Dad and Mom pressured Charlie, the more Charlie dug in his heels.

Charlie vented to Carolyn. "I wish they'd get off my back. Take a wild guess what they did."

"What?"

"Called Mrs. Vardon. Now I've got the college counselor breathing down my neck. She pulled me out of study hall yesterday." He had to report to her office every day until he finished filling out a stack of college applications, wrote essays, and gathered and made copies of recommendation letters from teachers, coaches, and his part-time employer. "Guess which university sat on top of the pile. Berkeley!"

"What have you got against Berkeley?"

"Nothing, except I'm not that impressed with their football program." He gave her a conspiratorial grin. "Don't tell anyone, but I've applied to USC." He'd already talked to the college coach and been assured he qualified for a football scholarship.

"I'm not telling them anything until I graduate. Let 'em sweat!" He grinned with defiant pleasure. "I can hardly wait to see Dad's face when I tell him I'm going to play for the Trojans."

Charlie followed through with his plans, but Carolyn could tell he felt rather let down when Dad gave his blessing. And his instincts about the football program proved true, when USC went to the Rose Bowl during his first year.

Oma said she'd never seen the Tournament of Roses Parade and this would be a good time to go since Charlie was on the USC team in the big game. "Why don't you try to get time off, Hildemara?"

"Don't you think I'd like to go? Every day I miss is a day off our vacation time."

"Do you mind if I take Carolyn?"

Mom's face tightened, and then her shoulders drooped. "It'd mean a lot to Charlie to have family at the game."

Dad said he couldn't take time off either, so Oma took Carolyn. They stood among the crowds along Pasadena's Colorado Boulevard, watching gorgeous flower-scented floats, marching bands, and horseback riders pass by. Later, they attended the big game, where they could barely spot Charlie among the other Trojan uniformed players "warming the bench." He'd been happy to make the team, and he said he'd help win it again next year. They spent the night at Aunt Cloe's Beverly Hills mansion. Her producer husband was on-set somewhere in England, and her step-children off at boarding schools.

1963

About the time Carolyn started eleventh grade, Dock came back in her dreams. Sometimes she awoke aroused and confused. Guilt and shame caught her by the throat. She knew the facts of life. She'd taken biology. She'd overheard whispered conversations about sex in the girls' locker room. Girls who "did it" were considered sluts.

What would people say if they knew she'd lost her virginity while playing games with the man who lived next door? She'd only been in kindergarten, but it didn't do any good to tell herself it wasn't her fault. She knew it was. She had gone over there day after day, hadn't she? She'd told Dock she loved him. She let him do what he wanted.

Carolyn went to church with her parents—and Oma, when she wasn't away on one of her trips. She knew God existed. She imagined Him as old, with a long white beard and dressed in long white robes, His eyes blazing, and ready to cast the damned into a lake of fire. Was that where she would end up? God knew everything, didn't He? He saw everything. God would know she boiled inside. He probably knew why, even if she didn't.

She listened to Rev. Elias talk about the peace of God and doing what was right. She needed desperately to talk to someone. When she went over to talk with Oma, she found her grandmother packing for another trip. Oma spent more time away than at the cottage. She went to visit Uncle Bernie and Aunt Elizabeth or Aunt Clotilde. She flew to New York to see Aunt Rikka when her paintings were shown in some famous gallery. This time she was going to spend a week in San Francisco with her old friend Hedda Herkner, whose husband had died of a heart attack. Oma smiled over her shoulder as she folded a dress into her suitcase. "You're all grown-up, Carolyn. You don't need me."

❄ ❄ ❄

Two days after Oma left for San Francisco, a student came into Carolyn's civics class and gave the teacher a message. Mrs. Schaffer burst into tears when she read it. "President Kennedy has been shot down in Dallas, Texas."

Everyone sat stunned for a few seconds and then started asking questions.

A few girls burst into tears. Even a few boys looked ready to cry, though they tried hard not to show it. Mrs. Schaffer said everyone was to go to the auditorium for a school assembly. The principal would tell them everything he knew.

The principal cried, too.

Carolyn felt hollow and numb inside. Shouldn't she be scared? Others were. Shouldn't she be angry? Others were. She heard the news and waited to feel something, *anything*.

The assembly ended after less than fifteen minutes. School was dismissed. Parents would know about it. Students with cars headed for the parking lot. Most headed for the buses lined up in front of the high school. Someone had already lowered the American flag to half-mast. Carolyn got on her bus and sat in the back row. She stared out the window while others talked, sobbed, cussed in whis-pers, made speculations about the future. What would Kennedy's death mean to America? Would the space program end? What about the Peace Corps? So much for those who dreamed of being astronauts or going to foreign countries and solving world prob-lems. So much for hoping the world would ever get any better.

One by one, students got off at their stops. As the rows of seats emptied, Carolyn moved forward row by row until she sat near the front. She could see the bus driver's face in the rearview mirror. Tears ran down his cheeks. She stepped forward and clung to the pole next to the steps. "This is my stop, Mr. Landers." She had the feeling he would have forgotten if she hadn't spoken. He pulled over, stopped, and opened the bus doors.

Carolyn walked up the long driveway. The birds still sang. Everything still looked the same. She wished Oma were home, so she wouldn't have to go into an empty house. She took the key out from under the flowerpot and unlocked the door. The place felt like a tomb—closed up, airless, silent.

Craving the sound of a human voice, she turned on the tele-vision. Every channel covered the assassination. She saw the joyful scenes before the shooting—people holding up welcome signs, others watching from windows and rooftops, the smiling president and his pretty wife waving from the car. Then three shots. A Secret Service man getting out of the car behind the president. People in the crowd screamed and cried; policemen looked up to see where the shots had come from. Shaking, she wanted to scream. She wanted to put her foot through the television. Instead, she shut it off and went into the kitchen.

Mom had filled the cookie jar with Oreos. Leftovers filled the refrigerator. A roast defrosted on the counter, blood pooling in the plastic wrap. Carolyn pictured Jackie with her husband's blood on her designer suit.

She went over to the cottage, wandered through Oma's flower garden, and then took the key from under the mat and opened the door. The cottage felt like an empty shell without Oma, even with sunlight coming through the windows. But it smelled familiar and felt cozy. She went to the bedroom and crawled under the covers of Oma's bed, wishing she could curl up against Oma as she'd done when she was a little girl. It was the only time she could remember feeling truly safe as a child.

Only a moment seemed to pass, and she heard someone call her name. She heard a door open.

"Carolyn." Mom's voice came closer, voice hoarse with worry. "Carolyn!" Carolyn felt someone shaking her. "We've been looking all over for you!"

"I'm here," Carolyn mumbled, mouth dry. Her head felt strange. What was she doing in Oma's bed? Then she remembered. The president had been shot. Despair engulfed her.

"Didn't you hear us calling?"

"I didn't hear anything." She felt sick. "I don't want to hear anything."

"Come on home, Carolyn." She pulled the covers down. "You can sleep in your own room." She stood in the doorway. "Be sure to make the bed before you come."

Inexplicably angry, Carolyn yanked the covers up again. "I'm not coming! I'm sleeping here tonight!"

Mom sat on the edge of the bed. "Carolyn, we're all upset. . . ."

Carolyn shifted away. "Dad will have the television on. He'll want to watch the news over and over again. You know he will. And you'll be mangling something." She started to cry. "I don't want to see Kennedy shot again and again. I don't want to keep hearing about it!" She covered her head with the blankets. "Just go away, Mom. Please. Just let me go to sleep and pretend it never happened."

Mom rubbed her back and sighed heavily. "You're not the only one who feels that way." She stood. "Are you sure you're okay here alone?"

Carolyn wanted to scream at her. Of course she wasn't okay. She had never been okay. What kind of a mother would leave her vulnerable little girl alone every afternoon? A mother who didn't care, that's what kind. Why should her mother care now?

No one was ever home when she got there. What difference did it make if she spent the night in the cottage—or anywhere else, for that matter? It wasn't like Dock would come back after more than ten years. Even he hadn't wanted her in the end. "I'm fine, Mom. Go away."

"Well, if you're sure . . ." Her mother sounded hesitant. Something in her voice caught Carolyn's attention. She pulled the blankets off her head, but her mother was already heading for the door. As it closed behind her, Carolyn wept. She lay in the darkness, wishing her mother had argued a little. She wished she'd sat on the bed for a few minutes longer.

But then, she'd have to care to do that.

1965

While everyone else in her class grew more excited with the approach of graduation, Carolyn dreaded it. It meant she would have to leave home. She didn't have any great desire to go to college, but it seemed to be what everyone expected of her.

Oma made calls and fanned out university and state college brochures and application forms on the kitchen table. "War or not, the world goes on, Carolyn, and you have to make plans." UC Berkeley was close. She could come home on weekends. So she applied there, for Oma's sake, as well as Chabot junior college and Heald College in Hayward.

Dad seemed stunned when Carolyn was accepted at Berkeley. Oma asked why, for goodness' sake. "Did you think your daughter was stupid?"

Her brother came home for her graduation. It passed in a blur. Dad took pictures. Mom made a nice dinner. Oma decorated a cake. Carolyn received cards of congratulations and money from Uncle Bernie and Aunt Elizabeth, Aunt Clotilde, and Aunt Rikka.

Charlie grew restless. He wanted to go into town and see friends, although most of them had gone elsewhere for the summer. Dad asked if he ever heard from Mitch Hastings. Charlie said they talked. Mitch's mom had died of cancer, and his dad had moved to Florida and remarried. Mitch had made the Ohio State team, second-string. Mitch wouldn't be coming back to Paxtown anytime soon, if ever.

Carolyn felt a pang of disappointment. She supposed it was silly to wish Mitch Hastings might come home someday and see her as someone other than Charlie's kid sister.

"What do you say we take a ride, Sis?"

Mom told them to go ahead and have some fun.

They drove into town. Charlie said he was proud of her. She had received an award for being on the honor roll every semester since freshman year. "Why so glum?"

"Just scared, I guess."

"Scared of what?"

"Whether I can make it or not."

"You'll make it." Charlie drove from the high school to the end of Main Street, turned around, and came back. He honked and waved at people he knew. Everyone remembered her brother. He talked about college friends and professors, classes and football games, beer busts and pretty sorority girls. Charlie, so full of confidence, afraid of nothing.

"I'm amazed Dad agreed to send you to Berkeley. It's a hotbed of subversives!"

"He was always after you to go."

"Yeah, well, you're another story. It doesn't seem like a good fit for you. USC is hard enough, even for a coddled football player. But Berkeley! Man, that place has a reputation for chewing people up and spitting them out."

"Oma talked me into it."

He laughed. "You're going to like living in another universe, Carolyn." He honked at someone else and waved before giving her a quick glance. "Just don't turn into a hippy."

"You're the one letting your hair grow." Dad had made more than one comment about it over the last few days. "How do you get away with it? I thought you had to keep it short for football."

Charlie scowled. He didn't answer immediately. "Football's something else that chews you up and spits you out. Seems like a stupid waste of time when you consider all the guys going to Vietnam and dying to protect our freedom."

Her body tightened. She stared at him. He gave her a quick glance, an odd look on his face. "Mitch joined the Marine Corps. Did I tell you that?"

Her heart sank. "You said he was playing football for Ohio State."

"He was. He quit."

Her heart started pounding. She kept looking at Charlie. "I hope the war ends before you finish college."

"It won't." He stared straight ahead. Someone honked. He didn't notice this time.

"I hope you don't get drafted."

"I won't get drafted, Carolyn."

She clenched her hands at the assurance in his tone. "Don't enlist, Charlie. Please, don't even think about enlisting."

"I already did."

She put her hands over her ears. "No, you didn't! Don't tell me you did! Don't!"

Charlie turned off at the end of Main Street and took the road past the fairgrounds, out to the road along the hills. "Take it easy."

Take it easy? Take it easy! She couldn't catch her breath.

"Someone has to go. Why not me? Why is it always someone else who has to do the dirty work? You're going to have to help me break the news to Mom and Dad."

When she tried to open the car door, he yanked her back. "What are you doing? Are you crazy?" Swerving to the side of the road, Charlie slammed on the brakes. "Are you trying to get us both killed?"

"You're the one who's going to get killed!" Sobbing, she jerked herself free, scrambled out of the car, and ran.

Charlie caught up with her. "Carolyn!" He pulled her around and locked his arms around her. "Hey. I didn't think you'd take it like this."

She felt half-smothered against his USC jacket. She clung to it, burying her face in his chest. "I don't want you to go, Charlie. Don't go. Please don't go."

"It's too late to change my mind, even if I wanted to, which I don't."

She hadn't heard the worst of it yet.

❄ ❄ ❄

"The Marine Corps?" Dad turned ghastly white. *"The Marine Corps?"*

Charlie looked confident. "Why not be among the best of the best?"

"Why did you do it?" Dad swore. "Because Mitch Hastings joined up?"

"No, Dad. I can think for myself. I'm doing it to serve my country." He sounded angry. "I thought you, of all people, would understand." He looked from Dad to Mom and gave a nervous laugh. "You raised me to be a patriot, didn't you? You've been talking about what it means to be an American for as long as I can remember. *You* served. Why shouldn't I?"

"I was a medic, Charlie! We went in after the damage was done, to clean up the mess. The Marines are always the *first* in, the *first* up the beach!" His voice broke.

Mom covered her face and wept.

Charlie looked embarrassed. "I'll be okay."

"Yeah. Every young man thinks he's going to be okay. You signed up to be cannon fodder!" Dad shoved his chair back and left the table. Mom looked at Charlie, tried to speak. Nothing came out.

"I'm doing the right thing, Mom."

Her mouth trembled. "It's not a football game, Charlie."

Charlie's face tightened. "Do you think I don't know that?"

"Why didn't you discuss this with us first?"

"I don't need your permission. It's my life. It's my decision." His defiance melted when Mom started to cry again. "Mom . . ." He reached out to her. She got up and headed for the bedroom.

Charlie pushed his chair back and gave Carolyn an apologetic look. "I've got to get out of here." He glanced toward the back of the house. "I wish they'd stop thinking of me as their little boy."

"Can I go with you?"

"Not this time. Okay? I'm supposed to meet a couple of the guys at the Gay 90s."

Carolyn sat at the table alone, listening to Charlie's red Impala speed down the gravel driveway. She wished she could run, too. She wished she could take off and go hang out with friends who would understand what she was feeling, maybe help her make some kind of sense out of the world.

She went to the cottage. Oma turned off the television and patted the space beside her on the sofa.

"Charlie's enlisted in the Marine Corps."

Oma let out a deep breath. "I knew he'd done something. He looked different."

Carolyn put her head in Oma's lap and wept. "I don't want him to go."

Oma stroked her hair. "It's not your choice, *Liebling*. All you can do is live your life and let Charlie live his." She rested her hand on Carolyn's head. "It's a lesson I've had to learn over the years."

"I'm going to worry about him every day."

"No. You're going to go to the university and study and meet interesting people. You're going to make dreams for yourself. You'll be so busy you won't have time to fret."

"They'll send him to Vietnam."

"We don't know that yet."

"They will, Oma."

"Then we'll pray. We'll get everyone in the church and all our relatives and friends praying, too. And we'll write letters to him so he knows we love him. Sometimes that's all you can do, Carolyn.

Love people for who they are, pray, and leave them in God's hands."

Carolyn wasn't sure she could trust God. After all, God hadn't done anything to protect her from Dock.

CAROLYN WORKED ALL summer serving hamburgers and milk
shakes at the local diner, and Charlie came in every day. He
didn't have to report to San Diego for basic training until the
end of summer. Mitch had already finished basic and transferred
to infantry training. Charlie drove down when Mitch called
and said he had weekend liberty. When Charlie came home, he
disappeared for a day without saying where he was going. He
came into the diner just before Carolyn finished work and gave
her a ride home.

"I decided not to wait. I'm flying to San Diego on Friday. I'll be
in basic by the beginning of next week."

She made fists in her lap and looked out the window. "Why are
you in such a hurry to die, Charlie?"

"I don't plan to die. I just can't stand hanging around here any
longer listening to Mom cry or having Dad sit and stare at the
news. It's better if I go. You want to be the one to drive me to the
airport?"

"No."

"Come on, Sis." He tried to coax her. "I'll loan you my car for four years."

"I don't want your car." She wanted to know her brother would be safe, and he'd just obliterated that hope.

He sighed dramatically. "I guess I'll take the bus and then a cab." She knew he expected her to give in.

Dad drove Charlie to the airport. Mom closed herself in the master bedroom and didn't come out all that day or that evening.

Three weeks later, Carolyn packed and tried to prepare herself to leave home.

Dad said Mom wasn't up to taking her, and he had to work. Her grandmother would make sure she got settled.

❄ ❄ ❄

Carolyn carried her things into the dorm. When everything had been put away in her small room, Oma suggested they go for a walk. "I'd like to see the campus before I leave." They wandered for two hours along the walkways past great halls and through plazas. Oma wanted to see Sather Gate, the Bancroft Library, and the Campanile. "I would've given anything to attend a university like this. My father took me out of school when I turned twelve. He thought education was wasted on a girl."

"You know more than most of the teachers I've met, Oma."

Oma gave a short, humorless laugh. "You don't give up just because someone says you can't do something. Sometimes telling someone she can't makes her want it all the more."

Oma took Carolyn's hand as they walked back to the old gray Plymouth. "Time for me to go." Oma hugged her tightly and patted her cheek. "You'll be learning from masters. Take advantage of every moment you have."

"I'll do my best."

"Your best is all anyone can ask."

❉ ❉ ❉

Carolyn kept her word. She attended every class, took voluminous notes, studied late into the night, turned in all her assignments on time, and passed her midterms.

Charlie made it through basic and came home on leave. He drove to Berkeley and took Carolyn over to San Francisco for a day. He'd changed since she'd last seen him. He didn't say much about training, but pressed her for information about her classes, how she liked Berkeley, if she was finding her way okay. She said everything was fine, just fine.

They sat on a bench along Fisherman's Wharf. Girls looked at Charlie as they walked by. He looked back at a few. She teased him. "Wishing your little sister wasn't here?"

He laughed and said being locked up in a barracks for weeks on end tended to make a man appreciate the scenery more. "What about you, Sis? Having any fun?"

"Fun? I'm concentrating on keeping my head above water."

"Oma said you made the dean's list."

Carolyn shrugged.

Charlie straightened and studied her. "You'll make it, Carolyn. You're a survivor."

What about him? Would he make it? "I love you, Charlie. If anything happens to you . . ." She wondered if school was even important anymore.

He put his arm tight around her shoulders. She rested her head against him. He didn't make any promises this time.

When Charlie dropped her off at the door, the resident manager asked to speak with her. Two students weren't getting along. "You seem to get along with everybody. Would you mind trying another roommate?" Carolyn didn't have the nerve to say no. The RM looked relieved.

Depressed, Carolyn went upstairs, bought a Coke from the vending machine, and settled down to study. The door burst open, banging into the closet. Without apology, a girl entered and swung a duffel bag off her shoulder, flinging it onto the striped bed. "Rachel Altman." She extended her hand. "Since we're now roommates, call me Chel." She had a gravelly voice with an Eastern accent.

Startled, Carolyn shook hands. The girl had an arresting, if not beautiful, face framed by a mass of long, curling red hair held back by a woven leather headband with beaded tassels. She wore a white low-necked blouse that was nearly transparent and would have been indecent if not for the bangles and beads. A macramé belt with more beads held up skintight, brown corduroy, hip-hugging bell-bottom pants. Pulling her hand free, the girl dropped onto the bed and gave it a few experimental bounces. Her gold circle bracelets jangled. "Well, it ain't the Waldorf."

Carolyn stared, speechless. Chel looked Carolyn over, from her white Keds and socks to her ponytail. Her mouth tipped in a sardonic smile. "Let me guess. You're an education major, *primary* education. Right?"

Carolyn confessed. "What about you?"

"Liberal arts, baby. I'm liberal, and I like art. Seemed a good choice at the time, though I've been thinking about changing it to psychology or sociology. Any *-ology* would do."

"How did you guess mine?"

Chel's smile turned sly. "I just looked around. All your notes in neat little piles, typed. Books lined up. No dust on your desk. Your bed is made. All you need is a shiny apple on your desk." She flung herself backward onto the bed and put her hands behind her head. "And you're wearing a bra! I'll bet when you get dressed up, you wear a skirt and a nice sweater and pearls." She muttered a curse and lunged up, startling Carolyn again. "Don't worry, babe. I don't bite. Not girls anyway." She grinned broadly. "You look pretty uptight. You want some pot?" She laughed. "You should see your face. Haven't tried it yet, have you?" She stood and headed for the door. "Let's get out of here for a while, have coffee at the student union. I promise to be on my best behavior." She dragged Carolyn. "Come on. Live a little."

Carolyn forgot all about her studies.

Chel talked all afternoon. She seemed high on life—or something. She told Carolyn she'd grown up at the Waldorf, cared for by a well-paid but disinterested nanny while her even more disinterested daddy went off to make his millions, and her bored, disinterested mother went off to ski at Saint Moritz or buy more designer clothes in Paris. "Heaven knows where she is right now, and I couldn't care less. They're both capitalist pigs polluting the air we breathe."

She had left New York City and come to Berkeley because "Berkeley is the center of the universe, babe. It's where everything is happening! Haven't you looked around at all? I want to be in the middle of it. Don't you?"

Carolyn surprised herself and admitted she'd never had the courage to be in the middle of anything. "I've always found a way to blend in."

"A skill I obviously don't have." When Chel laughed, people looked, and she didn't care.

Carolyn had seen free spirits around the campus, but she'd never been this close to one. Chel was like an exotic bird with wild, colorful plumage who'd managed to escape from a zoo and find her way to Carolyn's dorm room. Chel fascinated Carolyn and made her laugh.

Chel looked smug. "I think you and I are going to get along real well."

She hardly saw Chel during the day, but they talked for hours when she returned from classes or wherever she'd gone. She brought pot back to the room. She put a wet towel against the bottom of the door and opened the window. "Come on, Caro. It's not going to kill you." Carolyn took a tentative puff. Chel laughed at her. *"Inhale."* After a few drags, Carolyn found herself talking. Chel lounged on her bed and kept asking questions. When asked if she'd ever had sex, Carolyn told her about Dock. Chel stopped smiling.

Despite their vast difference in material resources, Carolyn found their backgrounds weren't that different. Absentee parents who, when around, were still so preoccupied with their own problems and projects they were blind to anyone else. Of course, Mom and Dad had never been blind to Charlie. But then, Charlie was something special. She talked a lot about her brother.

"You're like a marionette, aren't you, babe? Dancing to everyone else's tune?"

No one made Chel dance.

Carolyn wanted to be just like her.

1966

Once a week Carolyn received a letter from Oma, going over family news and whatever had been happening around Paxtown, which was never much. Mom called a couple of times a month, usually when Carolyn was away at class. The RM left notes in her box. *Your mom called. They're looking forward to having you home for summer break.* Carolyn groaned. She didn't want to go home, but she couldn't afford to stay in Berkeley.

"If you don't want to go home, babe, check in with the employment office. They can line up a job for you. We'll get an apartment, have some fun."

"I can't afford an apartment, Chel."

"Did I say you had to pay?"

Chel didn't let up on the idea until Carolyn gave in. She figured staying in Berkeley with Chel might be easier than explaining to her parents and Oma why her grades had dipped dramatically. Mom and Dad didn't put up a fight. That didn't surprise her. Why would they care? But when Oma didn't fuss about it, she wondered if anyone missed her. Chel told her to join the club.

Charlie, on leave after infantry training, came to visit one afternoon. He looked surprised when she answered the door. "I guess Berkeley is having its way with you."

"What's that supposed to mean?"

"Attitude, too." He grinned. "Mind if I come in? Or are you going to leave your poor brother standing out here in the hall?"

She threw herself into his arms and hugged him. "Come on in. Take a look around." Chel had rented the apartment furnished and added a few colorful pillows to the beige sofa, an Oriental rug under the coffee table. They'd nailed up posters of Venice, Paris, London, van Gogh's *Sunflowers*, and Monet's *Nympheas*, but it was Georgia O'Keeffe's *Grey Line* that dominated the living room.

Charlie gave her a troubled look. "Interesting decor."

"Glad you like it." Carolyn lounged on the couch. "Chel pays the rent. Or rather her dad does. His secretary dumps money in her account every month."

"Must be nice."

"I think she'd rather have parents who cared."

He wanted to know more about Chel. "She's the first real friend I've ever had, Charlie." She didn't want to talk behind her friend's back. "You want a glass of wine? We have Chablis or cabernet sauvignon."

"I'm driving."

She poured herself a tall glass and brought it back to the couch. He raised his brows. She lifted the glass. "Never seen a girl have a glass of wine before?" She drank deeply.

"Lots of times. Just not my little sister."

She laughed, relaxed after half a glass. She asked him a couple of questions, knowing he'd take over the conversation. He talked about training and his new buddies-in-arms. "We're all getting transferred to different bases. Dad says it was a lot different when he was in the military. They trained and went overseas as a unit. I'll be going alone."

Her muscles tightened. "Are you going to Vietnam, Charlie?"

"Not yet."

She finished the glass of wine and thought about having another. Instead, she put the glass on the coffee table and leaned her head against the sofa. She wanted to cry, but it would only make him wish he hadn't come.

Charlie tugged a strand of her hair. "Try not to worry about me so much."

She rolled her head toward him. "Do you ever worry about me, Charlie?" Did anybody?

"I will now." He leaned over and kissed her cheek before pushing to his feet. "It's getting late. I'd better get on the road. You have to work tomorrow."

Drowsy, she followed him to the door. "Tell Mom and Dad I'm doing fine." If they asked.

He grinned. "I thought I'd tell them your apartment smells like pot and you keep bottles of wine in your fridge and pornographic art on your living room wall."

"It's a flower!"

He laughed. "Yeah, right. Some flower."

She grinned, bolstered by the alcohol. "You have a dirty mind, Charlie."

"Relax. I'm not going to tell them anything. If they ask, I'll suggest they come see for themselves."

"Like they'd have time for that."

He hugged her and spoke seriously against her hair. "Don't mess around too much, okay? I'd hate for you to have regrets later on." He let her go.

She leaned in the doorway. "Didn't you mess around when you were at USC?"

"Yeah, but I'm a guy. It's permitted."

"Male chauvinist pig."

Punching the elevator button, her brother looked back at her. "Don't go too crazy, Sis." He jerked his chin up, gave her a sad smile, and disappeared into the elevator.

She went back into the apartment and poured herself another glass of wine. She cried and swore and wondered what the future held for each of them.

CAROLYN WENT HOME twice during the first part of her sopho-
more year, once for Thanksgiving and then for a few days during
Christmas break. Both times Mom and Dad commented on her
bell-bottom pants, embroidered blouses, leather fringed jacket, and
moccasins. She'd let her hair grow and left it hanging loose rather
than pulled back in a ponytail. They didn't approve.

"How're your classes going? Are they harder this year? What will
you be taking next?"

Carolyn had expected questions, but this felt like an interrogation. "My main goal right now is to get through finals."

"What do you mean 'get through'?"

Here it comes, Carolyn thought, trying to prepare herself. "I
didn't make dean's list last time."

"We know." Mom looked as grim as she sounded.

"I don't think I'd make a good teacher. I'm thinking about
changing my major."

Dad raised his head and looked at her. "To what?"

"I was thinking about liberal arts. I'm not sure yet. I'm still trying to find myself."

Dad stared, his eyes blazing. "'Find yourself'? What's that supposed to mean?"

Carolyn wondered what her parents would say if they knew how often she went to the Fillmore or that Chel had talked her into going on the pill. Carolyn had no plans to dive into the free love movement, but Chel insisted. She could be a bulldog about some things. "Never say never, babe. And better safe than sorry." Chel wouldn't let up until she got her way, which never took long. Carolyn had always been good at giving in. Chel—charismatic, fun, smart—made it even easier.

Mom and Oma started calling more frequently and asking more questions.

They also asked when Carolyn might come home for another visit. Carolyn found excuses to stay in Berkeley.

When Mom called and said Charlie had a month's leave, Carolyn knew what it meant. He'd gotten orders to go to Southeast Asia. "He's coming home, Carolyn. I know he'd love to spend time with you."

Chel offered to drive. "Save you from taking the bus." They piled into Chel's new red Camaro purchased with "Daddy's guilt money."

As Chel turned in to the driveway, Carolyn spotted Oma working in her English flower garden. Oma stood, brushing off her hands, and shaded her eyes. Chel slowed enough that she didn't leave a cloud of dust around Oma as they passed by and parked the Camaro behind the garage next to Charlie's Impala. "Come, meet Oma." Carolyn headed for the cottage.

Oma hugged and kissed her. "It's about time you came home for a visit."

"I've been avoiding everyone." Carolyn meant it to sound like a joke. She introduced Chel.

Oma looked her over. "Would you ladies like some tea?"

"My favorite drink." Chel grinned.

As they sat at the kitchen table, Oma turned her attention to
Chel. She asked one question after another. Carolyn's stomach
tightened into a knot, waiting for her friend to say something
outrageous, but Chel didn't seem to mind the third degree. She
easily avoided questions about her parents and talked instead about
her succession of nannies and private tutors. She'd been sent off to
a boarding school in Massachusetts, then to a finishing school in
France. "I flunked out, of course, though I learned enough French
to find my way around."

"Je parle français également." Oma told her she once worked for
a French family in Montreaux and spent a few days in Paris before
going to England and then on to Montreal. Chel started asking Oma
questions; and her grandmother told of her lack of formal education, her dream of owning a restaurant and hotel, her quest to learn
languages and business skills, her journey from one job to another
to make her own way in the world. She talked about buying and
running a boardinghouse, in which her future husband boarded. "I
taught Carolyn's Opa how to speak English." She told them about
life on a prairie wheat farm and how she ended up in California.

Chel drank it all in. So did Carolyn, who had heard only bits
and pieces of Oma's story.

"Well, I've talked enough for today. You ladies had better get
over to the house before your mother thinks I'm holding you
hostage." Oma walked them to the door.

"Your grandmother is the grooviest person I've ever met!" Chel
said on the way to the house.

Charlie sat in the living room, watching television. He looked
bored when Carolyn walked in. Then he saw Chel on her heels.
Carolyn had never seen that look on his face before.

Chel dumped her backpack and stepped into the living room.
She stopped in front of him, hands on her hips as she looked
at him. "So you're the superhero Caro talks about all the time."
Speechless, Charlie stared, a bemused smile curving his lips. Chel
gave her growling laugh and cast Carolyn a catlike smile. Carolyn
didn't have to guess whether her best friend liked Charlie.

Carolyn hugged Charlie and introduced them formally. "We'd better stow our stuff in the bedroom, Chel."

Mom stood in the kitchen making dinner. Her eyes widened when she saw them. Carolyn had already warned Chel her parents were uptight, workaholic, staunch Republican, churchgoing people. Mom managed a smile and a welcome. She looked at Carolyn, a flicker of desperation in her eyes. "Your dad will be home soon. He had to go into town on an errand."

Chel tossed her pack in the corner of Carolyn's bedroom. She looked around at the pink walls, lace curtains, white chenille bed-spread with pink and white pillows, and Carolyn's old rag doll. When she picked it up, Carolyn took it and put it on the dresser. "Oma made it for me."

"A woman of many talents."

They went back out to the living room. When Dad came up the drive in his squad car, Chel put her hand over her heart. "I haven't even done anything, and here come the police."

Charlie laughed. "Dad works for the sheriff's department."

She grinned at him. "I know, soldier." She glanced at Carolyn's face and leaned over to whisper. "You think he'll shoot me?"

Over the next few hours, Carolyn realized Chel could play a role perfectly. She resurrected all the manners she had been taught at the Waldorf Astoria in New York City and impressed Mom and Dad with her erudite views on the world. When Mom asked if she'd traveled much, Chel talked about a half-dozen cities in Europe, various museums, and historical sites.

Dad finally brought up politics, much to Carolyn's discom-fort. Mom didn't look any happier. Chel said openly she was against the war in Vietnam and talked about how America needed changes in civil rights. When Dad opened his mouth to speak, Mom tried to change the subject. Dad scowled, aware of Mom's ploy.

Chel must have noticed too, and she trumped her. "I'd like very much to hear your opinion, sir, and how you came by it." Her sincerity seemed to surprise Dad. In the space of a second, Carolyn saw her father look past the hippy garb, the wild hair, the bangles and beads and headband, to Rachel Altman. He laid down whatever weapons he'd taken up in his mental arsenal and declared a truce by talking fondly about his days at Berkeley.

Charlie could hardly keep his eyes off Chel, though he tried to hide his fascination from Mom and Dad. Carolyn understood how easily Chel could mesmerize people. She was bewitching Mom and Dad with stories Carolyn had never heard. She wondered how many of them were true.

After dinner, Chel started to help clear the table. Mom quickly protested. Chel suggested a drive. "I'd love to see the town that shaped you, Caro." She invited Charlie, of course, but Mom and Dad came up with some lame excuse to squelch that idea. Maybe they'd noticed more than Carolyn realized.

Paxtown hadn't changed at all. They cruised Main Street like high school girls and stopped in at the Gay 90s. Chel ordered beer and flashed her fake ID so fast the waiter didn't get a good look at it, but he said he wouldn't serve Chel unless she produced a birth certificate stamped with a government seal. Unrepentant, she grinned at him. "No law against trying."

Chel wanted to see the church Carolyn's family attended. "Think it's open?" Chel got out and went up the steps to try the door. "Locked tight as a vault." The windows were too high off the ground for her to peer in. "Where else did you hang out?"

Carolyn shrugged. "That's about it."

"Looks like the eighteen hundreds around here. You wouldn't be able to sneeze in a town like this without having everyone know about it." She grinned. "No wonder you're so uptight."

"Some things go on that nobody ever knows about."

Chel looked apologetic. "I forgot about Dock." She drove down Main Street again, past the high school. "I never would've made it in a town like this."

The porch light had been left on. They took off their shoes and tiptoed into the house. Chel used the bathroom first and came out in a Cal T-shirt that hit midthigh. Carolyn went in to brush her teeth. The hall clock chimed once. She heard low voices in the hallway between her bedroom and Charlie's. When she came out, Charlie stood leaning against his doorjamb, bare-chested, pajama bottoms hanging low on his hips. She caught an odd look on his face before he straightened, wished them both a good night, and closed his door.

Later, the sound of the door opening awakened Carolyn. She saw Chel's silhouette as she went out, closing the door silently behind her. Maybe she needed to use the bathroom again. Rolling over, Carolyn went back to sleep. Chel slipped carefully back into bed just before the hall clock chimed four. "Are you okay, Chel?"

Chel jumped and let out a soft four-letter word. "I thought you were asleep."

"How many times have you gotten up tonight?"

"Once."

Once? "Where have you been?" She felt a sudden premonition and wished she hadn't asked.

"I was giving Charlie a going-away present."

The hair rose on the back of Carolyn's neck. "You didn't—"

"Relax, Caro. I asked him first." She sounded amused. "He said yes."

"If my parents ever find out . . ."

"I'll tell them I felt it my patriotic duty."

Carolyn groaned. "You're insane!"

"Maybe I am." She gave a bleak laugh. "At least, it gives me a good excuse to do what I want. You should try it sometime." She turned her back to Carolyn. "We talked, too. We didn't just—"

"I don't want to hear what you did with my brother."

"Are you mad?"

"I don't know."

"I like him, Caro. A Marine, no less." She choked up. "Who would've guessed?" She let out her breath. "I'm going back to Berkeley in the morning."

"I'm not mad, Chel. Maybe I should be, but . . . you don't have to go."

"Yes, I do. You need time with your family. They care about you."

"Yeah, right."

"Maybe you can't see it, but I can. And I'm getting out of the way."

"They were more interested in what you had to say than anything I've ever said."

"Maybe that's because you have to be drunk before you'll open up and talk to anyone." She raised herself up and peered at Carolyn. "If they didn't give a squat, they wouldn't have come home every night or taken you on every vacation. They wouldn't have moved your grandmother into a cottage next door. So don't try to tell me they didn't care." She warmed to her subject. "They call every few weeks and ask when you're coming home for a visit. You want to know the last time my dad invited me home? I can't tell you because I can't remember. The last time I saw my father face-to-face was more than two years ago."

"You get letters."

"His secretary sends a form letter once a month and encloses a check. Money, Caro, that's what I get from my parents." Her voice broke. Carolyn could hear her swallow. "Money's the cheapest, easiest gift anyone can give. If I had a hint my father or mother loved me, I'd—" She sounded angry. She spit out a four-letter word and flopped down again. "I'm going back to Berkeley, and you're staying here, if for no other reason than this might be the last time you see your brother alive."

Carolyn could feel her shaking and realized Chel was crying. She'd never seen this side of Chel before, broken, in pain. "I'm sorry. You don't have to leave."

"I can't stand seeing what I've missed, Caro, what I'll never have. What you've had all your life and don't have the sense to appreciate."

She turned over and Carolyn could tell the conversation was over. She was awake for more than an hour, wondering what would happen in the morning. What would her parents say if they found out what Chel had done? Chel would learn there was no such thing as a *Father Knows Best* or *Leave It to Beaver* family.

❄ ❄ ❄

When Carolyn awakened, Chel was gone. So was her duffel bag. Mom sat at the table with a cup of coffee. "Your friend left about an hour ago."

"Why?" Had Mom or Dad guessed what happened last night and told her to leave?

Mom shrugged. "She didn't say. She thanked us and said she had to get back to Berkeley."

Carolyn avoided her gaze. "Is Charlie up yet?"

"I guess he's sleeping in."

After the first uncomfortable moments after Charlie got up, the two of them wandered the property, talking about all sorts of things. He'd kept up with friends and filled her in on what they were doing, not that she had ever been part of their group. He talked about the Marine Corps and Vietnam and how much he believed in what he was doing. Maybe he'd stay in and make it a career, but he wasn't really thinking beyond the years of his enlistment. "How about you, Caro?" When he used Chel's nickname, she knew her friend was on his mind even if he didn't bring her up.

The whole family went to church Sunday morning. Charlie wore his uniform. He looked every inch the Marine, fit and confident. Rev. Elias announced to the congregation that Charlie was going to Vietnam. People swarmed Charlie after the service. Everyone said they would be praying for him.

Carolyn decided to skip Monday classes and stay home another day. Surprisingly, Mom and Dad didn't quibble. Dad pulled out the slide projector, and they enjoyed pictures of trips to the beach and Colorado. That night, Carolyn dreamed of Charlie in dress blues standing in a field of white crosses. Awakening abruptly, she prayed it wasn't a premonition.

Before leaving on Tuesday morning, she went over to say good-bye to Oma. They talked briefly about Chel. "That girl is headed for trouble."

"You heard her story, Oma. Despite all the money, she hasn't had an easy time of it."

"She can use her parents as an excuse to ruin her life or as a reason to do better. It's up to her."

"Is that why you shared so much of your life story with her?"

Oma tipped Carolyn's chin. "You'd better watch out for yourself, *Liebling*. If you don't decide for yourself what you want from life, someone will do it for you. And you may not like the result."

Carolyn thought that over as Charlie drove her back to Berkeley. They talked about Chel on the way. Carolyn abruptly changed the subject. "I hate the war, Charlie. I'm protesting it."

His knuckles whitened on the steering wheel. "If Dad hadn't fought, where would we be now?"

"We're not talking about World War II and the Nazis."

"We can't all stay home hoping things will turn out right."

"Vietnam isn't our country."

"We can't turn our backs on what's happening in the world, Carolyn."

"I don't care what happens to the world! I care about what happens to *my brother*. I'm going to do everything I can to get you back home."

They didn't say anything more until he pulled up in front of the apartment house. He tugged her hair. "Don't become a radical."

"Don't be a hero!" She burst into tears.

He gathered her into his arms. His voice choked as he tried to reassure her he'd come back in one piece. He set her away from him and got out of the car. He opened the trunk and took out her backpack. Leaning down, he kissed her cheek. "Try to behave yourself."

Smile dying, he looked at the door into the building. "Tell Chel I'll write."

❄ ❄ ❄

Mom and Dad continued to pay college expenses, adding fifty
dollars a month so Carolyn could pay her share of the rent on the
apartment. When her grades dropped, they suggested she move
back into the dorm. Chel said she wasn't going back and have an
RM breathing down her neck, telling her what hours she had to
be in bed. But she agreed the apartment might not be such a good
idea. Too many parties going on. She found a small, run-down
American bungalow, furnished and within walking distance of the
university, and talked Carolyn into moving in with her.

Carolyn sent her parents a change-of-address card and the new
telephone number. Mom called and sounded furious. "We're not
sending rent for a house, Carolyn. We can't afford it."

"You can keep your money. Chel and I have it all worked out."

"Worked out? How? She pays for everything?"

"I might quit school. Get a job. Protest the war."

"For heaven's sake, Carolyn. Don't start rebelling now. We have
enough to worry about with Charlie in Vietnam."

"Which is precisely why protests are more important than
classes!"

"Charlie believes in what he's doing! Your father's a veteran.
How dare you speak against them! If you're going to turn into
some kind of hippy, don't expect us to pay for it!" She hung up.

Carolyn held the receiver in her hand. She protested the war,
not *Charlie*. And definitely not Dad. When had she ever said
anything against her father's service? The hurt rose up, gripping her
by the throat; and then the anger came, blistering hot, defiant. She
slammed the receiver down and went into the kitchen to pour a
glass of red wine. When the telephone rang again, she knew it was
her mother calling back. She probably wanted to lay down more
laws, make more demands, throw around more threats to make
Carolyn conform.

Shaking, Carolyn downed the wine like medicine and let the
phone ring.

11

1967

The small house became a gathering place for anyone disenchanted with the system. Carolyn went to classes when she didn't have other things to do, like canvassing the neighborhoods for signatures on petitions to stop the war, or attending protest rallies or giving blood.

As the fighting intensified in Vietnam, Carolyn grew more distracted. She flunked her midterms and stopped going to classes. She worried about Charlie all the time. She couldn't sleep. Chel encouraged her to smoke pot, but that didn't help either. Only alcohol worked, when she drank enough of it.

Mom called again. "Come home."

"You can't tell me what to do."

"Have you been drinking?"

She hadn't slept the night before, and her head felt like cotton. "What's it to you what I do?"

"Charlie would be ashamed of you!"

The words cut deeper than if her mother had wielded a butcher knife. Charlie had gotten drunk a few times after football games in high school. If Mom and Dad ever knew about it, they never said so. "I'm trying to stop the war! I'm trying to bring him home! But I guess that counts for nothing in your book! If you want to know the truth, Mom, you and Dad sent Charlie to Vietnam. All your talk of God and country."

"*Stop it!*"

This time, Carolyn hung up.

Dad called a few hours later. Chel answered and held out the telephone. "It's your father." Carolyn took the receiver and slammed it down.

When a letter arrived from Oma, Carolyn dreaded opening it. When she read it, she found no mention of Mom and Dad other than the usual "working hard." Oma went on about books she had read, the garden, and missing Carolyn every afternoon when she sat down to tea.

I hope you can make it home soon. I miss you.

She must be the only one. Carolyn wrote back.

Dear Oma,

I can't come home right now. I'm collecting signatures on a petition to end the war. Chel is writing for an underground press, sharing intelligence on how to protest the war more effectively. No one seems to be listening now, but I have hope that change will come. There are plans to march on Washington, and many of us are sending letters on alternative service for conscientious objectors.

Several of our friends burned their draft cards. A few are talking about moving to Canada. . . .

Carolyn thought she'd write back and argue.

Mom wrote and asked if she was coming home for Thanksgiving. Carolyn didn't answer. Mom wrote again a few weeks later and invited her home for Christmas.

Carolyn couldn't face them. She felt ashamed of her behavior, but also somewhat self-righteous as well. They didn't understand her, and with Charlie off in Vietnam, she wouldn't have an interpreter. She didn't want to face their disapproval and submit to endless lectures about her political views, her loss of faith, or whatever else they would find to criticize. She couldn't stand seeing them sitting in front of their television set, listening to the news reports and body counts. She didn't want to watch them worry and then have them take it out on her. She was doing everything she could to end the war and make a better world for all of them!

She wrote home and said she and Chel planned to go skiing in Tahoe. They had talked about it, so it technically wasn't a lie. They went to San Francisco, instead, the new happening place in America, and spent the night partying at a house in Haight-Ashbury. Cold as it was, they put flowers in their hair and danced in the streets to guitar music and bongo drums.

When they got back to the Berkeley bungalow, Carolyn had two Christmas cards, one from Mom and Dad with fifty dollars in it, and another from Oma with only a note.

Trust in the Lord with all your heart. Don't lean on your own understanding. Acknowledge Him in all your ways and He will make your path straight. Proverbs 3:5-6. Live by it and you'll have no regrets. I love you, Liebling.

Oma

Carolyn felt a sharp pang of guilt, realizing she hadn't sent a card to anyone, not even Charlie.

She wrote back.

God is dead, Oma. If He loved us, we wouldn't have wars and famines. People wouldn't die of disease or be born with deformities or mentally retarded. I don't believe in God anymore.

She sent it before she could change her mind and then felt eaten up by guilt, ashamed that she'd lashed out at Oma, who'd always loved her unconditionally.

1968

January blew cold and brought with it the Chinese Lunar New Year. While the Vietnamese celebrated Tet, the Vietcong and North Vietnamese army overran the city of Hue. Chel had bought a television, and a dozen friends and strangers were packed into their living room, high on pot and angst, watching buildings explode and wounded American soldiers carried out on stretchers. Conversation buzzed around Carolyn, but she felt cold inside. Was Charlie among the Marines trying to retake the city? She wanted to scream. *Shut up! My brother is in the middle of hell, and if you call him a baby killer or warmonger again, I'll kill you.* Maybe she did say it. It got quiet in the room.

"What's with her?" someone muttered angrily.

"Jesus . . . Jesus . . . ," Carolyn prayed, trying to grasp hold of faith again, a last-ditch effort to save Charlie. *Please, God, don't let him get killed.* Drunk, she pressed her hands against the television screen. She felt someone's arms around her.

"Easy, babe. He'll be okay, Caro. You gotta believe. He'll be okay."

Believe in what? God? They'd all been saying God didn't care or God was dead. When had faith ever been enough?

Carolyn didn't go to work. She sat glued to the television, searching faces, drinking, looking for Charlie on the screen.

Oma called. "Two soldiers are with your mom and dad." She spoke Carolyn's name, but couldn't get any more out.

Something cracked inside Carolyn. She fumbled the telephone back into the cradle. Her body started to shake violently. The phone rang again. Carolyn heard it from a distance. Another sound intruded, a terrible sound, like a wounded animal screaming in pain. She covered her ears, trying to block it out. Charlie! It was Charlie!

Chel came out of the bedroom, half-dressed, hair in disarray. She grabbed Carolyn's wrists and pulled her arms down. When the sound grew louder, Chel slapped her across the face. The screaming stopped. Carolyn sat silent, stunned. Chel cupped her face. "Charlie?" Unable to speak, Carolyn crumpled. Hands spread on the bare wood floor, she sobbed.

Uttering a sobbing cry, Chel rose. She screamed a string of curses. When the telephone rang again, she grabbed the cord and yanked it out of the wall. Snatching up the telephone, she hurled it through a window. Hunkering down again, she grabbed Carolyn's shoulders and shook her. "Caro. Caro!"

The radio played an Animals song. *"We gotta get out of this place if it's the last thing we ever do. . . ."*

"I tried so hard, Chel. And I couldn't save him."

Chel got dressed, then lit a roach with shaking hands. She pulled Carolyn up with one hand and offered her the rolled marijuana. "Take a drag, Caro. Come on, babe. It's better than barbiturates."

Carolyn filled her lungs with pot smoke. She didn't want to feel anything. The music kept playing its siren song. *"We gotta get out of this place . . ."* Too late. Too late.

Chel dragged her up. "Let's get outta here."

They didn't pack anything. They left it all behind. The last thing Carolyn remembered was riding across the Bay Bridge in the front seat of Chel's red Camaro, Janis Joplin screaming, Chel screaming along with her, tears running down her white face.

Oh, Rosie, where do I begin? Charlie is dead, killed in Vietnam, and my sweet Carolyn has disappeared. The pain is too deep for tears. Hildemara can't eat or sleep; she cries all the time. I fear for her health. I fear for Carolyn as well. God alone knows where she is and what she's doing to herself. Will I lose everyone I love?

Ever since Charlie joined the Marines, the family has been in conflict. Carolyn has set herself against the war, and unwittingly against Trip. He says anyone against the war is against Charlie and every other young American boy fighting this war. Carolyn says she'd do anything to bring Charlie home, but Trip says the protests are aiding the enemy and demoralizing the troops. Trip called her a traitor and said Charlie would be ashamed of her. She withdrew from the university to devote herself to the antiwar movement, and she has no job, no means of support other than her rich, abandoned friend Rachel Altman. I've never met a more damaged girl.

Soldiers came to the house. Hildemara and Trip didn't want to call Carolyn the first day, but I called her. She hung up without saying a word, Rosie, and when I called back, she didn't answer. I assumed she was coming straight home to be with her family. She adored her brother. Charlie meant everything to her.

She never showed up. I drove to Berkeley the next day to bring her home. The house was in disarray, the telephone connection ripped from the wall, the television and several windows smashed.

I can't tell Hildemara or Trip I called Carolyn. They'd believe she didn't care enough to come home. I know the child is broken and grieving. I don't know how to find my granddaughter. I lie awake at night and I pray. When I sleep, I dream of Elise.

God knows where Carolyn is, and I pray for His mercy on all of us. I don't know what else to do.

12

1970

The Summer of Love had ended by the time Carolyn ran away to Haight-Ashbury with Rachel Altman after Charlie's death. Things had already begun to change. Pot still reigned, but harder drugs rose in popularity. Guru psychologist Timothy Leary advocated acid to expand the mind, but after one bad trip that left Carolyn with residual hallucinations for weeks, she made alcohol and pot her drugs of choice. She spent days in a blur, drinking liberal amounts of wine, red or white, trying to drown her grief, wash away the anger, and stop the nightmares of running through a jungle with her brother.

Chel continued to foot the bill for the two of them, in addition to a succession of hangers-on and groupies who came and went from the house they shared, many of them young men. Chel began to be haunted by hallucinations from dropping too much acid. Sobbing, she'd beg, "I need you, Caro. I need you *sober.*" Carolyn tried, but craved alcohol like water. They tried to lean on one another, but it didn't help that everyone around them still used.

When the hallucinations finally stopped, they went outside and sat on the steps. Feeling the sunshine, they went to Golden Gate Park for the first time in weeks. "You've been there for me every time I've needed you, Caro, even when I didn't know what I was doing. You drove me clear across the country after Woodstock, when I couldn't have told you my name, let alone my address. We couldn't save Charlie, but you saved me. And what have I done for you?"

"You've been my friend."

"What sort of a friend am I?"

"You helped me after Charlie died."

"I should've left you in Berkeley. Your parents would have come and taken you home."

"No, they wouldn't."

"Oma, then."

Carolyn shook her head. "This is where I belong."

They found a park bench and sat. Chel put her head in her hands. "Sometimes I just want to call it quits." She gave a bleak laugh. "I'm sick and tired of being sick and tired. I'm tired of fighting a losing battle." She leaned back, hands limp in her lap. "I scare myself sometimes, Caro." She gave Carolyn a sad smile. "I don't think we've been good for each other."

Hurt, Carolyn couldn't look at her. "Am I going to lose you, too, Chel?"

"I love you, babe." Chel raised her hand in a halfhearted gesture. "See that family over there?" Her voice turned mocking. "Mommy laying out the picnic lunch while Daughter dear plays with her dolly and Daddy helps Sonny boy fly a kite? Makes a nice Hallmark card, don't you think?" Her voice choked off. She let out her breath slowly. "What do we have, Caro?"

"Our friendship."

Chel looked at her then, eyes clear for a change, wet. She looked away again. They didn't talk for a long while. "I called my father."

Surprised, Carolyn stared at her. "When?"

"A week ago. Apparently, he dumped my mother last year and

married his secretary. According to the new one, he's off on a honeymoon in Madrid."

"Where's your mother?"

"She lives in Paris. Plays in Monte Carlo. Who knows? The new secretary didn't have her telephone number, or she had orders not to give it to me. She said my father wanted to invite me to the wedding, but didn't know how to reach me." She gave a harsh laugh. "All he had to do was follow the money. He just didn't care enough."

"Maybe he figured you wouldn't want to come."

"Maybe. But it would've been nice to have the opportunity to tell him off one last time." She looked at Carolyn, eyes dark with pain. "Get this. I told that secretary I needed to talk to my father. She asked me if it was an emergency. I told her it was. She said, 'Give me your number, and I'll let Mr. Altman know you called.' I haven't heard from him yet."

"Maybe she forgot."

"She remembered. She called back. She asked me how much money I needed." She called her father a string of foul names. "He's too busy with his new trophy wife." Tears spilled down her cheeks. "If I was lying in a hospital bed, dying from an overdose, he'd tell his secretary to make sure I had a private room, private nurse, and send some flowers." She dug in her jean pocket and pulled out a worn business card. "I want you to keep this."

"Why?"

"If anything happens to me, you call my father."

Scared, Carolyn shook her head. "Nothing is going to happen to you, Chel."

"I'm not planning anything. You just never know when your time will come. I could decide to go swimming in that lake and drown. Or go down to the ocean and walk in with lead weights around my ankles."

"I don't like it when you talk so crazy."

"Don't I always?" Chel laughed again, sounding more like herself this time. "You really are something, you know that?" She cupped Carolyn's face. "I love you. You've been better to me than any sister I could've had." She dropped her hand. "Whatever happens, it's not going to be your fault." She gripped Carolyn's wrist tightly. "Remember that. It's *not your fault*."

Worried, Carolyn kept an eye on Chel over the next few days. Chel smoked pot and drank, but not to excess. She still danced to the music, tossing her head and turning the way she had when they first came to Haight-Ashbury. Ash, the self-appointed leader of their little commune, watched Chel, too, especially when she turned up the music while he spoke his poetry. When he asked her to turn it down, she turned it up and danced right in front of him.

Carolyn thought everything would be fine then. Chel's depression had lifted. She was back to the same smirking, defiant girl she'd been in Berkeley. Carolyn went to the park for some air, spending two hours in the sunshine. She sat on a bench and watched children play, thinking of Oma and Mom and Dad. Loneliness gripped her. Pressing the heels of her hands against her eyes, she tried not to think about Charlie.

When she got back, Carolyn went upstairs and found Chel's door closed. Carolyn put her head against the door, but didn't hear voices. She tapped softly. "Chel?" She opened the door. "I've been thinking—"

Chel lay sprawled across her mattress. Her face looked so serene, Carolyn thought she was asleep. Then she noticed the rubber tubing coiled like a snake on the floor and a discarded syringe next to it. "Chel!" She knelt on the bed and lifted her. *"Chel!"* She shook her. Chel felt boneless, heavy. Sobbing her name, Carolyn let her go and screamed for help.

Voices. Footsteps running in the hall. "Everyone out!" Ash ordered. The door closed firmly. Carolyn heard the lock set. Sobbing, hysterical, she tried to speak. He clamped a hand over her mouth. When she tried to bite down, he slapped her, grabbed her by the hair, and shoved her face into the mattress. "Are you going to be quiet?" He pushed harder and only let her go when she started to pass out. Gasping for air, she scrambled away from him.

He put his hand on Chel's neck, checking for a pulse. Taking his hand away, he looked furious, not aggrieved. He swore under his breath. "Stupid witch."

"You don't even care that she's—"

"You were supposed to watch out for her." He hit her. She tasted blood in her mouth. He shoved her from him and turned toward the window.

She made it to the door, but Stoner stood right outside, blocking her escape. "What's the matter, babe?"

"Chel's dead."

"Bummer. Who's gonna pay the rent?"

She stared at him.

Ash came up behind her, his hands firm. With a tone full of compassion, he reassured Stoner. "Everything will be fine." When she tried to move away, his grip tightened. "We'll call an ambulance. Someone will come and take her to the hospital. What was her name, Stoner?"

"Chel."

When Carolyn opened her mouth, Ash's fingers bit into her flesh. "Chel." Ash spoke low. "That's all we know. Her name was Chel."

Stoner shrugged. "Yeah, man. That's all I ever knew."

Ash slipped his arm around Carolyn, pulled her back into the room, and closed Stoner out. He shoved her toward the bed where Chel lay dead. "You'll do what I tell you, Caro. Got that? It's your fault she overdosed. You said she was your friend. Where were you? You should've been right here with her every minute. I told you to keep watch." He gripped her face in viselike fingers. "But you didn't, did you? You did your own thing and had your little walk in the park. You put flowers in your hair." He crumpled them and threw them on the floor. "And now *she's* dead because *you* didn't care enough to take care of her." He let go of her and stepped away.

She'd once thought herself in love with this man. But he'd tossed her aside and moved on to another girl.

Suddenly solicitous, Ash drew Carolyn to her feet. He stroked her cheek. "It'll be the way it was." He whispered words of comfort now, words of endearment. "You don't have to worry about anything. I'll take care of you." When he kissed her, she felt nothing but revulsion. He drew back, his dark eyes searching hers. "I'll call for an ambulance. Sit with me downstairs. Be at my side." He opened the door. Stoner and several others stood waiting. "We'll light candles for our sister. We will say prayers." He stroked Carolyn's arms as though trying to smooth away the bruises.

The ambulance came within minutes. Two men got out. They unloaded a gurney and locked the vehicle doors before heading up the steps. One looked at her. When they came out with Chel's body zipped in a black bag, she heard them talking. "Chel. Not much to go by."

One unlocked and opened the back door of the ambulance. "She'll be another Jane Doe."

"Too bad. Pretty girl."

Carolyn came down the steps.

"You need to move aside, Miss."

"Her name is Rachel Altman. She came from New York City. She was an A student at UC Berkeley. They'll have her records."

His face filled with pity. "A friend of yours?"

"My best friend."

"We'll take good care of her."

"You'll be the first."

Frowning, he searched her face. "Are you going to be all right?"

Carolyn walked away without looking back. He had a job to do. So did she.

❄ ❄ ❄

It didn't take long to beg enough money for a long-distance telephone call. Carolyn stepped into a phone booth and dialed the number on the card Chel had given her. She asked for Mr. Altman.

"Who may I say is calling?"

"My name is Carolyn Arundel. His daughter, Rachel, was my best friend. She died today. You can tell him that, or let me talk to him."

"One moment, please."

Less than a minute passed and a man's voice came on the telephone. "My secretary says you have news about my daughter." He sounded annoyed. Maybe she'd interrupted a business meeting. "Make it quick. What is it this time?"

"She died of a heroin overdose this morning."

Silence. Then hushed anger. "Look. I'm in the middle of an important meeting. What kind of sick prank is she playing this time?"

"They picked up her body a few minutes ago." Carolyn gave him the Clement house address. "I gave the paramedics her full name and told them the university has her records. But Chel said if anything happened to her, she wanted me to call you. So I've called." She hung up.

Stepping out onto the sidewalk, Carolyn wasn't sure where to go. She'd been happy in the park, walking in the sunshine, looking at the flowers. She didn't make it. She walked half a block and squatted next to an old run-down Victorian row house, where she covered her head and sobbed.

She could hear Chel's voice in her head. *It's not your fault, Caro. Remember that. It's not your fault.*

Carolyn wished she could believe it.

Dear Rosie,

Trip has given up on finding Carolyn. He went to Berkeley several times looking for her, even went to the police, but they told him he is among dozens of parents whose children have "dropped out" and disappeared. Many have moved to Haight-Ashbury in San Francisco. Trip took days off work to look for Carolyn, contacting her neighbors and classmates, but so many of these young "flower children" hate authority, and Trip looks every inch the police officer he is, so I'm convinced, even if anyone knew of her whereabouts, they wouldn't tell anyone who looks like a member of "the establishment" they despise.

I am grieved Hildemara has given up on Carolyn as well. She never mentions her, nor can she abide my doing so. I invite her to tea. She declines. She comes home from work and stays in the house while Trip hammers on something. They go to church on Sunday, where they have the dubious distinction of being the only parents in Paxtown who have lost a son in action. Being a star football player in high school made Charlie a favored son, but his death has made him a local hero to some, object of hatred to others.

No one mentions Carolyn. She is more dead to everyone than Charlie could ever be.

13

TIME PASSED IN a haze of misery. With no place to go, nothing to do, Carolyn wandered through Golden Gate Park. She loitered near the museums, knowing that was her best chance of finding food. Some people looked at her with pity. Others stared in disgust, drawing children's attention away. Most pretended they didn't see her at all. She wanted a drink, but had no money. Sick to her stomach and suffering tremors, she left the pathways and collapsed. When she heard someone coming, she crawled into the bushes. Curled up in her hiding place, she wished she could will herself to die.

She used the public restrooms to wash. She found better places to sleep. Her fringed leather jacket kept the dew from soaking into her upper body, though her skirt felt wet after sleeping on the grass.

Occasionally a police car passed by. She would sit still, arms wrapped around her knees, making herself as small as possible, like an animal hiding among rhododendrons and overgrown azaleas.

She had always liked it there among the trees and flowers. The gardens reminded her of Oma's cottage.

School buses pulled in every morning during the week, bringing children for field trips. Once when the children came out to eat their bagged lunches, Carolyn approached to beg, but a chaperone told her to leave the children alone. So she sat with her back against a tree and watched children laugh, eat, and casually toss their leftovers away.

Too hungry to have any pride, Carolyn rummaged in the garbage cans, looking for their scraps. Before a security guard ordered her away, she found a half-eaten bologna sandwich, a brown banana, a box of hardened raisins. One month rolled into another. She lived hand to mouth. Her stomach was empty most of the time, but the rest of her filled up to overflowing with shame. She grieved over Chel. Worse, the anguish over Charlie's death returned. When he began haunting her dreams, she tried not to sleep at all.

❄ ❄ ❄

One evening, Carolyn went to the end of the park and down to the beach. Sitting on the cold sand, she thought about Chel. She thought about Charlie, too, all the time now. She didn't try to stop. The sun dipped toward the west. The light on the water made her eyes hurt. Her stomach ached. She hugged her knees against her chest, trying to stay warm. The surf pounded, waves whooshing up the sand while seagulls keened overhead. Two landed nearby and approached her, then flew off again when she had nothing to offer. The sky turned a beautiful rose-orange with pink streaks across the horizon.

Carolyn closed her eyes and imagined what it might feel like to walk into the surf, to go out so far there would be no turning back. She could spread her arms and drift weightless on the current until the warm water closed over her head. She imagined sinking into the blue, fish swimming around her, seaweed wrapping her in its embrace.

A blast of sand stung her face. The churning, crashing waves sounded angry, no longer inviting. The sea had come up. The mist turned cold. She got up and walked to the edge of the waves. The foamy sea lapped at her feet. In her dreams, it was warm, but this water felt ice-cold, so cold her skin and bones ached.

Courage failing, she turned away and saw a man in a military jacket sitting on the seawall, head turned toward her. Her heart quickened. Charlie? No. It couldn't be. Charlie was dead. How long had the man been there? He swung his leg over the wall and stood on the walkway. He shouldered a duffel bag and guitar case and headed back toward Golden Gate Park.

Night approached, and it grew colder on the beach. Carolyn followed the same route the man had taken. The public bathrooms had been locked. She relieved herself in the bushes and washed her hands in a public drinking fountain. Leaving the sidewalk, she crossed a lawn and sat by a small lake. Guitar music drifted on the air as one by one the stars began to appear. Carolyn moved toward the sound. She spotted a black plastic lean-to and a sleeping bag spread out beneath it. The man sat on a log, head down as he played his guitar. Hungry, cold, desperate, Carolyn swallowed her fear and approached him. He lifted his head and smiled at her. "I hoped you'd follow me."

"I like your music."

"Thanks." He had a kind smile. He was young, about the same age Charlie would be.

"Do you have any food?"

"Not much, but I'll share." He got up and dug in his duffel bag. He held out a Hershey's chocolate bar. She would have to come close to take it from his hand. "It's okay, miss. I won't hurt you." Though his face was young, his eyes looked old and sad.

"Thanks." She opened it and ate half, offering the rest to him.

"You go ahead. You can share my fire, too, if you want." He tilted his head and looked at her. "You look lost."

"Are you a vet?"

"Yeah." He went on playing the poignant, unfamiliar melody. "I'm still getting used to being a civilian."

She thought of Charlie, and tears spilled over and slipped down her cheeks. "My brother died in Vietnam."

He stopped playing and put the guitar aside. "Tell me about him."

She did. She let the words and pain flow out of her, wondering why it felt so natural to tell a stranger. She felt something happen inside her, a spark, a tiny seed of hope planted.

He told her about friends he'd lost. When he offered to share his sleeping bag, she thanked him and stretched out beside him. She didn't ask his name and didn't offer hers. The ground didn't feel as hard beneath her. When he drew the flannel-lined sleeping bag around them both, she sighed. He kissed her; she kissed him back. He was kind. He was gentle. When it was over, he didn't let her go, but held her tenderly. He cried. So did she.

She awakened once during the night, kissed him on the forehead, and walked away, the morning mist drifting through the trees. She thought she could find her way back, but she got lost again.

Exhausted, frightened, crying, she lay on the grass. She must have fallen asleep, for she awakened when someone touched her. A man whispered her name. *Oh,* she thought, relief sweeping over her, *he found me.* He stroked her hair so tenderly. Her body relaxed beneath his caress. She didn't want to move. She didn't want him to stop. Warm and drowsy, she looked across the grass. Small white flowers bloomed like stars among the green blades. He touched her again, and she felt enveloped in love.

"I've been lost."

"I know."

"I couldn't find you." She pushed herself up.

The sun rose behind him. Glorious color shone all around him. Carolyn raised a hand to shade her eyes.

"I found you." Raindrops of sensation raced up and down her body. It wasn't the young veteran who had found her. She couldn't see His face in the light, but she knew His voice even though she had never heard it before. Her heart pounded wildly. He whispered again, and then He was gone.

❄ ❄ ❄

Carolyn sat on the grass in the morning sunshine, holding tight to that one single moment when she felt loved, cherished, and for the first time in her life, certain of what she was supposed to do next.

Finally, pushing herself up, she found her way back to the sidewalk. She ducked into a public restroom to wash. Someone had broken the mirror. She stared at her reflection, like a Picasso painting, hacked up and put back together at odd angles. She dragged her fingers through her long, snarled hair, trying to make herself decent. How did she do that after spending weeks living in the same clothing, sleeping on the ground, scrounging in garbage cans? Giving up, she went back outside. She walked for a while and then sat to rest on a green lawn that tapered down to a pond.

Jesus had told her what to do. She just didn't think she had the courage to do it.

A young mother came down the slope holding a blanket and large picnic basket. A little boy and girl raced ahead of her, each with a small plastic bag in their hands. Bread crumbs for the ducks. One quickly swam their way, eight fuzzy ducklings following in her wake.

"Not so close, Charlie!"

Pain gripped Carolyn. Her heart pounded again, hard, fast, fluttering strangely as though she had just come back to life. The little boy looked older than his sister. He took her hand and pulled her away from the edge of the small lake. Protective.

Carolyn wanted to get up and move closer, but she didn't want to alarm the mother. She knew she looked a fright, like any other alcoholic still craving a drink, a slut who slept with strangers to keep warm, a derelict who ate out of garbage cans and slept under the cover of bushes. What mother in her right mind would want someone like Carolyn anywhere near her innocent children?

The young woman spread her blanket and sat down a short distance away. She smiled at Carolyn. "It's a perfect morning, isn't it?"

Carolyn found it difficult to speak. "Yes." Perfect. She watched the little boy. "You called him Charlie. My brother's name was Charlie." She turned her face away so the lady wouldn't see the tears that came so quick. She wiped them away.

"Was? Did something happen to him?"

"He was killed in Vietnam."

"When?"

"During the Tet Offensive." January 1968. Had it really been more than two years?

The lady sat for a long time, hands in her lap, watching her children. Carolyn knew she should leave, but the normalcy held her. The little boy and girl ran up the grassy slope. "Mommy! We need more bread! The ducks are still hungry!"

Chuckling, the lady opened a package of Wonder bread and handed them each a slice. "Little pieces. And don't get too close. You'll frighten them away."

Carolyn remembered Oma letting her open packages of Wonder bread on the way home from Hagstrom's grocery store. Her stomach cramped with hunger now, and her mouth watered. The children ran down the slope and threw the food to the ducks. Carolyn put her forehead on her raised knees and swallowed despair.

"Would you like a sandwich?" The lady held one out. "We have more than enough."

Too hungry to be proud, Carolyn got up and went over to accept it. "Thank you." She started to move away, but the lady spoke again.

"Why don't you sit with us and share our picnic?" She set out sandwiches, a plastic container of potato salad, a bag of chips, another container of chocolate chip cookies, pints of milk.

Carolyn sat on the grass next to the blue blanket and tried not to stare at the food as she ate the peanut butter and jelly sandwich.

"You can sit on the blanket." The lady smiled at her again. "It's all right. The grass is still a little wet with dew, isn't it?"

"I don't want to get your blanket dirty."

The lady's brown eyes softened. "Sit. Please. Do you live close by?"

Carolyn noticed the gold cross at her throat. "I've been living in the park for a while."

She looked dismayed. "Why?"

"I didn't want to go back to the place where I'd been living."

"You don't have anywhere else to go?"

Carolyn shrugged and then shook her head. "I burned my bridges a long time ago." She licked jelly off her fingers. She'd only eaten half of the sandwich. "May I please have one of those pieces of cellophane?"

"You're not going to eat the whole thing?"

"I'm saving a little. For later."

The lady's eyes grew moist. "You can eat it. I'll give you another one to save, if you want." She reached into the basket. "I wondered why I felt such an impulse to make extra sandwiches this morning." When she looked up, her eyes filled. "Don't cry or I will, too."

"People usually tell me to get lost." As if she wasn't already.

"May I ask your name?"

"Caro." A piece only, but enough.

"I'm Mary." She extended her hand. Carolyn had to move closer to shake it. "It's nice to meet you, Caro." She passed over a pint of milk, then took a paper plate and fork from the basket, scooped potato salad onto it, and handed it to Carolyn. "Tell me about yourself."

Fear melted away and loneliness won. Carolyn told Mary she had family, but they wouldn't want her anymore. She told her about college, Chel, the protest rallies, the desperation to change the world before it was too late, and then Oma's call telling her it already was. She told her about living in Haight-Ashbury and moving to Clement Street, the drinking and drugs, going to Woodstock and the long drive home wondering if Chel would make it.

"Did she?"

"Yeah. But she died of an overdose a couple months ago." Carolyn put her hands over her face and cried. "I'm sorry. I don't know why I told you all that."

"I asked, Caro. Because I care."

The children raced up the slope again. The girl came over to Carolyn. "Hello."

Carolyn felt her face fill with heat. "Hello."

"Who are you?" the boy wanted to know.

"Don't be rude, Charlie. Caro, this is Sadie, my little lady." She ran a tender hand over the little girl's dark curls. "And this is Charlie, the man of the house." Smiling, she pinched his nose. "Caro is our guest."

The little girl looked curious. "Is that why you made so many sandwiches, Mommy?"

Mary laughed. "I guess so." She patted the blanket and they sat down. They prayed together before she gave them their sandwiches.

Charlie leaned closer to his mother and whispered loudly, "Why is Caro crying?"

"Because she has had a very hard time."

"You used to cry a lot. I still hear you sometimes."

"Crying can be good for you." She kissed him. "Eat your lunch."

They took their bread crusts and ran down to the lake, eager to toss them to the ducks. Sadie, the little lady, picked tiny white flowers from the grass while Charlie went frog hunting.

"You should go home, Caro."

Carolyn hugged her knees close to her chest again and rested her forehead on them. "I don't think I'd be welcome."

"Your mother and father would want you back. So would your grandmother."

"I don't think so."

"Take my word for it. They would. They'd want to know you're alive and safe, especially . . ." She turned her face away and watched her children. "They didn't just lose their son that day, Caro. They lost you, too. I can't even imagine what I'd feel like if I lost one, let alone both my children."

"They'll never forgive me."

Mary faced her. "I'm a mother, and I can tell you no matter

what one of my children did, I'd want them to come home. I would run to them and throw my arms around them and kiss them until they cried for mercy!" She gave a soft, broken laugh. "Don't leave your mother and father wondering if you're dead or alive. That's the cruelest kind of torment."

Carolyn had a hundred excuses not to go home. She didn't have a way to get there. She'd have to beg for money for bus fare. By the time she had enough, she'd be starving again. In truth, the thought terrified her. What would Mom and Dad say? What would Oma? They'd wish her dead if they knew half of what she'd done.

Mary gathered the containers and put them back in the basket. She suddenly seemed to be in a great hurry. When she stood, Carolyn shifted off the blanket. Mary shook it out and folded it. She called Charlie and Sadie. They came reluctantly. "Do we have to go home?"

"We're not going home. We're taking Caro to the bus depot. We're going to buy her a ticket so she can go home to her family."

Carolyn gaped at her.

Mary folded the blanket over the basket and picked them up in one hand. Smiling, she held out her other hand to Carolyn and helped her up. The children ran ahead to a van parked on the road.

"Why are you helping me? Why go to all this trouble for a stranger?"

"My husband has been MIA since Tet. I don't know if he's alive or dead. I may never know." She gave Carolyn a tremulous smile, eyes awash with tears. "I can't bear the thought of someone else going through the suffering I go through every day. Don't you see, Caro? You've been MIA. You've been a prisoner of war, too. In your case, it's just a different kind of war."

"Not an honorable one. It's not the same."

"Oh, Caro. How could any mother or father not want their child back from the dead?" She grasped Carolyn's hand, squeezing it. "I'll pray they're watching for you, and they run to you when they see you coming home. If they don't, you call me. I'll come and get you."

When the depot announced her bus was about to leave, Carolyn rose. Mary and the children walked with her. Carolyn's heart pounded heavily. Her hands sweated. "You don't have to stay."

"I'm not leaving until you're safely settled on that bus and it's on its way." She scribbled her telephone number on a slip of scrap paper and handed it to Carolyn.

When Carolyn found a seat, she saw Mary, Charlie, and Sadie waving at her. She waved back.

14

CAROLYN GOT OFF the Greyhound bus in Paxtown and ducked into the restroom to wash her face, arms, and hands. She raked trembling fingers through her tangled hair, pulling it back over her shoulders. She didn't even own a rubber band to secure it in a ponytail. Hoping no one would recognize her, Carolyn hurried out of the bus depot and walked quickly along Main Street with her head down. She felt people stare as she passed. She wanted to run, but knew that would only attract more unwanted attention.

She breathed easier when she reached the end of town. It was a two-mile walk to Happy Valley Road, but she had been walking for weeks. Exhausted, sweaty, she headed for Oma's cottage. Mom and Dad wouldn't be home from work yet. There was a car Carolyn didn't recognize in Oma's carport, but she didn't answer when Carolyn knocked.

Carolyn didn't feel she had any right to go inside without an invitation, not anymore. She went back to the main house and lifted the flowerpot. Mom still kept the key there. She thought about going in, taking a long hot shower, washing her hair, getting something to eat. But what right did she have to go into their house? She put the flowerpot on top of the key and sat by the front door. She was so tired. If her family didn't want her, where would she go? She awakened sharply when a car came up the gravel driveway. The hedge had grown high, and she couldn't see whether it was Mom or Dad. Footsteps crunched in the pebbles, soft footsteps. Mom. Carolyn stood slowly, heart pounding.

Her mother came around the corner, looking so familiar and professional in her white uniform and cap. Startled, Mom stopped. She stared at Carolyn and took a step back. Then her eyes went wide. "Carolyn?" Before Carolyn could speak, Mom dropped her purse and flew at her. Carolyn cringed, expecting a blow, but found herself in a fierce embrace. Uttering a sobbing gasp, her mother let go and stepped back. "I didn't know it was you at first. You're so . . . different."

Different wasn't the word.

"When did you get home? How did you get here? Where have you been? What happened? We've been—" She stopped abruptly, her eyes sweeping over Carolyn. She raised her hands. "Never mind." She frowned in confusion. "Why didn't you go inside? The key . . ."

Carolyn didn't know what to say.

"It's okay." Mom spoke quickly. She unlocked the door and pushed it open. "Come inside." She remembered her purse and went back for it. Holding her elbows, Carolyn waited just inside the door. "Come in." Mom threw her purse on the breakfast counter and started to pull out the bobby pins that held her nurse's cap in place. She headed for the back of the house. Mom always took a shower immediately after coming home from the hospital.

Mom stopped and wheeled around. She looked scared. "Don't leave, Carolyn."

"I won't."

"Promise me!"

"I promise."

Mom let out her breath. "Okay. I'll only be a few minutes."

A few minutes might be all her mother needed to change her mind about letting Carolyn into the house. And what then? Carolyn stood in the entry hall and raised her head. She caught her breath at the memorial wall in front of her.

An eleven-by-fourteen picture of Charlie in his dress blues smiled at her. Two small potted palms sat on either side of the elaborate gilt-framed portrait sitting on a shiny black table. The wall above was covered with framed photographs: Charlie as a baby, Charlie as a toddler on his tricycle, Charlie and Mitch standing by their bikes, Charlie and Mitch in their high school football uniforms, Charlie showing off his varsity sweater, Charlie in black cap and gown holding his high school diploma and scholastic award, Charlie in his Trojan football uniform, Charlie looking handsome in Marine greens. The pictures surrounded a glass-encased triangular folded American flag set against black velvet. Below it were several colorful military ribbons, a Bronze Star, and a snapshot of Charlie grinning broadly, arms flung around two Marine buddies, a bunker and palm trees in the background.

Carolyn's throat closed tight and hot. If she lived a hundred years, she'd never get over losing Charlie.

The foyer felt warm, sunlight shining in from the skylight. She glanced into the living room. Everything looked exactly the same as the day she had left home: curved beige couch and oval birch coffee table in front of the wall fireplace, two recliners with a table, the television set.

"Carolyn?"

She turned slowly, steeling herself for whatever her mother might do next. She'd changed into blue polyester pants and a red, white, and blue polyester blouse. Her mother had every right to scream at her and tell her to go back to whatever hole she'd been hiding in for the past thirty months. They stood staring at one another, both at a loss for words.

Carolyn chewed her lower lip and gathered enough courage to speak. "Can I use the bathroom, Mom? Would you mind if I took a shower?"

Mom blinked. "Yes. Of course." She pointed as though Carolyn might not remember the way.

Stripping off her tan leather jacket, tiered peasant skirt, and blouse, she stepped into the stream of hot water. It felt so good. She squirted Prell shampoo into her hand and scrubbed her hair. She lathered and scrubbed her body, washing until the water at her feet ran clear. Then she just stood and let the water beat down on her until it went from hot to lukewarm.

After drying off, she wrapped the towel around herself and found a toothbrush and Colgate toothpaste in the drawer. How long since she'd brushed her teeth? Her gums bled.

Gathering her clothes, she went into her bedroom. Nothing had changed in here either. She slid the closet door open and saw two dresses, a jumper, a few skirts and blouses she'd worn in high school, things she hadn't wanted to take to Berkeley. She found underwear, faded jeans, and Charlie's discarded purple and gold high school sweatshirt. He'd tossed it at her the day he graduated. *"It's all yours, Sis."* She could hear the echo of his voice.

The jeans hung loose on her hips. She found a pink belt in the closet and cinched it to the last hole, bunching the denim around her waist. The sweatshirt looked huge on her. She put her arms around herself, thinking of Charlie.

A brush and comb were still in the top drawer. Her scalp stung as she brushed the tangles from her hair. If she'd found scissors, she would have cut it all off, hacked it away in penance. It hung damp and limp to her waist, a curling mass of sun-bleached blonde. She couldn't stop shivering. Ice ran in her veins.

Charlie. Chel. Both dead.

She went out to face Mom. Carolyn could hear the *click, click, click* of the potato peeler and followed the sound to the kitchen. Strips of potato peelings flew into the sink. Six naked white orbs sat on the counter. Did they have company coming to dinner? Mom glanced over her shoulder. "There you are. How was your shower?"

"Nice."

"I put a roast on. Dad will be home in an hour. It'll be a while before we can eat. Do you want anything now?"

"A glass of milk?"

"Help yourself."

Carolyn poured a full glass and drank it without stopping. She felt Mom watching her.

"You look exhausted." Mom bit her lip. She peeled another potato and then made a sound of disgust. Tossing the peeler aside, she scooped up the potato peels and dumped them in her compost bucket under the sink. "I don't know what I'm thinking. Well, we'll have leftover potatoes for a few days, I guess." She gripped the edge of the sink and stared out the kitchen window. "Where have you been all this time?"

"San Francisco." Light-headed, Carolyn swayed.

Mom had hold of her before she knew her mother had even moved. "Why don't you lie down and take a nap? I'll wake you when it's time."

Time for what? To face her father? Time for Mom to get over the initial shock of having her daughter show up on the front doorstep like a filthy stray cat?

"Come on." Mom kept her arm firmly around Carolyn's waist. When they went into Carolyn's old bedroom, Mom let go of her and yanked back the covers. "Lie down before you fall down!" She pulled the covers up over Carolyn's shoulders. Carolyn felt her mother's cool hand on her forehead. "Sleep for a while."

She heard the sound of voices, but couldn't quite rouse herself. Someone kissed her forehead. She thought she smelled her father's Old Spice. More whispered voices. Then she sank into a dark pit and stayed there.

❄ ❄ ❄

Carolyn saw sunlight streaming in the bedroom window. How long had she slept? Her heart stopped when she heard Dad's voice.

She wanted to cover her head with the blankets and go back to sleep. But she couldn't hide forever.

She opened her door carefully and slipped into the bathroom while her parents talked in the kitchen. When she came out, she opened the door to Charlie's bedroom and stepped inside.

His bed still had the same blue spread. The red blaze roses bloomed around his window. His Monopoly game had been laid out on his desk, money neatly stacked on both sides of the board, as though he and a friend had just left the game. There were hotels on Boardwalk and Park Place.

A USC banner hung on the wall. The bookshelf Dad had built still held Charlie's favorite sci-fi novels. She opened his closet. His shirts and slacks still hung there. She stepped inside and held a shirt to her face, breathing in the fading scent of her brother. She took it off the hanger and sat on his bed, holding the shirt to her face. If she closed her eyes, she could pretend he still lived in this room, had just gone out for a drive in his red Impala.

Gulping down a sob, she bunched the shirt against her mouth to stifle the sound. If she'd been anywhere else, out of sight, alone, she might have keened and wailed and screamed the way she had the day she learned her brother had been killed. She might have torn her clothes and ripped at her hair, might have slashed herself with a knife, anything to release the balled-up, tight-fisted, raging grief inside her.

Jesus. Jesus! Why Charlie? Why not me? He had so much going for him. And I'm nothing.

She thought of all the things she'd done in the last three years and wondered if a person could die of shame.

"Carolyn?" Mom stood in the doorway, her face pale and strained.

"I'm sorry." Carolyn stood, legs shaky. She held Charlie's shirt clenched in one hand. If Mom tried to take it from her, she'd hang on and fight for it.

"Breakfast is ready."

Breakfast? Hadn't she been peeling potatoes for dinner?

Dad sat at the kitchen table. Charlie's death had aged him. His hair had turned gray at the temples, and he had new lines across his forehead, around his eyes, and in his cheeks, lines carved by sorrow. She met his eyes briefly and bowed her head. He started to rise and seemed to change his mind. He put his hand flat on the table. "Sit down."

Mom set two plates on the table, one in front of Dad, one in front of Carolyn. Carolyn stared at the mound of scrambled eggs, four strips of bacon, a blueberry muffin. Mom filled her glass with orange juice. She couldn't remember the last time she'd had juice.

Setting her own plate on the table, Mom sat. Dad said grace.

"You slept thirty-six hours."

Carolyn raised her head and looked at her father.

"You must've needed it." He forked eggs into his mouth, not looking at her.

"You need to eat, too." Mom waved at the plate.

Carolyn's hand shook when she picked up the fork, and her teeth hurt when she chewed. Her throat felt so dry she had to swallow orange juice to wash down the muffin. Though they didn't stare, she felt her parents' attention fixed on her. What thoughts ran through their heads? What names did they want to call her? *Druggie. Boozer. Hippy. Worthless slut.*

All true.

They didn't ask questions; the silence became excruciating. She'd prepared herself for anger, accusations, fury, fingers pointed at the door, but not this watchful tension, this nervous caution.

She'd been sent home by Jesus, bus fare paid by one of His saints. Now what? What could she say? What excuses could she offer?

She couldn't eat any more. She put her fork down carefully, head still bowed. She put her hands on the table, meaning to push the chair back. Dad grabbed her hand, pinning her at the table. "We're glad you came home, Carolyn." His voice sounded rough and hoarse. "You know that, don't you?"

She raised her head and looked at him.

"We're glad you're home," he repeated.

She pulled her hand away and covered her face. She gulped down a sob.

How long had she been running on empty? Since she'd run from Berkeley . . . or long before that? She'd tried to fill the void, but nothing had worked—not alcohol, not drugs, not sex. All of it emptied her even more.

She had one miraculous moment to cling to in all that mess. One single minute at dawn, the May flowers blooming like stars in the grass, and Jesus laying His hand on her head. Telling her it was time to go home.

Jesus. They'd never believe it, not in a thousand years. They'd think she'd had some kind of drug-induced hallucination.

A sound came out of Dad, ripped out.

"Trip." Mom spoke, frightened.

He pulled Carolyn's chair back. When she almost fell, he swept her up and sat down again with her in his lap. Hugging her tight against him, he wept.

MOM AND DAD stayed home from work. She knew they wanted to ask why she had disappeared, but didn't, perhaps waiting for her to volunteer the information. She hadn't been thinking about them, the grief they must have suffered, and the further grief she might cause. She hadn't thought about anything at all. How could she tell them that she simply couldn't bear seeing Charlie in a coffin?

"Oma's visiting Rikka back in New York. Your aunt is having another showing. We called them last night to let them know you'd come home."

What would Oma say when she returned?

"I went to San Francisco a half-dozen times," Dad told her. "I thought you might be in Haight-Ashbury."

She'd been drunk or stoned most of the time. She hadn't even stepped outside the house that first month. They left shortly after that. "Chel and I lived on Clement Street."

"Is she still there?" Dad sounded worried. Maybe he thought she'd change her mind and go back.

"She died of an overdose."

"What a waste." Mom's words summed up everything.

They gave up trying to make conversation and did chores around the house. Carolyn felt at loose ends, not knowing what to do. When she tried to help with the dishes, Mom told her to go into the living room and relax, but Dad had the TV on and Carolyn didn't want to hear the news. The Vietnam War was still going strong, more unpopular than ever.

She took a nap in the afternoon. Even after hours of sleep, she felt tired.

Mom awakened her. "Dad just brought Oma home from the airport. Why don't you go over and say hello?"

Oma stood on her front porch, watching Carolyn walk across the lawn. Dad gave her an encouraging smile as he headed for the house. When Carolyn came close, Oma put her hands on her hips. *"Die Verlorene kommt schliesslich nach Hause."*

Carolyn gave her a bleak look.

"I said, 'The prodigal finally comes home.'" She let out her breath. "I'd like to beat you to within an inch of your life, but you already look like you've been through enough. Come inside. We'll have some tea and talk."

Oma filled the teakettle and slammed it on the stove. She spoke German again and corrected herself. "I haven't any cookies, not even store-bought. Tomorrow, I'll make a cake. You look terrible. Did they tell you that?"

"No."

"Well, you do. You're skin and bones! What have you been eating? air?"

"Trash."

Oma scowled. "You look it. Do you know what you've done to your mother and father and me with all your foolishness?"

"I'm sorry."

"Sorry. *Sorry!*" She closed her eyes and shook her head. She sank into the chair as though her legs wouldn't hold her up anymore. "It was my fault. I should have come to Berkeley and told you in person, brought you home with me."

"It wasn't your fault, Oma."

"Tell me where you've been all this time and what you've been doing." She waved her hand. "And I don't mean San Francisco."

"You don't want to know, Oma. You really don't." Carolyn struggled to keep tears back.

She sighed heavily. "I guess it's none of my business anyway." She raised her head. "What happened to Chel?"

Leave it to Oma to ask. "Heroin overdose." Carolyn swallowed hard. "Suicide."

Oma looked ready to cry. "Too many young people are dying these days."

"Where's Charlie buried?" Carolyn hadn't dared ask her parents.

"He could've been buried at Arlington, but your parents wanted him up on the hill, close to home." Carolyn thought about Charlie and figured Mom and Dad had made the right decision. "Hildemara—" Oma corrected herself. "Your mother went up every day for the first year."

"Can I take some flowers when I go?"

"Cut as many as you want. Anytime." Oma got up and poured hot water over the tea bags and set the cups on the table. "Take a bottle of water along. You'll need to refill the vase."

They sipped tea together. Oma set her cup down. "What do you plan to do now?"

"I don't have any idea."

"You're going to have to do something. Sitting around is the worst thing you can do for yourself."

"I know."

Oma stood behind her, stroking her shoulders. She held Carolyn's head and kissed her crown like a blessing. "Every day is a new beginning, *Liebling*."

❀ ❀ ❀

Carolyn heard Mom and Dad talking in the morning.

"Maybe I should stay home a few more days."

"You can't keep watch forever, Hildie. Besides, your mother will be here. She'll keep an eye on her."

When Carolyn opened the door, they stopped talking. Dad was wearing his uniform. She felt relieved to see him in it. They'd been treating her like a guest.

"I've got to go into town and do some grocery shopping." Mom sounded apologetic. "Would you like to go with me?"

And have everyone in town staring at her? "I'd rather stay here."

After they both left, Carolyn went through the house. She couldn't find a single picture of herself anywhere. Mom and Dad might have had only one child—Charlie.

She wrote a note and left it on the kitchen counter. She went over and cut flowers from Oma's garden and walked to the cemetery. The gate had been opened so people could drive in, make the loop, and come out. Few did. Carolyn had been here before, exploring with Charlie, and never seen the caretaker.

It took some wandering before she found Charlie's grave. He rested on the slope facing town, a row up from the iron fence, a small American flag on the headstone.

Kneeling, Carolyn removed the dead flowers, refilled the black vase with water, and arranged the fresh bouquet. Looking at the patches of golden California poppies and blue and white lupines dripping like splashed paint down the hillside, she started to talk. She cried, too. She told her brother how she'd run away the day she heard he'd been killed. She told him about the veteran she met in the park and Jesus touching her in the morning. She told him about Mary and little Charlie and Sadie and the ducks swimming on the pond.

After a while, she even told him about Dock.

She felt better for all of it, purged.

Oma stood at the end of the drive, taking mail out of the box. "You must be hungry. You've been gone for hours. Come on up to the cottage. I'll fix you lunch." She sorted the mail as they walked up the driveway together. "Your mom called. She was worried when you didn't answer the phone."

"I left a note."

"I know. I saw it. I called and let her know where you went."

"I confessed all my sins to Charlie." She tried to make light of it.

"He'll keep your secrets." She handed her a few envelopes. "Put those on the kitchen counter and come on over."

After lunch, Carolyn sat on the floor in Oma's small living room and fingered puzzle pieces. She raked fingers through her hair and stared at the hundreds of pieces. Nothing seemed to fit. "I don't know what I'm going to do, Oma."

"You're going to eat right and get your health back. You're going to stop kicking yourself. You're going to get up and put one foot in front of the other and get on with your life. That's what we all have to do."

"You make it sound easy."

"Nothing is easy, Carolyn. Life isn't easy. We do the best we can with what God gives us."

"I've made a complete mess of everything."

"It's not about what you've done. It's about what you're going to do now."

❄ ❄ ❄

Mom, Dad, and Oma took her to church. Everyone greeted her parents affectionately and then greeted her, too, eyes curious. Some talked about how they remembered her as a little girl.

"So shy and quiet. Such a pretty little thing."

"I remember when you came to my Sunday school class the first time. You didn't say a single word. You haven't changed much."

A lie they all wanted to live with.

Oma tucked her arm through Carolyn's and stood closer. "Why don't we find a seat?"

Carolyn felt strangely at home. She closed her eyes and listened to the choir. She listened so intently to Rev. Elias's prayer, she felt as though she knew what words he'd speak before he said them. She listened to every word of the sermon. The message seemed to have new meaning after her experience in the park. She knew the One he talked about now. It all made sense. She had been blind. Now, she could see, even with her eyes closed. She had been deaf; now she could hear.

When the service ended, Carolyn made the long walk to the back door, where Rev. Elias stood, accepting parishioners' thanks for an excellent sermon. He spoke warmly to her parents and Oma. The smile didn't reach his eyes when he looked at her. "Carolyn."

"It was a wonderful sermon, Rev. Elias."

"How would you know? You slept through it." He spoke tersely, then smiled at the people behind her. She took the hint and went out the door and down the steps.

Carolyn kept going to church, but kept her eyes open. She looked at Rev. Elias, hoping he knew she was paying close attention. She didn't feel Jesus' presence in the building, although she saw Him in her parents and Oma and some of the people who talked with her. She felt closer to God in the cemetery sitting beside Charlie's grave or sitting on the swing her father had built. And she clung to the memory of her encounter with God in Golden Gate Park at dawn, May flowers blooming in the grass.

God loved her, even if no one else could.

MOM AND DAD's friend and dentist, Doc Martin, offered Carolyn a job as his receptionist, the last girl having quit the week Carolyn came home from San Francisco. Thelma, Doc's wife, worked as the hygienist. Carolyn learned quickly that Thelma knew everyone's business and didn't mind sharing.

About a month into her job, Carolyn started to get nauseated every time she came to work. She'd always been bothered by the sounds of drills; now the scents turned her stomach. She tried to keep busy answering phone calls, calling patients to remind them of appointments, taking messages, but the smell of hot enamel sent her running for the bathroom.

Thelma tapped on the door. "Are you all right, Carolyn?"

She retched again. "I'll be out in a minute, Mrs. Martin." Fighting the nausea, she waited a moment and hoped her stomach wouldn't heave again. She'd already lost her eggs and toast. Nothing else remained. She rinsed her mouth, patted her face with a damp paper towel, and opened the door.

Thelma stood right outside, expression curious. "You look awfully pale."

"I'll be all right." The telephone rang and she hurried to answer. Feeling woozy, she slid quickly into the office chair and picked up her pencil. She could feel Thelma's eyes fixed on her back. She jotted another message on the pad.

By lunchtime, she felt fine. The next morning, she felt sick again, and the morning after that. She wondered if she had grown allergic to something in Doc Martin's office. Thelma, maybe. Just being around the woman made Carolyn anxious, but the thought of having to look for another job made her even more so.

When she threw up Saturday morning, she knew it didn't have anything to do with the scents and sounds of the dentist's office. So what was it? Mom heard her heaving and suggested saltines and 7UP. "They'll settle your stomach." They did.

At church the next morning, she had to leave the service. She barely made it outside before she puked in the bushes next to the front steps. Mortified, gulping for air, she straightened and saw her mother standing on the steps above her. "I think I need to lie down in the car, Mom."

Mom walked her to the car. "How long has this been going on, Carolyn?"

"Two weeks."

She paled noticeably. "*Every* morning?"

Carolyn shrugged. "It's probably a flu bug or something."

"I don't think so." Mom looked stricken. "As if things aren't bad enough already." She opened the car door. "We're going to have to talk about this later. Don't say a word about it to anyone, not even Oma, and especially not your father. Not yet."

Carolyn slipped into the car.

"Let's just hope you're not pregnant." Mom slammed the door and headed back to church.

Carolyn fought another wave of nausea. Pregnant? Ash had used her for weeks, but that had been months ago. After him, she hadn't wanted anyone to touch her ever again. She'd been on the

pill up until she left the Clement Street house. She'd left everything
behind that day, but why would she have needed birth control
when she stayed clear of people, except to beg?

The young veteran sitting on the seawall the night she wanted
to commit suicide. He played the guitar. He'd given her a candy
bar. They'd talked. He kept her warm all night.

She understood now why Mom had that look on her face, why
she looked ready to curse and cry, why she thought things were
going to get worse.

Curling up on the backseat, Carolyn wept.

❄ ❄ ❄

Dr. Griffith confirmed Mom's suspicions. "She's about six weeks
along. I think it'd be wise to check for VD."

Dad sat stunned at the dining room table. He looked like
someone had punched him in the stomach. Pain first, then anger.
He punched back. Hard. "Do you even know who fathered it?" He
didn't wait for an answer before cursing her. Mom whispered his
name in an agonized voice, but he didn't hold back. "Charlie would
be ashamed to call you his sister! It's better he's dead so he can't see
what you've become." He put his head in his hands and wept.

Charlie had died honorably, a hero deserving of a shrine. No
shrine for Carolyn. She hadn't seen a picture anywhere in the
house, and she had looked. It would be worse now that she was the
cause of the second-worst catastrophe a parent could suffer. "I'm
sorry. I should've stayed in San Francisco." She'd probably be dead
by now, but maybe that would've been easier on everyone.

"Why didn't you say something?"

She looked at Mom. "I didn't know." Not that that was any
excuse. She felt the muscles tightening around her throat as though
her own body tried to strangle her. The pain kept getting worse.
She pushed it down the way she'd always done, but it was harder
this time.

Dad scraped his chair back. "Maybe you're right. Maybe you should've stayed in San Francisco. Maybe you should go back!"

"Trip!" Mom's voice cracked.

"How are we supposed to fix the mess she's made of her life? Tell me that!"

"Trip . . ."

He glared at Carolyn. "Get out of my sight!"

Carolyn got up and headed for the front door. Mom cried out, *"No!"* She came after Carolyn and gripped her by the elbow. "Don't leave. Just sit in your room for a while; let me talk to him." Carolyn turned like an automaton, guided by her mother's firm hand.

Closed in, curled up on her bed, pillow over her head, she could still hear them shouting.

Chel came to her in her dreams that night. She walked into the surf. When she reached waist level, she turned and held out her hand. Carolyn followed. As the sea closed over her, she found she could still breathe. She swam among the seaweed, feeling the silky strands try to catch hold. She saw the young vet at the bottom playing the guitar. Charlie sat and listened. Chel sea-danced, her red hair floating around her.

When she got up in the morning, Dad sat at the dining room table. She hesitated and stepped back. Dad glanced at her. "Sit down, Carolyn." Steeling herself for further judgment and condemnation, Carolyn obeyed. She was only getting what she deserved.

Dad looked miserable. "We'll figure things out."

Mom sat down with them. "We'll just carry on as usual. You'll keep going to work. Dr. Griffith won't say anything to anyone."

"Mom is going to make a few calls, see what she can find out about homes for unwed mothers."

It didn't surprise Carolyn that they would want to get rid of her, but it still hurt. She had deserted them at the worst time in their lives, and now she came back and presented them with more trouble than they ever deserved. What right did she have to expect them to help her through this crisis?

"It'll be some time before you show." Dad could barely get the words out. "At least we can keep it secret for a while."

Mom folded her hands on the table, knuckles white. "We don't have to make all the decisions now." She searched Carolyn's face, her own troubled. "Is there anything you want to say, Carolyn?"

Instinctively, Carolyn covered her womb. Only one thing mattered to her now. "My life is completely . . ." She used a foul expression she had never heard come from either of their lips, but had heard every hour of every day in her other life. "Please don't take it out on my baby." She got up and fled to her room.

❄ ❄ ❄

No one had to tell Thelma Martin the news. "You're pregnant, aren't you?"

It wasn't really a question. She could sniff out gossip faster than a bloodhound could catch the scent of an escaped prisoner. One of her chatty friends had been sitting in Dr. Griffith's waiting room and saw Mom's face before they left.

"I can see the guilt on your face. Your poor parents . . ." False sympathy oozed from her voice. "I'm so sorry about what they must be going through, Carolyn, but we can't have you working here. Not in your—" her lips pursed—"*condition*. People would think we approved." Thelma's eyes glinted.

When the telephone rang, Carolyn didn't answer it, but rather picked up her purse, took her sweater off the back of the chair, and headed for the door.

"Where do you think you're going?" Thelma demanded, loud enough for the two waiting patients to hear.

"Home."

"Answer the telephone."

"You just fired me. You answer it."

"I didn't mean you had to leave *today*!"

As Carolyn headed for Charlie's red Impala, she imagined what

Chel might say. Her friend would've known how to rock and shock Thelma enough to leave her speechless.

She drove home, hoping to get into the house and close herself in her room, where she could think, before Mom and Dad heard. Maybe she'd be safe for a few hours before the crap hit the fan. By tomorrow morning, the stench of her life would be all over town.

Oma called out to her. Carolyn wanted to pretend she didn't hear. "Carolyn!"

She stopped and closed her eyes for a second, wondering if Oma had heard the news yet. Why not tell her? She might as well get it over with and have the last member of her immediate family hate her.

"I'm pregnant. And no, I don't know who the father is. Mom and Dad wanted to keep it secret. Thelma figured it out. So the cat's out of bag. I just got fired. So much for Mom and Dad saving face by dumping me in an unwed mothers' home before the whole town knows."

Oma said something in German.

Dropping to her knees in the gravel driveway, Carolyn sobbed. She felt the sharp pain of stones cutting into her flesh.

Oma's strong hands pulled her tight against her. "It's not the end of the world."

❄ ❄ ❄

Mom and Dad sat in silence as they heard the news. Oma told them. Having spent most of the afternoon hugging the porcelain throne, Carolyn barely managed to sit at the table. She didn't eat, and neither did Mom and Dad after they heard Thelma Martin knew everything. Or thought she did. Carolyn kept her head down. "I'll find another job."

"What's the point?" Dad threw his napkin on the table. "Who'd hire you now?"

"That's a nice thing to say." Oma sounded disgusted and angry.

Mom sighed heavily. "Thelma Martin is the biggest gossip in town. It's bad luck Carolyn ended up working for them."

Dad looked at Mom. "Have you been able to find out anything about homes?"

"I have another idea, but I need a little more time."

Carolyn suspected she knew. She didn't want to add an even bigger sin to all the rest she had committed. "I won't have an abortion."

Mom and Dad stared at her. "We wouldn't suggest such a thing." Mom spoke for both of them, but the guilt on their faces told Carolyn they'd already debated that solution. "Just stay home until we can sort this out."

Oma left the table, slamming the front door as she went out.

❄ ❄ ❄

Over the next week, Carolyn watched her parents try to live a normal life. They went to work; Carolyn stayed home. Oma invited Carolyn to ride into town with her while she ran errands, but Carolyn declined. If Mom and Dad didn't want her showing her face, she wouldn't.

When Sunday rolled around, they shocked her by saying they wanted her to come to church with them. "Why?" She couldn't think of a worse idea. Thelma Martin was one of the deaconesses.

Mom looked determined. "People know what Thelma Martin is. And there are more people in that church than one nasty gossip." Clearly, she had a point to make, and it didn't matter how Carolyn felt. "You're not staying home."

People greeted them. Some gave pitying glances; others seemed embarrassed; most said nothing, just gave a nod and a faint smile. Mom led the way to the same pew they had occupied for years, six rows from the front, where they could see and hear everything. Oma told Carolyn to keep her head up. Rev. Elias stepped to the pulpit and gazed down at Carolyn, and then he looked at the rest of his congregants.

When the service ended, Carolyn just wanted to escape. Mom and Dad worked their way toward the door, where Rev. Elias stood. Carolyn saw Thelma whispering to several women. Oma stopped and glared at them.

Carolyn noticed her parents saying a quick, quiet word to Rev. Elias as they reached the door. He nodded grimly, shook Dad's hand, and patted Mom sympathetically. Oma took Carolyn's hand and pulled it through her arm. As they came to the door, Rev. Elias smiled at Oma, but ignored Carolyn. When he extended his hand to Oma, she ignored it and walked out the door.

"I'd like to shoot Thelma Martin." Mom stared out the window.

Dad started the ignition. "She's not saying anything that isn't true."

Mom and Dad went back to town that afternoon. Mom came home red-eyed from crying, but she was more serene than she had been in days. Dad seemed more relaxed, too. "Rev. Elias wants to talk with you, Carolyn. Monday is his day off. He said one o'clock would be convenient."

The church door stood ajar when Carolyn arrived. She stepped into the narthex and saw Rev. Elias in his office, writing on a legal pad. Tapping lightly, she waited for permission to enter. After several minutes, he tossed his pen on the desk, sighed heavily, and looked at her. "Come in." He sounded grim. "Sit down." Leaning forward, he steepled his fingers. "Your parents and I talked yesterday. Did they tell you?"

"No, sir." But she'd known, all the same.

"We had a long talk. I've never seen your father cry. You've broken their hearts. Mine, too." He sat back in his big chair. "I wonder if you have any idea how we feel. I've watched you grow up. I had such hopes. They brought you to Sunday school; they brought you to youth group; they've done everything possible to rear their daughter as a moral, upright, responsible girl. You've disappointed all of us, Carolyn, everyone in the congregation."

"I've disappointed myself, sir."

"Oh, let's not play games, shall we?" His tone hardened. "I

know what goes on in Haight-Ashbury. I can imagine what you've been doing since you took off. 'Doing your own thing.' Isn't that what you call it? And then you came back. I hoped. We all did. I thought maybe you'd repent. But then I saw you sitting in the pew with your eyes closed. You don't like hearing the truth, do you? You don't want to listen to the Word of God."

"I pray—"

"Don't lie to me. I wasn't born yesterday." He shook his head, mouth tight. "I confronted you. And you stared at me after that. Open defiance. I can see everything from where I stand. I can see *you*."

Her body grew colder as his tone grew hotter.

"You can look like a Christian on the outside, but it's the fruit that shows what you are." His gaze flickered down, resting pointedly on her abdomen, then back up to stare coldly into her eyes. "You can't hide now, can you? Everyone will know what you are."

She didn't think it could get worse, but he wasn't finished.

"When your brother died, you didn't even have the decency to come home for his funeral. You didn't care enough to show him the honor he deserved. You wanted your own way. Now you have to live with the consequences."

She bowed her head and cried.

"You're sorry now." Rev. Elias sounded weary. "You have regrets; you feel remorse. But I have yet to hear your confession. I see no evidence of repentance."

What kind of evidence did he want? She was about to ask, but one look at his face kept her silent. She didn't see even a hint of love or compassion in his eyes. He'd been the only pastor she'd ever known, but as she searched for Jesus in his face, she couldn't find Him.

The wall clock *tick, tick, tick*ed.

"Well, Carolyn? Don't you have anything to say? Or do you think it's all water under the bridge?"

What could she say? She had sinned, she was paying, and she'd keep paying as long as she lived.

Rev. Elias let out an impatient sigh. "Go on then. Have it your way. I'll pray for your mother and your father, but I won't pray for you. I'm giving you over to Satan. Let the devil sift you."

Carolyn sat in Charlie's Impala, gripping the steering wheel. She wanted a drink. Not just one, a whole bottle, and it didn't matter if it was wine or whiskey. She wanted a drink so badly, she shook and broke out in a cold sweat. She wanted a joint. She wanted acid. She wanted oblivion!

The only thing that stopped her from driving to Hagstrom's grocery store and buying booze was the child tucked beneath her heart.

When Carolyn entered the house, Mom stood in the kitchen fixing dinner; Dad stood nearby talking with her. Mom glanced over her shoulder. "Did you have your talk with Rev. Elias?" She sounded hopeful.

"Yes."

Dad's mouth tightened. "I hope you took everything he said to heart."

"I have." She'd never set foot in a church again.

Carolyn went into her bedroom and closed the door. She thought she might have some respite, but Dad tapped on her door and said to come out in the living room. They had something to tell her. She went on leaden legs.

Dad sat, hands gripping the arms of his recliner. Mom spoke, hands clasped in her lap. "We've found a place for you to live until the baby comes." She looked so relieved. "Jasia Boutacoff is an old friend of mine. We went to nurses' training together. She lives in the San Fernando Valley. I called and told her the situation. She said she'd be happy to have you come and stay with her. She'll take good care of you, Carolyn." She actually smiled as though things couldn't have worked out better. "What do you think?"

Dad's face darkened. "It doesn't matter what she thinks. It's what's best."

Mom covered her anger quickly. "You'll be much better off with Boots."

"Boots?"

"Jasia's nickname."

Dad's fingers stopped digging into the arm of his chair. "Charlie's car is yours now. I had it registered in your name." Dad glanced at Mom. "Boots gave you directions, didn't she?"

"Yes." Mom took a map and short note off the side table and held them out. "She said it would be easy to find. Her telephone number is at the bottom."

Carolyn took the map and directions in trembling fingers. They didn't have to say any more. She understood. They couldn't wait to get rid of her.

Dear Rosie,

I thought things might work out between Carolyn and her parents. Trip had softened, and I saw a desire on all sides to bridge the chasm. No matter the circumstances, this baby could have bound them together in love.

Trip and Hildemara sent Carolyn to Rev. Elias. The poor girl looked like something had broken inside her. She won't tell me a word of what the man said, but I can guess. I will never set foot in that church again as long as that sanctimonious hypocrite stands in the pulpit!

If that wasn't bad enough, this morning I learned Hildemara has sent Carolyn away. She and Trip decided Carolyn would be "better off" in Southern California among strangers than in Paxtown, "where she would be the brunt of cruel gossip." I asked Hildemara Rose if she cared more about what others think than how their daughter feels. She told me she knew what it felt like to be cast out, but that wasn't what she was doing to her daughter.

I am in Yosemite. I needed fresh air. I needed a walk in the mountains. My heart is broken, Rosie. I wanted to make my girl strong, not hard. . . .

17

WINDS GUSTED AS Carolyn drove over Altamont Pass. Spotting the Speedway sign, she remembered how much Chel had wanted to go to the concert. They'd both been too stoned to make it. Just as well. They missed the Hells Angels, the brawls, the fights and chaos. A steady stream of commuters headed back the way she had come, going west to Hayward and Oakland, maybe even as far as San Francisco.

August heat made the inside of Charlie's car feel soupy, even with the windows down. She turned south and kept on, pushing, wanting to speed, and then wondering why she was in such a hurry to get to a stranger's house. Before long, the Tehachapi Mountains loomed ahead, the Grapevine winding upward like a gray snake half-hidden by the inversion layer of smog and haze.

By the time she reached the San Fernando Valley, five o'clock traffic clogged the gray macadam arteries. She'd driven in traffic before, but not like this—six lanes, bumper to bumper, cars weaving, nosing in, taillights flashing red, horns honking if you hesitated a few seconds before making your decision. Adrenaline rushed in her veins. She developed a splitting headache. Her fingers ached from clutching the steering wheel. But she made the right exit and got on the right freeway.

It took forty-five minutes to go eleven miles, but she found her way to Canoga Park. She pulled into a shopping mall and bought her first meal of the day, Kentucky Fried Chicken. She didn't want to arrive on Jasia Boutacoff's doorstep hungry and begging for food. She reread the directions while she ate, and she had them memorized before she got back in the car and headed for Topanga Canyon.

The tan, two-story house with a Spanish red-tile roof stood at the end of a cul-de-sac, desert mountains looming behind. Carolyn parked, opened the trunk, took out her duffel bag, and hefted it onto her shoulder. The landscaping looked professional, trimmed juniper trees between boulders with river-rock ground cover. Two large terra-cotta pots with topiary privets and two Talavera pottery frogs sat on either side of the large mission-style door.

Carolyn had barely rung the bell when the door opened. "Jasia Boutacoff?"

"Call me Boots, honey." The tall, slender woman with gray-streaked black hair smiled warmly. She wore white slacks and a flowing purple tunic with a gold chain belt. "And you're Carolyn." She waved her in. "Come on in. It's hotter than Hades out here."

The air-conditioning hit Carolyn like a cold front, but she welcomed it after hours in hundred-degree heat. She smelled something wonderful cooking. The foyer had dark hardwood flooring, painted cabinets, Talavera sconces on the walls, and a large, frosted-glass Mexican star hanging from the ceiling. An archway opened into a dining room furnished with a painted country-style wood sunflower sideboard, a wrought-iron chandelier hanging over the painted table, and eight blue chairs.

"You must be exhausted after that long drive." She took Carolyn's bag. "I'll show you the way to your room. You can freshen up a bit, if you like, and join me in the living room." She led the way down a corridor without pausing for breath. "You

were six months old the last time I saw you. Your dad was changing your diapers." She laughed. "He gagged. Men are so helpless
sometimes."

Carolyn caught a glimpse of the huge Southwest-style living
room with a curved white fireplace and sliding-glass doors to
the backyard. Boots kept talking about Carolyn's dad and mom
as she walked down the hallway and opened a door into a large
bedroom, crossing the plush, tan carpeted floor. She put Carolyn's
duffel bag on the end of a four-poster queen-size bed with a crazy
quilt. Carolyn took in a Tuscan dresser on one side of the room,
marble-topped side tables, a comfortable chair with a stool near
the windows, a small table beside it with several books, one a Bible.
A watercolor of a field of sunflowers hung on one wall, an Italian
coastal town on the opposite.

Boots opened the big armoire. "You can put things in here,
or use the closet." She opened one of the sliding-mirror doors.
A dozen white silk hangers hung on the rod. "You have a private
bathroom." Boots leaned in and flicked on a light, revealing a
luxurious white marble bathroom with a big tub, separate shower,
and cubby room for the toilet. A thick terry-cloth robe lay over the
vanity chair. Mirrors lined the marble counter. Two sinks. Carolyn
had never seen anything so gorgeous.

"I'm so glad you're here, Carolyn. I'm looking forward to spending time with you. I want you to be comfortable. If you need
anything, you tell me. I want you to feel at home."

Overwhelmed, Carolyn burst into tears.

"Oh, sweetie." Boots held her close and rubbed her back.
"Don't worry. Everything is going to be fine. Things have a way
of working out the way God intends. I know this isn't your home,
but I'm going to do my best to make you feel as though it is.
You're not the first girl who's faced having a baby. You're not alone.
Believe me." She drew back and cupped Carolyn's face, leaning
down slightly to look into her eyes. "You're the daughter of one of
my oldest and dearest friends, and I promised Hildie I'd take good
care of you. Now I'm promising you."

She let go of Carolyn. "Why don't you freshen up and unpack? Come on in the living room when you're ready. We'll have a few minutes to talk before dinner is ready."

❄ ❄ ❄

Carolyn expected to hide out until the baby was born, but Boots dispelled that notion over a gourmet breakfast the next morning. "I've invited some friends over this afternoon. They've been a great comfort to me through some rough times. Kept me accountable. You're going to like them, and they're going to love you."

"I've never had many friends."

"Hildie said you had one that meant a lot to you." Boots looked at her.

What else had her mother told Boots?

"I can see what you're thinking. Your mother called me because she didn't want you among strangers. She knows my life hasn't been pristine. I was a party girl when we knew one another. She always walked the straight and narrow, but I dated every new intern who came to the hospital. No one was ever good enough for me, or so I thought. It took me a long time to realize I loved myself more than I'd ever loved anyone. And along the way, I found plenty of opportunities—and excuses—for getting drunk."

Boots lifted her glass of orange juice. "It never occurred to me I might become an alcoholic." She set the glass on the table. "No one sets out to bring that kind of misery into their life, and it takes more than willpower to stop." Completely relaxed, Boots smiled at Carolyn. "By the grace of God, someone dragged me to my first AA meeting. I heard about a higher power. I call Him Jesus. He's become the love of my life. And I made friends. You'll meet a few. I've been going to meetings ever since."

"The ladies who are coming today?"

"Only one, but none would claim to be perfect." She reached over and patted Carolyn's hand. "The thing is, we all struggle, some harder than others. Some of us make trouble for ourselves."

Carolyn hadn't just brought trouble on herself; she'd carried it home to her parents. She wondered how she'd support herself and her baby. She hadn't finished college, had no real job skills. Could she earn enough as a waitress or mall shopgirl to pay for a small apartment? What about doctor and hospital bills? If she kept her baby, she'd have to find work. She'd have to arrange day care. Would she end up raising her child in a ghetto neighborhood? There was always adoption, but Carolyn wanted to weep at the mere thought of handing her baby over to strangers, never to see her child again. Just thinking about all the decisions made her want to get drunk or high.

"I understand."

She hadn't realized she'd spoken the last aloud. Mortified, she closed her eyes.

"You don't have to figure everything out today, honey."

"I don't know if I can figure anything out."

"Take it one day at a time."

Carolyn wasn't used to trusting people, especially someone she'd known for so short a time, but she felt at ease with Boots. She felt safe. She'd been fighting temptation since she left the Clement Street house. If she'd had any money, she would've spent it on booze and drugs while living in the park. She had nothing then; she had nothing now, but the temptation hadn't lessened. Only the baby kept her straight.

"Can I go to an AA meeting with you sometime?"

"We'll go tonight."

❄   ❄   ❄

Mom called once a week. She'd ask Carolyn how she was feeling. "Fine." She'd ask how things were going with Boots. "Great." She'd ask if Carolyn needed anything. "No." Then she'd ask to speak with Boots.

Sometimes Dad got on the phone, but not often and never for long. Oma never called. She wrote letters, filling them with newsy tidbits, what she had seen, what grew in her garden. She didn't ask Carolyn if she'd made any decisions about the baby.

Dr. O'Connor, the husband of one of Boots's many friends, told Carolyn the baby had a strong heartbeat. She'd gained ten pounds in two months, largely due to Boots's great cooking. They went on morning walks together before the heat trapped them inside the house. Sometimes they went out again in the evening. Boots insisted on "playing tourist" with her. They went to the Los Angeles Zoo, Santa Monica Pier, La Brea Tar Pits, Malibu. When Boots asked her if she'd like to go to Disneyland, Carolyn told her about the trip with Oma. She no longer had to worry about hurting Charlie's feelings.

They attended AA meetings twice a week. Carolyn listened, but never talked. No one pressed her.

Boots tapped on her door early one morning. "We're going to the beach before the crowds get there." She drove Topanga Canyon Road like a NASCAR driver. They arrived at dawn. Joggers ran along the water's edge.

"Come on." Boots got out and headed across the sand with a basket and blanket. Dumping them, she kicked off her shoes and continued on toward the waves lapping the beach. Carolyn followed. Boots stopped at the edge of the wet sand. Hands on her hips, she lifted her face and closed her eyes. "Listen to that. There's something about the sound of the sea, isn't there? Soothing."

They walked along the beach together, not saying anything. Boots didn't seem worried about the blanket. When they turned back, she bent and scooped up a stick, twirling it in her hand like a baton. "You're eating yourself up with guilt and worry, Carolyn, and it's got to stop." She stopped and jabbed the stick into the moist sand. "Write down every sin you've committed right here in the sand. Let it all out." She walked up the beach onto dry sand, spread the blanket, and sat. "Take your time!" she called out. She lay back, arms beneath her head, and crossed her ankles.

Carolyn barely managed to write a few words before a wave came and washed them away. She wrote more, and the waves came in again, erasing her words. She wrote and wrote, and each time the sea came and swept away her confession. She didn't know how long she bent to the task before she finished. Her feet were numb from the cold water. She tossed the stick into the surf and watched it carried out. For the first time in weeks, her chest didn't feel like someone was sitting on it.

"Finished?" Boots called.

"For now."

Boots came down and stood next to her. "You can always come back." She smiled at her and then looked out at the sea. Surfers rode the small waves. "I listen to the sea and hear the Lord, Carolyn. Jesus said He came to save us, not condemn us. He took our sins upon Himself. He paid the price to set you free. God is like those waves, honey. He washes away your sins. He offers you the free gift of grace, the added bonus of the Holy Spirit dwelling in you, and eternal life as well. You have decisions to make, but the biggest one is what you're going to believe about Him. Ask Him in, and He'll take care of the rest."

They stood side by side looking out at the ocean. Carolyn felt a fluttering sensation—angel wings. She put her hands over her abdomen. Boots saw the movement and turned to her. "The quickening?" Carolyn laughed for the first time in months. It sounded odd to her ears. Boots laughed with her.

❄ ❄ ❄

Carolyn's heart pounded during AA meetings. She could feel the tension grow inside her. Sitting on her hands, she kept her head down, listening, soaking in the words.

One evening the silence lasted so long, she broke out in a sweat. She knew it was her turn to open up, but didn't know if she could speak a coherent sentence.

She took a breath and confessed she started drinking to deal with the stress of attending UCB. She drank more when her brother was sent to Vietnam, then started smoking pot with friends while protesting the war.

Everyone listened. No one judged her. Several came over to talk with her after the meeting, sharing similar stories.

"First time is usually hardest," Boots told her on the way home.

It took another month before she could talk about Charlie. She'd stayed drunk or stoned the year after he died. "I can only remember bits and pieces; most I'd rather forget. . . ." She cried when she told them about Chel.

Mom called again. Carolyn might not be able to talk with her mother, but Boots never had a problem. "She's filling out, has a nice basketball growing." Boots took pictures of Carolyn. When December rolled around, Mom and Dad sent money. So did Oma. Carolyn wrote and thanked them. Boots took her to the mall. As they wandered through the stores, Boots picked up a sweater. "Good godfrey! What a price!" She folded the sweater back onto the table. When she wasn't looking, Carolyn bought it for her.

Boots cried when she opened the box Christmas morning and found the red cashmere sweater. "You must have spent all your Christmas money on this."

"You like it, don't you?"

Boots put the sweater back in the box. "I love it, of course. But now you listen. Your mom and dad have been sending me money every month. I never asked for a penny, but they insisted. And then you go and buy this. I should take it back to the store."

"Please don't."

"Okay. I won't." She grinned, eyes brimming. "I'll throw you a shower instead."

Oma and Mom sent their regrets, inclement weather keeping them from making the long drive south. Oma had a bad cold, and Mom was keeping an eye on her.

A half-dozen friends of Boots showed up bearing gifts, most of which turned out to be for Carolyn and not the baby. A peach suit, white shell blouse, a pair of taupe heels and purse. "For job interviews." A jogging suit "to get back in shape after the baby." A classic camel-hair coat.

They couldn't have been kinder, though their expectation was clear: adoption was the best option. Only Boots gave her money to spend as she wanted.

Braxton Hicks contractions came often. Carolyn knew she didn't have much time left. She cried more now than she had during the earlier months, and she dreamed of sleeping in Golden Gate Park, lying on a sleeping bag beneath a black plastic lean-to. When she awakened, she reminded herself of Jesus speaking in that loving voice, His hand upon her, the tiny starlike flowers blooming in the grass, and dawn coming.

Mom finally asked the dreaded question. "Have you decided what to do?"

Carolyn noted her mother didn't ask what she *wanted* to do. Her eyes burned. She swallowed hard and wiped tears from her cheeks. "I guess." Give up her baby to someone else to rear. Everyone seemed to think that best, except Boots, who said things had a way of working out. Carolyn didn't see how. Had they worked out for Chel?

"You can stay with me as long as you want, Carolyn. You want to keep the baby, we'll work things out so you can."

Carolyn felt ashamed. Chel had paid for everything after they'd left Berkeley. She didn't want someone else paying her way now. It was just another way to run and hide from the real world. She had to grow up sometime, had to bear the consequences of her actions, no matter how painful. And wouldn't her baby be better off with someone else, someone less screwed up? someone who could offer a home and love? In three weeks, more or less, she'd give birth. She had to stop dreaming.

She called the adoption agency. They said they'd draw up papers. She cried all the way back to Boots's house.

Carolyn went out for a long walk alone the next morning. She had memorized the Serenity Prayer and said it over and over.

"A package came for you last night," Boots told her over

breakfast. "I forgot all about it when you came home so upset. I put it on your bed."

Boots had sliced open the cardboard box. Carolyn lifted out the big pink- and blue-papered box. When she opened the card, she recognized her mother's neat handwriting.

Dad and I hope this helps you make your decision. We love you.

They'd sent a baby car seat.

❄ ❄ ❄

My dearest Carolyn,

I had a quiet Christmas with Bernhard, Elizabeth, and Eddie. I'm in Truckee now, enjoying snow-covered mountains, remembering the days I took long walks in the Alps with my friend, Rosie. She has been my faithful friend through all these years. She knows all my faults and failures and still loves me. May Boots prove such a friend to you.

I'm in no hurry to go home. All I do is sit alone in the cottage. Your mother is working long hours at the hospital. Your dad comes home and goes right to work building the retaining walls for the terraces he has planned. Rikka wants me to come to New York City in the spring. A gallery will be showing her work.

You and my first great-grandchild are in my constant

prayers. God grant you peace in whatever decision you make. I love you. That will never change. And I will love your child, too, no matter what happens.

Life has its twists and turns, Carolyn. As for me, I am surrendering all to Jesus and trust Him to make it all straight in the end. Whatever you may think now, God promises to use everything that happens for His good purpose in making you into the woman He designed you to be. Just love Him. Lean on Him. Remember He loved you first and always. As do I.

Love,
Oma

❄ ❄ ❄

1971

Labor started in the middle of the night on February 6. Boots acted as Carolyn's coach. Boots washed the baby and wrapped her. The moment Carolyn held her newborn, she roused from exhaustion and wept with joy. She fell in love for the first time. Her daughter fit perfectly in her arms. Carolyn felt a tug at her breast as tiny fingers closed around her thumb. God had given her this child the night she had almost thrown her life into the sea. Tangible evidence of His grace.

Boots's eyes shone with tears over her surgical mask. "Well, you can't name her Charlie now, can you?"

"Her name is May Flower Dawn." She knew it sounded like a hippy name, but she didn't care. She couldn't call her the only other name that fit—Epiphany.

She'd conceived the baby the night before she saw Jesus, and she would always consider this child an undeserved gift from God.

❄ ❄ ❄

Mom called every few days to check on things. "Everything is ready." After a month, she lost patience. "It's time to come home, Carolyn. Boots has done enough."

May Flower Dawn slept most of the way. Carolyn stopped every couple of hours to nurse and change diapers. When she arrived home, Mom and Dad came outside. Oma came out of the cottage. Before Carolyn could get out of the car, her mother opened the passenger door and lifted May Flower Dawn from the car seat.

Her parents had turned Charlie's room into a nursery. They'd painted the walls pale green. Mom had hung airy white curtains. Dad had put up new pull-down shades and set up the white crib. Oma had bought the mobile with Disney characters. Dad had painted the bookcase white. Charlie's sci-fi books were gone and in their place, two stacks of diapers, Vaseline, baby powder, baby shampoo, bath soap, and some children's books.

May Flower Dawn still in her arms, Mom opened the closet. "Your grandmother has been sewing since she found out she has a great-granddaughter."

"So have you," Oma said from the doorway.

They had even bought a rocking chair. Mom sat in it. She laid May Flower Dawn on her lap. "She's beautiful." When May Flower Dawn started to whimper, Mom lifted her to her shoulder.

Carolyn stepped forward and reached out. "She's hungry."

Reluctantly, it seemed, Mom relinquished May Flower Dawn. Carolyn waited until her mother, father, and grandmother filed out of the bedroom before sitting on Charlie's bed to nurse her baby. She looked around the room again, taking in all the work her parents and Oma had done.

They might not love or want *her*, but Carolyn had no doubt they wanted May Flower Dawn.

18

CAROLYN SAT AT the dining room table, Dad at the head, Mom sitting opposite with May Flower Dawn in her arms again. While she cooed softly to Carolyn's baby, Dad did the talking. "It's not going to be a free ride. You'll have conditions to meet if you're going to live here." He folded his hands on the table. "We expect you to finish college and get your degree. And we expect you to work and pay rent."

Panic bubbled. "How?"

"You got yourself into this mess, and you're going to have to work your way out. Here's how things are going to be."

"You'll have two more months to rest and take care of the baby." Mom spoke without lifting her head. "By then, our little lady here will have had the most important benefits of nursing." When May Flower Dawn grasped Mom's thumb, Carolyn felt a twinge of jealousy. "I'll step in then."

"Step in?"

"Your mother is giving up her career in order to stay home and take care of your daughter."

"I didn't ask—"

"No, you didn't ask, but what did you think, Carolyn?" His eyes darkened in anger. "You could live off other people because you have a child?" His voice became tighter, harsher. "We can't take care of you for the rest of your life. You have to learn how to pay your way."

Mom raised her head. "Trip . . ."

Dad glanced at her and at the baby in her arms. His shoulders sagged. He looked back at Carolyn, his expression bleak. "We're not trying to punish you, Carolyn. We want to help you put your life back together. You need to finish school. Berkeley is out of the question, so we filled out the application for State College in Hayward. All you have to do is sign it. The college has an employment office. They'll help you find a job that will work into your school schedule."

Mom looked at her sadly. "It isn't going to be easy."

"Life isn't easy." Dad's mouth flattened. "We won't be around forever, picking up the pieces. You need a way to support yourself. Without an education, you're not going to get much of anything. We tried to tell you—"

Mom cleared her throat.

May Flower Dawn began to cry, a whimper at first, then louder, her little mouth opening and quivering as she wailed. Carolyn wanted to do the same thing. She started to stand. "Let me take her, Mom."

Mom stood, too, and shook her head. "She'll be fine. You and Dad need to talk." She took the baby into the back bedroom and closed the door, leaving Carolyn alone in the dining room with her father. He hadn't finished laying down the rules.

"You'll pay us rent. Not much, and not until you start working, but after that, we want eighty percent of whatever you make. It'll go for room and board and to repay the money we sent to Boots. And the hospital bill."

The full weight of what he expected fell on her like a load of bricks. How many years would it take to pay off her debts—ten?

twenty? May Flower Dawn would be grown and gone by then. She could hear her baby crying and wanted to go after her, wanted to grab hold of May Flower Dawn and run.

"Excuse me." Carolyn stood.

"Where are you going?"

"She's hungry."

She didn't tap at the bedroom door. She walked in. "She needs to nurse, Mom."

Mom smiled. "Sit here beside me and I'll give her to you."

Were there going to be conditions on everything now? Maybe there always had been. She hadn't understood the rules she had to follow to earn love. When Mom didn't rise from where she sat on the edge of the big double bed, Carolyn obeyed. Mom handed over May Flower Dawn, but didn't leave her alone.

Mom put her hand on Carolyn's knee. "I know you probably won't believe this right now, but Dad and I aren't doing this to ruin your life. We're not trying to make things even harder for you; we're trying to help you learn how to stand on your own two feet."

Carolyn looked into her mother's eyes and saw compassion. She also saw pain, and she knew she had caused it. "I know, Mom."

She also knew the price they asked: May Flower Dawn.

❄ ❄ ❄

What her parents demanded wasn't in writing. They didn't ask for her signature on any document. But it was a binding contract nonetheless, and Carolyn agonized over it. She could see no way out, nor did she feel she had the right to seek one. For the next six weeks, she pondered what she would have to do to make a way for herself and her daughter. If she went back to Boots, she would destroy a friendship that had weathered more than thirty years. She couldn't do that to her mother or to Boots.

So Carolyn signed the college application, put May Flower Dawn into the car seat, and drove into Hayward to hand-deliver it. Every course she had completed at UCB would count at State.

At least that was something, though she would still have two and a half years of coursework to complete while working part-time. If she went to school half-time, it would take her five years.

Could she do it? She spoke with the employment office. They assured her they would be able to find something for her when the semester began.

Time passed too quickly. She grasped every moment with May Flower Dawn, holding her, playing with her, watching her sleep. When Mom gave two weeks' notice at the hospital, Carolyn wept.

The first week of separation from May Flower Dawn proved agonizing. Her milk came in when she would have been feeding her, and the pain was excruciating. By the time she returned home, her mother had given May Flower Dawn formula, bathed her, changed her, and rocked her to sleep. Carolyn was left to take a warm shower and watch her milk flow down the drain.

She got a job in the library. She worked twenty-five hours a week, minimum wage. At the end of the month, she signed over her paycheck to her father. Dad had given her an accounting. Most of her check would go toward the hospital bill and Boots repayment, then toward room and board. Once the hospital bill and Boots had been taken care of, Carolyn could chip away at what she owed for tuition and books. He gave her twenty-five dollars to call her own. What she didn't spend on gas for Charlie's Impala went into a savings account.

Depressed, driven, Carolyn thought about drinking again. At least drunk she wouldn't feel the pain, the loneliness. Frightened by the craving, she found an AA meeting in Hayward. It helped to have friends who understood, a place where she could draw hope from others' experiences. But it took another hour out of her day, an hour she might have spent with May Flower Dawn.

Between classes, work, and AA meetings, Carolyn missed every milestone in May Flower Dawn's first year. Carolyn wasn't there when her baby daughter rolled over, learned to grasp a toy, sat up, or began to crawl. She didn't hear her say *Mama*. Mom and Dad began calling her daughter Dawn, and when she needed comfort

or wanted something, she didn't reach out to Carolyn. She wanted
Granny.

❈ ❈ ❈

1974

Finally growing weary of her library job, Carolyn used a portion of
her savings to buy business attire and applied for part-time work
as a receptionist in a real estate office owned by Myrna Wegeman,
an attractive, ambitious overachiever, who hired her and started
Carolyn at fifty cents more an hour than she'd been earning.
Carolyn still had nights and Sundays free to study and attend AA
meetings, but hardly any time at all with three-year-old Dawn.
Mom and Dad didn't complain, and Dawn didn't miss her.

With a constant stream of new listings, Myrna handed Carolyn
an expensive camera and sent her out to take pictures of properties.
Carolyn studied the houses from every angle before shooting the
pictures. Myrna couldn't have been more pleased with the results.

"I'm getting more calls on the properties you've shot than the
ones I've done. You have a talent for this. Ever think about becoming a real estate agent?"

The more Carolyn did for Myrna, the more Myrna expected
of her. When Myrna began asking her to oversee open houses on
Sunday afternoons, Carolyn asked for double pay. Myrna reluctantly agreed.

This time, Carolyn ran into resistance at home. Mom balked
at the idea of longer hours. "You're hardly ever home as it is."

Dad didn't like the idea either. "Your mother could use a break
once in a while."

So could I! Carolyn wanted to say. She never had a day off, not
that she dared ask for one. "I can take May Flower Dawn with
me." The idea of having her daughter to herself for an entire afternoon excited her, but Mom nixed that idea.

"Maybe she should take Dawn with her, Hildie. Give Carolyn
a chance to find out how hard it is to take care of a child."

Mom gave Dad a quelling look. "You make it sound like labor. I love taking care of Dawn. She's no bother at all!"

Dad gave up on Mom and directed his logic at Carolyn. "You've got plenty of time. You don't have to be in such a hurry. You're making good enough headway on your debts."

Carolyn realized they had no concerns over how much time she'd already lost with May Flower Dawn.

Oma came over early one Sunday before heading to church. She no longer attended church in Paxtown, but drove to a neighboring town. Mom had commented on it once. "Oma can't stand to be in the same building with Thelma Martin. Not that I blame her. But I'm not letting that gossip drive me away."

No one ever suggested Carolyn return. Certainly Rev. Elias never did.

Oma set her purse on the breakfast counter. "When was the last time you spent more than an hour with your daughter?"

"I don't have an hour, Oma. I have classes. I have to study. I have to work."

Oma watched Carolyn write notes. "Your mom and dad are doing what they think is right. They're doing the best they can for both you and May Flower Dawn."

Carolyn looked up from her textbook. "I know. I'm not complaining. It's just the way things are." Flipping the page in her text, she tried to refocus on her studies. "Sorry. I don't mean to ignore you, but I only have a couple of hours to study before I have to leave for an open house." She could feel Oma looking at her. How long since they had sat on the patio and had tea together?

"Maybe you should speak up about what you're feeling, Carolyn."

"Feeling?" Carolyn gave a bleak laugh. Speaking up wouldn't change anything. It would make things a hundred times worse! Oma didn't move. Frustrated, Carolyn stopped writing and looked at her. "And you don't have to say it. I already know. By the time I have a place of my own, Dawn won't be mine anymore."

"It's never been about possession."

"Maybe not, but that's the way it's turned out. And I'm losing ground with every day that passes." No matter how little time she spent with her child, she loved her. She longed to have her back in her arms. Why else did they think she worked so hard? She wanted her life back, a life that centered on May Flower Dawn.

Oma reached over and gripped her wrist, eyes flashing. "I took care of you when you were little more than a toddler. You *needed* me. Do you remember? But that didn't change the fact that your mother is still your mother!"

"Yes. I remember." Carolyn put her hand over Oma's. "But I learned to love you more, didn't I?"

Oma's eyes flickered. She had an odd expression on her face. Picking up her purse, she stood. "It never stopped you from loving her." She went quietly out the door.

Dear Rosie,

I see more clearly now how things I thought I did for good caused harm. Remember when I moved in with Hildemara when she was ill with consumption? I wanted to help, but ended up taking over. I became so attached to Carolyn, I didn't see the damage I did to my daughter.

Now I find myself watching Carolyn suffer as Hildemara must have. The girl is working so hard to put her life back together and earn love, all because Trip laid out a plan for her to "get back on her feet" and "fly right." They want to help, just as I did. But these conditions have left no time for Carolyn to be with her child, no time to be part of the family. I hardly ever see Carolyn anymore. We barely have time to exchange a greeting, let alone sit under the arbor and have a cup of tea. How can I encourage her? I have no answers.

I have never seen Hildemara so happy (other than her complaints that Carolyn no longer attends church). I understand her happiness because I felt the same when I took care of Carolyn. I felt the loss of my daughter's affections far less when I could freely pour my love out on my granddaughter. And there is the dilemma!

Did I have the right to usurp Hildemara in Carolyn's affections as I now see her doing with May Flower Dawn? Hildemara is in her glory. She does all the things a mother longs to do for her child. Of course, Carolyn does not complain about anything. She has always been reticent about sharing her feelings. Yesterday she surprised me and said her mother never had time for her, but all the time in the world for May Flower Dawn. She didn't say it with bitterness, but resignation.

I've been pondering Carolyn's words ever since. I wonder if Hildemara feels the same about me. . . .

19

1976

Time moved too quickly. Carolyn's mother had enrolled Dawn in nursery school and stayed as a volunteer. Carolyn pushed harder than ever as she went into her senior year of college. Myrna urged Carolyn to study for a real estate license. "I have more clients than I can handle, and you've already learned how to write proposals and put the paperwork together." Myrna had seen to that. "You'd make a lot more money than you do as my receptionist."

Adding another goal chewed into what little time Carolyn had left. She wished she could quit college, but Dad wouldn't hear of it. "Real estate markets go up and down. A college degree lasts forever." The last few months proved to be the most taxing, and then she got the word she had made it. She told Dad, knowing he would care more than Mom. Only one hitch.

"What do you mean you're not going through the graduation ceremony?"

Carolyn shrugged it off. "It's not important. I'll get my diploma in the mail."

"Don't you think you owe it to us to walk across that stage?"

She wanted to remind him she had already given him and Mom everything he demanded—and the one thing that mattered most to her, May Flower Dawn. "The test for my real estate license is on the same day, Dad. I have more chance of making a living at real estate than as an officer manager." She'd already checked. It was still a man's world. All her business degree would get her was a menial job in a big corporation and low starting pay. She didn't have any more time to waste.

"Doesn't it matter to you, Carolyn?" Her father looked troubled. "You've worked so hard. You should be proud. I'd think you'd want to wear that cap and gown and have the whole world see you get your diploma."

The whole world? Who was he kidding? Carolyn felt a sudden rush of anger. "It mattered more to you than it ever mattered to me."

"Why didn't you say something?"

"And where would I've been if I had? I'd have done *anything* to stay off the streets. I've done everything you and Mom asked of me, and you're still not satisfied."

Dad winced as though she'd slapped him across the face. She had to clench her teeth before she lied and retracted every word.

❄ ❄ ❄

Real estate license in hand, Carolyn gave Myrna Wegeman notice. "You're quitting?" Myrna couldn't believe it. "After all I've done for you?"

Carolyn thanked her. "You've taught me more about business than all my classes put together. You're the one who believed in me and made me feel I could do so much more." She wanted to work in the valley, close to May Flower Dawn. She wanted time with her daughter.

Myrna wasn't mollified. "You owe me for the opportunities I've given you!"

Carolyn had had enough. She didn't want to hear how much

she owed Myrna—or anyone else. She'd been working on her debts for five years! "I'm sorry you feel that way. I hoped we could part as friends." Forget the two weeks' notice. She headed for the door.

Myrna came out from behind her desk and called out to her to wait a minute. "Can't we talk about this?" Carolyn didn't even look back as she went out the door and closed it firmly behind her.

She'd already lined up a job in a real estate office in Paxtown. Real estate boomed over the East Bay hills, too, and Ross Harper had been willing to hire her, despite having been warned by others of her less-than-pristine reputation. He'd heard of Myrna Wegeman. "If you survived three years with that tiger, working with me is going to be a piece of cake."

She no longer had to get up at the crack of dawn to commute to the Bay Area. She no longer had night classes. She didn't have to spend every spare minute studying and writing papers. She could breathe a little, as long as she scoured the valley in search of people willing to list property with a young, untried real estate agent. And then she had to promote those properties to other agents and show the houses.

America's bicentennial came, and Carolyn managed enough time off to attend the fireworks and celebration at the fairgrounds. Five-year-old May Flower Dawn was frightened by the explosions and bright, showering lights. When Carolyn tried to snuggle her close, she cried harder. Straining away, Dawn called out for "Granny" and wouldn't be calmed until sitting on Mom's lap.

A week later, Carolyn sold her first listing and used every bit of her commission to pay off the last of the debt she owed her father and mother. She felt a moment of ecstasy when she handed Dad the check.

"Against all odds." His eyes glistened with tears. "You did it, Carolyn." He smiled broadly. "I'm proud of you."

She had never expected those words to come out of his mouth, not in a million years. Embarrassed, she stammered. "I have some buyers interested in another listing. If all goes well, I'll have enough to move out on my own." She glanced toward the living room, where May Flower Dawn played with Barbie dolls while Mom read a story.

Mom left the book on the table and came through the foyer. "What are you two talking about?"

Dad showed her the check. "She's debt-free."

Mom held the check in both hands and stared at it. No congratulations were forthcoming. Carolyn stood a little straighter. "I was telling Dad if I make another sale, I'll be moving out with May Flower Dawn."

"Moving out?" Mom raised her head, her face paling.

"She won't be going far." Dad seemed oblivious. "She works for Ross. Remember? It's not like she'd be moving to the San Fernando Valley."

Dad didn't seem to notice Mom's pained glance back at the child playing on the living room rug. Carolyn did, and she understood only too well. Her mother wasn't worried about losing her. She just didn't want to lose May Flower Dawn.

❄ ❄ ❄

When Carolyn came home the next afternoon after showing houses all morning to prospective buyers, her mother and father said they wanted to talk with her. Mom's red-rimmed eyes warned her something was wrong. "Where's May Flower Dawn?"

"She's fine." Mom wiped her cheek. "She's at Sandy's house."

"Sandy?"

"Her best friend from nursery school. They live on First Street."

"Nice family," Dad added. "They go to our church."

Carolyn knew less than nothing about May Flower Dawn's classmates. That would soon change. She clasped her hands tightly in her lap. "You wanted to talk to me about something?"

He smiled. "Actually, we wanted to give you something." He slid a bankbook across the table. When she didn't touch it, he nodded at it. "Go ahead. Take a look. It's yours."

She took it and wondered what catch her parents had attached to this. She put it back on the table and pushed it away. "I don't need a loan. I just wrote an offer on a house today. If it goes through, I'll receive a good commission. I've had my eye on an American bungalow out on Vineyard Avenue—"

Mom cut her off. "It's not a loan, Carolyn. It's yours."

"Every penny of it." Dad pushed the bankbook back to her. "It's every dollar of the rent money you've given us since you came home."

She stared at them. She didn't know whether to believe they could extend such kindness or pull defensive armor around herself. "I don't understand."

Dad leaned forward. "We knew you'd need a nest egg, Carolyn, something to give you a good start when you finished school. So we've been setting aside the rent money from the beginning."

Carolyn looked at her mother and saw a war of emotions. Did she understand this gift would become the means to take May Flower Dawn away from her? Mom's sad smile hinted she did; then her words confirmed it. "You should have enough to put a down payment on that bungalow you want."

"If I can talk them into selling, I will." Carolyn took the bankbook with trembling fingers. "Thank you."

Carolyn felt no qualms about embracing her father or soaking his shirt with tears. Hugging her mother proved more difficult. As soon as Carolyn put her arms around her, Mom stiffened and turned her face. Hurt, Carolyn took the hint and withdrew. Her mother's eyes filled with pain. She took Carolyn's hand, patting it. "You'll do fine."

❄ ❄ ❄

Carolyn wasted no time. She went to the Zeiglers, who owned the house she liked, and asked if they might be interested in selling. She expected resistance, but they surprised her and agreed. They had been thinking about selling for over a year. "Our daughter would like us to move back to Ohio and live with her family. She has a big house on a lake, with a granny unit."

Everything moved quickly. Mrs. Zeigler called Carolyn and asked if she would be interested in buying some of their furniture. "We won't have room for most of our things." The only thing they wanted to take east was their bedroom set, a gift to each other on their fortieth wedding anniversary. Carolyn bought their sofa, wing chairs, bookshelves, a dining room set, a large mahogany coffee table, two standing tulip lamps, and the brass fire screen and utensils. She had made another sale and went out to find something special for May Flower Dawn. She purchased a French provincial twin canopy bed, white dresser, desk, and two matching side tables.

Carolyn used every spare moment to get the house ready for May Flower Dawn. She washed walls and painted; put up new drapes and sheers; had the wood floors in the living room sanded, restained, and sealed; and bought an imitation Persian rug. She added wall-to-wall carpeting in the bedrooms. Mom had told her May Flower Dawn's favorite colors. She painted the walls of her daughter's bedroom pink with white trim, bought pink sheets and blankets and a purple comforter set with pillow shams. She hung white lace curtains and bought new Barbie and Ken dolls with half a dozen changes of clothes.

Carolyn worked far into the night every night, wanting everything to be perfect before her daughter moved in. By the end of her first month of home ownership, she was ready. "Everything's been done, Mom. I want to make things as easy as possible for both of you. Do you want to bring May Flower Dawn, or shall I come and get her?"

"Dad and I will bring her to you. We'd like to see what you've done to the place."

When her parents arrived, Carolyn watched her daughter's face, hoping to see some hint of pleasure. May Flower Dawn looked scared. She clutched her grandmother's hand and avoided Carolyn's eyes. Mom had a forced smile plastered to her face. She talked in an overbright voice, pointing out what a nice house Dawn would be living in. "What a lovely bedroom. Your mother painted it your favorite colors, honey."

"I don't want to live here, Granny." May Flower Dawn spoke in a low voice.

"This is your home now, Dawn."

"I want to stay with you and Papa."

Every word stabbed Carolyn's heart. Mom was clearly grief torn. Dad looked grim and somewhat irritated. "We'd better go, Hildie. Now."

"Just give me a minute with her."

Carolyn wanted to scream. *You've had her for five years, and I've given you weeks to prepare her!* Pushing the pain and anger down, she quietly left them alone and went outside with Dad. He gazed back toward the house. "Don't expect Dawn to adjust overnight, Carolyn."

She tried to be fair. "I suppose it's going to be difficult for Mom, too."

"You have no idea."

Mom came outside alone, eyes streaming tears. "If you need us, just call." She slipped quickly into the car and covered her face, shoulders shaking. Carolyn watched them drive away before she went back into the house. She found May Flower Dawn curled up and crying on her new bed.

Sitting on the edge, Carolyn put her hand on her daughter's shoulder. "I love you, too, you know."

"Why can't I live with Granny and Papa?"

"Because I'm your mother. You belong with me."

She peered up at Carolyn, eyes red-rimmed, face awash with tears. "You've never wanted me before."

Carolyn drew in a sharp breath of pain. "That's not true, May Flower Dawn. I've always wanted you, from the first moment I knew you were on the way. Everything I've done has been for you." She looked into her daughter's blue eyes and knew she didn't believe her.

"My name is *Dawn*."

"Your name is May Flower Dawn Arundel. Dawn is your middle name."

Her daughter's lip quivered. "The *Mayflower* was a ship."

"You weren't named after a ship."

"Papa said it's a hippy name."

Carolyn supposed that was how her father and mother might perceive it. She felt wounded by the reminder of their condemnation. "May . . . Flower . . . Dawn. Three separate words, each with precious meaning."

Her daughter blinked and stared at her face. "I like the name Dawn."

Should she explain how she had come up with the name? Perhaps it was better not to look back. Other questions might come up, like who her father was. "All right. Dawn, it is."

"Can I see Granny and Papa?"

"Of course." She tried not to let the hurt show. "It's not like we've moved to the other side of the moon."

Even that assurance didn't ease things for more than a little while. Carolyn heard her daughter crying that night—and every night that followed. Dawn didn't like anything she cooked. When she asked her daughter what she did like, she shrugged. Carolyn knew it wasn't the food that mattered, but the hands that prepared it.

Other more serious problems quickly developed.

Carolyn had to pick up Dawn from school and keep her at the office for the afternoon. A kindergartner didn't have homework to keep her occupied, and coloring didn't hold May Flower Dawn's interest for long. Her daughter wandered and got in the way. When she accidentally knocked a stack of files off Ross's desk, he called Carolyn into his office.

"You're going to have to make other arrangements for your daughter, Carolyn. I can't have her in here."

Carolyn remembered coming home to an empty house when she was May Flower Dawn's age. She remembered gravitating to

Dock's warm welcome and how that had turned out. "She just needs a little more time to adjust, Ross."

"No. A child shouldn't be cooped up in an office all afternoon. She should be outside playing with friends."

Stung, Carolyn asked for a few days to work things out. She called her grandmother. "Oma, I don't know what to do."

"Of course you do. Ask your mother to babysit."

"I'd be handing May Flower Dawn back to her."

"No. You'd be sharing her."

Carolyn wanted to weep. Sharing? Over the past five years, how much time had Mom allowed with her daughter? "You don't understand."

"I understand better than you do, Carolyn." She sounded sad and tired. "Don't make it a tug-of-war."

When Carolyn hung up, she put her head in her hands and wept. Gulping down sobs, she looked up and saw May Flower Dawn standing in the doorway, frightened and upset. Carolyn wiped her face. "It's okay. You're going to get what you want."

Running up the white flag, Carolyn called her mother. She could hear Mom's relief and pleasure. "Of course! I can pick her up after school. She can stay here until you're off work. You can drop her off anytime you need to show houses. I'd love to have her!"

She hadn't had May Flower Dawn back for a month before she lost her again.

Life went more smoothly after that. At least Mom and Dawn were happy.

1977

It had been seven years since Carolyn left San Francisco and came home. Seven years of demolishing the old and constructing her new life. She'd hoped it would become easier with time. She hoped people would forget her past and allow her to raise her head without feeling censorious eyes upon her.

With only one bank in town, Carolyn often saw someone who knew her past. Today, that person just happened to be Thelma Martin. She came in shortly after Carolyn got in line to wait for a teller. She could feel Thelma's eyes boring into the back of her head. They hadn't spoken since Carolyn left the dentist's office. Carolyn's muscles clenched tight as she focused on not turning around. The woman had spread more poison in Paxtown than anyone, and she still seemed to delight in dredging up Carolyn's history for anyone curious enough to listen.

A teller opened up, and Carolyn made a beeline to her window to make her deposit. "Can I do anything else for you, Miss Arundel?"

Carolyn said no thank you, stuffed her checkbook into her shoulder bag, and headed quickly for the door. She barreled right into someone standing just outside. The man steadied her.

"I'm so sorry." She stepped back from his touch, face hot. "Excuse me."

"Carolyn?"

Flustered, she looked up. She hadn't seen this tall, broad-shouldered, red-haired stranger around town, but he looked familiar. In the split second she looked into his green eyes, her pulse shot up. She tried to place him. Had she slept with him in Haight-Ashbury? She hoped not, but the memories of those awful days came fresh to mind every time she saw Thelma Martin's condemning glare.

"Mitch Hastings." He smiled at her. "Remember me now? Your brother and I rode bikes together, until he got a red Impala."

She had driven the Impala until Dad had said it wasn't safe to drive anymore. She hated seeing it towed away, hated even more the payments for another used car.

When she didn't say anything, he went on. "We played football together in high school. I played offensive lineman so he could score all those touchdowns."

His smile made Carolyn's insides quiver strangely. That alone made her want to run. She glanced away and saw Thelma Martin heading straight for the door. "Nice to see you again, Mitch." She didn't even extend her hand. "I have to run." She stepped around him and walked quickly toward her car.

"Wait a minute." He caught up with her easily and fell into step beside her. "What's your hurry?"

"I have to get back to work."

"Can I call you?"

"Sorry." She got into her car. If he kept standing where he was, she'd run over his toes. She glanced at him as she backed out. Cranking the wheel, she shot out of the parking lot. She glanced in her rearview mirror. Mitch stood, hands on his hips, looking bemused. He turned his attention to Thelma Martin when she came up to him and extended her hand. No doubt Thelma Martin would feel it her civic duty to warn Mitch off having anything to do with the town slut.

The telephone rang within minutes of her return to Ross Harper's agency. His wife, Candace, answered. "Yes, she is. She just walked in the door. One moment please." She smiled at Carolyn. "Call on line two. He has a nice voice."

"Carolyn Arundel. How can I help you?"

"You can go with me to my class reunion tonight." Mitch Hastings didn't waste time.

She couldn't imagine anything worse than a Paxtown class reunion—it didn't matter what year. "No, thank you."

"I know it's short notice. If I'd known you were back in town, I would've gotten in touch sooner." He chuckled. "It was providential we ran into one another."

Clearly, Thelma had given him an earful about her past. He wasn't the first eager beaver wanting to go out with her and see how far he could get on a first date. Hence, she never went out. "I wasn't in your class."

"We're out of high school. The age difference doesn't matter anymore."

Meaning what? She'd been jailbait when she had a crush on him? "Try someone else." She hung up.

When she picked up May Flower Dawn that afternoon, her mother told her Mitch Hastings had been there for a visit. "He was a sight for sore eyes. I haven't seen him in years." She looked pleased and speculative. "He said he saw you in town."

"We bumped into one another."

"Did he tell you he's a certified financial planner now?"

"We had about two seconds to exchange greetings, Mom. I had to get back to work."

"He told Dawn stories about Charlie and had us all laughing. He has a place up north of Healdsburg; Alexander Valley, I think he said. He's in town for the class reunion. He said he asked you to go with him, but you said no. If you'd like to change your mind, he left his number. He's staying at the Paxtown Hotel. We can keep Dawn for the night. . . ."

"No, thanks."

"I always liked Mitch. He's a solid young man, Carolyn. Why don't you go? All you do is work. It wouldn't hurt to have some fun once in a while."

Carolyn had to bite her tongue to keep from telling her mother Thelma Martin had gotten to him first and poisoned the water. And how did anyone know what Mitch Hastings was? Mom just said she hadn't seen him in years. Carolyn didn't feel safe with what he'd stirred in her in less than a minute. "I don't need any more complications in my life." She preferred loneliness to feeling used. Several of her brother's friends still lived in the valley. When they called her out of the blue, she knew why. She could hear it in the seductive tones they used, the way they promised her a good time. Saying no hadn't changed her reputation. What man wants to admit he's been shot down? Better to smile and let people believe things went exactly as people like Thelma Martin expected. She didn't go out with anyone. She didn't trust herself where men were concerned. All she had to do was look back. Why open the door to more hurt?

Mitch called the office again on Monday. "How about lunch?"

"I thought you just came for the reunion."

"I decided to stay a few extra days."

Carolyn's body responded to the warmth in his voice, which made her more wary. "Well, enjoy yourself. I'm busy."

"You have to eat sometime."

"I brought a sandwich."

Ross turned and looked at her, brows raised. Thankfully, another line rang, distracting him. Candace had gone on break and wasn't around to answer.

Mitch cleared his throat softly. "Did I do or say something to offend you, Carolyn?"

"No. It isn't that." When another line started ringing, Ross glanced at her. "Sorry, but I have another line coming in. Can't talk." She hung up and hoped he'd take the hint and leave her alone.

Someone wanted to see a house in Paxtown Heights. "I can show you the property now, if you'd like." She jotted down the prospective buyer's address, grabbed her keys, and headed for the door. She didn't return until midafternoon.

Ross nodded toward her desk. "Mitch Hastings called you back. He wants to see one of your properties out on Foothill Road."

She threw her shoulder bag into the bottom drawer of her desk and kicked it shut. "Why don't you take him?"

He grinned all too knowingly. "He didn't ask for me."

"He isn't interested in buying that house, Ross. He already has a place up in Sonoma County somewhere."

He leaned back in his swivel chair. "So?"

Candace decided to join the conversation. "People have been known to buy more than one house."

"Nothing ventured, nothing gained." Ross smiled. "Go talk to him."

Fuming, Carolyn got her purse out of the drawer and left again. On the way to the hotel, she tried to rehearse what to say. Heart pounding, she waited while the clerk called and told him, "A lady is in the lobby, Mr. Hastings." He listened and hung up. "He said he'll be right down."

When Mitch appeared, she opened her mouth, but he put his hand at the small of her back and guided her toward the dining room, not the front door. She dug in her heels. "I was told you wanted to see a house out in the foothills."

"Ross said you hadn't had a chance to eat before you went out to show the other place."

"I'm not hungry."

"Yes, you are. Your stomach just growled."

The host looked as though he expected them. "Right this way." He led them to a small private table overlooking the gardens.

Mitch held her chair. "We can talk over lunch."

She couldn't refuse without making a scene. Accepting the

proffered menu, she pretended to read it. "So what would you like to know about the house?"

"Give it a rest."

Too nervous to eat, she ordered a small salad. Mitch ordered a steak. Her palms sweated when he looked at her over the table, green eyes glowing. She figured it was time to lay out the ground rules. "I don't go out with clients."

"No problem."

"And I don't like games."

"No game intended. I couldn't think of any other way to get you to go out with me."

"You might not be so interested if you knew the facts."

"So tell me."

Okay. Better now than later, when it would hurt more. "While Charlie was being a hero in Vietnam, I was burning my bra, smoking pot, and protesting the war in Berkeley, not that it did any good. The day my parents got the news Charlie had been killed, I took off for Haight-Ashbury. Everything you've heard goes on there? I did it all. I don't even remember how many guys I slept with. I was too stoned to care. When my best friend died of a heroin overdose, I left the commune and lived in Golden Gate Park. I slept in public restrooms, on park benches, and under bushes. I ate out of garbage cans. You met my daughter, May Flower Dawn. How'd I get her? I was cold one night. A stranger offered to share his sleeping bag. My baby is the only thing about my life I *don't* regret."

She tossed her napkin on the table.

Mitch caught her wrist before she could get up. "Past history, Carolyn. We all have regrets."

"Regrets? That's what you call it? Let go!"

"Not unless you give me equal time."

She held her breath, afraid he could feel the pulse in her wrist. "Please let go of me." His fingers loosened enough for her to slip free.

His mouth curved tenderly. "Please don't run." He managed

to sum up his life in less than two minutes. After a minor football injury put him on the bench, he quit college and joined the Marine Corps. "Maybe Charlie got the idea from me. Neither one of us knew what we wanted out of life other than *more*. I got tired of drinking beer, chasing girls, and playing football." He thought joining a cause would give his life purpose. It did, for a while. "I was in the jungle when Charlie was killed in Hue. I did two tours of duty before getting out, then went back to college. I finished at Ohio State with a business degree, then found a good job in Miami." When his father and stepmother were killed in a car accident in Key West, he inherited their home in Vero Beach. "I sold in a seller's market, invested the money, and took off on my motorcycle to see America."

Carolyn relaxed enough to eat. "What brought you back to California?"

He studied her for a long moment as though debating with himself before answering. "I'm a Californian at heart. Every place else seemed a little too tame. Healdsburg reminded me of Paxtown twenty years ago. I bought a ranch house on twenty acres in Alexander Valley, planted a vineyard, and went to work for a wealth management firm." He laughed. "They were impressed with my portfolio." The day he came to Paxtown, he went to visit Charlie's grave. He talked about Charlie after that, the fun they'd had riding bikes, hiking the foothills, playing football, cruising Main, and honking at girls. He made Carolyn laugh, something she hadn't done in a long time.

His gaze caressed her face. She tried to ignore the strong attraction. He smiled as though he knew exactly what she was feeling. Heart hammering, she glanced at her wristwatch. Gasping, she pushed her chair back. "I have an appointment." She grabbed her purse. "I'm sorry to eat and run, Mitch. Thank you for the lunch and for the journey back in time to more innocent days."

"Wait." He signed the check hastily and rose. "I'll walk you to your car." He took her hand as they went out the door. "How about dinner and a movie this evening?"

She pulled her hand free. "I can't."

"May Flower Dawn is welcome to come along."

She fumbled the key into her car door. "It's been nice, Mitch, but . . ."

Mitch turned her around. "Look at me, Carolyn." She saw the strength in his face, the confident man he had become. Again, she felt the jolt of attraction between them.

"You asked what brought me back to California. *You* did. I've been in love with you since I was fifteen." He gave a self-deprecating laugh. "You were eleven. Charlie didn't know then. He figured it out when you were in ninth grade. I dropped a class just so I could be in a study hall with you."

"Mitch . . ."

He slid his fingers into her hair, his eyes never leaving hers. "The thing is, I never got over you. I left for Ohio figuring that was it, I'd never see you again. And then I decided to come back and find out what happened to you." When he leaned down, she thought he meant to kiss her. She caught her breath. He stopped just short. "Just dinner. Okay? That's all I'm asking for right now." His breath caressed her face. "Say yes."

"Yes."

"Thank God." His hand slid down her neck, across her shoulder, and away. When he smiled, his eyes lit up and glowed with warmth. "Let's go someplace quiet where we can talk."

"Why don't you come to my place, and I'll fix dinner?" The moment the words escaped her lips, she couldn't believe she'd suggested it. What was she thinking? Worse, what might he think?

"Perfect. What time?"

Short of withdrawing the invitation, what could she say now? "Six thirty?"

He opened her car door. "I'll be there."

She made it to her appointment on time. When she drove out to pick up May Flower Dawn, Mom asked if she wanted a cup of tea before going home. Her mother looked surprised and pleased when she said yes. Carolyn had always had trouble talking with her mother, but today she felt like giving it a try. They sat in the living room while May Flower Dawn picked up her Barbies and put them back in her room. She never touched the dolls Carolyn bought.

"Have you heard from Mitch?" Mom sipped her tea.

"He called the office and asked to see a house."

"Is he planning to move back to Paxtown?"

"No. It was a hijacking."

Her mother laughed. "I guess he's not a man to take no for an answer." A frown flickered across her face, and Carolyn wondered what she might be thinking. She didn't want to give her mother any wrong ideas.

"We talked a lot about Charlie. I asked him over for dinner this evening."

"Why don't you let Dawn spend the night here?"

"I wouldn't want to give Mitch the wrong idea."

Setting her cup down, her mother looked at her. "I'm sure his intentions are honorable, Carolyn. If not, you *can* say no."

Carolyn couldn't help but laugh. "*Honorable.* I don't know what that means these days."

Her mother frowned, clearly troubled. "He was Charlie's best friend, Carolyn. He misses your brother. He probably just wants a quiet evening to talk with someone who loved him as much as he did."

If only that was all there was to it. She didn't want to say too much and have her mother speculating on what they might do, other than talk about Charlie.

Mom chuckled as she sipped her tea again. "Dawn was just telling me a while ago she'd like to ride the bus to school just once. If she stayed overnight, she could ride to school tomorrow."

"I don't know, Mom."

"Please!" May Flower Dawn spoke up from the foyer.

Her daughter seldom asked for anything from her. How could Carolyn say no?

❄ ❄ ❄

Home and alone, Carolyn decided to call the whole evening off. She phoned the Paxtown Hotel and asked to be put through to Mitch's room. The telephone rang ten times before the clerk came back on the line and said he was sorry, but Mr. Hastings seemed to be out for the afternoon. In a panic, Carolyn rummaged through her refrigerator, wondering what to fix for dinner. She threw together a meat loaf, put two potatoes in to bake, and made a tossed salad. She'd just finished setting the table when she heard a motorcycle out front. Her pulse rocketed. Her heart would have gone into orbit if it hadn't been encased in her chest.

The doorbell rang. Swiping the perspiration from her palms, Carolyn fixed a smile on her face and opened the door. "Hi, Mitch. Come on in." Her voice sounded so chipper, so high school. Mitch looked entirely too handsome in a black leather bomber jacket, casual blue henley shirt, black leather belt, Levi's, and boots. He held a bottle of red wine in one hand and a bouquet of lilies in the other. Swallowing hard, she opened the door wider and waved him in. "Can I take your coat?"

"Better take the wine and flowers first."

She blushed. "Of course."

As soon as his hands were free, Mitch stripped off his jacket, tossed it on the sofa, and followed her into the kitchen. "Something smells good."

"Does it?" She rattled off the menu. "Sorry. Nothing fancy."

"Got a corkscrew? I'll open the wine."

She fingered through her utensil drawer until she found a can opener that included one. "Here you go." His fingers brushed hers, and she dropped it. "Sorry." She stooped to pick it up and put it on the counter. Did he have to watch her like that? Her heart kept knocking wildly. She arranged the lilies in a vase and took it back into the dining room. She took a wineglass from the built-in china cabinet and put it on the table.

"Only one glass?"

"I'm a recovering alcoholic. An ex-pothead."

He grimaced. "Sorry."

"I'll try not to drool while you enjoy it." She tried to make it sound like a joke, but the words came out flat. "Dinner won't be ready for another forty-five minutes. Why don't we sit in the living room?" She waved toward the sofa, where he'd tossed his jacket. Mitch sat and watched her. Tense, she picked up his leather jacket and then wondered what to do with it. She should hang it up, but she didn't have a hall tree. She thought of her bedroom and discarded that idea. Giving up, she folded it over the sofa again.

She sat in one of the wing chairs, back stiff, hands clasped in her lap. "So. What shall we talk about?"

"You want to tell me why you're so nervous?"

"I've never invited a man over for dinner before." She smoothed her skirt over her knees. "You want to talk about Charlie?"

"Is May Flower Dawn going to join us?"

"Nope. She's spending the night with my parents." She felt her face flame up to her hairline as she considered how he might take that news. "It wasn't my idea."

His mouth tipped ruefully. "I'm sure it wasn't. I'll bet it was you calling my room this afternoon, trying to call the whole evening off."

So he had been there. "Why didn't you answer?"

"Why do you think?"

The look in his eyes didn't give her any room for speculation. Her mind flashed images of other men who had wanted her. Dock popped into her head, first. As she fled thoughts of him, Ash emerged from the pit, beautiful, charismatic, and on a power trip. More pain. More shame. How many others had she slept with who wanted her body, but cared as little about her as they did about the weather? She'd become the wasteland after the hurricane, the refuse washed up onshore, the broken trees, the crushed houses. And now, Mitch Hastings, Charlie's best friend, sat on a secondhand sofa in her living room, eyes full of a consuming fire, asking her what she thought.

She put her hands on the arms of the chair and pushed herself up. "I'm not much of a hostess. I didn't even think to offer you something to drink. I have Coke, 7UP, iced tea, lemonade, well water. Or you can start on the wine you brought."

"Nothing, thanks."

She sank into the chair again. Now what? She sought desperately for something to say. She dredged down into the darkness and came up empty. Thankfully, Mitch came to her rescue.

"You mentioned Charlie. We wrote letters back and forth after we left high school, kept up the correspondence when he went into the military. He wrote about you."

"I'll bet."

"He loved you, Carolyn. He worried about you."

She pressed her back against the chair and lifted one shoulder. "His dumb, screwed-up sister gone hippy." More cause for grief. "Mom and Dad said I made him ashamed."

"He never told me he was ashamed of you. He said you were trying to stop the war. He said you wanted to be his savior. He worried about your relationship with Rachel Altman. She seemed to have a lot of influence on you."

She bristled. "Charlie only met her once."

"Yeah, and it was that one meeting that made him worry. Apparently, she came into his bedroom in the middle of the night."

She blushed. "I know. She told me after the fact."

"He beat himself up over what happened. He said she was totally screwed up, and he took advantage."

Carolyn gave a soft laugh. "I think it was the other way around, Mitch."

"Whatever the case, Charlie liked her. A lot. He said there was something about her . . ."

"Chel sang a siren song." Like Janis Joplin, her idol, who died of a drug overdose less than a year after she did.

"They exchanged letters. He planned to look her up when he came home."

"Did he?" And now both of them were dead. She wanted Mitch

to get things straight. "No one can blame Chel for the things I did, Mitch. Some people are born into a mess. Some people find ways to mess up their own lives. It's the one thing at which I've always excelled."

"You put your life back together, Carolyn. That takes courage."

Mitch deftly turned the conversation to other things, managing to make the mundane interesting. She asked about his travels. He talked about riding cross-country on his Harley, interesting people he'd met in diners and campgrounds, sights he'd seen. Carolyn relaxed and enjoyed listening to him. When the timer went off, she put the food on the table. She poured him a glass of wine and set the bottle down before taking her seat across from him. He asked if it would be all right if he said grace. Surprised, she said please, and when he finished, she asked when he'd become a Christian.

"Always have been, just never went to your church." He'd attended Sunday services all across the country, checking out different denominations. "Thing about knowing the Lord is you have friends and family everywhere. You recognize them when you meet them."

She didn't know about church, but she'd found the same rapport in AA meetings. People cared. They didn't use the Christian jargon, but had their own lingo and simple slogans to get through each day. *First things first. Think! Easy does it. Let go and let God.* She'd felt Jesus' presence there. No one looked down at her from the pulpit or told her she wasn't welcome. She could say, "My name is Carolyn and I'm an alcoholic" and hear "Welcome, Carolyn," instead of being shown the door and told not to come back until she had proof of repentance. She would have crashed and burned long ago if she hadn't found a meeting close by.

Mitch ate as though he enjoyed the food. "What was it like in Haight-Ashbury?"

She told him about the pot and alcohol, the constant parties, the confusion and angst. She told him about Woodstock and the long, frightening drive home with Chel still half out of her mind in the backseat. She told him about Ash and his brand of enlightenment, though she left out the drug-induced sexual exploits, the rapes. Some things should be shared only with God and her dead brother.

"Were you in love with him?"

What she'd felt for Ash couldn't be called love. "No. I saw him for who he really was the day Chel died. In a way, her death freed me."

"But you're still not free of all of it, are you?" His eyes filled with compassion. "You're still carrying a truckload of guilt and shame."

She stood and started clearing the table. Mitch helped. He insisted on washing the dishes. She dried and put things away. She thought he would leave then, but he said he'd love a cup of coffee. She apologized for not making a dessert. She'd forgotten. She didn't even have ice cream or store-bought cookies to offer.

He grinned. "We could always go for a ride on my Harley. There's a Baskin-Robbins in Walnut Creek."

She thought of sitting behind him on that powerful bike, her body pressed against his, her arms wrapped around his waist, holding on tight. "I don't think so."

She filled two mugs and carried them back into the living room. She asked him more questions about his travels, about the churches he'd visited, the pastors. He laughed. "Oh, there were a few who took one look at my Harley and black leather jacket and tried to bar the door, but for the most part, I felt welcome." He glanced at the mantel clock. "It's getting late. I'd better go."

She stood, amazed at how quickly five hours had passed. Would he think her too forward if she asked him over again? "When do you head back to Healdsburg?"

"Tomorrow morning."

"Oh." She felt the prick of tears, the sting of loss. "Well, it's been wonderful seeing you, Mitch."

"Thanks for dinner. It's been a great evening." Smiling at her, Mitch shrugged into his black leather jacket. "I'm coming back, Carolyn."

Relieved, she walked him to the door, remembering what he'd

said about never getting over her. Even if that had changed, at least she knew she had a friend.

Mitch put his hand on the doorknob, started to turn it, and then let it go. He turned toward her. He looked uncertain. "Would you mind if I did something I've been dreaming about for years?"

"What?"

"Kiss you."

She caught her breath, but didn't move. He raised his hand tentatively, giving her the opportunity to say no. He cupped her cheek and bent down slowly, still giving her time to decide. She held her breath. When his mouth touched hers, sensation flooded her body. He raised his head and looked into her eyes. "Nice."

He kissed her again. She stepped close, her hands slipping inside his leather jacket. He let out a soft groan, and his arms came around her, fitting her to him. She didn't have to wonder if he was affected. Her body went hot.

She didn't know how long they stood there, bodies straining to get closer, but she didn't want him to stop.

Finally Mitch put a few inches between them. "Better than any fantasy I've ever had." He gave a hoarse laugh and kissed her below the ear. "Nice to know your heart's beating as fast as mine." His breath sent tingles down her spine. When his hands moved over her back, she instinctively arched against him. He set her away from him. "I need to get out of here." He opened the door this time.

"Mitch . . ." She didn't have to say any more.

"If I stay, I won't stop. And then you'll wonder. I don't want you questioning yourself or having any regrets after we're married." He went out.

She stepped out onto the porch. "What did you say?"

"You heard me." He grinned at her as he pulled on his helmet. "I'll call you tomorrow." He swung his leg over and kick-started the motorcycle.

He'd already kick-started her heart; it roared more loudly than his Harley.

21

MITCH CALLED EVERY evening, right after May Flower Dawn
had gone to bed. Sometimes they talked until past midnight. He
came back every weekend, driving a sedan instead of his Harley so
they could include her daughter on Saturday outings. He found
activities they all could enjoy: hiking in the hills, a drive into San
Francisco to see the Steinhart Aquarium, horseback riding, a baseball game. Carolyn always offered to fix dinner on Friday night,
but Mitch said it'd be safer to go to a restaurant. "I have to keep
my hands off you in a public place." He attended church services
in Walnut Creek and always invited her. She always refused. She
assured him she had her own fellowship to attend. She went to
AA meetings every Wednesday night and read the Bible Oma had
given her years ago. Sundays were her day of rest, and rest meant
staying home and working in the garden while everyone else in her
family went to church, including May Flower Dawn.

"Someone really hurt you, didn't they?"

She shrugged. Why tell him the pastor she'd known all her life
said she wasn't good enough to enter God's house? Why tell him

Thelma Martin was still a deaconess and Rev. Elias still ruled from the pulpit? What right did she have to judge?

When Mitch invited Carolyn and May Flower Dawn to spend a weekend with him in Alexander Valley, Carolyn agreed. Directions in hand, one small suitcase for herself and another for May Flower Dawn, Carolyn drove up.

She had been prepared for a nice ranch house with a vineyard, but gaped when she turned onto his stone paver driveway and saw the Spanish-style mansion at the end. Mitch came out to welcome them. Opening her door, he helped her out, kissed her, and then frowned. "What's wrong?"

"That." She pointed.

Dawn stood with her mouth gaping. "Do you live here?"

"Yep. Come on. I'll show you around." He took Carolyn's hand.

Her entire house would fit in his family room. The master suite wasn't much smaller. He had a formal parlor living room, four bedrooms with private baths, a kitchen a professional chef would envy, and a solarium with French doors opening to a trellised patio that looked out on terraced gardens, a swimming pool, and a gazebo. She spotted two Hispanic gardeners at work, undoubtedly full-time. She gleaned he had four full-time employees working in the vineyard, more in the winery.

"We can take a look at the operation later, if you'd like."

Carolyn said never mind. She'd already seen enough. He took them back inside the house and asked if Dawn would like to play a video game in the family room. "You have video games!"

Mitch sat with Dawn until she knew how to use the system and play the game, then left her to it. Carolyn stood in the kitchen, taking in the shiny stainless-steel appliances. He touched her arm. "You want a Coke? lemonade?" He gave her a teasing smile. "Well water?"

"Right now, I'd go for an eight-ounce glass of bourbon straight up." She sank onto a suede stool and looked around at the gorgeous granite counters and custom-built cherrywood cabinets, the Mexican tile floor.

"I told you I did well with investments, Carolyn."

"Slight understatement, I'd say. Are you sure you don't have a wife and twelve children hiding somewhere? The place is big enough."

"Only four bedrooms."

Not counting the maid's quarters, complete with kitchen and living room. She didn't know what to say.

He smiled at her as he put a tall glass of iced lemonade in front of her. "I want a family. I tend to plan ahead. I've only ever wanted one wife. You." His eyes warmed. "We're going to make beautiful babies together and have fun doing it."

Fighting down the heat he roused in her so easily, she shook her head. "I don't know, Mitch. I don't have your confidence."

"Yes, you do." He came around the counter, turned her on the stool, and cupped her face. "You knew before I brought you up here." He kissed her firmly. "I'm not letting you chicken out."

❈ ❈ ❈

1978

They'd been talking to one another every night and seeing one another every weekend for six months. Finally, one evening in May, Mitch told Dawn over dinner that he wanted to marry her mother. "How do you feel about that?"

"Does she want to marry you?"

"I think so." He winked at Carolyn. "But I haven't formally asked her yet." He looked back at Dawn. "I wanted your permission first."

"I guess it's okay." Dawn seemed bemused at the idea, and she clearly had no idea how it might change her life. Carolyn wondered if she should explain that it would mean leaving Granny and Papa. It would mean moving away and seeing them only on occasion. Would May Flower Dawn be so indifferent then?

"Maybe we should talk about this later." Carolyn gave Mitch a pleading look. "Alone."

But once alone, talk wasn't uppermost on their minds. "Good thing you brought Dawn with you."

"Our chaperone has been asleep for an hour."

He put his fingers over her mouth. "Don't tempt me. Let's set a date, Carolyn. How much time do you need to put together a church wedding?"

She broke out in a cold sweat. "Why don't we just go to Reno?" A church wedding implied a minister who would be willing to perform the ceremony, a white gown, bridesmaids, flowers, music, a church organ or piano playing, a congregation of witnesses, a reception in the social hall.

"I'm in a hurry, Carolyn, but not that big a hurry. Every woman wants a nice wedding and you're going to have one."

"If that's the condition, the answer is no."

"No? You're in love with me, aren't you?"

"What has love got to do with it? What would I wear, Mitch? Black? Who'd stand up with me? You think my parents would want to foot the bill for my wedding? And who'd want to come?" Fighting tears, she pushed away.

Mitch turned her around, his eyes dark with pain. "I could name a hundred people who'd want to come."

"All *your* friends." No one knew any of hers. AA was an anonymous program. First names only.

"Yours, too. You have more than you realize. I'll bet Candace would jump at the chance to stand up with you. Dawn could be part of the wedding party. I'll pay for it."

"No."

He rubbed her arms. "We'll keep it small—family, friends. Your grandmother, your parents, aunts, uncles, cousins . . . They're going to want to come, Carolyn. You can't cut out the people you love. Only one thing I won't bend on. I want my pastor to perform the ceremony. If you don't want it in a church, okay. We can have it here, in the gazebo. How about August, just before Dawn has to start school?" He held her shoulders. "What do you say?"

When she looked up at him, she knew May was still a month

of miracles. May, the month Jesus sat with her on the grass in Golden Gate Park, spoke her name tenderly, and sent her home. She hadn't known she carried a child then, but God had. "That sounds perfect, Mitch." She placed her hand on his chest and felt his warmth, his strength, the steady beat of his heart. God had given her a man she could trust. Even so, it took courage to say the words. "I love you."

"I know." His mouth tipped in a teasing smile. "But I've loved you longer."

"You're getting the raw end of the deal, Mitch."

"No, I'm not. And don't ever say that again." He touched her as though she were the most precious thing in the world to him. "I'm getting the woman I want. I feel as though I've loved you forever."

She knew he meant it.

❄ ❄ ❄

Their wedding day turned out to be a perfect, sunny day. Carolyn's father gave her away while Mom and May Flower Dawn sat in the front row of folding chairs. Dawn didn't want to be her flower girl, so Carolyn didn't have one. Mitch's pastor performed the wedding ceremony before a gathering of Mitch's close friends and Carolyn's relatives. She was surprised they all came, including Aunt Rikka, who flew in from New York. Boots drove up from Topanga Canyon. Mitch had arranged for a professional photographer who took candid shots as well as formal poses. He'd also hired a catering service to put on a wedding luncheon.

Oma patted Carolyn's cheek before she and Mom and Dad headed home. "You've done well for yourself. I'm proud of you." Mitch bent down to receive her kiss of blessing. "Take good care of my girl." He promised he would. He had a honeymoon planned, but wouldn't tell Carolyn anything about it. May Flower Dawn was "going home with Granny and Papa." Mitch reminded Dawn home was now Alexander Valley, and he and her mother would be picking her up in ten days. Dawn looked less defiant after that.

Mitch saw the last guests out while the caterers cleared everything away. Within a few hours, the folding chairs and tables, the linens, trays, and china had been loaded into vans, leaving the gardens and house spotless and silent.

Mitch took Carolyn's hand and led her to the master suite. She felt a bubbling fear in her belly as all the old memories rose up. Mitch sensed something was wrong. He didn't push. He took his time. Even so, he knew she hadn't experienced the pleasure he had. He didn't ask questions, just held her close. Emotionally exhausted, she fell asleep in his arms. He awakened her with kisses and coffee at three thirty in the morning. "Time to get dressed."

"Where are we going?"

"Hawaii. A limo is picking us up."

"What? I haven't packed!"

"Your mom took care of that. Anything you don't have, we'll buy when we get there."

Dear Rosie,

Carolyn and Mitch are married. I am so happy for them. The wedding was lovely and held in the backyard of Mitch's rather palatial home in Alexander Valley. The place looks like a Tuscan villa, with cypress trees lining his driveway and a vineyard on the hills behind the house with all its grand landscaping, pool, and gazebo. Bernhard was all praises about it. I was equally impressed. I remember Mitch when he was a skinny, freckled redhead on a bicycle, riding off with Charlie to do some mischief and, later, a gangly young man with eyes for Carolyn, though she never seemed aware of his adoration. He has grown handsome, competent, confident—a man who always did know what he wanted: Carolyn. My prayers for her are answered. Mitch sees her as a gift from God and will treat her accordingly.

Carolyn asked May Flower Dawn to be her flower girl, but the child refused. She sat in the front row and sulked. Hildemara made no effort to correct her rude misbehavior. I wanted to turn both of them over my knee. Dawn will stay with Hildemara and Trip until Carolyn and Mitch return from a Hawaiian honeymoon.

Hildemara understands she must relinquish May Flower Dawn. Or says she does. I wonder.

I tried to talk with Hildemara about our past, but she cut the conversation short. All I can do is keep holding out the olive branch and hope one day she will accept it.

Oh, Rosie, I look back and wish I had handled things differently. . . .

22

Mom and Dad greeted them on their return from a glorious week in Hawaii. While Dad took Mitch into the living room, Mom took Carolyn into the kitchen. She looked worried. "What's wrong, Mom? Where's Dawn?"

"In her room. We explained everything to her, but she doesn't fully understand." She offered Carolyn a cup of tea or coffee. "This is the only real home she's ever known."

What about the house on Vineyard Avenue? Carolyn wanted to say. *Didn't that count?* "She doesn't want to go with me. Is that what you're trying to tell me?"

"She's only seven, Carolyn."

"She's my daughter."

"I know that. It's just going to be very hard for her to adjust to all these changes."

Mom's red-rimmed eyes told Carolyn her daughter wasn't the only one having a hard time.

"I'm sorry about that, but I think the sooner we go, the better."

"You won't even stay for dinner?"

"Is she packed?"

May Flower Dawn clung to her grandfather. Pried loose and strapped into the backseat, she cried for an hour. Carolyn and Mitch tried to reassure her. It didn't help. When she finally fell asleep in the backseat, Mitch took Carolyn's hand. "Give her time."

Mitch carried their things into the house. Carolyn unpacked Dawn's clothes, hanging her dresses in the closet and putting the rest into the dresser. She left the Barbies and doll clothes in the box for Dawn to unpack the next morning. When she told Dawn to get ready for bed, she did. As she tucked her in, Dawn started to cry again. "I want to go home!"

"This is your home."

"I want *Granny*!"

Pierced through the heart, Carolyn bent down and kissed her daughter's head. "Sorry, May Flower Dawn. You're stuck with your *mother*."

*May
Flower
Dawn*

23

WIDE-AWAKE AND MISERABLE, Dawn lay curled in a ball in the middle of her fancy new bed. Her mother had turned off the light and closed the door, leaving only a tiny night-light in the bathroom to contend against total darkness. Even though she was seven and a half, Dawn was a little nervous in this big, dark, silent room. Unlike her mother's bungalow on Vineyard Avenue, Mitch's house stood at the end of a long driveway lined with cypress trees, too far from the road to hear cars or see headlights.

Dawn didn't want to live in this house so far away from Granny and Papa. Her mother wouldn't have time for her. She'd never see her school friends again. Granny said she and Papa would come to visit soon, but what did "soon" mean? Tomorrow? Next week?

Dawn wiped away angry tears. She had initially liked Mitch, but now that he'd married Mom, she wasn't so sure.

A soft wind and moonlight cast frightening shadows outside her window. Dawn huddled deep under the blankets, covered her head, and cried herself to sleep.

❄ ❄ ❄

Mom opened the door the next morning and came in, all smiles and cheer. "Breakfast will be ready soon."

Dawn hated that her mother looked so happy when she was so miserable. "I'm not hungry."

"I'm making bacon and waffles."

Dawn set her jaw, refusing to be tempted by her favorite breakfast. "I'm not going to eat anything until you take me home." She felt triumphant when the joy dimmed in her mother's face.

"You *are* home, Dawn. If you want to go on a hunger strike, that's fine. If you want to come out and sit with us, even better. Either way, I won't force you." Her mother quietly closed the door behind her.

Dawn stared, furious. When fifteen minutes passed and Mom didn't come back, Dawn shoved her covers off and went into the pink, green, and white bathroom. Her hair looked like a blonde mop on her head. Granny used to brush it for her every morning. Her clothes lay in a mess on the floor where she'd dropped them. Granny would have picked them up and folded them for her. Her mother always expected her to do everything herself! She'd probably force her to do dishes, too!

As Dawn approached the kitchen archway, she heard Mom talking. "A private Christian school is too expensive, Mitch. She's my daughter. I wouldn't feel right having you pay tuition—"

"Whoa. What's mine is yours now. Remember? You need to get that into your head, Carolyn. We're partners."

"She's been going to a public school. I'm not sure I want her in a Christian school."

"Why not?"

Her mother spoke too quietly for Dawn to hear. Dawn walked around the corner and through the archway into the kitchen.

Mitch grinned. "Well, good morning, sleepyhead." Dawn glared at him. His brows rose. "Oops. I guess you're not a morning person."

Her mother studied her coolly. "I thought you weren't hungry."

"I won't eat if you don't want me to. I can go back to my room and stay there and starve, if that's what you want!"

Mitch breathed out a laugh. "Trying hard to be a pita, aren't you?"

"Pita?"

"Pain in the . . . Never mind." He stood, pulled out a chair, and bowed. "It would please us humble folk to have Your Majesty grace us with your presence at our table." He waved his arm for her to sit.

Dawn stayed where she was, trying not to cry. Mitch had always been nice to her. She wanted him to like her, not think she was a spoiled brat.

His face softened. "Relax, Dawn. Sit with us." Mitch scooted her chair in comfortably when she did. He squeezed her shoulders before he took his seat again. Mom put two strips of crisp bacon and a golden brown waffle on her plate, but Dawn had lost her appetite. She kept her head down, blinking back tears. Mitch and Mom had already finished breakfast. They hadn't even waited for her.

Mitch sighed. "Think I'll leave you two alone." He cleared his dishes while Mom loaded the dishwasher. "Are you going to be okay?" Mitch spoke tenderly. Dawn glanced up and then realized he wasn't talking to her. He had his arm around Mom's waist. Mom shrugged. He kissed her. Grimacing, Dawn looked away. Mitch came over to the table and leaned down to plant a kiss on top of her head. "See you later, alligator. . . ."

She used to laugh and say, "After a while, crocodile." That was before he married her mother.

Mom poured another cup of coffee and returned to the table. "Something wrong with the waffle?"

Granny's waffles were darker and crisper. "It's okay, I guess." She nibbled the edges.

Her mother sighed. "If you're done, you can put your plate on the counter." Her mother put her hands around her coffee cup. "I was going to wait a few days to put you in school. Now, I think the sooner, the better. The sooner you make new friends, the sooner you'll settle in."

"I want to go to my old school with all my friends!"

"You'll make new friends at your new school. Go get cleaned up, and we'll head over there. They'll probably even let you start today."

Fear coursed through Dawn. "It'll be just like when Susan came." The girls had whispered about her and made her cry. It had been a game at first, one that made Dawn uncomfortable, but she hadn't wanted to go against the crowd. "Nobody wanted to be her friend."

Her mother stood and looked at her. "Well, let's hope the people you meet in Healdsburg will be nicer than the 'friends' you had in Paxtown."

Dawn felt as though her mother had slapped her.

Mom's expression softened. "I know life isn't easy, May Flower Dawn. Believe me, I do. I could fix your hair in a French braid and help you pick out a skirt and—"

"I don't want to look like you!" She fled to the doorway. "And don't call me May Flower Dawn. It's a stupid, hippy name! I'm *Dawn*."

❄ ❄ ❄

Granny called that night. Dawn poured out her loneliness and anger over having to live so far away. Granny said she was sorry about that, too, and then asked if she liked second grade. "Did you make any friends today?" Several girls had come up to her and wanted to be friends. Dawn had been surprised at how nice they were.

Granny called again the next night—and the night after that.

After a few weeks, Dawn realized she enjoyed riding the bus to school with her friends. Getting off the bus after school proved harder. Granny wouldn't be waiting at the house. She had always given Dawn a snack, then played board games or let Dawn watch TV. Mom told her to play outside or with her Barbies. "You've been sitting in a classroom all day. I don't want you sitting in front of a television all afternoon."

Every evening, Granny called right about the time Mom started clearing dishes. After a while, Mom stopped answering the telephone and let Dawn run to her room and catch it. At least she had her very own phone. That was one nice thing about living in Mitch's house.

❄ ❄ ❄

Dawn knew something was wrong the moment she heard Granny's voice. "What is it, Granny?" Her heart began to pound. "Is Papa sick?"

"No. Papa is fine." Granny sniffled. "Everything is fine."

"No, it's not. I can tell." Something had made her grandmother cry.

"I'm going to stop calling you every evening, honey. I'll call you once a week instead."

"Why? Are you mad at me?"

"No! Of course not. It's just that . . . your mother says— "

"She's so mean!" Dawn was crying now too. "I want to come home! Please come and get me!"

"Honey, I can't. I love you so much, but she's your mother." Granny sniffled again. "She and Mitch love you very much, Dawn. I have to go now." Her voice broke. "I'll talk to you in a week."

Dawn marched down the hall to the kitchen, where her mother was putting the last plate into the dishwasher. "You made Granny cry!"

Mom turned and looked at her. "I'm sorry about that, but—"

"You're not sorry! You're not sorry at all! You said she couldn't call me anymore!" Hands in fists, she screamed. "And I hate you! I wish you were dead so I could go home and live with Granny!"

All the color drained from her mother's face, leaving her skin the color of ashes. She opened her mouth, but no sound came out. Her blue eyes filled with tears, and she turned away.

Feeling sick rather than triumphant, Dawn fled to her room.

❄ ❄ ❄

Someone tapped on the door. Limp from crying, Dawn sat up, expecting her mother to retaliate. She tensed when the door opened. Mitch stood in the doorway, looking grim and unhappy. "May I come in?"

She shrugged, trying to pretend she didn't care. Her palms felt moist. Had her mother told him what she'd said?

Mitch crossed the room, took her desk chair, and turned it around, straddling it and resting his arms on the back. "So, Pita. Feeling any better now that you got things off your chest?"

He'd called her Pita. Dawn heard the disappointment in his tone and felt the heat of guilt pouring into her face. She decided to lie. "I don't know what you mean."

"I was home, in my office. I heard every word you said. Not *said*—screamed, like a spoiled two-year-old having a tantrum."

"She told Granny not to talk to me anymore!"

"That's the second lie you've told me, unless your grandmother lied to you."

"Granny never lies!"

"Then how about the truth this time?" He spoke gently.

Dawn plucked at her skirt, eyes smarting with tears. "I want to go home."

"Granny isn't the only one who loves you. She's not the only one who cries. Your mother loves you, too."

She covered her face and sobbed. Mitch sat for a while, silent. He got up, put the chair back, and came over to her. She felt too ashamed to lift her head. "Your mother loves you, Dawn, and so do I." She felt him kiss the crown of her head. "Maybe you could give us a chance."

❄ ❄ ❄

Dawn didn't sleep well. Gathering her courage the next morning, she headed for the kitchen to say she was sorry. Her mother was at the sink.

Dawn stood in the doorway, chewing her lower lip, not sure what to do. "Where's Mitch?"

Her mother's head lifted slightly. "He went to work." She turned mechanically, removed the lid from a frying pan, and scooped a portion of scrambled eggs onto a plate. She brought it to the table, poured a glass of orange juice, and moved away.

Dawn poked at her breakfast. The hollow feeling in her stomach had nothing to do with hunger. She didn't know what to say to break the silence. Her mother went back to the sink and stood there, staring out the window, arms wrapped around herself. Did she have a stomachache, too? After a few minutes, she went into the laundry room off the kitchen and began sorting clothes.

Dawn scraped her uneaten eggs into the garbage disposal. Rinsing her plate and silverware, she put them in the dishwasher. Trembling inside, she went to the laundry room door. She gulped. "Can I talk to you for a minute?" Her voice came out tight.

Her mother went still. She didn't look up. "If you want to talk, call Granny when you get home from school."

It didn't matter that she'd won. Dawn felt awful. She wanted to say she was sorry; she didn't hate her; she'd just been so mad. She wished she could take the words back, but they still hung in the air like a foul stench. *Mommy,* she wanted to cry out. *Mommy, I'm sorry.* "I . . . I . . ." She couldn't get the words past the hard, hot lump in her throat.

24

Dawn called Granny as soon as she got home from school. "Mommy said I can call you—"

"I know, sweetie. Your mother called me. She didn't tell me what made her change her mind. Do you know?"

Dawn knew, but didn't want to say. "She said she knows I love you." That was true, at least.

"Oh. Good. I was afraid . . . Oh, never mind. Why don't you tell me all about your day, honey? I'm eager to hear everything. Who did you play with?"

Dawn didn't want to tell Granny it was the worst day of her life. Her teacher asked a question twice before Dawn realized she was supposed to answer. Everyone laughed. She spent recess crying in the back stall of the girls' bathroom. On the way home, she sat in the back of the bus, worrying about how things would be when she got home, but Mom acted normal, even asked how Dawn's day had gone. Dawn could muster only one word: "Fine." Her mother sighed and said she could go call Granny.

"You're a little quiet tonight, sweetie."

Dawn couldn't think of anything to say. "I have homework, Granny." It was true.

"I suppose I should get Papa's dinner going. I'll call you tomorrow. I love you, honey."

"I love you, too." Dawn hung up and put her head in her arms.

When Mitch came home, he stuck his head in her room to say hello. "Apologize yet?"

She shrugged. "I tried."

Later, Mitch called her to the dinner table. He talked easily about his day. Mom paid close attention to everything he said. She glanced in Dawn's direction several times, passed serving dishes, asked if Dawn wanted more milk, more mashed potatoes. But whenever Dawn looked at her, Mom turned away without meeting her eyes. When Mom started to clear dishes, Dawn picked up her own. Mom held her hand out for them. "I can do that."

Mom carried the dishes to the sink. Dawn looked at Mitch, hoping he could do something to make things better. He gave her a sad smile. Pushing his chair back, he went to her mother. He draped his arm around her shoulders and whispered something in her ear.

Feeling left out, Dawn wandered away from the table.

❄ ❄ ❄

Without consulting her, Mom registered Dawn for soccer. "Your friends play, don't they? Mitch is going to be your coach."

"Assistant coach," Mitch clarified. "Football is my game. Joaquin Perez is coach. He knows everything there is to know about soccer." He grinned at Dawn. "We'll both be learning from scratch."

On the first day of practice, she spotted four classmates: Torie Keyes, Tiffany Myers, Leanne Stoddard, and Susan Mackay. They had all played soccer since kindergarten. "Swarm ball," Torie laughed.

After several practices, Coach made Dawn a forward. "You're a natural." Mom encouraged Dawn to invite her friends over to play. Soon they were practicing soccer on the big lawn behind the house.

Dawn's days filled with activity. She went to church with Mitch, though her mother never attended, staying home alone. Mitch said Mom liked being alone with God, and she had fellowship when she went to AA twice a week in Santa Rosa.

❅ ❅ ❅

1979

Dawn dumped her backpack in her bedroom, changed for soccer practice, and went searching for Mitch, eager to leave. "Mitch! Where are you? It's time to go!"

"We're in here!"

She found Mom and Mitch sitting close together in the family room. Mitch had a grin on his face. Her mother looked oddly uncomfortable. "What's going on? We're going to be late for practice."

"Sit down, Dawn. We have some good news to share." He kissed Mom's temple. "Go ahead. Tell her."

"She'll take it better from you."

Mitch laughed, his eyes alight. "We're going to have a baby! You're going to have a little brother or sister about six months from now. What do you think of that?"

Dawn didn't know what to say. "That's great." But was it?

"I think she's in shock." Mitch kissed Mom again and stood. He clapped his hands on Dawn's shoulders. "You'll get used to the idea." He turned her around. "Let's go."

"Go where?" Her mind had gone blank.

"Soccer practice!"

Mitch told Coach Joaquin, and a few players overheard. Soon everyone knew Dawn's mother was pregnant. Dawn swung between embarrassment and worry. Where would she fit into the family after a baby came?

"Oh, wow, do I pity you," Torie said. "It's bad enough when

you have a brother or sister close to your own age, but eight years apart . . . The baby will be the star, and you'll be the babysitter."

Soon after soccer season ended, Granny called and asked to speak with Mom. Dawn knew something was wrong. She handed the telephone over to Mom and stayed around to watch and listen.

"What? When? Why didn't you call us sooner?" Mom sounded shaken. "We'll come right down. . . . Why? . . . Does he have to be so stubborn? This weekend then." She listened again, her expression growing more troubled. "I don't know, Mom." She glanced at Dawn and then turned away. "The weekend. A couple of days." She hung up.

She held up calming hands at Dawn's flurry of questions. "Papa had a mild heart attack, but he's okay. He's spending another two nights in the hospital just to be sure."

Dawn started to cry. Didn't people die of heart attacks? When her mother put her arms around her, Dawn stiffened at the unexpected show of affection. Mom let go and stepped back.

"He'll be home for a while," Mom added. "On bed rest. We'll go see him this weekend. Granny wants you to stay at the house."

Papa looked more disgruntled than sick when Dawn came flying into the house. He was in plaid pajamas and a robe, wearing old, worn leather slippers and sitting in his recliner in the living room. When he started to get up, Granny told him she'd march him straight back to bed if he did. He grinned at Dawn. "Granny's got her nursing cap on. Heaven help me. Climb on up here and give me a hug!"

Mom had noticed Oma's car was missing. Granny said she was gone again. "She came home to see Trip—I mean Dad—and then decided to spend a week with Uncle Bernie and Aunt Elizabeth."

Mom and Mitch asked Papa questions, but Granny answered. Papa glowered. "I'm still alive. I can speak for myself. It's not as bad as she makes it sound."

Granny scowled back at him. "It was bad enough."

Granny's lips trembled. Papa took her hand and kissed it and suggested she start dinner.

Mom offered to help. Granny said she could manage, then asked Dawn to set the table. Papa kissed Dawn's cheek before she got off his lap. Mitch and Papa talked in low voices. Mom didn't say anything. In the kitchen, Granny ran her hand over Dawn's hair. "Papa looks better now that you're home."

Papa was too tired to sit at the dinner table. Dawn went along while Granny walked with him back to the master bedroom and settled him into the hospital bed they'd rented. She prepared a dinner tray for him. "Why don't I make up a tray for you too, honey? You're better medicine for Papa than anything the doctor prescribed." Granny stayed at the dining room table with Mom and Mitch.

While they ate dinner together, Papa asked Dawn how she liked living in Alexander Valley. She had grown to like it a lot, and she told him about her new friends, about Mitch acting as assistant soccer coach. She loved soccer. Did he want to know how many goals she'd kicked? Twenty-six! Mitch was teaching her to swim now, and she practiced every day in the backyard pool. Papa's eyelids drooped, and he fell asleep while she was talking. She kissed his cheek, then left the bedroom. She heard Granny talking in the kitchen.

"Well, you could ask her, couldn't you? The school year is almost over. She wouldn't miss anything."

"We didn't plan on leaving Dawn behind, Hildie."

"Well, I told Carolyn—"

"We were talking about this weekend, Mom. Two days, not the whole summer."

Dawn walked into the kitchen just as Mom got up and left the table. Mitch gave Granny a grim look and pushed his chair back, following Mom into the living room. Mom picked up her sweater and pulled it on, then picked up her shoulder bag. They spoke in low voices. Dawn asked Granny what was wrong. Granny said nothing, nothing at all; it was just a little misunderstanding and nothing to worry about. Mom stood in the entryway. "We'll be at the Paxtown Hotel. We'll be back in the morning, Dawn."

Granny looked furious. "You're leaving now? What about dessert? I made a chocolate cake. It's your favorite!"

"It's Dawn's favorite." Mom turned to Dawn. "We'll be back tomorrow." She went out the door.

Mitch said he'd be right with her. He leaned down and whispered in Dawn's ear. "Be wise. Don't take sides."

"It's just like your mother to run away!" Granny stacked dinner dishes and headed into the kitchen. She asked if Dawn wanted to play a board game. Dawn hadn't played games since moving to Alexander Valley. There were too many other things to do now. When she didn't say anything right away, Granny added, "Or we could watch TV."

Granny checked on Papa and joined her in the living room. She talked more than she watched. She and Papa sure missed Dawn. Wouldn't it be nice if she could stay longer than the weekend? How long before school ended? Two weeks? She didn't have any plans for summer, did she? Remember how much she loved the county fair? And with the baby coming, her mother would have all kinds of things to do: doctors' appointments, getting the nursery ready, shopping, that sort of thing. She wouldn't have time for Dawn, not like Granny and Papa. They would have all the time in the world for her.

Dawn knew what Granny wanted. Maybe she *should* spend the summer. Granny seemed so certain Papa would get better fast if she did.

She loved Granny and Papa, but this wasn't her home anymore. She wanted to be in Alexander Valley with Mom and Mitch. She wanted to be there when her baby brother or sister was born. But how could she say that to Granny without hurting her feelings?

Mom and Mitch came back in the morning. Granny said she would have breakfast ready shortly, but Mitch said they'd eaten at the hotel. Granny seemed hurt. She said she thought Dawn wanted to spend the summer. Mom said that didn't surprise her. Mitch asked, "Is that what you want, Dawn?"

"Granny said Papa will get well faster if I'm here."

He frowned at Granny. "No one can argue with that without sounding like a heartless wretch."

Granny's face turned beet red. "I wasn't pressuring—"

"It's probably true, Mitch," Mom said quietly. "Dad will do better if Dawn is here. But she has two more weeks of school. I'm not leaving her now."

"That'll be fine." Granny smiled, relieved. She hugged Dawn against her side. "We'll have all summer together."

"One month, Mom. Not the whole summer."

"What about the county fair?"

Mom turned to Dawn. She held her gaze for the first time in months. "One month or the whole summer, Dawn?"

Mitch interrupted. "Your little brother or sister is expected the middle of July. Remember?"

"I . . ." Dawn looked from Mom to Granny and then at Mitch. "Um . . ." She felt pulled and torn. "I . . ." She wanted to cry. No matter what she decided, someone would be hurt and upset.

"One month," Mitch decided. He smiled at Granny. "I'll miss her too much. She can come home the end of June and stay until the baby comes. Then she can make up her mind about the rest of the summer. Is that agreeable to everyone?" He looked to Mom to answer. She nodded.

Granny harrumphed. "I guess I don't have anything to say about it."

Papa spoke from the doorway. "I think you've had too much say already."

❊ ❊ ❊

Dawn enjoyed her time with Granny and Papa, but was ready to go home by the end of June. Mitch drove down to get her. Her friends had been calling. When she asked how Mom was doing, he said, "Bursting at the seams."

She settled in again and spent hours on the telephone with Torie and Tiffany. She swam every day. She rode double on Torie's horse. Mom vetoed any idea of having one of her own. "I just can't imagine you mucking out a stable. . . ."

"Dawn!" Mitch awakened her in the middle of the night. "Baby's coming. Up and at it, sugar. I've already called Tiff's folks. They're expecting us." He dropped her off on the way to the hospital, Mom huffing and puffing and saying they'd better hurry.

Two days later, Tiffany's mom brought her home. Dawn charged into the house, dumped her duffel bag. "I'm home! Where are you?"

Mitch appeared at the master room door, finger to his lips. Mom sat in a new rocking chair by the windows, holding the most adorable creature Dawn had ever seen.

"May Flower Dawn, meet your brother, Christopher Charles Hastings." Dawn had never seen that look on her mother's face. She was enraptured, in love, her lips curved in a soft smile. She held the baby so close, as though he were the most precious human on the planet.

Mitch put his hands on Dawn's shoulders. "So? What do you think of your baby brother?"

She looked at the baby again, her mouth wobbling. "He's so cute." She stepped forward. "Can I hold him?"

Mom seemed slightly alarmed at the idea. "Not yet. In a few days. We'll see." She studied Dawn's face and looked relieved. Gazing down again, she ran a tender finger along the baby's smooth cheek. "I think your sister likes you." His tiny mouth worked.

"Uh-oh." Mitch laughed. "He's hungry again." He ushered Dawn out of the room so her mother could nurse the baby.

❄ ❄ ❄

Dawn decided not to go back to Paxtown. She wanted to stay in Alexander Valley with Mom, Mitch, and her new baby brother. Christopher fascinated her. He had the cutest little ears, and he was so soft. She loved when he grasped her finger, holding on tight.

Mitch let her hold him once, but Mom took him back after a few minutes.

Once, she snuck into the master bedroom to watch him sleeping in his crib. She touched his hand and watched him start, his fingers opening wide, then closing on her thumb. Leaning down, she kissed his forehead. He even smelled good.

Granny and Papa came at the end of August. Mom didn't hand Christopher over to Granny, not even for a minute. She did let Papa hold him once. When Mom placed Christopher in his arms, Dawn watched his face soften.

Mom smiled. "I need to step out for a few minutes. Are you going to be okay alone with him?" He nodded, gaze fixed on his grandson.

Tears ran down his face as he cupped Christopher's head and leaned down to kiss him. "You look just like Charlie. . . ."

❄ ❄ ❄

Granny and Papa came up for Thanksgiving and stayed four days. Mom didn't relax until they left. Mitch invited them back for Christmas. Mom invited Oma, too, but she said Aunt Cloe had already insisted she come to Hollywood. Dawn overheard Mom talking to Mitch in the kitchen. "Something's wrong, but she won't say what."

Over Christmas Eve dinner, Papa announced he'd put in for retirement. He figured it was about time. He didn't want to have another heart attack. Besides, the law was now working against police officers. Arrest a criminal and the courts would let him loose.

"We've been thinking about moving," Granny said.

"Moving?" Dawn gaped. "But you love Paxtown!"

"Well, of course we do, but we love our family more. We only get to see you a couple of times a year."

That wasn't true. They came to visit for every holiday, and Dawn spent time with them every time she had a school break.

Mom set her knife and fork down. "What about Oma?"

"We invited her to come with us." Granny sawed at a tender slice of turkey like it was shoe leather. "She said no."

Papa put his hand on Granny's wrist. "I told you not to bring it up, Hildie." He faced Mom. "We haven't made a final decision yet. We wanted to ask if it would be all right with you if we moved closer."

Dawn couldn't bear the look on Granny's face. "That'd be great, Mom! Wouldn't it?" *Say something!* Mom opened her mouth, but no words came.

Mitch spoke. "It'd be great to have you two closer. You're the last set of parents I have."

"Thanks, Mitch," Papa said. Granny relaxed a little. Papa glanced at her, his face softening. Then he looked at Mom. "We've missed you more than you know, Carolyn."

Mom winced. Dawn jumped in again to break the tension. "You could live right next door!"

Papa laughed. "Sorry, honey. We can't afford this neighborhood."

Granny's shoulders relaxed. "Healdsburg seems like a nice little town."

Christopher started to fuss in his high chair. Mom got up quickly and released him, lifting him in her arms and holding him closer while Papa talked.

"I was thinking of something a little farther out. We don't want to park ourselves on your front doorstep."

Mitch poured more sparkling cider. "Stay with us while you're looking. We have plenty of room."

When Dawn came into the kitchen the next morning, she found her mother sitting at the table, rubbing her forehead while she talked on the telephone. "I'd feel better if you were coming, too." When she saw Dawn, she got up and took the portable phone into the family room. "We have plenty of room. You could live with us. Mitch would . . . Why not? Why would she care?"

Dawn knew Mom was talking to Oma. Pouring herself a bowl of cereal, she lingered and listened.

"Just think about it, Oma. Please?" Mom pleaded.

Dawn knew her mother loved Oma, but she didn't know why. Granny stayed away from her, so Dawn did too.

Dear Rosie,

My daughter doesn't know how to let go. She has decided to sell the big house and property (including my cottage) and move to Sonoma County. She would like it if she could live right next door to May Flower Dawn, though I think Trip will put his foot down over that. I'm not sure what I will do. I had hoped to live here for the rest of my life. I should have seen this coming when Trip put in for retirement.

I'm not sure where I will live now. Hildemara said I can come with them, but doing so might make it look like I approve. She doesn't consider how this will affect Carolyn's budding relationship with Dawn. In truth, I think Hildemara is a little jealous, though she would never admit it.

Bernhard and Elizabeth think I should move in with them. Clotilde offered a condo in North Hollywood. Rikka invited me to stay part of the year in her Soho apartment. She has many artistic friends, all like tropical birds chattering about their flights of fancy. Two weeks and I'm ready to migrate back to California.

As much as I love my children, I can be on my own.

Why do they think I need a keeper? I may have gray hair, wear glasses, have certain limitations, but I am not in my dotage. I still have dreams. They say I'm being stubborn. So be it.

I miss the Central Valley. I miss the heat, the scent of sand, orchards, and vineyards. I miss putting flowers on Niclas's grave. Merced is centrally located. I can afford a bungalow there. I could drive to Yosemite in an hour and enjoy the mountains for a day. Who knows? Maybe, after all these years, I could finally go to college. . . .

25

1980

Granny and Papa's Paxtown property sold quickly. A moving company stored everything while they stayed in Alexander Valley and looked for another home. They stayed in the second suite at the other end of the house from Mom and Mitch. Dawn was in-between. Granny made afternoon and evening appointments with their Realtor. That way, Dawn could go with them to see houses. Granny wanted to live at the north end of Healdsburg. Papa wanted to look at Cloverdale. Granny said that was too far away. So were Windsor and Santa Rosa. Granny said maybe they'd find something on Dry Creek Road.

Finally Granny decided on a house in Healdsburg. She talked about the nice guest bedroom with private bath, the neat houses along the street, the small, easily maintained backyard. And it was so close to Dawn's school. "You could have lunch with us!"

Papa looked at Dawn in the rearview mirror and didn't say a word until they got back to Alexander Valley. "Go on in the house, Dawn. Granny and I are going to have a little talk before we come in."

They sat in the car for almost an hour. When Granny came inside, she headed straight for the guest suite. Papa went into the family room and sank into an easy chair. Mitch raised his brows. "Is everything okay?"

"We're going to take a long drive tomorrow, by ourselves, and see a little more of the area." Mom came into the family room, Christopher in her arms. Papa looked at her with a sad smile. "Healdsburg is a nice little town, but I'd like to be forty-five minutes to an hour away. Somewhere on the coast, if we could afford it."

Papa found just the house he wanted at the end of the Russian River in Jenner by the Sea. The house was tucked into a hillside, almost hidden by a row of overgrown, shaggy cypress trees. He said the place needed some work, but he claimed it would have a "million-dollar view" when the trees were topped and the dead-wood cut out and hauled away. Granny argued vehemently against buying it, but Papa won in the end.

❄ ❄ ❄

Just before Christopher's first birthday, Mitch flabbergasted Dawn by asking if he could adopt her.

Her stepdad was the coolest guy she knew, and she loved him, but she was torn. She asked for some time to think about it. Her mother didn't like that, but Dawn didn't want to make a rash decision and hurt anyone's feelings. She went out to Jenner by the Sea for the weekend and talked it over with her grandparents. She hoped they'd give their blessing.

Papa didn't say much about it other than, "It's up to you, honey." Granny remained silent on the subject until the next morning, when she insisted she and Dawn go to the beach for a walk. They hadn't gone to the beach in months, so Dawn knew Granny had something to say. Granny let loose in the car on the drive over. She reminded Dawn that Mitch wasn't her father; that Papa had paid all the bills for the first five years of her life; Papa had rocked her to sleep. Papa had read stories to her; Papa had played with her. Of course, he'd been hurt when Dawn told him about Mitch's offer. How could he not be? Of course, he'd hide his feelings and say it was up to Dawn! Granny parked and wiped tears away. Besides all that, Dawn was the last Arundel in the family. Yes, of course, she'd get married someday and take her husband's name, but until then, it meant a lot to them.

Dawn couldn't bear to hurt her grandparents, and she knew Mitch would understand.

When she came home, she told Mitch she was honored, but thought she'd like to leave things as they were. Mitch looked disappointed, but accepted her decision with grace. He even kissed her cheek. "Don't worry about it."

Her mother stood silent, eyes glacier blue. She opened her mouth to say something, then pressed her lips together and left the room without speaking. Mitch followed her, closing the door of the master suite behind them. Her mother talked then, loud enough for Dawn to hear the tone, but not the words.

Dawn tried to talk to her the next morning. She wanted to explain it had nothing to do with Mitch. She loved Mitch. "I'm sorry if you're upset, Mom. I just don't want to hurt anyone's feelings."

"You don't want to hurt Granny's feelings. You don't care who else you hurt."

"Mitch seemed okay with it."

"They're your *grand*parents, Dawn! Isn't that enough?"

"*They've* always been there for me."

Her mother blinked. "So you hurt Mitch to get back at me?"

"No!"

Mom turned her back and continued making Dawn's bag lunch. She didn't have to say she didn't believe Dawn; her posture said it all.

"Can we talk about it, Mom?"

"Why? You made your decision. Everything will be the way Granny wants it, and it'll stay that way. It always does." She shoved the sandwich into a Baggie and put it in the paper bag. "You'd better get your stuff together, or you'll be late for the bus."

❅ ❅ ❅

1985

Dawn struggled with feelings of ecstasy, anger, and misery. She had kicked the winning goal in the final junior high team championship soccer game, and Mom wasn't even in the stands. Mitch had come. Her stepfather always made an effort to support her. Just once, couldn't Mom make the effort, too—especially since this was the last and most important game of Dawn's life? Of course, Mom would have an excuse. Chris always had something going on somewhere else. Mom hadn't even bothered to show up at Mary's Pizza Shack for the season-ending party. When Dawn and Mitch came into the kitchen, there they were, sitting at the table, Mom smiling over something Chris had said. She glanced up. "How'd it go?"

"Dawn kicked the winning goal. I got it all on film."

"That's great. Congratulations, Dawn. Chris's game started late. We just got home. He wanted to stop at Burger King."

Mitch ruffled Christopher's curly red hair. "How'd you do, Tiger?"

"We lost." Her little brother—still adorable at almost six—never got upset about anything. "Can we watch Dawn's game?"

"Whenever you're ready."

Christopher was on his feet, hamburger forgotten. He and Mitch trooped into the family room while Mom gathered up the remains of their take-out meal. "You seem upset."

"No, Mom. Why would I be?"

"Where are you going?"

"To my bedroom."

"Aren't you going to watch the game video?"

"I *played* the game, remember? Seeing it on video isn't the same as being there, is it?"

Her mother stood at the trash compactor. "You had a cheering section. Mitch went. And Granny and Papa were there."

"Why should it matter whether Granny and Papa are there? It'd be nice to have you and Chris at one of my games."

"Well, Chris couldn't come. His team needed him."

"He's in peewees! They play swarm ball! Just once, just for a couple of hours, couldn't *I* be first in your life?"

"You came first for a long time, Dawn. Not that it ever mattered to anyone, especially you."

Dawn gave up. Storming out of the kitchen, she went down the hall and slammed her bedroom door. She sat on the end of her bed and cried. Someone tapped on the door. Dawn shouted, "Go away!"

Sometimes she wished her mother would yell back instead of walking away—or responding in that cool, calm tone. Dawn wondered sometimes: How could she miss her mother so much when she'd never had her love in the first place?

26

1986

Dawn still felt adrift after nine months as a freshman. High school had turned out to be a complete bust. She'd gone from junior high Sky Hawks star soccer player to outcast and dweeb. The girls who had been her friends since second grade left her behind by mid-September, charging like forwards into new groups. Torie Keyes now ran with the Mexican gangbangers. Dawn saw her every day in the corridor, draped around Juan Alvarez like a bun around a hot dog. Susan Mackay hacked her hair into a butch, donned button-down shirts and black pants, and "came out of the closet" as a lesbian. Two other buddies from the Sky Hawks soccer team, Tiffany Myers and Leanne Stoddard, still hung out together. They smoked pot behind the modular buildings lining the football field. If Dawn wanted to go to a big party where booze and drugs and sex would be in abundance, all she had to do was ask Tiff and Lee. They'd know where to find one.

She scribbled more loops on her notepaper. Summer break loomed a week away with the promise of endless boredom.

She'd be stuck at home for three months without even Christopher's company. Her little brother had an army of little buddies; hence, places to go and things to do. In addition to friends, Mom signed him up for swimming lessons and, not one, but four different vacation Bible schools. Why? Because he had four "best friends," all in different churches, and he didn't want to play favorites. *Must be nice to be so popular, not to mention the blessing of being the first and only son.*

Even more annoying, Mom, who never went to church, would volunteer at every VBS. She'd take snacks, help with art projects, do whatever she could to be involved in Chris's life. She acted like a mother bear sometimes, as though someone might snatch Christopher away and molest him.

Tossing the pen aside, Dawn rubbed her forehead. Thinking about her mother always brought on a stress headache—ironically, the one thing they had in common. After they argued, Mom always retreated into the master suite and put cold compresses on her head or went to an AA meeting.

But their arguments were infrequent. You had to have feelings for someone to fight with them. Her mother didn't seem to care one way or the other about Dawn. She didn't hover over her; she just stepped back and watched from a distance, if she watched at all.

Mitch made time for her. Every month, they went on a "date." The last time, they couldn't find a movie worth watching and ended up eating dinner at the Western Boot. He talked about Uncle Charlie all evening. She loved hearing about Uncle Charlie. He sounded so cool. He and Mitch had gotten away with major mischief that left her laughing and in awe.

"And what about Mom? Did she get into any trouble?"

"She was a good girl."

"Yeah, right. She never did anything wrong."

"Nope."

"She waited until she got to Haight-Ashbury."

Mitch didn't say anything to that.

"Does she ever talk to you about those years?"

He shook his head.

"And you don't ask?" When he just looked at her, she pressed a little harder. "Shouldn't you know?"

"Your mother laid her life bare in less than a minute the first time I managed to corner her for lunch. She tore the skin off old wounds, and no, I am not going to betray her trust and tell you anything."

"Did she say anything about my father? Does she even know who he is?"

Mitch put his napkin on the table and signaled the waiter.

Dawn hung her head. "I'm sorry." She looked up at her step-father through her tears. "I don't want to go yet, Mitch. Please. I'll behave."

Mitch told the waiter they'd like to see the dessert selection. Dawn looked at the menu, but she wasn't hungry. Was it so wrong for her to want to know? "I must remind her of things she'd rather forget."

Mitch put the menu aside. "You should sit down with *her* and ask your questions, Dawn."

"She'd never tell me anything. Every time I even hint, she changes the subject or says she has to go to a meeting. Maybe just talking to me makes her want a drink."

"I'm not going to get in the middle."

"Mom and I don't even speak the same language."

Dawn tried to put herself in her mother's shoes. How would she feel if she had a kid out of wedlock, living proof of how she'd messed up her life and needed her parents to pick up the pieces and put her back together? As painful as it might be to go over the past, Dawn wanted to know something about her biological father. Not that Mitch wasn't a great dad; he was the best. But she didn't come from his gene pool.

Rubbing her temples, Dawn stared at the wall clock, noting another fifteen minutes before study hall ended. Maybe she'd ask her mother if she could sign up for summer school; at least it would be something to do. She'd already checked at McDonald's about a job, but she had to be sixteen. If she didn't find something to do, Granny and Papa would expect her to spend the summer at Jenner by the Sea again, just like last summer and the summer before that and every summer since they'd moved from Paxtown. She loved them dearly, but three months around their house with nothing to do wore her down.

They had books, of course, lots of them, most about building a house from foundation to roof, how to remodel, how to make repairs, plumbing and wiring, etc. Granny collected cookbooks. Dawn wouldn't have minded learning to cook, but they had a "one-butt kitchen," as Papa called it, and Granny liked being the only "butt" at the sink and stove. Last summer, Dawn found herself so desperate, she weeded every inch of Granny's garden below the house.

The class bell rang, jolting Dawn from her reverie. She stuffed her notebook into her backpack, slung it over her shoulder, and headed for the door.

If she wanted to stay home this summer, she was just going to have to spell it out. She'd beg if needed. If Mom said no, she'd enlist Mitch and Christopher's help. They always had better luck with Mom than she did.

❄ ❄ ❄

Dinner was almost over before Dawn gathered enough courage to say she wanted to spend summer at home. Mom glanced up, surprised. "But you always spend the summer at Jenner."

"I know, but I'd rather stay home this year."

"What's Granny said about this?"

"I haven't told her yet." Avoiding her mother's look, Dawn smiled at Christopher. "Maybe I can help keep an eye on Little Dweeb when you have an open house."

"I only do open houses on the weekends, and Mitch is here."

So much for trust.

"What do you plan to do for three months?" Mitch cut a piece of roast beef and forked it into his mouth.

She batted her eyelashes at him. "You could teach me to drive."

He laughed in mock horror. "No way! Besides, you're not old enough."

"I could learn to drive one of your tractors."

"And risk my vineyard? I don't think so."

"I can help with laundry and cooking."

Mom spooned a second helping of mashed potatoes onto Christopher's plate. "Your grandparents will be disappointed. They expect you to spend time with them."

"I could go out one weekend a month. It's not like I'm saying I don't want to spend any time with them."

Mitch gave her mother a look. "It might be nice having Pita here for a summer. She's not going to be around that much longer, you know. Three more years and she'll be off to college."

"I'm not looking for a fight, Mitch. You know how things are."

Mitch put his napkin on the table. "I'm going to be late for the elders' meeting." He leaned down and kissed Dawn on the cheek. "It'll be good to have you around this summer, Pita." He came around the table and kissed her mother full on the mouth. "Won't it?" He kissed her again. He ruffled Christopher's thatch of curling reddish brown hair. "No dragging your feet about going to bed tonight, buster. You still have a couple of days of school left."

Her mother sent Christopher to take a bath and gathered the dinner dishes. She glanced at Dawn's plate. "You didn't eat much."

"Wasn't hungry. I can help around the house, Mom. Do the dishes. Do the laundry."

"That'd be nice." Mom stood at the sink. "Okay." She turned and looked at Dawn. "On one condition."

"Anything."

"*You* have to tell your grandparents."

Dawn gave her a half-pleading smile. "I was hoping you would help me with that."

"No way." Her mother turned to rinse the plates before putting them in the dishwasher. "They wouldn't believe me if I told them you'd rather be here than out there with them."

❋ ❋ ❋

Dawn worried and rehearsed the call for two days.

"Was it your mother's idea to make you stay home all summer?"

"No." *Just say it, Dawn!* She let her breath out slowly. "I've never been home for an entire summer, Granny."

Silence.

"You'll still come out on weekends, won't you?"

Dawn chewed her lip. "Not every weekend, Granny."

Another silence.

"We were thinking about taking you on a trip to Yellowstone. Papa isn't getting any younger. This will probably be the last year for doing this kind of thing."

Granny knew how to apply the screws. "I know you and Papa will have a great time." She plucked at her bedspread. "I love you, Granny. I'll call you soon." She hung up before Granny could add anything else to make her feel even more guilty.

"Everything all right?" Mom stood in the doorway, expression guarded, hands tucked into her apron pockets.

"Everything's fine."

"Good." Her mother took her hands out of her pockets and smiled. "Come on in the kitchen. You can go through my cookbooks and decide what you want to fix for dinner tomorrow night."

"Tomorrow night? But I don't know how to cook."

"Cooking is easy. All you have to do is follow directions."

Panic set in.

Her mother walked ahead of her down the hall, pulled several cookbooks off a shelf, took a pad of paper and a pen from a drawer, and dropped them on the kitchen table. "Figure out what you'd like to cook, make a list of ingredients, and I'll pick up whatever you need tomorrow morning." Her mother slung her purse onto her shoulder.

"Aren't you going to help me?"

"I can't. Chris's class is having an end-of-year party." She opened the refrigerator and took out a bowl of potato salad.

"Mom?"

Her mother paused in the doorway and looked back at her. Dawn wanted to say she hadn't stayed home to be alone, but to spend time with her mother. The silence stretched, the words sticking in her throat.

Her mother's expression softened. "Don't look so worried, Dawn. You'll do fine without me."

Dawn listened to the garage door open and close. She flipped open the *Joy of Cooking* and turned the pages. Shoving the book aside, she put her head in her arms and cried.

Two weeks at home felt like a year. Christopher had a packed social calendar, Mom as chauffeur, while Dawn got to hang around the house, do laundry, plan and fix meals. At least she had company today. Christopher had a rare day at home, and Mom trusted her enough to act as lifeguard while he swam in the backyard pool.

Dawn rubbed sunscreen on her legs while keeping an eye on her little brother. Christopher stopped and sputtered, wiping hair back from his face and treading water in the deep end. Tossing the tube of Coppertone aside, she stood. "Need me to fish you out?"

"No!" He set off again.

Dawn walked to the end of the pool and waited for him. When he grabbed hold of the edge, she tapped him on the head. "Enough already, Chris." He cleared his eyes and looked at her. She held his wrist. "You're doing great. Just take a rest, would you please? You've done four laps. If you do another, I'm going to have to drag you out and give you mouth-to-mouth resuscitation."

"Gross!" He let her haul him out of the water. Christopher's wet feet slapped along the smooth concrete. He threw his towel around his shoulders, but still looked like a half-drowned mouse.

She grabbed her towel off the chaise longue and rubbed his hair dry. "I couldn't even do one lap when I was six."

"If I can do six laps without stopping, I can be a dolphin. And then I can learn to dive." Her little brother flipped out his towel and sprawled on his stomach. "Dawn, will you go to VBS with me tomorrow?"

"I'm too old for VBS, buddy."

"You could be a helper."

"Doing what? Handing out graham crackers and apple juice? Taking kids to the potty?"

"Come on. Please." He put his hands together and gave her his practiced puppy-dog look. "Pretty please. I'm supposed to invite someone."

"Someone from kindergarten to fifth grade, Chris. I'm telling you they don't sign up sophomores for VBS."

"High school kids come. They have a band! They help in the classes; they play outdoor games with us."

"Sounds like VBS has more than enough help already."

"I told the band kids I have a sister. I said you were pretty."

"Thanks."

"I said I'd bring you tomorrow."

When she glared at him, he stuck out his lip. He could be cute. "Do you get extra points or something?"

"No. But if you go to VBS, you can't do the wash and Daddy won't have to wear pink T-shirts." He grinned broadly.

"Okay. That's it!" Dawn jumped up, grabbed him by an arm and a leg, and headed for edge of the pool. "Time for a few more laps!" He squealed with laughter as she swung him back and forth and launched him into the deep end of the pool. He popped up quickly, grinning from ear to ear and hollering for her to do it again.

❄ ❄ ❄

Cornerstone Covenant Church turned out to be a large warehouse with metal roll-up doors in the Windsor Industrial Park. Volunteers had pitched two huge tents in the empty back lot. It looked more like a circus than a church.

Christopher grabbed Dawn's hand. "We have to go to chapel first!" He hauled her into a huge concrete-floored room with basketball hoops on either end. No pews, just folding chairs. Bright colored banners hung on the walls. *Faith. Hope. Joy. Love One Another.* The largest was purple with gold names appliquéd: *Mighty God, Everlasting Father, Wonderful Counselor, Prince of Peace, Jesus, King of Kings.*

Mom laughed. "It's not exactly what I expected either." She carried a tray of iced cupcakes and nodded toward a door. "The kitchen is that way."

"No, Mom. Dawn has to come with me." Christopher pulled her into the throng of kids. "Come on! They're going to start in a minute. My class is down front."

Her heart jumped when she spotted Jason Steward, one of the best-looking guys at school, on the raised platform with four other teens. They wore black Levis and canary yellow T-shirts with *Christ is Lord* emblazoned in red letters. Kim Archer, a pretty brunette who was a cheerleader at Healdsburg High, and another girl, Sharon something-or-other, had been in Dawn's PE class. Both had seemed nice. One of the guys plugged a guitar into an amplifier while the other did a drumroll and hit the cymbals. Jason caught a hand microphone tossed by a man near the stage. Raising one hand, he held the mike to his mouth. "Good morning, everybody!"

The children shouted back. "Good morning!"

He laughed. "Is that the best you can do?" He put his hand to his ear. "I can barely hear you!" The guitar player made a loud, warbling chord that had everyone shouting good morning again. Jason called out, "This is a day the Lord has made!" Another loud chord, more cheering. "Let's rejoice and be glad in it! Let's hear you! *Good morning!*"

Dawn wanted to cover her ears.

"That's better! Come on, everybody! Let's worship the Lord!"

The drummer went wild, his head bobbing up and down, while Jason and Sharon sang and Kim played keyboard. It seemed more like a rock concert than vacation Bible school.

A hundred children, plus teachers and volunteers, clapped their hands and sang the words projected on an overhead screen. Christopher kept pulling her forward, waving wildly. "Hey, Jason! I brought my big sister!"

Dawn wanted to duck down among the throng and hide. She pulled Christopher's arm down. Too late. Jason Steward looked straight at her and smiled broadly as he sang.

"What do you think you're doing?"

"That's Jason Steward! He told me to bring you! Isn't he the coolest?"

"I'm going to kill you."

"Don't go!" Christopher grabbed her hand again. Dawn pried loose and looked for escape. Boxed in with children all around her, there was no path out of this mob. Christopher joined in the clapping and singing. Dawn locked her attention on the overhead screen and lip-synched the words.

She'd spotted Jason her first day of high school. Who wouldn't? He was drop-dead gorgeous with black hair, hazel eyes, and olive skin. He looked a mix of Caucasian, Hispanic, and Asian. He'd been standing in the corridor of lockers, talking with a couple of guys. He had a contagious laugh. Later, she had seen him sitting at a picnic table under the redwoods, having lunch with a group of kids. She caught a glimpse of him every day on her way to English class. He'd caught her staring at him once and smiled. Mortified, she'd been careful not to stare after that.

Instead, she'd sit where he wouldn't notice her, watching him toss a football back and forth with the jocks during lunch break. Jason Steward was nice to everyone—geeks; pretty, popular cheerleaders; and even gangster types. She'd see him standing under the redwood trees near the student parking lot, talking with people. She'd seen him alone only a couple of times during the whole year, and she had never had the courage to utter hello.

Was her face still as red as it felt?

After three more songs, Jason handed the microphone over to Pastor Daniel Archer, who prayed, made some announcements, and then dismissed the children by groups.

"I'm going to go help Mom."

"No, you're not!" Christopher grabbed her hand again. "You have to come to my class."

"What am I? your show-and-tell?"

"I told Jason you'd help."

She let her brother lead her out of the chapel into the blinding morning sunlight and through the gate in the cyclone fence. "Come on!" He pulled her along. Glancing back, he let go, and his face broke into a broad smile. "Hey, Jason!"

Dawn gulped, but didn't turn around. She prodded Christopher. "You have to get to your class. Where is it?"

"Wait for Jason."

She wanted to throttle him. "We've gotta go."

Jason caught up with them. "Hi." He smiled at her, and she felt the heat rising into her cheeks again.

"Hi." She cast a quick smile in his general direction. "Bye." She ducked inside the tent after her brother. Heart knocking, she stayed in back as Christopher grabbed a square of carpet and ran forward to sit among a gaggle of other leggy boys and girls his age. His teacher, Mrs. Preston, had a felt board. *Oh, boy. Oh, boy.*

Jason came inside the tent and stood beside her. "Christopher said he'd bring his sister today. You go to Healdsburg High, don't you? I've seen you around."

"Yeah." Gawking at him, most likely. She glanced up briefly and then fixed her gaze on the back of Christopher's head.

"Chris didn't tell me your name."

"May Flower Dawn Arundel." Her face went hot again. What possessed her to say her whole name? "People call me Dawn."

"People call me Jason." He stepped in front of her and held his hand out. "Nice to meet you, Dawn. Thanks for agreeing to help." When his fingers closed around her hand, she tingled all over. His expression turned curious. "Arundel? Not Hastings."

Once he released her hand, she breathed easier. "Christopher is my half brother."

"He's a great kid."

"He has his moments." She swallowed hard. "Now that I'm here, I'm just not sure what I'm supposed to do."

"Help me set up the art project." He smiled and gestured toward two long tables covered with butcher paper on the left side of the tent. "They're making burning bushes today." While Mrs. Preston gave a dramatic reading of Moses fleeing into the wilderness, Jason laid out the trays of supplies. "They're going to glue down twigs to make a bush, drop paint, and use a straw to blow it around like flames."

"Clever."

His dark eyes shone with amusement. "Yeah, well, tomorrow's lesson is on the plagues of Egypt. They're making green paper-plate frogs. You are coming back to help, aren't you?"

"Let's see how today goes." She'd be back. She just didn't want to sound too eager. She laid a piece of paper and a small pile of twigs by each folding chair.

Jason put out paint, brushes, and straws. "Christopher told me he wants to be in a rock band."

"Last week, he wanted to be an astronaut; yesterday he wanted to be a dolphin in swim class so he can learn to dive."

Jason laughed. "Reminds me of myself at his age." It took them less than five minutes to put everything needed on the table. "Our work's done for the moment." He pulled out a folding chair for her, turned another around, and straddled it. Crossing his arms on the back, he looked her straight in the eyes and smiled warmly. "What about you?"

She was close enough to see the flecks of gold in the green, the rim of brown around his pupil. "What about me?"

"Do you know what you want to do with your life?"

"I haven't got a clue. Have fun, I guess." Could she have said anything more inane and shallow? "You'll be a senior, right? You probably have your future all planned out."

"I have a couple of ideas. My mom would like me to be an engineer. Pastor Daniel thinks I should go into the ministry. Maybe I can figure out a way to do both."

"How?" They seemed diametrically opposed.

"There's a lot more to ministry than just working at a church. God needs workers in all kinds of businesses, too. I've been asking Him to show me which direction to go, and I know He will."

She'd never heard anyone talk so naturally about God, though she didn't see what God would have to do with Jason's decision. Wasn't it all about free will? "Why would God care what you do? I mean, doesn't He want us to decide for ourselves? That's what I've been told. It's up to us to find out what makes us happy."

He tilted his head to one side. "Well, yes, God wants us to be happy. But there's a whole lot more to it than that."

"Really? What do you mean?" Jason Steward sure wasn't what she had expected.

"God gave each of us specific talents and abilities. He has plans for us. He has a purpose for your life."

"My life? I'm not so sure about that."

"You can be. It starts with being in an intimate relationship with Him. Then, just like any other relationship, it will influence what you want, what you do, what you believe."

The conversation was starting to make her uncomfortable. "*Intimate* isn't exactly a word I'd use about God."

Jason stood. "Hey, just think about it. If you open the door and let Him in, everything in your life is going to change. I promise."

Maybe that's why he'd told Christopher to bring her. To evangelize her. She didn't care one way or another about God. She just wanted to keep Jason talking. "Is that what happened to you?"

His eyes glowed. "Yeah." He looked behind her. "Ready or not, here they come." He swung his chair back into place as Christopher and his friends surrounded the table and found seats. Dawn helped her brother get started on his project, then helped a couple of the other kids. Jason introduced her to Mrs. Preston, who said Christopher was a terrific kid and a pleasure to have in class. As if Dawn hadn't heard that a thousand times before.

It didn't take long to finish the burning bushes. Mrs. Preston called the children together and took them outside, where she handed them over to other volunteers who gave them a choice of games to play.

Jason stood beside Dawn. "Do you go to church?"

She said, "Of course," and told him where. When he asked about their youth group, she shrugged and said with a congregation of less than a hundred and comprised mostly of people older than her stepdad, who was in his forties, there weren't enough teenagers to have one.

"Come to ours then. We meet here tonight at seven thirty. We hang out, play basketball, eat junk food, and have a Bible study. Give it a try. See what you think."

"I'd have to ask my mother." Mom might disapprove, but she wouldn't have grounds for argument. She was bringing Christopher to VBS here, after all.

"Do you need a ride?"

Her heart fluttered. Would he offer to pick her up if she said yes? "We live in Alexander Valley."

"I can introduce you to someone who lives up that way."

"Never mind."

A piercing whistle came from the parking lot. Jason gave a wave. "I have to get back to the sanctuary and set up for the closing. Thanks for helping today, Dawn. Hope I see you tonight . . . and tomorrow."

She looked for Jason when she accompanied Christopher's class back into the warehouse. He stood on the platform, talking and laughing with the two girls who had been onstage with him while the classes settled into their designated seats. Pastor Daniel had the microphone again and encouraged everyone to get settled quickly. He explained how the children's offerings would buy books for an orphanage in Mexico. He asked if anyone had a guest. Dawn held Christopher's hand down. Pastor Daniel went on. "Keep giving out those invitations! We have plenty of room for more."

He tossed the microphone to Jason, who had everyone up and singing again. After several songs, Jason gave a short closing prayer and called out, "See you all tomorrow!"

Dawn grabbed Christopher's hand and headed for Mom standing against the wall with several other women. She came toward them and smiled at Dawn. "I see you survived."

"It was okay, I guess." She didn't want to sound overly enthusiastic and have Mom wonder why. "I said I'd help again tomorrow. One of the guys invited me to youth group tonight."

"Invited?" Her mother gave her a quick glance. "As in asking you for a date?"

"No. He just said to come. He thought I might enjoy it."

"I'd rather you didn't go."

Dawn bristled. "Why not?" Christopher could do anything he wanted, but she asked for something and the answer was no?

"You have a church."

"So does Christopher, but that didn't stop you from signing him up for VBS at Cornerstone."

"Because Mitch's church doesn't have one."

"It doesn't have a youth group either."

"VBS only lasts three more days, Dawn."

"I'm not asking if I can join the church, Mom. I just want to see what youth group is like. I'd like to hang out with kids my own age, Christian kids."

"Let me think about it."

THE CCC YOUTH group consisted of fewer than twenty kids, mostly girls grouped together and talking while five guys played basketball. Another guest invited by Jason, Tom Barrett, had come to stick his toes carefully in religious waters. As soon as he was introduced, Jason took him to join in the basketball game. Kim Archer, the pastor's daughter, took charge of Dawn, inviting her to grab a folding chair from those stacked against a wall and join the gaggle of girls. Dawn knew some of them already, their names at least. She'd seen Sharon Bright, Pam Preston, Linda Doile, and Amy King at school, not that they would recognize her.

"Hey," Sharon said. "You were in my PE class. Dawn ran right past everyone during track."

Dawn added her chair to the circle. "I played soccer for six years. Coach Perez made us run a mile before every practice."

Pam twisted her hair up and put a clip in it. "Why didn't you try out for the team? We could use you."

"Thought I'd take a break. Try something else."

"Such as?"

"Studying."

"That's where I've seen you." Linda crossed her ankles. "In study hall. You sat in the back row by the windows."

"Yep."

The girls talked about school and how their summers were shaping up. Dawn took quick, surreptitious glances at Jason playing basketball with the guys. Sharon said her family was heading for Tahoe next week for a family gathering. Linda had a job in a pizza parlor near the downtown mall. Amy wished she had a job at the mall. She was working as a nanny for three children. She almost hadn't come this evening. Bed had looked pretty good, and she had to be back at the Johnsons' by six thirty in the morning. Kim answered the church telephone. She was filling in for the church secretary, Mrs. Carson, who was in Los Angeles helping move her mother into a residential care facility.

"What about you, Dawn?" Kim asked. "What are you doing this summer?"

Dawn pulled her gaze away from Jason. "Not much. I don't have a driver's license, and we live out in Alexander Valley." She shrugged. "I'm doing laundry and cooking for the family. So far, no one has died."

Pam laughed. "My mother says you were a big help in her VBS class this morning."

"All I did was put out some art supplies."

"I'll say thank you anyway. You saved me from being drafted into duty." She shuddered expressively.

The basketball bounced their way. "Hey, ladies!" Jason called. "Save us some steps?" Dawn got up, caught it, and gave it a light kick so that it landed right in his hands. "Good kick!" He grinned and dribbled the ball halfway down the court, passing it to Tom Barrett, who took two steps, jumped, and shot it smoothly over the heads of three others. It dropped perfectly into the basket. Jason and Tom gave each other high fives.

Sharon laughed as Dawn sat down. "Well, we all know why you came tonight."

"What?" Dawn pretended not to know.

"Jason Steward." Sharon stretched out her long, jean-clad legs. "Join the club. We've all had a crush on him at one time or another."

When she glanced over, Jason was looking at her. He quickly looked away. Raising his hand, he called out to Tom, who passed him the ball.

❄ ❄ ❄

When Pastor Daniel came in, everyone made a circle of chairs. Everyone but Dawn had brought a Bible, even Tom Barrett. Kim said not to worry about it and shared hers. The pastor called on the regulars to read portions of the book of Daniel, then pointed out how a few teenagers made an impact on a godless society. He challenged them to make a difference wherever they were: high school, mall, babysitting.

When the study portion ended, everyone hung around, nibbling chips, eating leftover VBS cupcakes, drinking sodas, and talking. Jason had picked up Tom Barrett. They walked out and stood talking to a couple of the guys in the parking lot. Dawn spotted her mom's tan Suburban and headed for it. Pam Preston caught up with her. "I'm glad you came tonight. Can I meet your mom?"

"Sure. I guess." Dawn opened the car door. "Mom, this is Pam Preston; Pam, my mom, Mrs. Hastings."

Pam leaned in to shake her hand. "It's nice to meet you, Mrs. Hastings. We live on the north side of Healdsburg. I could pick up Dawn next week."

Mom looked dubious. "It's nice of you, but—"

"I've had my license for two years and haven't gotten a ticket. My mom says I drive like an old lady. You can ask her when you bring Christopher to VBS tomorrow."

Mom smiled politely. "I'll take your word for it, Pam." Dawn got into the car and closed the door. "She seems nice enough. How well do you know her?"

"She's on the high school soccer team." Dawn watched Pam talking to Kim and Pastor Daniel.

"So what was it like?"

"We read about Daniel." Dawn leaned back as her mother drove out of the parking lot. "There's a lot more to him than surviving a night in a lion's den. I felt like such an idiot. Everyone had a Bible. I don't even know where mine is."

"I'm sorry they made you feel inferior."

"No, Mom." Dawn didn't want her getting the wrong idea. "It wasn't like that at all. It's just that I've been going to church with Mitch since second grade, but I don't know a fraction of what those kids know."

"Granny and Papa read you Bible stories when you were little, didn't they?"

"Yeah. Simplified versions with pictures. Pastor Daniel made something written thousands of years ago sound like current events. Rev. Jackson doesn't exactly light my fire when he preaches."

"Boots gave me a Bible when I lived with her."

"Wasn't she Granny's friend? the one who died of cancer a few years ago?"

"Yes. She was my friend, too. She's the one who encouraged my interest in Scripture."

"I didn't know you even had a Bible, let alone read one."

"I didn't mean to shock you."

"Well, it's not like I've ever seen you reading it."

"I have a quiet time every morning. In the privacy of my room, so I can think about what I'm reading."

"But you never go to church."

Mom kept her eyes straight ahead.

"Why don't you?"

Her mother lifted one shoulder and shifted her hands on the steering wheel. "I'm not comfortable in church."

"Did Boots go?"

"Christmas and Easter. Like me, she felt more at home in AA meetings. We both have the same Higher Power: Jesus."

"AA isn't the same as church, Mom."

"How would you know?"

Dawn hadn't meant to sound critical. This was the first time her mom had talked to her about anything remotely personal. Dawn didn't want to ruin it. "Is it?"

"For me, it's better." She gave Dawn a bleak smile. "We all know we're sinners in AA. No one wears a mask."

❄ ❄ ❄

Every Wednesday, Dawn hitched a ride to Cornerstone youth group with Pam Preston. After meetings, they hung out until Pastor Daniel locked up and headed home with Kim. Then Dawn piled into Pam's Honda with Sharon, Linda, and Amy; and they all went to Taco Bell to have sodas and nachos and talk about boys, movies, movie stars, clothes, makeup, and the latest diet craze. Tom Barrett called Dawn for a date. So did Steven Dial. Dawn made excuses, hoping Jason would call. He didn't. She saw him at youth group, but he didn't talk to her much.

Pastor Daniel started a new summer study on chastity and talked at length about running from sin and avoiding youthful passions and how rebellion against God led to a ruined life. "Joseph had to run from Potiphar's wife when she tried to seduce him. Learn from Joseph. God wants you to be pure, and that's not going to be easy in a world that encourages promiscuity."

Jason glanced at her once, but she didn't look back at him. Discussion moved to advertising, movies, music, attitudes at school, the media, new provocative styles of dress.

Jason didn't come to the next meeting.

"He can't come for the rest of the summer," Kim told Dawn. "My dad knows someone at Raley's, and they helped Jason get a job there. He's working nights stocking shelves and cleaning floors."

"Oh. That's great." Dawn tried to sound enthusiastic. "So he's not coming back?"

"Not until school starts. Maybe not then either. He has to save money for college."

She felt niggling jealousy. She liked Kim. She liked her a lot, but she seemed to know quite a bit about Jason's private life. "Well, say hi when you see him."

"I don't see him. He comes by and talks with my dad." She gave Dawn a knowing smile. "If you want to see him, you'll have to come to church."

"I can't."

Kim's brows went up. "Why not?"

"I promised my mother I'd keep going to Mitch's church if she let me come to youth group."

"Oh." Kim looked sympathetic. "Then I guess you're going to have to wait five weeks until school starts." She gave Dawn a curious look. "You said 'Mitch's church.' Doesn't your mom go with you?"

Dawn shook her head. "No."

"Why not?"

"I have no idea. My grandmother said she used to go all the time, and then she just quit."

She couldn't get Jason out of her mind for the rest of the week. The thought of going through the rest of the summer without so much as a glimpse of him depressed her.

"Why so glum, Pita?" Mitch asked over dinner. "The spaghetti and salad are great. You're becoming a fine cook."

Dawn lifted one shoulder and poked at her food. "Doesn't take a lot of talent to boil noodles, dump Ragu on them, and tear up a head of lettuce."

He chuckled. "Maybe you need to challenge yourself more. Try some fancy French cuisine tomorrow night."

She sighed heavily. "Getting through the rest of summer is going to be challenge enough."

Mom frowned as she lifted her glass of ice water. "Since

Christopher won't go to camp for two weeks, I thought this might be a good time to go down to Merced and see Oma." She sipped and set her glass down without looking at Dawn. "We'll be back in plenty of time for camp."

Christopher's exuberant mood collapsed. He groaned and launched into excuses. He wanted to play with his friends. He wanted to swim and Oma only had sprinklers. He wanted . . .

Mom glowered at him. "Be quiet, Christopher."

Mitch leaned back in his chair. "Why don't you take Dawn this year?"

"She wants to stay home for the summer."

"Granny called." Christopher jumped in again. "She and Papa are coming in to pick Dawn up and take her out to Jenner by the Sea for the weekend."

Dawn's heart sank. She'd forgotten all about it. "You could go instead of me. Granny and Papa would love to have you spend a weekend with them. Or a week, for that matter."

"The beach! Cool!" Christopher turned a bright smile on Mom. "Could I, Mom?"

"No." Her tone came out flat and hard enough to keep Christopher from asking again. Dawn wondered why it was fine for her to spend an entire summer, but her mother wouldn't even allow Christopher to spend a night. What sense did that make? They were his grandparents, too, for heaven's sake.

Mitch spoke up. "Christopher can stay home with me. Take Dawn. You two haven't had a trip alone together in a long time." Dawn wanted to snort. They had never been on a trip together. Mitch looked at Christopher. "What do you say we make it men only for a week?" He winked. "Pizza delivery, steak at the Western Boot, rent a dozen movies. We could play some golf. What do you say, buddy? Wanna stick around the hacienda with dear old Dad?"

"Yeah!" Christopher turned to Mom and made prayer hands. He stuck out his lower lip and made it quiver pathetically. "Please, Mom." Not waiting to see if his playacting worked, he jumped up and wrapped his arms around her neck and kissed her cheek three or four times.

Mitch laughed. "How can you turn the boy down?"

Mom, mouth twitching, rolled her eyes at Mitch. "Okay, Christopher, okay. . . ." She laughed.

Sometimes Dawn felt like an outsider watching the three of them. She was a cuckoo left in a warbler's nest.

"Only promise me one thing, Mitch."

His eyes grew warm as he looked at Mom. "Anything."

"Please don't take him out on your Harley."

"Aw, Mom!" Christopher groaned.

Dawn chewed her lower lip. Her mother was going to Merced for a week. Just because she'd agreed to leave Christopher home with Mitch didn't mean she wanted to take her daughter with her. Dawn remembered how Mom and Oma would have afternoon tea on the wisteria-covered patio in Paxtown. Granny never sat with them, and when Dawn had, the conversation felt stilted. Mom and Oma always seemed to have things to talk about. And Mom was one of the most reticent people Dawn knew; she hardly talked to anyone, except Mitch, and then mostly in quiet voices or behind closed doors.

While Christopher came up with a dozen more ideas on how he wanted to be entertained for a week, making Mom and Mitch laugh, Dawn spoke up. "Can I go with you to Merced, Mom?" She held her breath as her mother considered it.

"I think it's time you did."

29

Mom wanted to leave early. Dawn packed shorts and tops, sandals and toiletries in a duffel bag and set her alarm for five. She didn't want Mom leaving without her. She lay in bed wide-awake thinking about Jason. He'd be working right now, stacking cans on shelves or sweeping and polishing the floors of the grocery store. He'd probably met some pretty checker a couple of years older and wiser, some fast girl who'd promise him a good time and know how to keep herself out of trouble. Rolling over, Dawn punched her pillow. She hoped Jason had been listening to Pastor Daniel. She hoped he'd run like Joseph did when Potiphar's wife tried to seduce him. *Run, Jason! Run!*

Bleary-eyed in the morning, Dawn dressed and took her duffel bag into the kitchen. Mom sat with a cup of coffee, a pensive look on her face. She glanced up in surprise. "I thought I'd have to wake you."

"I set my alarm. I didn't want you sneaking off without me."

Her mother gave a soft, humorless laugh. "I wouldn't do that. Would you like breakfast before we leave?"

"I'd rather eat along the way. Could we?"

Mitch came out in sweatpants and a T-shirt, his red hair sticking up all over his head like a little boy's. Mom's eyes softened and glowed.

"Didn't want you going without a kiss."

Dawn rolled her eyes. "I'll be in the car." She grabbed her duffel bag. One thing hadn't changed in the eight years Dawn had known Mitch. He still couldn't keep his hands off her mother.

It would be nice if Jason felt that way about her. Just thinking about him made Dawn's blood warm.

Mom followed her out. "I thought we'd take our time and use country roads. Do you know how to read a map?"

"Not really."

Mom opened a California map and refolded it. "We're here. Just follow the yellow highlighted roads. We're going to follow this little black line to Calistoga and meet up with Highway 29 through Yountville and Napa." She traced the route with her finger. "We connect here with Highway 12 and then head east through Rio Vista."

"Great." Dawn tried to make sense of the map. "Have you gone this way before?"

"Yes, but you haven't."

"We could end up in Sacramento with me as guide."

"You'll be fine."

Christopher probably talked Mom's ear off when they went on their excursions. Dawn didn't feel much like talking. She kept thinking about Jason, trying to figure out a way to see him before school started. She looked out the window at the hedgerows of blooming roses. Mitch had rosebushes all around his vineyard too. He told her they drew bees for pollination, but were sensitive to disease and gave vintners early warning so they could take preventive measures if necessary to save their vines.

The road went through Napa and took them south of town onto Highway 12. Dawn watched for signs. "There's the turnoff to

Now that Dawn had a name from her mother's past, she wanted to know more.

"Haven't you?" Mom didn't raise her eyes. "I thought Granny might have mentioned her."

"Nope." If Granny had, Dawn couldn't remember. "Are you still in touch with her? I mean, if you were best friends and all . . ."

"No." The word came out firm and flat. End of conversation. Her mother poked at the fruit and speared a piece of melon. "What classes are you taking this year?"

"English, geometry, social studies, PE, biology." She'd be studying human anatomy and physiology this year, too.

"What about Spanish? You'll need a foreign language if you want to go to a university."

"Spanish, too. I forgot. Not that I'm all that excited about going to college."

Mom glanced up. "What do you want to do?"

"I want to get married. I want to have children. I want to be a housewife." Dawn laughed at herself. "Hardly considered a worthy goal, is it? I'm supposed to want a career." Dawn forked eggs into her mouth, pleased to have shocked her mother. At least she was getting some reaction out of her.

When they headed off again, Dawn yawned. "I'm so tired." She looked at the map. "I hardly slept last night."

"I wouldn't have left you behind."

Dawn had hoped they'd talk all the way down, but the silences grew longer. She might as well take a nap so the time would go more quickly. As she dozed off, she thought she felt her mother's fingers lightly brush the hair back from her face.

❄ ❄ ❄

Dawn awakened when the car stopped. "We're here!" Mom sounded light and happy. They were parked in front of a small house with a single-car garage. Dawn got out and went around the back for her duffel bag. She stood on the sidewalk looking down a long, straight street lined with old elm trees and small houses that all looked alike except for the color and landscaping. Oma's house was yellow with white trim and a bright red door. Red, yellow, and white roses bloomed profusely below a front window. A cement walk led to the front steps and postage-stamp porch.

The front door was opened by a wizened old lady with permed white hair and wire-rimmed glasses. She was wearing a blue dress with white polka dots and collar. "It's going to be a scorcher."

Mom hurried up the steps and hugged Oma. Dawn felt shy. Oma's hands looked like bird claws on Mom's back. "It's good to see you, *Liebling*. And I noticed you brought someone special with you."

Mom straightened and turned, eyes glistening with tears. "Dawn asked to come along."

"Did she?" Oma smiled at Dawn. "Well, come on in where it's cool."

An oscillating fan whirred on a stool set up in the kitchen doorway, stirring the heavy air across the tiny, simply furnished living room. A gilt-framed print of snow-covered mountains and green meadows hung on the wall. A recliner sat near the windows with a white crocheted afghan tossed over one arm. A reading lamp stood on one side and a side table stacked with books on the other.

Oma waved toward the short hall. "Carolyn, you can take the front bedroom." Mom disappeared around the corner with her suitcase. "Dawn, the family room is through the kitchen and down the steps on your right. You can use the hide-a-bed."

Dawn stepped around the stool with the oscillating fan and went into the kitchen. She liked the glossy yellow walls with white trim and colorful chicken-print curtains. An ancient gas stove and a small, round-fronted refrigerator were on her right. Three red vinyl, chrome-leg chairs and a table covered with a blue- and white-checkered oilcloth sat against the back wall. A big window looked out onto a large backyard with a stretch of green lawn and a tree loaded with lemons, oranges, and limes.

Dawn went through the side doorway at the back of the

kitchen and stepped down into the family room. It looked more like a library. Shelves laden with books covered the back wall. Dawn dumped her duffel bag beside the green hide-a-bed with needlepoint pillows and took a closer look at Oma's collection. Each shelf held books on a different topic: the ancient history of Egypt; Babylonian, Assyrian, Chinese, European, and British history; American history; biographies. Several shelves held books on farming and business management. One shelf held novels, all classics, all on Dawn's college preparatory reading list.

The backyard beckoned. Stepping outside, she inhaled the sweet scent of wisteria, roses, and sweet alyssum mingling with freshly mown lawn. Bees buzzed in the Joseph's Coat roses climbing posts supporting the white lattice patio cover. Two white wicker chairs with green- and white-striped cushions and a yellow and white couch swing looked inviting. Red, purple, and pink fuchsias spilled from hanging pots.

The kitchen window slid open. "May Flower Dawn!" Oma called out to her. "Iced tea or lemonade?"

How long since anyone had called her May Flower Dawn? Only Mom ever did it, and not very often.

"Lemonade, please." She came back inside and found Mom sitting at the kitchen table with a glass of iced tea. She looked so relaxed and pretty, her blue eyes shining. "It's so good to be here, Oma." She clearly meant it.

Oma's hand shook, spilling some lemonade, as she set a glass in front of Dawn.

"Drat it all. Lucky I didn't spill it all over you. I'm shaking worse than ever."

"What did the doctor say?" Mom wanted to know.

"He said I'm getting old." She snorted. "As if I didn't know. I see myself in the mirror every morning when I put in my dentures." She scowled. "But let's get serious. Angel food cake now or after supper?"

Mom laughed. "How about now *and* after supper?"

"That's my girl." Oma winked at Dawn. "Still has her sweet tooth. How about you, Miss May Flower Dawn?"

Just Dawn, she wanted to say, but stopped herself. She'd never seen her mother in such a lighthearted mood and didn't want to spoil it. "Any time is a good time for dessert."

"Good answer."

Mom told Oma to sit; she'd take care of serving. Oma eased herself into a chair. While Mom cut the cake, Oma asked about Christopher and Mitch. One question from Oma and words spilled from Mom's mouth. Dawn had never heard her mother talk so much or so easily. Nor had Dawn ever tasted anything as good as Oma's angel food cake. Granny's didn't come close.

"And what about you?" Oma asked Dawn. "What's going on in your life?"

"Not much." Dawn shrugged. "Other than I have a massive crush on a gorgeous guy I met at a youth group." She couldn't believe she had blurted out that bit of news. Oma was practically a stranger.

"And you left him all alone to come down here and visit an old lady? I'm flattered."

"Unfortunately, Jason barely knows I exist."

Dawn collected the empty plates and put them in the sink. "Would you mind if I sat outside on your patio? It's so pretty out there, and I love your swing."

Oma waved her hand. "Make yourself to home."

Dawn stretched out on the swing, one foot on the patio to push off. She gazed dreamily through the red, orange, and golden blossoms of the Joseph's Coat above her. She hadn't known what to expect, but she liked it here. Granny said Oma could be unapproachable and rather cold, a woman who expected perfection, but so far, Dawn hadn't gotten that feeling. Maybe age had mellowed Oma. If her great-grandmother had always expected perfection, why would she and Mom be such bosom buddies? Mom had broken moral laws and Granny's heart right along with them.

With the kitchen window cracked open, Dawn could hear

Mom and Oma talking inside the house. Though words were indistinct, the constant babble and frequent laughter told her clearly how well they got along, how much they loved each other.

It had always been that way. Granny said they had a private club with only two members and it was no use trying to break in. But Oma had welcomed Dawn today. She had seemed genuinely glad to have her come down for the week. Dawn hadn't really expected that.

The back door opened and Oma came outside. "Mind if we join you?"

Dawn grinned at her. "As long as I don't have to give up the swing."

"You stay put. I have to move the sprinkler." She went out and pulled on the hose.

Mom came outside, carrying two frosty glasses of lemonade. She set one on the side table near the swing. "I thought you might like a refill." She sat in one of the white wicker chairs. "It's hot out here, isn't it? Like a sauna."

Oma dragged the hose, the sprinkler flipping over and over. "So what do you think, Dawn?" She snapped the hose and the sprinkler righted itself. She headed back for the covered patio.

"About what?"

Oma settled into the other wicker chair. "Being down here with your mom."

"I'm glad I came."

"Good." Oma put her head back and let out her breath. Her mouth curved into a Mona Lisa smile.

_30_

THE THREE OF them sat in the family room that evening and watched _Jeopardy!_ Oma knew every question in every category before the contestants. Amazed, Dawn asked if she'd ever tried to go on the show. "You'd make a fortune, Oma!"

"Might have made sense thirty years ago when I needed the money, but I have more than I need now. What would I do with a fortune other than leave it to my kids and ruin their lives? And don't give me that cheeky grin. It'd be even worse giving it to grandchildren or great-grandchildren. Take away all your incentive to make something of your life. It's the hard days of scrambling for enough that you'll look back on with fondness when you're a dinosaur like me."

"Granny says every parent wants to make things easier on their children."

Oma turned the volume down with the remote while a commercial played. "Making things easier on your children is sometimes the worst thing you can do. Of course, sometimes it's easier for you. But what does it do in the long term?" She put the remote aside. "Take your granny as an example. She was a sickly baby. If I'd kept on coddling her, she'd have grown up weak. But she's strong. She developed dreams of her own and went after them."

Dawn winced. "I forgot. She said to say hi to you."

Oma grunted. "Next time you talk to her, tell her I'd rather have a call from her than a relayed message."

Mom patted Oma's hand and kissed her cheek before getting up. "I'm going to bed."

"Sleep as long as you want, Carolyn. You're on vacation."

Mom wished Dawn a good night and went up the steps into the kitchen. Oma moved to give Dawn more room on the sofa. "Since this is your bedroom, you let me know when you want it all to yourself."

"How late do you usually stay up?"

"Depends on what's on television. Not much these days. I usually end up reading in the living room, but I'm between books right now."

Glancing toward the back wall, Dawn gave a quiet laugh. "You must love reading."

"Did you find anything to interest you?"

"I have to read *Ivanhoe* next year in English."

"Have to?" Oma got up and pulled the book from the shelf. "It wouldn't be a classic if it hadn't won the respect and hearts of generations." She dropped it on Dawn's lap. "Read fifty pages. If you're not hooked, put it back. If you enjoy it, take it home as my gift."

They watched a mystery in companionable silence. When it ended at ten, Oma flipped through channels, giving terse critiques. "Rerun. Stupid. Copy of a better show. Trash. More trash. I give up!" She shut off the television and put the remote on the cabinet. At home, if nothing caught Dawn's interest, she could always load a favorite video. Oma didn't have a VCR, let alone a library of movies.

Oma struggled to her feet and headed for the kitchen steps.

"How about some hot chocolate? Now that it's cooled off, we can sit outside and enjoy the stars."

Dawn sat in a wicker chair, fascinated as her great-grandmother pointed out stars and constellations and told the mythological stories that went with them.

"How do you know all this, Oma?"

"I'm interested. I have *Bulfinch's Mythology* in my library if *Ivanhoe* doesn't catch your attention." She waved her hand. "There's a whole universe of things to learn." Crickets chirped love songs while Dawn sipped cocoa and listened to Oma until she wound down and sighed.

"You made your mother very happy by coming down here."

"I had to beg her to bring me," Dawn admitted. "She prefers Christopher's company."

"Christopher never said, 'I hate you. I wish you were dead so I could go home and live with Granny.'"

"What?" Dawn spoke weakly.

"Oh, it was a long time ago. You'd just moved to Alexander Valley. Your mother said she understood. After all, you'd spent more time with your grandmother than you had with her. And your grandmother had built her life around you."

Dawn didn't hear any condemnation in Oma's voice, but felt close to tears anyway. She hadn't thought about that in a long, long time. She remembered feeling ashamed. She remembered wanting to apologize. She remembered her mother telling her if she wanted to talk, she could call Granny. She hadn't told Granny what she had said. She'd been too ashamed to admit it. "Sometimes people say things they don't really mean."

"You meant it at the time." Oma reached out and patted her hand. "I've said things I regret, too, my dear. We all do."

"Granny's always loved me."

"So has your mother."

Dawn wanted to believe it. "Not like Granny does."

"And why would that be, do you suppose?"

Why not be frank? Maybe she'd get the truth from Oma. No

one else wanted to talk about the past. "Because I wasn't planned, I guess. I was a mistake in a long line of mistakes she made."

"When has she ever said that to you?"

"She never says much of anything to me."

"Your mother doesn't say much of anything to anyone, other than Mitch."

"She talked with you all afternoon." Dawn hadn't meant to sound resentful or jealous. "I've never heard her talk that much to anyone, not even Mitch."

"She's safe with me."

Dawn looked at her, waiting for more. She could see the sheen in Oma's eyes as she looked at the sky.

"Your mother has never had to guard words with me. She can speak her mind without fear I'll love her less." Oma gazed at the stars in silence for a few minutes, then spoke again. "We all make mistakes. It's how we learn. I'm quite certain your mother would admit to making her share of mistakes. Though I'm also certain she does not consider *you* to be one of them."

"She'd probably still be in Haight-Ashbury if she hadn't gotten pregnant with me."

Oma scowled. "Well, now, I don't know how you can believe that when she didn't even know you were on the way until a month *after* she came home."

"Granny said she came home pregnant."

"Yes. She did. But being pregnant isn't the same thing as knowing you're pregnant. Your mother found out the same day your granny did."

Dawn tried to think back on things Granny had said to her. "Maybe I got it wrong."

Oma relaxed again. "You wouldn't be the first."

Dawn chewed her lip for a moment. "Do you know who my father is?"

"I never asked. Have you?"

"Yes," Dawn said in frustration, "but she always changes the subject."

"Then you might ask yourself when and how you asked."

"I just want to know the truth, Oma. Don't I have a right to know?"

"That's all well and good, but what would you do with the truth if it was given to you?"

Oma talked in riddles! "I don't know what you mean."

Oma pushed herself up from the wicker chair. "Then you have something to ponder, haven't you?" She picked up her empty cup, said good night, and went back inside the house.

❄ ❄ ❄

Over a breakfast of scrambled eggs, sausage, and biscuits the next morning, Oma talked about what her other "kids" were doing. Dawn couldn't help but laugh at the idea of Granny, in her sixties, still being considered a kid. Uncle Bernhard had received a long-deserved prestigious award for grafting lime, lemon, and orange trees. Business boomed and their son, Ed, now managed vendor and customer accounts as well as advertising so Bernie could concentrate on his horticulture experiments.

Rumors circulated in Hollywood that Aunt Clotilde would be up for an Oscar. "Apparently the costumes she designed for some science fiction movie were out of this world," Oma joked.

Aunt Rikka still lived in her apartment in Soho. "She says she has good light for her painting and plenty of subjects. She's doing portraits now. She just finished one of a hoodlum from the Bronx with a tattooed neck and arms. She's calling it *Simon the Zealot*. She's talked an IRS officer into posing as Matthew the tax collector. I don't know who will buy these portraits, but she doesn't care. She says she's saved enough to paint whatever she wants for a while. If she runs short on money, she can always weld some more scrap metal together, give it a fancy name, and put it in that art gallery that loves her work. She told me she has a friend who mounted a urinal on a slab of wood and sold it for two hundred thousand dollars!" Oma shook her head. "People will make complete fools of themselves trying to keep up with whatever the latest art craze is."

Mom took Oma's grocery list and headed off to the store, leaving Dawn alone with Oma. Oma smirked at Dawn as Mom went out the door. "Am I babysitting you or are you babysitting me?" She got up from her recliner. "I have some watering to do. Would you like to go out in the backyard with me? We can keep an eye on each other."

Dawn lounged on the swing. "You had four children, Oma, and they're all so different."

"More similar than you might imagine." Oma tipped a watering can over a box overflowing with blue and red petunias. "All four were bright and good-looking. They all found their God-given talents. Clotilde and Rikka are both artists. Bernhard and Hildemara took to science."

Dawn put her arm behind her head. "I don't think I have any talent."

Oma straightened and glowered at her. "How would you know? You haven't tried anything yet. Other than soccer, which your mother said you play very well."

"Yeah, well, I don't think they have any professional women's soccer leagues."

Oma set the watering can down and eased herself into a chair. "You probably have a good idea already what you want to do with your life."

Get married. Have children. She didn't want to say all that after Mom's nonresponse. "I'm only fifteen. How would I know?"

"Your granny was reading books on Florence Nightingale at fifteen. I left home at fifteen. I knew what I wanted, or thought I did, and made steps to go after it."

Dawn couldn't imagine leaving home right now, let alone leaving her country. How had Oma done that? "What did you want, Oma?" Had she run away like Mom? Maybe that was part of the bond between them.

"I wanted a chance to make something of my life, and my

father thought educating a girl was a waste of time and money. He made me quit school at twelve and sent me to work at whatever menial job he could find. He didn't think I'd amount to anything. He sent me to housekeeping school in Bern to learn how to be a servant. It wasn't what I wanted, but I found ways to make good use of the training. I was going to own something as grand as the *Hotel Edelweiss* someday."

"*Hotel Edelweiss?*"

"My friend Rosie's family had a hotel. It's still in the family as far as I know."

"So you had to give up that dream?"

"Not completely. I owned a boardinghouse in Montreal and helped build a forty-acre ranch specializing in almonds and grapes. If my father had pampered and petted me, I might have ended up staying in Steffisburg and waiting on him for the rest of my life." She snorted and shook her head.

All Dawn wanted to do was get married and have children. It didn't seem like much when compared to Oma or Granny or even her mother, who had become a successful Realtor. In less than three years, Dawn would be eighteen. She'd need some kind of workable plan for her future until her dreams came true, if they did. "The idea of going out on my own scares me." The thought was daunting.

"Probably because you're too comfortable." Oma chortled. "Nice big room in a big fancy house with a swimming pool, everything taken care of for you. Why would you want to leave? The people I loved most told me to go. My mother told me to fly. Rosie couldn't wait for me to have adventures. Even my employers, Solange and then Lady Daisy, both said I had to go. They loved me, but put their needs aside for my good. People either weigh you down or give you wings. I had to shove your granny out of the nest. If I hadn't, she'd still be single and living on the farm, thinking she had to take care of me." She looked annoyed at the memory. "I love every one of my children, and I did the best I knew how in raising them. I just wasn't always the mother they wanted." She let out a soft breath. "I tried to mend the rift with your granny, but . . ." She shook her head. "It's easier to put up a wall than build a bridge."

"Are you sorry you never got your dream, Oma?"

"I can't complain. Sometimes we realize our dreams in ways we never imagined. I never thought I'd ever marry, let alone have children. I wanted an education more than anything. I don't have a high school diploma, but I can speak three languages, and I've read more great books than most college graduates. It's a good thing God isn't limited by what we have in mind for ourselves. His plan is so much bigger. When you're as old as I am, you have time to sit still and take a long, thoughtful look back over your life and see how God's plan was also a whole lot better."

"Jason talks about God the way you do."

Oma raised her brows. "And how's that?"

"Like God cares."

"And you don't think He does?"

"Well, I suppose so, but . . ."

"It's too hot out here for a philosophical conversation." Oma fanned herself. "Let's go inside."

Dawn followed Oma back inside the house. They sat at the kitchen table, the oscillating fan turned on high. "As I get older, I miss the Alps more. Then again, maybe it's just the heat."

"Have you ever gone back?"

"Once, when I was eighty-four. Rikka went with me and made drawings of the old Lutheran church, the schoolhouse where I went, Thun Castle. I was offered a job there once."

"In a castle?" Dawn was impressed.

Oma snorted derisively. "As a maid who'd've been paid a pittance for the honor of working there." She snorted again. "I said no."

"I never knew any of this. You should write all this down."

Oma pushed herself to her feet, took an old leather journal from a kitchen drawer, and tossed it on the table in front of Dawn. "Rosie gave that to me as a going-away present before I left for Bern. She told me to fill it with adventures." Oma chuckled. "I didn't expect to have any. So I filled it with bits and pieces of useful information, things I thought would get me where I wanted to go. And eventually, I suppose some of my 'adventures' made it into the pages too."

Dawn opened the journal. Oma's German script was as small and perfect as the Declaration of Independence, and she had made the most of every page. "Can you read some of it to me?"

Oma put her hands on her hips. "*Ivanhoe* will be a lot more interesting, especially for a girl with romantic inclinations. Jason, is it? He's the one you want to marry?"

Dawn blushed. "I can hope." Covering her embarrassment, she gave Oma a smug smile. "I finished *Ivanhoe* last night."

"Did you now? Well, aren't you the smart little cookie?" Oma looked pleased. "Go ahead and read my journal. It's only the first section that's in German. I started practicing my English as soon as I could. If nothing else, it'll help put you to sleep."

Dawn flipped through pages. "Any recipes for love potions or advice on how to win a boy's heart?"

Oma laughed. "You're on your own there, my girl. I only went out with one man and ended up marrying him. But there's advice on how to mend fences and build bridges. Not that I've ever been good at either."

31

THAT NIGHT, AFTER Mom and Oma had gone to bed, Dawn stayed up reading the worn journal. The first pages, in German, looked like lists and maybe recipes. The journal switched to English beginning with a heading, "Tea Service for Lady Daisy." A recipe for spicy chicken sandwiches was followed by advice on how to wash linens, polish silver, and clean wood floors. Sometimes a line would be written that wouldn't fit in among the rest.

Another year and I will forget why I came to England. Do I want to be as hopeless as Miss Millicent?

She'd filled one page with information on crop rotation and how to prune almond trees and grapevines.

I bought a car today. Niclas is not happy. I am!

More menus followed, along with a list of "Summer Bedlam Activities." Oma had filled the last two pages with Scripture.

Trust in the Lord with all thine heart; and lean not unto thine own understanding. In all thy ways acknowledge him, and he shall direct thy paths. Proverbs 3:5-6

Oma had made a vine and grape border around this Scripture. The second stood alone with more space around it than anything she had written on the other pages.

When I was a child, I spake as a child, I understood as a child, I thought as a child: but when I became a (wo)man, I put away childish things. For now we see through a glass, darkly; but then face to face: now I know in part; but then shall I know even as also I am known. And now abideth faith, hope, love, these three; but the greatest of these is love. 1 Corinthians 13:11-13

Dawn turned the last page.

I have lived out my mother's hope and pray I have given wings to my daughters' dreams.

Leaving space, she wrote again.

A coddled child grows up crippled.

The last entry put an ending to the journal.

I lived and loved the best way I knew how, trusting God to keep His promise never to lose one of His own. I hold fast to what Mama taught me. In Him, we live and breathe. In Him, we will one day find one another again. In Him, we are one. In this life, we will not love perfectly. In the next, God promises we will. I hold to that hope. I cling to that dream.

❄ ❄ ❄

On the way home to Alexander Valley, Mom fell into her habitual silence. It didn't bother Dawn as much this time, not after a week with Oma. "Can I go back with you next summer?"

Mom smiled, eyes straight ahead. "So you enjoyed yourself."

"Very much." She didn't want to be left out or left behind again. "Christopher and I could camp outside on Oma's lawn."

"He'd like that."

Well, her mother hadn't said she couldn't come. "Oma knows more than anyone I've ever met." She gave her mother a teasing smile. "Even Mitch."

Mom let out a soft laugh. "She's lived decades longer."

Dawn enjoyed the new rapport between them. "Could we go to a stationer's on the way home? I'd like to get a thank-you gift for Oma."

"What do you have in mind?"

"A diploma."

They stopped on the way through Santa Rosa. "I want something that looks like a real diploma. It has to look authentic. This one." She pointed. "'This certifies that Marta Waltert has graduated magna cum laude from the University of Hard Knocks.'"

Mom laughed. "She's going to love it!"

When they picked up the framed diploma, Dawn wrote a

note and put it in the box before sending it by Federal Express to Merced.

> Dear Oma,
>   I learned more from you in one week than I've learned in ten years of school. I hope to visit again soon.
>
>   Love, Dawn

Ten days later, a package arrived Priority Mail from Oma. Dawn opened it at the kitchen table with Mom watching. "A leather journal! Just like the one her friend Rosie gave her." Dawn ran her hand over the beautifully etched tan cover. When she opened it, a note fluttered to the floor. Mom picked it up and handed it to her.

> If you learned more from me in one week than you learned in ten years of school, you weren't paying attention! Open those lovely blue eyes and look at the world around you! Open those cute shell-shaped ears and listen! Get busy on going after your dream. Thank you for my diploma. I have it hanging on my bedroom wall where I can admire it every night and pray for the blessed child who sent it.
>
>   Love, Oma

Dear Rosie,

Carolyn brought May Flower Dawn with her this year. I had given up hope of ever getting to know my great-granddaughter. She was such an obnoxious child, so full of herself, so spoiled by Hildemara and critical of Carolyn—not that it was entirely her fault. Christopher usually comes with Carolyn, but Dawn asked to come this time. I see that as a miracle. I didn't think she liked me.

Dawn has a "crush" on a young man who barely knows she exists. I doubt that. The girl is a beauty—long blonde hair, blue eyes, nicely proportioned. I was taken aback. She is the mirror image of Elise. Thankfully, she is very different in temperament. May Flower Dawn and I had several very nice, long conversations. I was surprised to discover she has a teachable spirit. I am quite taken with her. She may very well turn out to have the best of Hildemara Rose and Carolyn in her, and perhaps a little of me as well. Not too much, I hope.

Dawn sent a gift. According to the diploma she had made, I graduated magna cum laude from the University of Hard Knocks. I laughed and wept when I saw it, and I wept more when I read her sweet note. May Flower Dawn wants to come again. I am filled with joy! Dare I hope she might be the one to bring my daughter home to me? Oh, how I would love to sit and serve Hildemara, Carolyn, and May Flower Dawn tea on my patio. Think of it, Rosie! Four generations of women together at last. We could drink in the scent of summer roses and talk. Oh, how I would love that. . . .

32

THREE WEEKS LATER, Granny called. When Oma didn't answer her telephone, her neighbor had gone over to check on her. She found Oma sitting in her recliner. She'd died peacefully, Alexis de Tocqueville's *Democracy in America* open on her lap.

The memorial service took place in a Methodist church in Merced, the front two rows packed with relatives and the rest packed with friends. No air-conditioning and late August heat made the sanctuary almost unbearable. Uncle Bernie and Aunt Elizabeth; Ed; Granny and Papa; Aunt Cloe and her producer husband, Ted; and Aunt Rikki and an old friend and widower named Melvin were all there. Dawn sat beside Mom in the pew behind Granny and Papa. Mitch sat on the other side of Mom, his arm wrapped around her as though holding her together. Christopher sat on the other side of Mitch, leaning against him.

Dawn had never lost anyone, and she felt more regret than grief. She'd liked Oma immensely and wished she'd spent more time with her. But the depth of her mother's grief frightened her. Mom had cried for three days after Granny called with the news.

She hadn't eaten in a week. Now, she sat ashen-faced, tears streaming down her cheeks as the minister spoke of heaven and the hope God gave everyone who believed in the crucifixion and resurrection of Jesus Christ our Savior and Lord.

Granny glanced back at Mom, her expression pained, almost angry. Dawn had overheard her speaking to Mom in the pastor's office before the service. "Are you going to be all right, Carolyn?" She had sounded impatient.

"She'll be fine, Hildie." Papa put his arm around Granny's waist. "Come on. We need to go in and sit down."

"No." Granny stepped away from him and kept staring at Mom. "If you can't hold yourself together better than this, Carolyn, maybe you should stay in here and cry your heart out."

Mom gasped as though struck.

Mitch's face darkened. Dawn had never seen him so angry. "There's no shame in grieving over someone she loves!"

"No shame at all." Papa took Granny firmly by the arm. Granny's face crumpled before she turned away.

Mitch looked chagrined and muttered the first foul word Dawn had ever heard him say. He folded Mom in his arms and whispered to her. Christopher looked confused and distressed. Dawn put her arm around him and told him everything would be okay, though she wondered if it would.

Now, as the service wore on, she studied her mother's worn face and wanted to weep. She took her hand and found it cold. While the minister droned on, Dawn remembered things Granny had said. "Your mother was always going off by herself, even as a little girl. She liked being on her own in her dream world. She'd play outside with the dog for hours."

Dawn thought that meant her mother hadn't cared deeply about anyone but herself, that she didn't need anyone. Clearly, she cared deeply about Oma.

Mitch decided they would leave Merced shortly after the reception started. "She's taken all she can take," he told Papa.

"We have to stay," Papa said. "The lawyer will be going over the will tomorrow morning. Apparently, Oma managed to make some good investments."

Mom stared out the front passenger window on the drive home. Tears streamed down her white cheeks. Mitch looked worried. Christopher put his head in Dawn's lap and slept most of the way. Dawn didn't know what else to do but pray. *God . . . God . . .* Even then, words wouldn't come.

❄ ❄ ❄

During the last two weeks before school started, Mom went about her daily chores like an automaton. Even Christopher couldn't lift her spirits with his cheerful inane chatter and repertoire of new puns and knock-knock jokes. When Granny called, Dawn escaped to Jenner by the Sea. Papa asked how her mom was doing, and Granny jumped in.

"You know very well how she's doing, Trip. I told you I called a few days ago and Mitch said she wasn't up to talking to me."

"Maybe she's feeling better now."

"She won't even speak to me!"

"She isn't talking to anyone, Granny." Fighting tears, Dawn went into the blue bedroom off the kitchen and closed the wooden folding doors. She could hear her grandparents talking in low voices at the table. Papa raised his voice.

"You're madder at Carolyn for grieving than you're sad over your mother dying."

Dawn heard Granny crying and then quick footsteps retreating to the back bedroom. Opening the door slowly, Dawn peered out and saw Papa still sitting at the kitchen table, staring out at the Russian River. When she sat with him, he gave her a pained smile and quipped, "Women. You can't live with them, and you can't live without them." He let out his breath. "Things wouldn't be nearly so bad if everything had been sorted out between your granny and Oma years ago."

"What wasn't?"

He scratched his balding head. "Nothing that's ever going to get fixed now."

❄ ❄ ❄

Home again, Dawn left Mom alone and went out to wander through the garden and vineyard alone. Mitch had started building a new tasting room last spring, and now he pitched in with the carpenters. Maybe he just wanted to be out of the house so Mom could grieve in private.

Hot and tired, Dawn came back inside and found her mother sitting at the kitchen table with a cup of steaming hot tea. Dawn sat with her. "Is there anything I can do for you, Mom?" She'd already finished the laundry and folding. She wouldn't need to start dinner for another three hours.

"It'll just take time." Mom put her hands around the cup. "I wish you'd known her better."

"So do I. It's my fault I didn't." Dawn hurt for her mother. She hurt for Granny, too. They should be comforting one another. Instead, they didn't even speak. "Do you want to talk about Oma? Would that help?"

Mom raised her head and offered a sad, rueful smile. "Maybe you should think about being a shrink."

Dawn gave a soft laugh and started to cry. Angry with herself, she covered her face. "I'm sorry. I just wish I could make things easier on you and Granny. She cried all weekend."

"Did she?"

Dawn wiped the tears from her cheeks. "She'd smile and pretend everything was fine, and then she'd disappear into the garage and cry."

Mom rubbed her temples. "You'll be a great comfort to her."

"What about you, Mom?" Dawn could see the effort it took for her to sit at the table. Her mother leaned forward, heels of her hands pressed hard against her eyes. Was she trying to stop another onslaught of tears?

"I won't run away to Haight-Ashbury," she half whispered hoarsely. "I won't run . . ."

It seemed such an odd thing to say, but Dawn didn't want to make things worse by asking what she meant. "Christopher needs you, Mom." Maybe that would be enough to shake her out of despair.

Her mother raised her head with an effort, eyes bleak. "And you don't."

Dawn felt impelled to admit what she never had before. "Yes, I do." She slid her hand across the table, lifting her fingers in invitation, hoping her mother would understand. Silent, pale, her mother stared. Dawn waited, counting the seconds. Just when she'd almost given up hope, her mother slid her hand across the table and wove her fingers into Dawn's. The first spark of life came back into her mother's eyes as they held tight to each other.

33

"YOU HAVE MAIL." Mom came into Dawn's room and handed her two envelopes. Dawn set Jane Austen's *Pride and Prejudice* aside and tore open the large envelope first. Members of the CCC youth group had sent a condolence card with wishes she would return to meetings soon. Even Pastor Daniel had signed it. The second envelope held a note from Jason Steward.

Dear Dawn,

Kim told me about your great-grandmother passing on. I'm sorry for your family's loss and hope you take comfort in the Lord Jesus. I hope to see you when school starts again. If you'd like to talk, I'd listen.

Sincerely yours,
Jason Steward

She spent the rest of the afternoon obsessing about Jason's note. Did he want her to call? Was he inviting her into a relationship? If so, what sort? friendship only or something more?

It took all night and most of the next day to gather enough courage to look up his telephone number. Her heart pounded in her ears as she pushed the numbers. Losing her nerve, she hung up after two rings. She picked up her portable phone half a dozen times before she finally had the nerve to try again.

A woman answered. Stammering, Dawn asked if she could please speak to Jason Steward. The woman's voice became cold. "Who's calling?"

"Dawn Arundel."

"Just a moment." Dawn could hear muffled voices. Time stretched and with it Dawn's nerves. Had she made a mistake calling Jason? Maybe he'd sent the note only to be polite.

"Dawn?" His voice made her pulse skyrocket. She hadn't talked to him in weeks.

"Hi." She winced at the high-pitched tension she heard in that one word. She let out her breath and tried to calm down. "I just called to thank you for your note." When he didn't say anything, she wondered if they'd been cut off. "Jason?"

"I'm here. Hang on a second." Again, the muffled receiver, the indistinct voices. Then he came back on. "How are you doing?"

"So-so, I guess. Better than my mother. Oma's death has hit her hard. They were extremely close."

"Was it expected? Her death, I mean. Your grandmother's. I mean your great-grandmother." He let out a tense breath.

He sounded more nervous than she was. That pleased her, for some odd reason. "She was in her nineties. It wasn't exactly unexpected."

"Oh. Yeah. Dumb question."

"I didn't mean that. My mom and I spent a week with Oma this summer. She was really, really cool." Dawn rolled her eyes, thinking she sounded really, really dumb.

Jason's mother said something. He told Dawn to hang on a second again.

"Dawn?"

"Yes?"

"I have to go. I have something I have to do before I go to work tonight."

"Okay." Dawn felt heat flood her entire body. "Bye." She clicked the phone off and tossed it on the bed. She shouldn't have called. How would she face him when school started?

Kim called later that evening. "Did Jason call you?"

"No," Dawn drawled cautiously. "Why would he?"

"Well, I don't know, but he called me an hour ago and asked for your number."

"He did?"

Kim giggled. "Dad thought Jason wanted to ask me out. I didn't dare tell him he wanted your number."

"I guess your dad doesn't like me very much."

"Oh, it's not that," Kim said quickly. "It's just that Jason is exactly the sort of guy my father wants me to marry. Are you coming back to youth group? Jason said he had Wednesday night off this week."

When Jason didn't show up, Kim shrugged. "I guess he had something else he had to do."

❄ ❄ ❄

Dawn took special care getting ready for the first day of school. She wanted to catch Jason's attention and make a lasting impression. When she came out for breakfast, Mitch leaned back in his chair and gave her a wry grin. "Who's your prey?"

She blushed. Angry, she pulled her chair out and sat down. "I don't know what you mean."

"Ah, Pita. I see trouble ahead." Mitch tossed his napkin on the table and stood. He kissed Mom on the cheek. "I'll buy a shotgun on the way home." Laughing, he headed out of the kitchen.

Mom raised her brows at Dawn.

Dawn stared back at her. "What?" She had chosen jeans that fit her like a second skin and a pink scoop-neck T-shirt that showed off her tan. She'd left her hair down and put on touches of eye shadow and glossy pink lipstick. It wasn't that big a deal, was it?

"You look very nice. That's all I was going to say."

As the bus turned off Prince Street into the school driveway, Dawn caught a glimpse of Jason in the student parking lot with Tom Barrett and Kim Archer. Slinging her backpack over her shoulder, Dawn got off the bus.

"Dawn! Wait up!" Kim caught up with her. Jason held back with Tom, talking while looking at Dawn. Did he like how she looked? His expression showed nothing. He didn't even wave at her. "He bought a car!"

Dawn pulled her gaze from Jason. "Who?"

"Jason! Who else? He gave me and Tom a ride to school." She kept talking as they went inside together to their lockers. Dawn wished she lived in Windsor instead of Alexander Valley. Then, maybe, he would offer her a ride.

Jason and Tom came in the door after them. She stood with her back to them as she opened her locker. Every nerve quivered when Jason came closer. "Hi, Dawn." He spoke quietly. She gave a quick glance over her shoulder without meeting his eyes and gave what she hoped was an equally nonchalant greeting.

After that, she didn't see Jason until the lunch hour. He was with Kim and Tom again, sitting at a table in the cafeteria. Matt Cavanaugh came over and blocked her view. "I don't think I've seen you around school. My name's Matt. And you're . . . ?" He left the question hanging.

"Dawn Arundel. I was here last year."

He grinned at her. "How did I miss you?"

"Maybe you were too busy getting dents in your football helmet."

He laughed easily. "Where are you sitting for lunch?"

She peered around and saw the seats at Jason's table had already filled up. Sharon glanced toward her in question. "Outside, I guess." She headed for the door, not expecting Matt to follow.

He got to the door ahead of her and opened it. "You can sit with me in the senior court."

Joe Hernandez and two other seniors joined them. They flirted outrageously, each trying to outdo the other, which gave her a feeling of power and made her laugh. She finished her lunch quickly and excused herself, going back inside the cafeteria. Sharon, Steven Dial, Pam Preston, Linda Doile, and Amy King still sat at the table. Kim, Tom, and Jason had left.

"Where have you been?" Sharon asked.

"Sitting with Matt in the senior court."

"If you're looking for Jason, he and Kim and Tom went to do a Bible study in one of the courts. I'm not sure which one."

Dawn spotted Jason in the hallway as she headed for her Spanish class. He barely looked at her as he passed by.

The next few days were no different, other than she managed to avoid Matt and his friends. Jason hung out with Tom and Steven Dial, and sometimes Kim. He made no effort to single Dawn out or even speak to her. When she sat down, he got up and left the lunch table. She wasn't the only one who noticed.

"What's with you and Jason?" Sharon kept pace on the way to class. Dawn had just spent another miserable lunch hour of wondering why Jason seemed so determined to avoid her.

She shrugged off Sharon's question. "I've got to get my books."

Spanish passed slowly, Dawn struggling to concentrate on conjugating verbs. She kept glancing at the clock. She wouldn't see Jason until tomorrow, and he'd probably ignore her again. When the bell rang, she headed for biology and then realized she'd forgotten her textbook. She hurried to her locker and grabbed the book she needed. Turning, she bumped into Jason. Her heart jumped and she stepped back, embarrassed. "Sorry. I didn't see you."

"My fault. Can we talk?"

Now he wanted to talk? After almost a month of acting as though she didn't even exist? "I'm going to be late." She stepped around him, but he moved to block her.

"I tried calling you."

"When?"

"This summer. After you called me."

"Thanks for reminding me."

"Once I stayed on the line long enough to hear your voice on the answering machine. I didn't leave a message."

She looked at him. "Why not?"

"I chickened out." A muscle tensed in his jaw.

"Your note said if I wanted to talk, you'd listen. I guess I know now that was bull." She stepped around him and raced to class, slipping into the room just as the bell rang.

She didn't expect to see Jason waiting for her when she came out.

"Would you like to go for a soda after school? We could talk then. I have a car. I could drive you home."

After so many weeks of nothing from him, she couldn't quite take in his sudden warmth. False hope and wrong conclusions would just add to the hurt. "I know you have a car. Kim told me you've been picking her up every day."

His eyes flickered, and then he smiled, looking relieved. "I've been picking up Tom Barrett, too. But she and Tom decided to ride the bus together instead. It takes longer to get home."

She blinked, not sure what he meant. "Are you saying they like each other?"

"Yeah. Is that so surprising? Tom's a great guy."

"I know he is, but Kim is Pastor Daniel's daughter, and Tom is barely a Christian."

"The three of us have been doing a Bible study every lunch hour. Tom is talking to Pastor Daniel about getting baptized."

A Bible study every lunch hour? Was that why Jason had been leaving the table? Maybe his departure had nothing to do with her.

The warning bell rang. Jason took her books. "I'll walk you to class."

Bemused, she fell into step beside him. "You don't know where I'm going."

"You're going to algebra, which is just down the hall from my trigonometry class." He saw her to the door. "Do you want to go have a Coke after school?"

"Yes."

His eyes warmed. "Wait for me after class. We'll get your stuff and go." He headed back in the other direction.

Dawn couldn't wait for class to end. Every minute felt like torture. When the bell finally rang, she slapped her book closed, gathered her things, and headed for the door. A few minutes later, she spotted Jason weaving his way through the throng of students. When he smiled at her, Dawn went hot all over.

"How was algebra?"

"Agony."

On the way to student parking, Dawn spotted Kim and Tom walking hand in hand. "How did I miss that?"

Jason laughed as he opened the car door for Dawn. "I guess you had other things on your mind."

Jason. That's what she had on her mind. Every day, all day, and nighttime, too. She slid into the white Honda, admiring the pristine, beige interior. Jason tossed his backpack into the trunk and slid into the driver's seat. She smiled. "It's so neat and clean."

"I bought it from a lady in the trailer park. She's in her eighties and can't drive anymore." He started the engine. "She only put seven thousand miles on it and had records on oil changes and services." He put his arm on the seat behind her, backed out of the parking space, and pulled into line behind others waiting to exit the cyclone-fenced lot. "My mother is less than happy about it."

"Why?"

"I dipped into my college savings." He pulled out onto Prince Street. "She was pretty ticked off. But I'm still working five to nine as a bagger five days a week. It's good pay."

"What about a Doyle Scholarship and Santa Rosa Junior College? That would give you two extra years to save." She didn't want to think about him leaving the area in less than a year.

"My mother has her heart set on me going to the University of California."

"Which UC campus? Berkeley? Davis?" Both were close enough that Jason could come home on weekends.

"Berkeley. The hotbed of radicals." He pulled into McDonald's and asked if she wanted something to eat. She was hungry, but said no. She didn't want him spending what little money he had buying her junk food. He bought two sodas and a large order of French fries.

Jason drove to Memorial Beach. They walked across the grass and sat on the beach above the Russian River. He insisted she share the fries. They talked about their classes and teachers' expectations. He asked about her summer, and she talked about Oma.

"You're blessed." He looked at the river, expression wistful. "I've never met my grandparents."

"Do they live far away?"

He wadded up his empty bag and pitched it into a garbage can. "San Diego." He rested his forearms on his raised knees. "They don't speak to my mother."

"Why not?"

Jason turned his head and looked at her solemnly. "She had me." When her mouth fell open in surprise, he stood abruptly and walked down to the water's edge. Dawn got up, dusted off her jeans, and followed him. Jason shoved his hands in his pockets. "I thought you ought to know."

Dawn moved closer, her hand brushing his arm. "My mother came home from Haight-Ashbury and found out a month later she'd brought an unexpected package with her. Arundel is Mom's maiden name."

Jason stared at her. "I wouldn't have guessed."

"It's not something to advertise, is it? Have you met your father?"

"Once, when I was five or six. We ran into him at a park. He kept staring at me, and I asked why. Mom told me he was my father. I ran over to him and asked. His friends laughed." He gave a bleak laugh. "He told me to get lost. We moved a few weeks later. I haven't heard of or seen him since." He tilted his head. "What about you?"

She shook her head. "I have no idea who my father is."

"Have you asked?"

"Once or twice. My mother won't tell me anything."

"Maybe the memories are too painful."

"Or she doesn't know who he is."

He winced. "Ouch."

"Well, she was a hippy. Free love and all that. . . ." She lifted her shoulders. She wondered why she was telling Jason. It wasn't something she'd ever wanted to discuss with anyone.

Jason turned to her and gripped her arms. "Dawn, I've been wanting—" At the sound of a car crossing the bridge, he let go of her and stepped back. Looking grim, he glanced at his watch. "I'd better drive you home. I need to get to work." They walked slowly up the sandy hill and under the shade of the redwood trees, neither in a hurry to leave.

"When are you going to do homework, Jason?"

"Study hall, and I get up early." He opened the car door for her. When he slid into the driver's seat again, he turned to her. "I'm not going to have a lot of free time, but what I have I'd like to spend with you. How do you feel about that?" He searched her face.

Everything bloomed inside her. "I'd like that very much."

34

JASON MET DAWN at the bus stop every morning and walked her
to her locker and first class. They ate lunch together with other
members of the CCC youth group, then met every afternoon,
after their last class. Filling their backpacks with textbooks and
homework assignments, they'd head for the parking lot and drive
to the library. They'd find a small, empty table and sit opposite
one another. When she had trouble with math assignments, Jason
moved his chair beside hers, leaning close and whispering help. The
brush of his shoulder against hers and warmth of his body made
her blood race. She savored the exquisite torture of being so close
to him. When he looked at her, she studied the gold flecks in his
eyes, the black depths of his widening pupils.

Dawn was disappointed, but not surprised, when Jason said
they couldn't study at the library anymore. "I'm not getting my
work done, and I've got to keep my grades up."

They hung out at school every day, and he called her every
night on his work breaks. Sometimes he called when he got home,
but his mother never allowed him to talk long. Dawn could hear

her. "You need your sleep, Jason." "You have to get up at four thirty tomorrow morning to finish that report." "You'll see her in school. Get off the phone!"

Sometimes he called her back. "Mom's asleep. We can talk now." And they did, for two hours sometimes.

Pastor Daniel came by. Jason fumed over the telephone. "Mom must have called him. He said rebellion against God leads to a ruined life."

"You haven't rebelled against God."

"I told him that, but he's right, too. I'm not exactly where I was a year ago. I can't go to youth group because of work, and I'm not reading my Bible every day like I was. I'm not praying like I did either. Other than getting my homework done, all I think about is you."

"Maybe we both have a problem." Dawn rolled over and tucked her arm beneath her pillow. "We'll bring our Bibles to school and find a nice quiet place where we can be alone and study. Do you think that will help?"

He gave a hoarse laugh. "When I'm with you, the last thing on my mind is studying."

The sound of his voice stroked her senses, and she knew hers did the same to him. Stirring him up stirred her as well. She liked the rush of blood in her veins, the warmth in her belly. "I wish you were here, Jason."

"Imagine I am."

"Dawn?"

Dawn jumped a foot off the bed. "Christopher!" She hissed in annoyance. "You scared me!"

Her little brother stood in the doorway in his pajamas. "I had a bad dream."

She wanted to tell him to go back to bed, to leave her alone, but he looked so distressed, she stretched out her arm. "Speaking of dreams, I think my little brother just had a bad one." She made room for him. "He likes to curl up in bed with me when that happens." Christopher climbed in and snuggled close.

"Lucky Christopher." He wished her a good night and hung up. She tucked the telephone back in its cradle on her bedside table.

"You love Jason, don't you?" Christopher pressed tight against her.

"More than anyone."

"More than Granny and Papa? More than Mom and Dad and me?"

"It's a different kind of love, Chris. It doesn't take love away from anyone else." She pushed down the palm tree of hair tickling her nose and kissed his head. "Now, go to sleep."

❄ ❄ ❄

On Thanksgiving Day, Granny and Papa arrived for the annual gathering. Mom and Granny acted like polite strangers. No one mentioned Oma. Before the table had even been set, Granny said she wanted to have the family come out to Jenner by the Sea for Christmas. Mom said she'd think about it. Granny said she had all the rooms ready and decorated. Mom and Mitch could have the downstairs apartment with Christopher in the small sitting room.

"I'll put a nice little tree downstairs with ornaments and lights." Dawn would have the blue bedroom upstairs, of course, just as she always did. Mom kept laying out silverware, not saying anything.

"Well, Carolyn?"

"I said I'd think about it."

"I know what that means." Granny stood by the table, fiddling with the silverware Mom had carefully laid out. "Why don't you ask Dawn what she wants to do?"

Dawn hated to be pulled into the middle of the argument. When Mom glanced at her, she winced. She didn't want to tell her grandmother she'd rather stay home. She knew Jason would be working extra hours over Christmas break, but she still wanted to be at home in case he had time to see her.

"It's not up to Dawn." Mom laid out the last set of silverware and left the dining room. Dawn heard her telephone. She'd turned the volume up on the ring so she wouldn't miss it. Excusing herself quickly, she ran down the hall, swinging her door shut before she grabbed the phone.

"Hello."

"You sound like you've been running," Jason said.

"It's crazy around here. Granny and Mom are circling one another with me right in the middle."

"We're going over to the Archers' for dinner."

Uh-oh. "Pastor Daniel probably wants a private talk with you."

"Why do you say that?"

"Because he talked to me last night after the meeting." Pastor Daniel had done a lot of talking about relationships over the last few youth group meetings. He said if anyone thought they were standing strong, they'd better be careful not to fall. Sometimes he'd look right at her when he talked. Last night, Pastor Daniel called her aside after the kids dispersed. Sharon cast a worried glance and said she'd wait in the car.

Pastor Daniel got right to the point. "Georgia tells me you and Jason are seeing a lot of each other."

Dawn felt her cheeks heating up. She had met Jason's mother only once. She'd sensed Georgia Steward didn't like her very much. "We see each other at school. That's about it." Pastor Daniel didn't say anything, but Dawn could tell he was waiting for more of a confession than that. "And we talk on the telephone." Clearly, he already knew that.

"My intention wasn't to upset you, Dawn."

"I'm not upset." What did he want her to say? "We haven't done anything wrong."

"I didn't say you had. You're members of our youth group, and I care about you both. I'll see you next week?"

She forced a smile. "Sure." She watched him walk away. His words had seemed bland enough, but she felt a stab of guilt. Hadn't he read last week that Jesus said thinking about sinning was tantamount to committing the sin? Well, then she sinned all the time! Not a day passed that she didn't wonder what it would be like to make love with Jason.

"What'd Pastor Daniel say?"

"He said he heard we were seeing each other. I got the impression he thinks I'm some kind of Delilah tempting Samson."

Jason didn't laugh. "Mom must have talked to him. She told me the other day she thinks I'm losing my focus."

"And that's my fault?"

"She didn't say that. She just reminded me that I have to keep my focus on where I want to be in five years. We've had this same conversation a hundred times before you and I started hanging out."

She could hear Jason's mother speaking in the background. "You need to get off the phone, Jason. We have to go. You can talk to her at school. . . ." *Yada, yada.*

"I've got to go, Dawn. Can I call you tomorrow?"

"I don't know." Her voice choked up. "*Can* you?" She hung up.

❄ ❄ ❄

Mom fixed turkey with all the trimmings, but Dawn didn't feel like eating. As soon as everyone finished, Mom started clearing platters. Mitch, Papa, and Christopher went into the family room to watch football. Granny stayed to help clear the table. "You've been quiet all evening."

"I just have a lot on my mind." Dawn stacked Villeroy & Boch dinner dishes and headed for the kitchen. She didn't feel like talking about Jason or his mother. She wondered if he was having a good time with Kim. His mother probably would have no problem with Jason going out with Pastor Daniel's daughter. Mom positioned herself at the sink so Granny couldn't step in and wash anything. The dishwasher door yawned, wide-open, from the wall on the other side.

Granny asked what she could do to help. Mom suggested she go relax with Papa and Mitch and Christopher; everything would be done in a few minutes.

"What about the pies? I could cut the pies," Granny insisted.

Dawn wanted to scream at both of them. Why couldn't Mom give in and Granny shut up?

The doorbell rang. Relieved, Dawn said she'd go, then fled the kitchen.

"Don't just open the door," Granny called after her. "Check the peephole first."

Jason stood on the front door stoop. He looked like a *GQ* model in his navy blue sports jacket and gray slacks. He'd loosened his tie and unbuttoned his shirt collar. Her insides knotted. He was clearly upset. "Jason." Her voice came out breathy. "I thought you were going to the Archers'."

"I did. I left." He stepped closer. "Dawn, I—"

"Ask him in." Mitch spoke from behind her. "Jason." He extended his hand in welcome. "Come on into the family room. Dawn's grandparents are visiting."

Jason winced. "I'm sorry. I didn't mean to interrupt your Thanksgiving. I should've called first."

"I'm glad you came," Dawn said quickly.

"We've already finished eating or we would've invited you to join us." Mitch put his hand on Jason's shoulder and half pushed him toward the family room. "Dawn? Are you coming? You can make the introductions."

Jason's arrival distracted Granny from trying to help Mom. Papa shook hands with him. Mitch told Jason to sit and relax. Dawn sat beside him, every nerve stretched tight while Papa asked questions like a police detective. Granny told him to stop interrogating the boy. Mitch seemed to be enjoying the scene. Mom came out of the kitchen and sat. She listened and watched, but didn't say anything.

Dawn gave Mitch a pleading look. How long did they have to sit and make small talk before they could escape and Jason could tell her why he had come?

Christopher provided the way when he insisted Jason had to see his latest LEGO creation. Thankful, Dawn followed and sat on Christopher's bed while Jason hunkered down and admired Christopher's castle and knights. Her little brother chattered on and on about King Arthur and Sir Lancelot, Galahad, Gawain, and Perceval. When Jason glanced at her, Dawn rolled her eyes. "Mom's reading him a book on the knights of the Round Table."

"You want to see it?" Christopher jumped up.

Jason straightened. "Maybe another time, Chris. I came to talk to your sister."

Dawn preceded him down the hall. "We can use the library." The double pocket doors were open. As Jason moved into the center of the room, she closed them quietly. He stood on the yellow and blue Aubusson rug. He glanced around at the mahogany bookcases with colorful amphoras and expensive American Indian pottery tucked in here and there. When he turned, his expression was pained. "I keep forgetting . . ."

She came toward him, drinking in the sight of him. He had left the Archers and his mother and driven all the way to Alexander Valley on Thanksgiving to see her. That had to mean something, didn't it? "Forgetting what?"

He shook his head. "It shouldn't matter, but it does." His gaze swept the room again, pointedly, and she understood.

"It *doesn't* matter." Dawn stood right in front of him. "I'm sorry I hung up on you." She lowered her voice. "I was upset."

"I know."

"Do you want to sit down?"

"No." He reached out, his hand sliding down her arm and taking hold of her hand. He toyed with her fingers. When she looked at him, he let go and stepped away. Sitting on the couch, he rested his forearms on his knees.

Dawn sat beside him. "What happened?" She put her hand on his arm.

"We weren't there five minutes before Pastor Daniel invited me into his office. When he closed the door, I knew something was up. He picked up right where Mom left off on our drive over, and I saw red. I asked if Mom had asked him to talk to me. He said she had concerns. He started talking about how he met his wife. I know all that. He didn't even date until he was a senior in college.

He met her in class and didn't ask her out until he'd asked around about her and knew she loved the Lord as much as he did. They didn't kiss until they were engaged. I didn't want to hear the whole story again." He raked his hands into his hair and held his head. "I lost it."

"What did you say?"

He looked at her bleakly. "I asked him whatever happened to trusting in the Lord, and then I left."

"What about your mother?"

"She's still there." He grimaced. "I can imagine what she's going to say." He came to his feet as though he couldn't bear to sit still any longer. "I've never done anything like that before. I don't know what's the matter with me. I'm going to have to go back and apologize." He stood at the window, looking out. "And if they find out I came here to see you, it's going to make things a hundred times worse."

His words hit like a punch to her stomach. "Oh." She closed her eyes tightly, fighting tears. "I guess they don't like me very much."

Jason turned around to face her again. "They're just trying to protect us."

"Not *us*, Jason." She blinked away tears. "*You*. They don't think I'm good enough."

Someone tapped on the door and slid one side open. Mitch held out the phone. "Your mother wants to speak with you, Jason."

Jason's face darkened as he took the telephone and walked over to the window again, facing out. Mitch pushed the pocket doors into the walls and motioned Dawn over. "Leave the doors open."

Dawn glared at him. "We're not doing anything!"

His gaze narrowed. "Maybe not, but emotions are running a little too high in here."

Jason came back and handed the telephone to Mitch. "Thanks, Mr. Hastings."

"Everything okay?"

"Just some things that need sorting out." Tense, angry, Jason said he had to leave. He apologized to Mitch for the interruption and went into the family room to say good-bye to Mom and tell Granny and Papa it was a pleasure meeting them. Frustrated and worried about whatever his mom had said, Dawn walked with him to the front door. "Will I see you at all this weekend?"

He took her hand. Out of sight of the others, he didn't pretend he wasn't upset. "I doubt it. I'll probably be grounded."

"And it's my fault."

"No, it isn't. This has been brewing for a long time. It's got nothing to do with you, Dawn." He leaned down and whispered, "Can I kiss you?" She said please. His mouth was firm and warm, moving tentatively over hers. When he straightened, she drew in a shaky breath. They stared at one another, and then he stepped closer and kissed her again. His arms slid around her, and she felt his heart pounding against hers. At the sound of footsteps, they broke apart, panting softly, shocked that their feelings could skyrocket so fast. He stared at her, eyes dark, face flushed. "I'll call you." He went quickly out the door, closing it behind him.

Dawn turned and found her mother standing in the archway. "Is everything all right?"

Heart pounding, body swimming with sensation, Dawn shrugged. "No. Not really." Not yet, anyway, but things were going to change. She felt ecstatic and triumphant. When Jason kissed her the second time, she knew his mother and Pastor Daniel wouldn't be able to keep them apart.

35

JASON DIDN'T CALL. She didn't see him until Monday morning at school. He'd gone back to the Archers' and apologized to everyone. When he and his mother got home, she exploded. Yes, he was grounded. For two weeks. No telephone privileges, no going anywhere with friends. *Friends*, Dawn knew, meant her.

Every morning when Dawn got off the bus, Jason stood waiting for her. They hung out under the maple trees along Prince Avenue before going to their lockers and on to class. They met as often as their schedules allowed. They sat alone together on the field during lunch hour, rather than eat with their friends. He never kissed her, but sometimes he held her hand when they walked around campus.

Dawn still attended youth group with Sharon on Wednesday evenings, but she barely paid attention to what Pastor Daniel had to say. She came to be with her friends, not listen to him lecture. Kim and Tom sat together, but didn't touch, and Kim still rode home with her father after the meetings while the rest of the kids, including Tom, met up at Taco Bell or McDonald's to talk for another hour or two. "Does Pastor Daniel know you and Kim are going out yet?" Steven Dial asked, stirring up trouble.

"Yeah, he knows." Tom shrugged. "He was pretty cool about it."

"Cool? How so?"

"He invited me to a baseball game. We spent most of the time talking."

Steven laughed. "You mean *he* talked."

"Not all the time. He asked me if I loved Kim. I said I did. He told me love between a man and woman can be a beautiful thing, but it's fragile, too. It only takes one mistake to turn life into a tangled mess." Everyone knew what he meant, though few believed him.

Two weeks felt like two years, but finally Jason's mother paroled him. Jason called Dawn that night. He called on breaks at work. He called when he got home, when he finished his homework. They often talked until after midnight. She worried about him. He seemed so tired all the time. She'd tell him not to call, to go to bed; she'd see him at school first thing in the morning. He said he liked hearing the sound of her voice just before he went to sleep, although sometimes they talked about things that kept them both awake long into the night.

Christmas break approached, and Dawn went shopping with Sharon, Amy, and Kim. Kim bought Tom a Bible and a silver chain and a cross made of nails. Dawn bought a gold identity bracelet with *Forever* engraved on it for Jason.

The day school let out for winter break, Jason drove her out on Dry Creek Road and parked in the empty visitors' center lot at the base of Warm Springs Dam. The skies opened up, rain pounding the roof of his Honda and sheets of water pouring over the windshield. He kept the car running and the heater on, though it wasn't necessary. The knowledge they were alone and the desire swimming in their bellies kept them warm. Eager to see if he liked his gift, she insisted he open hers first. As soon as he opened it, she took it from the box and attached it around his wrist. "So everyone will know you're mine."

Jason gave her a small white box tied with a red ribbon. He seemed nervous. "I hope you like it." She told him she'd love anything he gave her, but drew in a soft breath of pleasure when she saw a delicate gold bracelet coiled on the cotton. She touched the small heart and glistening white pearl. She asked him to put it on her wrist. As he did, she kept her gaze fixed upon his face. "I love it, Jason. I'll never take it off." When he raised his head, she leaned toward him, lips parted.

The windows steamed up. The rain pounded harder and faster, as though trying to keep pace with their hearts. Murmuring his name, she clutched his shirt. He pressed her back against the seat. She wanted him closer. Pushing his jacket open, she slipped one hand beneath his sweater. She felt the smooth skin of his back, the hard muscle from lifting boxes of canned goods. His hand went under her thigh, gripping, sliding her down on the seat. She gave a soft cry as her head bumped hard against the armrest. Jason pulled back abruptly. "Are you okay?"

"Yes." Her voice came out raspy. She rubbed her head as he pulled her back up.

"I'm sorry."

"Don't be." When she leaned toward him again, he drew back.

"We've got to stop." He shifted over and shut his eyes tightly, then opened them again, face taut. "We'd better go."

"We were only kissing, Jason. There's nothing wrong with that, is there?"

"No, but I wanted more."

Swallowing hard, pulse pounding, she looked straight into his eyes. "I wouldn't have stopped you."

"That's why we have to leave." He released the emergency brake and put the car into reverse.

She pressed the heels of her hands against her eyes and gulped a sob.

Jason stopped, rammed on the emergency brake, and put his arms around her. "Don't cry. It's my fault. I shouldn't have brought you out here. It's my fault things got out of hand." He tipped her chin and kissed her softly. "I'm sorry, Dawn. I won't let it happen again."

She believed him, which only hurt and frustrated her more. "You're good all the time, Jason. All the time you're good. And all I want is you."

Jason touched her arm gently. "It isn't what God wants for us, Dawn."

God again. "Sometimes you talk as though He's in the backseat."

"He's closer than that. He's inside us."

Us. Maybe that was the real problem. The Holy Spirit did live inside Jason. She had no doubt about that.

But she wondered . . . what about her?

❄ ❄ ❄

Granny called, trying to wear Mom down about having the family Christmas dinner at Jenner by the Sea. Failing, Granny called Mitch at his office. Dawn arrived in time to overhear the end of the conversation. "I'll talk to her, Hildie. Sure, I understand, but . . ." He rubbed his forehead. Dawn slipped into the chair in front of his desk, mouthed *no*, and shook her head. "What's wrong with Trip? If it's serious, Carolyn is going to insist you two come in." He gave Dawn a pained look. Dawn leaned forward. Mitch shook his head and mouthed, *He's okay.* She put her head back against the red leather wing chair. Just Granny applying the emotional screws again. "Let me talk to her. If she agrees, she'll call you. Okay? That's the most I can promise. I love you, too."

Hanging up, Mitch gave her a wry grin. "And how was your day?"

"Are we going to Jenner for Christmas?"

"You heard what I said. Maybe. We'll see. It's up to your mother."

"Then we'll be going. I'm surprised she's held out this long."

"You don't look pleased about it."

"What's wrong with Papa?"

"He doesn't feel up to driving in and spending a few days in Alexander Valley. He wants to stay home."

Dawn went into her bedroom and dumped her backpack. Flinging herself onto her bed, she stared at the ceiling. Jason had hoped to take her out over break, but it all depended on his work schedule and what plans his mother made.

Mitch had probably told Mom about Granny's call by now. She decided to go to the kitchen, hoping to encourage her mother to hold her ground and insist Granny and Papa come in this year.

"Well, at least, let me bring something. . . ." Mom was on the phone, perched on a kitchen table, knees together, feet up like a little girl.

So much for that idea. Dawn returned to her room and threw herself across the bed again.

Mom announced at dinner that they'd be going to Jenner by the Sea for Christmas Eve dinner. "She wants to serve dinner at six instead of four."

"Then we'll stay over," Mitch decided. "It'll be after ten before we finish unwrapping presents. No point in driving back in the dark on a windy road with the weather such as it is."

"With the weather such as it is, they should come in," Dawn said. "You know how Jenner gets this time of year. If there's a real storm, we could end up stuck out there."

"Too late, Pita." Mitch gave her a cajoling smile. "Your mom agreed, and rightfully so. Granny said this is probably the last year she'll have the family gathering, and she has her heart set on it." He looked across at Mom. "She'll pass you the baton."

"Did she say that?" Mom sounded hopeful.

"Not exactly, but it's only a matter of time."

"It's not about time, Mitch." Mom looked defeated. She glanced at Dawn. "You'd better pack extra clothes. They'll want you to stay through New Year's."

Dawn's heart sank. "Maybe Christopher could stay this time."

"No, Christopher can't. Besides, you haven't spent a weekend out there in over two months."

Before Dawn could protest, Mitch spoke up. "If Jason wants to see you badly enough, he'll drive out."

❄ ❄ ❄

Christmas went exactly as Dawn expected. When Mom tried to help, Granny acted like a pit bull guarding her territory. Only Dawn was allowed into the kitchen "so she'll know what to do when she has a home of her own." Sometimes Dawn wondered if Granny just wanted Mom out of the way and things back to the way they used to be when she was a little girl and Granny was her nanny.

After hours of labor, dinner disappeared in less than thirty minutes. Mom insisted on doing the dishes. "You cooked; I clean." It started to turn into an argument before Papa and Mitch stepped in. Mitch said he'd help, and they'd open gifts when the dishes were washed and put away.

Papa took Granny by the arm and escorted her into the living room, where she sat nervous as a cat, staring at the closed door to the kitchen. She couldn't stand to be idle. Papa told her to put on one of her old Christmas movies. "How about *Ben-Hur*?" Dawn suggested, knowing it was one of her favorites.

"There's no time for *Ben-Hur*," Papa grumbled.

"How about *How the Grinch Stole Christmas*?" Christopher piped up.

"We don't have that one," Granny said.

"How about *A Christmas Story*?" Christopher tried again. "The one where the boy wants a rifle."

"A BB gun," Dawn corrected him.

"We don't have that one either," Granny said.

"How about *Hatari*?" Papa said. "We have *Hatari*."

"It's not a Christmas story."

When Papa put his head back and let out a heavy sigh, Granny got up. "We can have some nice Christmas music."

Things eased up after Mom and Mitch came into the living

room. Mom looked more relaxed. Mitch held her hand. When
they sat on the couch, he put his arm around her and pulled her in
tight against him. Christopher played elf and passed out the presents. Papa put out a big box so they could wad up wrapping paper
and "shoot baskets." Christopher pleaded to camp out in the living
room so he could enjoy the colorful Christmas lights on the tree
and the fire burning low in the fireplace. Mitch thought that was
a grand idea and whispered something in Mom's ear that made her
blush.

"How's Santa going to come if you're here in the living room?"
Papa teased Christopher.

"He's not coming. We already opened all the presents."
Christopher grinned. "Besides, Papa, how'd he get down your
chimney with a fire burning?"

They all laughed, even Granny, who sat with the robin's-egg
blue velvet robe with embroidered trim Mom had given her. She
kept stroking it.

Mitch stood, drawing Mom up with him, and bid everyone
good night. Granny smiled and nodded and told them to feel free
to sleep in the following morning, then watched Mom leave the
room, a pained and wistful look on her face.

Long after Granny and Papa had gone to bed and Christopher
had settled down in a sleeping bag on the living room floor, Dawn
lay awake.

Jason didn't call.

❄ ❄ ❄

Mom, Mitch, and Christopher piled everything into the Suburban
and headed home after breakfast the next morning, leaving Dawn
at Jenner with Granny and Papa. "We're going to have such a good
time together," Granny promised, and Dawn didn't want to disap-
point her. While Papa dozed in front of the television, Granny
made an angel food cake. Dawn sat at the kitchen table and talked
about Jason. She showed off the bracelet he'd given her, though

she left out personal details of what had happened during their gift exchange.

"Your first love." Granny smiled. "It's a milestone."

"He's my last love, too, Granny."

"That's the way it was for me and Papa. He was the first man I dated and the only one I've ever loved." She slid the angel food cake into the oven. "I think it was that way with Oma, too. Fidelity must run in the family, just skipped one generation."

Dawn recognized the reference to Mom's hippy years and ignored it. "What was Opa like?"

Granny sat across from her. "He was grand. Tall, blond, handsome. He was at least a head taller than Mama. And strong as Atlas. I remember him lifting me as though I didn't weigh more than a feather. He worked hard. So did Mama, of course, but my father enjoyed life more. He didn't allow things to worry him the way Mama did. He sang in the orchard. My mother never sang, except in church. And he had the patience of Job, especially with Mama. She'd get so het up about things, had to have her way."

Dawn held back a smile, thinking Granny could fit that description, not that she'd like hearing it. "Do you have any pictures of him?"

"Just a couple. There's one in the bedroom on my dresser. They had it taken before Bernie went away to college. Bernie had copies made later on. Photographs were expensive in those days, and they never had a lot of money to spare. Rikka drew pictures of Papa and Mama and had them framed. They're probably in one of the storage boxes out in the garage."

Dawn followed Granny into the bedroom later while she put some towels away. She picked up the portrait and sat on her grandparents' old king bed to study it. Oma, with dark hair cut short and pushed back from her plain face, stood straight, shoulders back, chin up, eyes straight ahead, lips curved into a taut smile. She stared straight into the camera lens, expression grim, as though having her picture taken was the last thing she wanted to do. Opa, on the other hand, looked at ease, a relaxed smile on his lips.

Strikingly handsome in a dark suit, white shirt, and tie, he stood with one shoulder behind Oma, his head tilted toward her. Dawn imagined he had his arm around her waist, holding her in place. "Opa was sure handsome."

"Blond hair and blue eyes." Granny tucked away the towels and came out of the pink- and black-tiled bathroom. She took the picture and studied it with a smile. "Bernie got his looks. All the girls at school fell in love with him. Cloe and Rikka got his coloring, too." She set the picture firmly on her dresser. "I took after Mama."

36

Jason called two days after Christmas. "We just got back from LA." When she asked if he'd gone to Hollywood or down to Disneyland, he said no. His mom wanted him to walk the campuses at UCLA and USC and Pepperdine.

"I thought she wanted you to go to Berkeley."

"We're not talking about Berkeley anymore." He changed the subject before she could ask why. "When are you coming home?"

"New Year's Day." She turned her back on Granny when she came into the kitchen. She lowered her voice. "I miss you, Jason."

"Would your grandparents mind if I came out to see you?"

Heart singing, she told Granny and Papa her boyfriend was coming for a visit. She was so excited she couldn't sit still. She changed from sweats to fitted jeans and a pink sweater. She put on a touch of makeup. Maybe they could visit with Granny and Papa for a little while and then go over to the beach.

How long before he got there? It only took forty minutes and it had been forty-five. She sat at the kitchen table watching cars come around the bend before crossing to tiny Bridgehaven with its trailer park—flooded now—two-room motel, and restaurant overlooking the river.

The rain started again. So much for taking a walk on the beach.

An hour passed, and then another. "Road might be closed," Papa told her while eating a sandwich at the kitchen table. "Aren't many places to stop and call."

Finally, she spotted his car zinging along Highway 1. When the car slowed through Jenner and turned right onto Willig, she darted out the back door to unlatch the gate. Swinging it open, she stayed under the wooden cover and watched him park. Heart knocking, she smiled as he got out of the car. "I was worried you got stuck somewhere!"

"I didn't want to come empty-handed." He leaned back into the car, sweater stretching taut over his shoulders, jeans snug, and lifted out a cellophane-wrapped potted poinsettia and box of Russell Stover chocolates. When she reached for the chocolates, he drew them back and grinned at her. "For your grandparents, not for you." She laughed. He looked toward the house and then leaned down to brush a kiss against her cheek. "Not sure I can stay long. There were a lot of fallen limbs on the road, and water just after Guerneville."

"If the road closes, you can always stay over."

"I don't think my mom would go for that idea."

The sky opened up, rain pounding the roof and streaking down over the living room windows. Papa said he'd better go down and get some presto logs out from under the garage in case the power went off. Jason insisted he'd take care of it. "Nice young man," Papa said.

"And handsome, too," Granny added. Dawn felt smug. At least she had her family's approval.

Granny suggested an early afternoon dinner "so Jason can eat before he heads home." Jason became so engrossed in Papa's World War II stories that Dawn went into the kitchen to help Granny make a tossed green salad and a casserole of turkey, dressing, and gravy. They all sat to eat at three. By four, the sky had darkened.

The rain hadn't let up. Jason gave Dawn an apologetic look and said he'd better go. Papa said he'd better call highway patrol first and see if the road was open through Guerneville.

It wasn't. Papa said Jason would have to take the road south through Bodega and go back through Sebastopol in order to get the highway north to Windsor.

Granny protested. "It's dark. And that's too far to go in driving rain, especially if you aren't familiar with the coast highway. Jason should stay here with us." She suggested he call his mom so she wouldn't worry. Dawn suggested Granny go on into the living room with Papa and let her take care of washing the dishes. For once, Granny didn't quibble. Maybe she understood how desperately Dawn wanted to be alone with Jason, even if only for a few minutes, before his mother insisted he get back in his car and come home no matter how bad the weather.

Jason sighed. "She'll be ticked off."

"It's not like you started the storm, Jason."

"No, but she told me it was a bad idea coming out here."

Dawn wondered if she'd been talking about the weather or seeing her. Jason punched in the numbers. His mother must have been sitting by the telephone because it barely had time to ring before Jason said, "Hi, Mom."

Dawn squirted dish soap into the old porcelain sink, turned on the hot water, and pretended not to listen.

"The road's closed. I'm going to have to stay out here." He listened briefly. "It'd take two hours to go that way, and I only have half a tank of gas. . . ." Jason turned away. Elbows on knees, shoulders tense, he hunched over the receiver and growled. "Jeez louise, Mom, would you rather I ended up over a cliff in the ocean—"

Apparently his mother cut him off. Dawn added some cold to the hot and grabbed one of the glasses.

"Nice to know how much you trust me." Jason grew more angry. "We're not alone out here, Mom. *Both* of Dawn's grandparents are with us, and it's a small house. Two chaperones. Is that good enough?" He listened for another few seconds. "Okay. I'm sorry, but—" He sat up and let out a steamed breath. "Yeah, I hear you. First thing in the morning. Okay, okay. Yes! I'll drive south if the roads are still closed. I promise." He hung up. His expression looked faintly triumphant. "Need some help with those dishes?"

"Sure." She smiled. He'd be here all night! "The towels are in that drawer." When he stepped close beside her, she looked up, melting inside. He told her how much he liked her grandfather as he dried glasses and then silverware, asking where things went. Dawn daydreamed. Someday, when they got married, they'd stand like this every night and do dishes together.

They'd just finished putting everything away when Granny came into the kitchen with a pile of burgundy sheets, a pillowcase, and flannel pajamas. "Here's an extra pair of Papa's pajamas for you, Jason, and Dawn can make up the bed downstairs."

Jason looked blank. "Downstairs?"

"The apartment. There's an electric blanket on the bed, but we'll keep the heat on so you don't get too cold. You'll be snug as a bug down there."

"Please don't go to any trouble. I can sleep on the couch."

"Nonsense." Granny dumped the pile into Dawn's waiting arms. "We like our guests to be comfortable." She went back into the living room.

Dawn headed for the back door. "Come on. I'll show you where you'll be." He opened the door for her as she called out to her grandparents that they would be back in a few minutes.

The frosty air of the downstairs apartment struck Dawn as she stepped inside. Jason followed her. Mom had folded up the hide-a-bed—Chris hadn't slept in it anyway—and put the coffee table back. Granny's small writing desk sat in the corner. A Victorian lounge chair sat in the back room facing the stripped queen-size bed. Mom had left the thermal and electric blankets and blue chenille spread folded neatly across the end. Jason straddled the flowery lounge and watched Dawn shake out the bottom flannel sheet. She worked quickly. "You look like you know how to make a bed."

She laughed, excited to have him here, even more excited at

the thought of him sleeping just down the stairs from her room. "Granny taught me how to do square corners. She was a nurse." Shaking out the top sheet, she glanced at him and saw something in his expression that made her breath catch.

She unfolded the electric blanket, making sure it was plugged in properly, before spreading it over the burgundy sheets. Dawn didn't notice any cold air now, and no warm air blasted yet from the heating vent. Jason got up and helped spread the thermal blanket over the top. They didn't speak. Pillowcase fitted, she plumped the pillow, pulled the bedspread up, and tucked it neatly under.

They stood on opposite sides of the bed, staring at one another.

Jason came around the side of the bed and took her hand. "Can I kiss you again?"

Trembling, she looked at him. "I wish you would."

Tilting his head toward her, he whispered, "I was afraid your grandparents might get the wrong idea. . . ." When his mouth covered hers, she stepped closer, putting her arms around his neck and pressing her body fully and firmly against him. His soft groan lit a fire inside her. His hands moved down her back to her waist and hips and then up again, encircling her tightly. He dragged his mouth away. "I don't think I'm going to get much sleep down here. I'll be lying awake, staring at the ceiling, knowing you're right above me." When he kissed her again, she fitted her body to his and heard his sharp intake of breath. They were both shaking when Jason finally set her away from him. "We'd better go upstairs before your grandparents wonder what's going on down here."

Granny and Papa stayed up later than usual. When Papa pushed himself out of his recliner and said it was time to hit the sack, Jason stood and said he'd better go to bed, too, and thank you for everything. Dawn said good night to him from the couch and watched him go out the back door. He glanced back at her through the glass before heading for the wooden steps to the downstairs. Granny paused in the bedroom doorway and looked at her. "Are you staying up, Dawn?"

"I'm not sleepy yet. I thought I'd watch television for a while."

"Turn down the thermostat when you go to bed." Granny wished her a good night and closed the French glass doors with their sheer privacy curtains. Dawn pulled a crocheted afghan around her shoulders. She lowered the volume and changed the channel. She heard Papa's loud snores. He always fell asleep the moment his head hit the pillow. It wasn't long before Granny made it a duet. Dawn waited another fifteen minutes before turning off the television and resetting the thermostat. She took a quick shower and slipped on her nightgown. Pulling the covers back, she rumpled them and stuffed two pillows underneath in the off chance Granny awakened and felt the need to look in on her.

She closed the accordion doors before carefully opening the back door. She made sure it was unlocked before quietly closing it behind her. Then she hurried tiptoe down the wooden steps, feeling the icy drops of rain soaking through her cotton gown. A soft light shone above the apartment door. She hesitated. Then, shivering with cold, she pushed the door open. Her heart lurched as it creaked. As she stepped inside the door, Jason turned on the bedside light. "What are you doing?" Throwing the covers off, he got out of bed.

Jason looked so comical in Grandpa's pajamas, Dawn giggled nervously. "I couldn't sleep."

"Shhh. . . . You'd better go before they—"

"Listen!" she whispered, pointing up. Papa snored so loudly, they could hear him downstairs. She grinned at him. "They both sleep like logs. They won't know a thing."

"You're shivering." He put his arms around her. "You're wet!"

"It's raining." She inhaled his scent. It went right to her head. "I'm freezing." She shivered, loving the feel of his arms around her. His heart pounded harder. "I'd be warmer in bed."

"Not a good idea."

"We won't do anything." She slipped her arms around him. "We'll just talk."

Beneath the covers, Jason held her close and asked if she was warm enough. She said no and snuggled closer, pressing her body against the length of his. She heard his breath quicken. They did talk, for a little while. Then they kissed. Heating up fast, they had to push the covers off. Niggling doubts flitted into Dawn's mind as passion grew.

Fear gripped her at the last. Too late. She sucked in her breath at the unexpected pain. Jason stopped, rasping an apology. She said, "It's okay; it's okay." They both knew it wasn't. Worse, they couldn't go back.

This wasn't how she imagined it would be.

When it was all over, Jason sat on the edge of the bed, head in his hands. Dawn pulled the blankets up to her chin. Silent, rigid, eyes welling, she felt sick with regret. What had she done?

Jason was silent so long, she felt driven to speak. "I love you." That's why she'd done it. "I love you, Jason." She sounded like a frightened child afraid of being chastised.

"I love you, too." Jason's voice was thick with tears. And regret.

Ashamed, Dawn shoved the covers off and fled to the door. Jason caught up with her and wrapped his arms around her. Pulling her firmly against him, he whispered against her hair, "It's my fault." He drew in a ragged breath. "I should've gone home."

Hurt by his remorse, ashamed of her own behavior, she spoke tersely, voice breaking. "I wish you had."

❄ ❄ ❄

Of course, Granny insisted Jason have breakfast before he left. Jason glanced at her once when she came out of her bedroom. He had dark shadows under his eyes, as though he hadn't slept any better than she had. Dawn could tell it took concentrated effort for Jason to smile and act normal, to talk with her grandparents as though nothing had happened last night.

Sitting there at the table, Granny and Papa chattering away, Jason giving distracted answers, she kept thinking, *I had sex with Jason downstairs last night in the bed Mom and Mitch slept in a few days ago. Granny and Papa were right upstairs. They all trust me. They respect Jason. What would they think of us now if they knew?* She felt cold prickles along her arms. What if Jason confessed what they'd done to Pastor Daniel? What if he told Tom Barrett and Tom told Kim?

She hadn't expected to feel sick with guilt and shame. She knew Jason felt even worse than she did. He didn't hurry, but he didn't linger over breakfast the way he might have if she'd stayed in her own bedroom last night.

"I'd better get going." Jason said his good-byes and thank-yous. Dawn followed him out to his car. She stood under the overhang, arms wrapped around herself, afraid of what he might say. Jason gave her the same chaste peck on the cheek that he had when he arrived yesterday. Only his eyes looked different. "The sheets are . . ." He winced. "They're going to know."

Dawn's face went hot. "I'll strip the bed and wash them." Thank goodness Granny had given her burgundy sheets rather than white ones, or she'd never be able to wash away their sin.

Sin!

Shocked, Dawn felt the word stab her heart like a spear, leaving her wounded. *We sinned. I sinned.*

"I'm sorry, Jason." She pressed her lips together, tears spilling from her eyes.

He stepped close, his hand at her waist as he whispered into her ear. "I love you. Nothing's going to change that."

But something already had.

37

1987

Dawn didn't hear from or see Jason until school started again. He stood waiting when the bus pulled in and fell into step beside her as she headed inside to her locker. "We have to talk."

"You could've called." Hurt, angry, she walked on.

"I couldn't. Mom and I had a big fight when I got home."

The blood drained from her head, and she felt faint with fear. "Did you tell her?"

"No." Glancing around, he leaned closer while she worked the combination and opened her locker. "How long before we know if you're . . . ?" She could feel his embarrassment. She looked at him and let him see her fear and hurt, and he frowned. "Things will work out." When Jason took her hand, she wove her fingers through his and held tight, afraid he'd fall out of love with her as quickly as she had fallen in love with him.

Every day, he gave her that questioning look, and she shook her head. After three weeks had passed, he said he'd try to get a home pregnancy test. "I might not be able to buy one this week. Bill is working the same shift I am, and if he sees, he'll say something to Mom." Agitated, he raked a hand through his hair.

Mom awakened Dawn Saturday morning. "Your grandparents are going to be here in an hour."

Dawn sat up and rubbed her eyes.

"Are you all right?"

Fear shot through her. Did her mother know? Had she some extrasensory perception that she could guess? "I'm fine."

She showered, dressed, and threw her hair into a ponytail. A car honked loudly, and she drew back the sheer curtains. Granny and Papa had arrived in separate cars, Papa in a white Buick and Granny in their shiny black Sable. When Dawn opened the front door, Granny dangled the keys. "The Sable is all yours."

Papa grinned. "Happy sixteenth birthday!"

"What?" Dawn stared. "You're kidding, aren't you?"

"Of course not." Granny took her limp hand and dropped the keys into it, closing Dawn's fingers around them. "We wouldn't kid about something like that."

Dawn shrieked and threw her arms around Granny and then Papa. "Thank you, thank you!"

Mitch, Christopher, and Mom appeared and asked what was going on. Dawn darted out the door and ran her hands over the freshly polished Sable. "They said it's mine!" she called back, happy for the first time in weeks. "I have wheels!"

Mom's eyes widened. "You should've talked to me about it first."

Granny scowled. "We're doing it as much for you as for Dawn, Carolyn. You have Christopher in sports and music lessons and church group. Dawn can't take a bus everywhere, you know. She needs a car. Now she has one."

Mom's face reddened. "It's not for you to make that decision." She turned to Mitch, who stood beside her. He looked grim.

Dawn came back, wanting the freedom the car offered. "You won't have to drive me to Jenner, Mom. I can drive out all by myself."

Granny beamed. Papa patted Dawn's shoulder. "Everything's been checked out. It's a good car, Carolyn."

"I know, Dad. That's not—"

"That little baby won't need any repairs for a long time to come. All the paperwork is in the glove compartment, Dawn. This car will run for another hundred thousand miles easily. You won't find a better used car anywhere, and it gets good gas mileage."

"It's beautiful, Papa." She kissed his cheek and embraced her grandmother. "I love it."

Mom headed for the house. Granny's expression soured. "Oh, for heaven's sake, Carolyn . . ." She stepped around Dawn and went after her.

Papa looked worried now. "Maybe we did get a little ahead of ourselves."

"Yeah," Mitch said solemnly. "You did. But it's too late now to take it back, isn't it?"

Dreading the argument she knew was brewing, Dawn went to the kitchen. Granny stood with her hands gripping the back of a kitchen chair, making her case, while Mom stood, back to her, at the sink peeling potatoes. "I'm sorry if I've done something wrong." Granny sounded exasperated, not sorry.

"Can I say something?" Dawn pleaded. The swelling fear of the last three weeks made her feel even more vulnerable when Granny and Mom were at odds. "I really, really want the car, Mom, but I won't even ask to drive it until after I have my license and you and Mitch are both satisfied that I'm a safe driver."

Mom turned slowly and studied her. "What about insurance and gas?"

"We'll pay for her insurance and give her an allowance, since it seems you won't."

Spots of pink bloomed in Mom's cheeks. "No, we won't, and you won't either." She blinked as she said it, as though surprising herself. Granny's lips parted.

Things were going from bad to worse, and Dawn knew she was in the middle of the battlefield. "I have some savings, Granny, and

I can get a part-time job after school at Java Joe's." At Granny's blank expression, she added, "It's a coffee shop near the square." She looked between them. "It'd be fun. It'd be good for me."

"We'll talk about it later, Dawn." Mom turned her back to both of them and resumed peeling potatoes.

Granny pulled the chair out and wilted into it. "I should've asked first. I'm sorry, Dawn, but maybe . . ."

Mom put her hands on the sink. "Dawn can keep the car." She sounded tired and defeated.

Dawn stood between the two women she loved most in the world and wanted to weep. Oma suddenly popped into her mind like a specter. "Wouldn't it be nice if we all had tea?" Oma had said the same thing every day when she and Mom visited her in Merced. Mom turned toward her. Face crumpling, she muttered a soft excuse and left the kitchen.

"She hasn't gotten over Oma yet." Dawn spoke into the silence.

Granny's shoulders drooped. "I don't think she ever will."

Mitch and Papa and Christopher carried the conversation through dinner. When Mom got up to clear the table, Mitch suggested they all go into the family room. Papa kept glancing at Granny, who sat silent and distracted. Mom called everyone into the kitchen. She had set out a sheet cake decorated with pink flowers and *Happy 16th Birthday, May Flower Dawn* written in white across the icing. "Chocolate!" Dawn forced a brightness into her voice that she didn't feel. "My favorite." She smiled at her mother and thanked her. She felt Mitch squeeze her shoulder.

Leaning down, he kissed her cheek the way Jason had the morning before Dawn changed everything between them. "You're growing up, Dawn."

Maybe more than he could even imagine.

She opened Christopher's gift first and raised her brows at him. "A soccer ball? Are you sure this is for me?"

"You played really, really well." He grinned impishly. "You can teach me."

"Thanks, sport." She ruffled his hair and gave him a hard hug.

Mom and Mitch gave her a pearl necklace and pearl stud earrings. "Pearls for innocence." Dawn felt Mitch's hand on her shoulder.

Her mother spoke from across the table. "They're also a rite of passage into womanhood."

Dawn couldn't raise her head for fear of what they might see in her face. She wasn't innocent anymore, and she didn't feel like a woman either. She touched the luminous pearls and swallowed the tears gathering and almost choking her. "They're beautiful. Thank you."

She lay in bed that night crying softly, silently confessing her sin and pleading with God that no baby had been made. Startled, she heard a tap on the door, and Mom came in. She sat on the end of Dawn's bed. "What's wrong, Dawn? Are you upset because Jason didn't remember your birthday?"

"I didn't tell him." She'd forgotten all about it. Her mind had been too filled with worries and fears to think about anything else.

"Do you want to talk about what's bothering you? You haven't been yourself for the last few weeks."

"I'm okay." *One lie.* "I just feel so stirred up all the time." *True.* "I don't know what's wrong with me." *Another lie.* They didn't come as easily after she'd just been begging God for mercy.

"I'm just worrying about the future." That was true, at least. She wanted to bury her head in the pillow again and sob, but she couldn't do that with her mother sitting so close. Dawn felt her mother's hand through the blanket.

"You won't turn eighteen for another two years. You have plenty of time to make decisions."

Dawn gave a hoarse laugh. "I know." She'd already made one. A bad one.

Her mother squeezed her foot. "You can talk to me, you know." She waited a moment. "About anything." She waited again. Minutes passed. She let out a soft sigh and got up. "Good night, May Flower Dawn." She stood at the open doorway. "If you can't talk to me, you know you can always go to Granny." She closed the door quietly behind her.

After two more days of feverish prayers of repentance and promises of chastity and obedience, God answered her prayers.

Jason met her at the bus stop the next morning. His mouth curved in an uncertain smile. "Everything okay?"

"Everything is perfect!"

For the first time, Jason kissed her there in front of everyone. He took her hand as they walked into school together, both forgetting the door they had opened and the untamed beast that now prowled loose.

❄ ❄ ❄

Mitch and Mom thought it would be a good idea if she got a part-time job. Java Joe's manager, Dennis Bingley, didn't even ask her to fill out an application, but hired her on the spot. "The boys will be lining up for coffee when they see you." She worked Monday through Friday afternoons from three to five. Jason drove her downtown, bought one coffee, and stationed himself at one of the small tables tucked in a back corner, where he did homework until four thirty. Boys did line up, but she didn't pay any attention. Whenever she cleared and cleaned a table, she'd stop by Jason's. Mitch picked Dawn up on his way home.

After six weeks, and hours of practice driving with Mitch, Dawn felt ready to face the DMV test. She passed with flying colors and drove the Sable home. Mom told her over dinner that night she could drive the car to school. Dawn said she'd take turns with Sharon driving to youth group, but she wanted to continue riding the bus to school. That way, she'd save money for the next insurance premium as well as gas.

"And Jason will still give you a ride to work." Mitch gave her a smirk that said she wasn't fooling anyone. She conceded that was part of her reasoning.

The first Saturday after she gained driving privileges, she drove to the Windsor Trailer Park. The double-wide looked old, but well-tended, with potted flowers on a small deck with green- and white-striped awning and a pebble driveway, where Jason's Honda was parked. Jason, dressed in sweatpants and a sleeveless T-shirt, opened the door before she even knocked. He came out barefoot and admired her car. An elderly lady opened her screen door just across the way. "A friend of yours, Jason?"

"Study partner," he called back. "How are you doing this morning, Mrs. Edwards?"

"Can't complain." She sat in a rocker on her little porch.

Jason opened the front door, and Dawn entered a carpeted living room with a worn green plaid couch, two matching chairs, and a coffee table facing a small television on an old cabinet. Beige drapes and sheers let a shaft of light through the front window.

"It must feel claustrophobic to you," Jason said grimly.

"It's cozy. Comfortable."

A small Early American table with two chairs was cluttered with books, an open binder, and papers. "You're studying."

"Every spare minute." He drew her into his arms. "I needed a break." He kissed her. One gentle, tentative kiss led to another and another.

Breathless, she began to worry. "Where's your mom?"

"Working. Until noon."

"Maybe I should go." When he didn't let go, she wondered if she had said the words aloud or just thought them. He asked if she wanted to see his room. Of course, she did. Things quickly got out of hand, not that either tried to stop, not until someone rapped on the door. Jason pulled away and got off the bed. "It's probably Mrs. Edwards." Another rap sounded, louder this time. "If I don't answer, she's going to think something's going on."

Think something is going on? Dawn wanted to laugh hysterically. "Wait!" She ducked into the bathroom and leaned against the door. Adjusting her clothing, she raked fingers through her hair. She could hear Mrs. Edwards.

"I don't think your mother would want a girl here when she's not."

Jason said they were just talking. "Then where is she? I don't see her sitting on the sofa."

Dawn flushed the toilet and ran the water noisily before stepping out of the bathroom. She pretended surprise. "Oh, hi." Mrs. Edwards muttered something to Jason and went down the steps. "What'd she say?"

He gave a brief laugh. "She told me I'd better behave myself."

Blushing, Dawn shrugged her purse onto her shoulder. Neither one of them had been doing a good job of that lately. "I'd better go."

Jason walked her to her car. He said he wished she wouldn't go. They stood and talked awhile. Mrs. Edwards sat in her rocker watching them. Jason asked if Dawn was planning to go on the mission trip to Mexico. She said she was and had already gotten the financial backing she needed from Mom and Mitch and her grandparents. "Plus I'm putting in some of my own money," she added, proud of herself. "What about you?" He said he wasn't sure yet, but he hoped so. Before Dawn got into her car, she waved at Mrs. Edwards and said it was nice meeting her.

The following Saturday, Dawn brought her backpack full of books, and they did study, for a little while. She left an hour before Georgia Steward was due home. The Saturday after that, they didn't even bother to open a book.

38

THE NEXT SATURDAY, Georgia Steward's white van with *Georgia's Housekeeping Services* painted in red on the side was parked behind Jason's white Honda. Disappointed, Dawn figured she and Jason would just have to study today. At least they'd be together. Grabbing her book bag, Dawn slid out of her Sable. Mrs. Edwards wasn't sitting on the porch this morning, but movement in the front curtains told Dawn the old lady was still watching. Annoyed, Dawn went up the steps and tapped at the door, expecting Jason to answer. His mother opened the door. "Hello, Dawn."

"Hi." Dawn plastered a smile on her face despite the cool look on Georgia's. "I'm here to study with Jason."

"Come in." Georgia opened the door all the way. The drapes had been pulled back, allowing sunlight to stream in. Jason's bedroom door was wide-open. She had seen his car in the drive-way. Where was he? "Have a seat." Georgia closed the front door.

Dawn felt her body tense. She put her book bag down and took a seat at the table. "Where's Jason?"

Georgia sat across from her and folded her hands. "He's gone for the day."

"Gone?" Dawn's heart pounded in alarm. Why hadn't he called her? She felt increasingly uncomfortable under his mother's scrutiny.

"He and Pastor Daniel took a little fishing trip. He didn't know he was going until early this morning."

Dawn felt the urge to take flight. "I should go then." She reached for her book bag.

"Not yet." Georgia's tone was firmer this time, colder.

Leaving the book bag on the floor, Dawn eased back into the seat, knees trembling beneath the table. "Is something wrong?"

Georgia's expression turned to one of disdain. "You could say that, couldn't you?" Her knuckles whitened. "I knew what was going on between the two of you when Jason came home from Jenner. He couldn't look me in the eye. I watched him sweat for a month and thought maybe the two of you had learned your lesson. And then Mrs. Edwards told me yesterday that you've been coming over every Saturday . . . to study."

"We do study."

Georgia reached into her pocket and put a crumpled, empty condom wrapper on the table between them.

Dawn felt all the blood draining from her face. She met Georgia's glare. "I love him. And he loves me."

Georgia's face flushed. Her brown eyes grew hotter. "You don't know anything about love! You're a spoiled, self-centered little girl who wants what she wants and wants it *now*." She leaned forward. "Your *love* has single-handedly ruined most of Jason's chances to escape this trailer park. His grades have dropped. He no longer has the qualifications to get into UC Berkeley—or get a full scholarship to Stanford. He spent most of his savings buying that car so he could take you out. He hardly reads his Bible anymore, and his relationship with God used to be *the most important thing in his life*!"

Dawn flinched as Georgia stood abruptly and stepped away from the table. After a moment, she continued in a taut, restrained tone. "If you get pregnant, Jason will do the right thing. But I'd like to give you a picture of what your lives will be like if that should happen." She sat again, more in control, eyes like black ice.

"Jason will have to give up all his dreams of college. He'll have to find a job to support you and your baby. And what sort of job will he find with only a high school diploma? Minimum wage. Of course, he won't make enough working nine to five to pay rent on a place as grand as this." Her eyes swept the room derisively. "So Jason, being Jason, will want to do better. He'll get a second job, which won't please you because you'll never see him. He'll be working all the time just to keep a roof over your head and food on the table for the three of you. And then there are the utilities and medical expenses. Of course, you'll be lonely. You'll carry the full responsibility of taking care of your baby: changing diapers, nursing, getting up at all hours of the night. You'll be exhausted. You'll feel overwhelmed. The baby will be your only company. After a while, you'll get bored sitting around the trailer. When Jason finally does make it home, you'll complain he's never around. He's no fun anymore. He doesn't make you happy."

Dawn started to cry.

"Tears don't work with me, honey."

"Why do you hate me so much?" Wrapping her arms around herself, Dawn fought for control.

"I don't hate you. I just don't like you. Why should I? *You're ruining my son's life!*" Georgia sounded distraught, close to tears. She released her breath slowly. "He's in love with you. Anyone can see that. He's so in love he can't think straight. He won't listen to a word of caution. You've stripped him of his dreams, taken his innocence, and now you're on the road to destroying his potential." She let out her breath in frustration.

Dawn couldn't raise her head.

"Look at me, Dawn." When she managed to raise her head, Georgia stared at her. "What I see in front of me is a very pretty sixteen-year-old girl with no character and no substance. You have nothing at all to offer Jason, and you're too willfully stupid and selfish to see or even care about the damage you're doing to him. That's not love. Not by any stretch of the imagination. You think you can live with your romantic daydreams. Fairy tales always end with 'happily ever after,' don't they? You don't know how wrong you are."

When Georgia didn't say anything more, Dawn spoke in a small voice. "Can I go now?"

"Please do. And don't you dare come into this house again, not unless *I* invite you."

Dawn got up quickly and headed for the door.

"One last thing." Georgia still sat at the table, face turned away. "You'll probably run straight to Jason and tell him everything I've said to you . . . or those parts that serve your purpose." She looked at Dawn then, eyes glistening with unshed tears. "But remember this: Someday, Jason will grow up. And when he does, he'll see the truth for himself."

❄ ❄ ❄

Dawn's first instinct was to go to Granny and sob out her woe, but she quickly dismissed that idea. Dawn knew she could do no wrong in Granny's eyes. Granny always took her side. If Granny knew she'd seduced Jason in the downstairs apartment, she'd be deeply hurt. She might start thinking Dawn was the kind of person who could live the wild life in Haight-Ashbury like her mother had.

What was Pastor Daniel saying to Jason right now? Was he hearing the same things Georgia Steward believed? *That girl isn't good enough for you. She has nothing at all to offer. She's selfish, spoiled, carnal, and probably not even a Christian. What are you thinking, Jason? Why would you want to be with her?*

She drove aimlessly for an hour, then went home. Her mother had an open house. Mitch and Christopher had gone bowling. Dawn went straight to her bedroom. Stripping off her clothes, she took a long, hot shower. She scrubbed and still felt unclean. Hunkered in the corner of the shower, she sobbed as the water pounded her. The air thickened with steam. She felt no better when she stepped out and dried off. Pulling on sweats, she got into bed. She lay there for the rest of the day, going over and over what Jason's mother had said.

"Dawn?" Mom tapped at the door. "Dinner's almost ready."

"I'm not hungry." When Mom opened the door, Dawn covered her head with a pillow.

"Are you sick?"

Lovesick. Heartsick. Sick with shame. "Just go away, Mom. Please." She half hoped her mother would press harder this time, but she left quietly, closing the door behind her.

❄   ❄   ❄

Hours later, the door opened again, a spear of light from the hallway intruding. Mom came in this time. She didn't turn on a light. She sat on the end of the bed, but didn't say a word.

After fifteen minutes, Dawn couldn't bear the silence. She whispered, "Would you hate me if I told you Jason and I have been having sex?"

"No." No questions, just a firm response, then silence again.

Dawn sat up slowly, bunching the pillow tight against her chest, thankful for the darkness. She wouldn't be able to see her mother's disappointment. "I went to see him this morning. He wasn't there. His mother talked to me."

When Mom still didn't ask anything, Dawn went on talking, slowly, painfully, until everything spilled out in a flood of tears. When Dawn finished, she pressed her face into the pillow already damp from an afternoon of weeping. She felt her mother's hand on her head.

"Words can be a sword to the heart, Dawn." Mom ran her fingers gently through Dawn's hair. "Sometimes there's truth in them. Sometimes there isn't. Go over what Jason's mother said to you. If there's any truth in it, you'll have to decide what to do with it. As to the rest, try to let it go." Her hand lifted.

Dawn curled into a fetal position. Her mother stood and pulled the covers up, tucking them in around her as though she were a little girl again. Leaning down, she kissed Dawn and whispered, "And try to forgive."

❋ ❋ ❋

Jason called Sunday night. He said his mom told him she'd come by. He apologized for not being there. "Pastor Daniel took me out to the coast. I didn't know he was coming until he showed up."

She said it was okay. She and his mother talked. He wanted to know what about. She said nothing much. Just small talk. *No character. No substance. Nothing to offer . . .*

"Dawn . . ." She knew by his tone what was coming. "I think maybe we should stop hanging out for a while."

She couldn't have prepared for the pain his words brought. She tried to press her lips together to keep from crying out. She hunched over, mouth open in agony. Shutting her eyes, she wanted to beg. She wanted to remind him they said they loved each other. Instead, she heard the echo of Georgia's voice. *Someday, Jason will grow up. And when he does, he'll see the truth . . .*

"Are you okay with that?" Jason sounded uncertain. Did he want her to say no? Did he want her to talk him out of it? And if she did, what then?

You'll ruin his life. . . .

Dawn had spent all of Saturday night and all of Sunday thinking about what Jason's mother had said, seeing the awful truth in it. Only one thing was false. She did love Jason.

She'd dreamed about Oma last night. She'd come like a vision, speaking words of wisdom. *"When you know what you want in life, May Flower Dawn, go after it. Sometimes it doesn't end up the way you planned. Trust God and it'll turn out better."*

Dawn knew what she wanted. She wanted to be Jason's wife. She wanted to have his children. She wanted to spend her life with him. And now she'd ruined it all. What had she brought into his life? Sin. Regret. Fear. Shame.

"Dawn? Are you there?"

Her breath caught softly, throat thick with pain and tears. "I think you're right."

She went into the kitchen and told Mom and Mitch she and Jason had broken up. She asked if she could transfer to the independent study program. She didn't have to explain why. Mom said she'd call the school Monday morning and do everything she could to make that happen.

❄ ❄ ❄

Dawn didn't return to youth group until Kim and Sharon told her Jason wouldn't be coming back because of his job. "About the only time I see Jason is at church on Sunday," Kim told her. "He comes with his mom. He doesn't come by the house and talk with Dad anymore."

A month after Jason broke up with her, Dawn came home from independent study and found a message on her answering machine. "I love you, Dawn." His voice roused all the pain and longing she had tried so hard to push down. He cleared his throat as though having trouble speaking. "I'll love you forever." *Click.* She sat on the bed and replayed it, letting herself wallow in regrets.

She didn't know what to do about the Mexico mission trip over spring break. She'd received pledges of financial backing from Mitch and her grandparents. She had a certified copy of her birth certificate. But if Jason was going, she knew she shouldn't. It would be too hard to be together. Sharon asked her why she hadn't said yes or no, and Dawn admitted her dilemma. Sharon called the next day. "I talked to Jason. He's not going to Mexico. He has to work. He said you ought to feel free to go now that you know he isn't."

Pastor Daniel might not share that opinion. She had no doubt Georgia Steward had talked with him about Dawn's relationship with Jason. He might not want someone like her to be part of his team. Dawn needed to know one way or the other, but it took days to gather the courage to call him.

Pastor Daniel seemed surprised by her question. "Of course, I want you on our team."

Maybe he didn't know everything. Maybe Georgia Steward hadn't wanted to share that information. "I didn't want to take anything for granted, Pastor Daniel."

"God loves a broken and contrite spirit, Dawn." His quiet words dispelled any illusions about whether Jason's mother had spoken to him. They also reassured her that Pastor Daniel wasn't going to throw stones.

After all the talk of how a mission trip could change a person's outlook on life, Dawn didn't know what to expect. Hearing about poverty or seeing it on television ads wasn't the same as being in the middle of it, smelling it, tasting it in the air. They drove down streets with houses tucked tight together, garbage dumped and rotting in the streets. Some people lived in shelters that couldn't even be called shanties. What surprised Dawn most was the people: They smiled and shouted greetings as the Amor ministry team arrived. Children ran alongside the van, waving and calling out in Spanish.

After a night's sleep, she and the others rose early and went to work building a twelve-by-fourteen-foot house for the Guttierez family. Dawn's hands blistered, her back ached, and she smelled of sweat like any common laborer. When Pastor Daniel told her to take a break, she sat in the shade and watched some children kicking an old soccer ball back and forth. She wasn't a great hod carrier or carpenter, but she knew how to play soccer. Dawn joined the children and showed off a few tricks she'd learned while playing for the Sky Hawks. Soon, children swarmed around her whenever she wasn't working on the house.

On the last night, house complete, Senor and Senora Guttierez insisted on hosting dinner for the entire team. Leftover boards propped up on sawhorses acted as a dining table. Senora Guttierez and her teenage daughter, Maria, made a big pot of beans and chicken enchiladas with cheese. Senor Guttierez stood at the head of the table, tears running down his rugged cheeks, as he told them in broken English what it meant to him to have a house for his family. Senora Guttierez added her shy thanks, as did their five children.

Dawn went outside, sat hunched against the wall, and wept. Pastor Daniel came out and sat beside her. "What's on your mind?"

"My bedroom is bigger than their entire house." She covered her face. Had she ever once said thank you for the blessings she had received? Not that she could remember. And the Guttierez family hadn't stopped thanking all of them since the day the team arrived.

"From those to whom much is given, much is required."

And there it was again, that piercing stab of conscience. "I think they spent everything they have to put on this dinner." What had she ever given to anyone?

"Probably, and they're proud and pleased to do it. They count the ability to give as a blessing, too." He got up and smiled at her. "Come back inside when you're ready."

Dawn sat for a while longer. These people worked hard and barely managed to get by. They wanted the opportunity for a better life for their children. Georgia Steward popped into her mind. *"Your* love *has single-handedly ruined most of Jason's chances to escape this trailer park."* Dawn leaned her head against the wall she'd helped build. Was that true? Not entirely, but enough so that it stung. Jason still had opportunities. So did she.

Before leaving the next morning, the CCC crew left the remaining food supplies, bottled water, building materials, and some tools. As soon as they crossed the border and started the long drive north to Anaheim, where they would stop and spend a day at Disneyland as reward for their labors, everyone fell asleep except Pastor Daniel, Mr. Jackson in the passenger seat, and Dawn in the back. While they talked, she sat in the back row, staring out the window and praying.

Who am I, God? Who do You want me to be? Oma said the plans

You have are better for us than the ones we make for ourselves. My plans led me into sin and pain and regret and fear. God, I want to become a woman of character and faith. I don't want to be a selfish, spoiled little girl with nothing to offer. Change me, Lord. Please change me.

Weary, head aching, Dawn leaned her head back against the seat. Pastor Daniel looked at her in the rearview mirror. His eyes crinkled the way they did when he smiled.

❄ ❄ ❄

Back in Windsor, everyone piled out of the church van and started unloading. Some met up with waiting parents. Dawn had left the Sable in the church parking lot. Running a finger over the dusty trunk, she imagined what Papa would say and decided to go through a car wash on the way home. She stowed her duffel bag. Closing the trunk, she found Pastor Daniel standing by the car. "Thanks for going with us, Dawn."

"My pleasure."

"You worked harder than anyone on the team." He gave her a teasing smile. "I didn't know you had it in you."

She gave him a sad smile. "Neither did I."

Maybe it was a start.

When she pulled into the last space in Mitch's four-car garage, Christopher bounded out to greet her. Mitch took her duffel bag. He said Mom was manning an open house. "You look worn-out, Pita."

"I'm exhausted." Dawn hugged him around the waist. "Thank you for my big, beautiful bedroom and the beautiful home and yard and pool and good food on the table and for loving me even when I'm a pain in the—"

"Wow!" Mitch laughed. "What happened to you?" He put his arm around her shoulders and steered her toward the door into the house. "It's been my pleasure, Dawn. You look dead on your feet. They must've worked you hard in old Mexico. Why don't you take a nap?" She thanked him and headed down the hall to her room. Mitch called after her, "Forgot to mention it, but you'll never guess who stopped by my office for a visit."

"Who?"

"Jason. He stayed more than an hour."

Just the mention of his name was enough to make Dawn's heart race. "Did he ask about me?"

"Briefly. He had some questions. He has to make decisions about his future. He's weighing all his options. He said to say hi."

❋ ❋ ❋

Independent study helped keep Dawn's mind occupied. She didn't have to worry about facing Jason. She didn't have friends or class disturbances to distract her. She could fix her mind on the work ahead. Rather than coast by, Dawn dove into her studies. She only had to go to Healdsburg High once a week to check in with the independent studies supervisor, turn in work assignments, and take exams.

All Sharon, Amy, and Pam talked about at youth group was the upcoming prom. Kim and Tom were going together. Steven Dial had asked Pam. Sharon held out hope hunk-of-the-month football fullback Tomás Perez would ask her. Amy worried that if anyone did ask, she wouldn't be able to afford a dress. Dawn wondered if Jason was going and with whom, but didn't ask.

Prom came and went, and conversations at youth group turned to finals and graduation, summer jobs and college plans. Half the members were finishing high school. Sharon and Kim were graduating and going to college. Amy's father had been offered a better job in Dallas. With so many of her friends leaving, Dawn wondered if she'd even attend the CCC youth group next year. She felt out of it, on the edge again, not really part of anything anymore. She didn't know what was happening on the Healdsburg High campus, nor did she care. What did all that matter, especially now that Jason was going away to college? "Somewhere in

Southern California," Sharon told her. "I just can't remember which college. And he's working construction over the summer. Down in San Jose, I think, with a friend of a friend of Pastor Daniel."

Dawn had the feeling Jason Steward had walked out of her life. Whatever plans God might have for her now clearly did not include him.

She didn't think her grief could go any deeper until Granny called on a hot August morning and said Papa was dead.

39

THE APPALLING CALL about Papa's death sent Mom into panic
mode. They needed to get out to Jenner *now*. Dawn insisted on
going with them. Mitch called the Eckhards and asked if they
would keep Christopher. They dropped him off on the way out.
Dawn sat in the backseat in a state of shock. When they arrived,
they found Granny sitting in the corner chair in the living room.
Face white, eyes red, she pointed to the closed French doors to the
bedroom. Mom stepped back and bumped into Mitch. He grasped
her shoulders and whispered something.

Trembling, Dawn went into the bedroom first. She refused to
believe Papa was dead. He apeared to be asleep. She went closer
and laid her hand on his forehead. He felt so cold. He wasn't
breathing. She drew in a sharp breath as though to do it for him.
She felt warmth behind her. Mitch, standing ready. "He looks
peaceful, doesn't he, honey? He's with the Lord." Sobbing, she
turned and fell into his arms.

Granny spoke in the living room. "He said he was tired. He
gave me a kiss good night. He was snoring when I went to bed.

And then when I woke up this morning, it was so quiet." She cried. "It was too quiet. I knew."

Mitch ushered Dawn back into the living room. Mom's face twitched. Her fingers pleated her tiered skirt. Face ashen, wide-eyed, she turned toward the bedroom, but didn't move. Dawn sat next to her on the couch. They didn't look at one another. They didn't touch. Mitch seemed the only one in the room capable of thought. "Have you called anyone, Hildie?"

"I called you." Granny blew her nose.

Mitch went down on one knee beside her and put his hand over hers. "I mean about his body."

She jerked. "No. I'm not ready to send him away yet."

"You'll be able to say good-bye at his memorial. . . ."

"There's not going to be a memorial service!" Granny sounded broken, but adamant. Her hand fluttered like a wounded bird. "We don't know anyone up here." It had been too far to drive in from Jenner to church on Sundays. She and Papa only made it to Easter cantatas— and one Christmas pageant when Christopher had played a little shepherd boy.

Mom shook, hands clenching her skirt. "You can have the service in Paxtown, Mom." She spoke in a dull voice. "Mitch can call Rev. Elias." Her face was shuttered. "Dad was one of his elders. He would want to officiate."

Granny dabbed her eyes. "Rev. Elias retired five years ago. He and Janice moved up to Silverton, Oregon. I think. I don't remember. We haven't even exchanged Christmas cards with them in the last few years."

"You have friends in Paxtown. The MacPhersons, Dr. Griffith, Doc and Thelma Martin." Mom's voice came out flat as she listed names.

Granny glared at her. "As if any of them remember us."

Mom raised her head, clearly distressed. "Is that my fault?" She sounded as though she thought it might be.

"No! Did I say it was? Did I? Thelma Martin was never my friend."

"Hildie." Mitch spoke gently.

Granny cried again. "We *had* friends, Carolyn. We've been gone eight years. Life goes on. People move away. People *die*." She started to sob.

Mom stared at Mitch with huge eyes. She was like a frightened little girl, frozen in her seat, afraid to move. Dawn couldn't bear seeing her like that or Granny crying her heart out. Someone had to do something! She fled into the kitchen, pulled out the telephone directory, and flipped frantically through pages. Scrubbing away tears, she read the number for Cornerstone Covenant Church and punched it into Granny's ancient phone.

Kim answered. She must be standing in for the church secretary again. Dawn started talking and knew she was making no sense. She started to cry. Pastor Daniel came on the line. "What's wrong, Dawn?" Fighting down the tears and rising hysteria, she told him her grandfather had died and his body was still in his bed and Granny didn't want a service and Mitch was going to call the mortuary and have his body taken away and she couldn't bear the thought of that being the end of him and—

"I'm on my way," Pastor Daniel interrupted her.

Mitch called the mortuary as soon as she hung up the telephone. Dawn went outside and paced on the deck, watching the road. When she saw Pastor Daniel's blue Chevy coming, she stood outside the gate. He got out of the car and held her close. "Did he know Christ, Dawn?" She nodded against his shirt, soaking it with her tears. "Then you know where he is right now."

"It doesn't help."

"It will."

She led him into the house and introduced him to Granny. He sat on her hassock and talked to her. Mom went outside and stood on the deck. Mitch went out and wrapped his arms around her, holding her tight against him. Dawn sat on the couch, hands pressed between her knees, not knowing what to do. *Jesus. Jesus.* That's all she could think to pray. Just His name over and over again.

"Why don't you get your mother and stepfather, Dawn?" When they came inside, Pastor Daniel led them all into the bedroom, where they gathered around Papa. Pastor Daniel held Granny's hand and talked about Jesus' life and death and resurrection and the promise He made, a promise that would never be broken. Mom kept looking at him. Granny grew calmer as he spoke.

Pastor Daniel stayed until after Papa's body had been taken away. He had been the one to remember to ask for Papa's wedding ring. He said he'd come and talk with Granny again if she liked. Would she be staying with the Hastings?

Granny shook her head.

Mitch leaned forward on the couch, one hand still holding Mom's, the other resting on the arm of the sofa closest to Granny. "Why don't you come home with us, Hildie?"

"No." Granny gripped the arms of her corner chair, letting everyone know she wouldn't be pried from her home. "I'm staying right here."

"You shouldn't be alone, Hildie."

Granny glared at Mitch, a stubborn tilt to her chin. "It's my home. I'm going to have to get used to being alone, aren't I?"

Dawn could tell Mitch was exasperated and torn. She knew he would take good care of Mom, who seemed as undone as she had been when Oma died. But Granny shouldn't be alone. When Pastor Daniel stood, Dawn took his place on the hassock. "I'll stay."

❄ ❄ ❄

Dennis Bingley gave her time off. Over the next week, Dawn cried almost as much as Granny. Instead of sleeping in the blue room, she slept with Granny. Once, while Granny slept in the easy chair, Dawn went downstairs and sat on the bed where she had given herself to Jason. She then cried for other reasons. If she'd followed Jesus instead of her own desires, she wouldn't be spending the rest of her life living in regret.

On the sixth morning, she awakened when Granny brushed

hair back from her face. Granny smiled faintly, head on her own pillow. "You're a very sweet girl. Do you know that?"

"Are you going to be all right, Granny?"

"Yes. I'll have to be because you have to go home today."

Dawn took her hand and held it against the mattress. "I'll call you every night and come out next weekend."

"I know you will." Granny's hazel eyes filled with tears. "All this is just part of life. Still it feels unexpected. You'll have to call home for a ride. Maybe your mother will come out and pick you up." She sounded hopeful.

Mitch came for Dawn. On the way home, he asked how things went. She told him Granny was going to have a hard time, but was too stubborn to talk about moving into town. "How's Mom doing?"

"She's bottled up inside again. It's going to take time. One good thing came out of all this."

How could anything good come from losing Papa? "What's that?"

"She asked me to take her to your church this morning."

1988

Senior year proved grueling as Dawn combined afternoon college courses with her remaining high school requirements. The previous year she had taken one class at Santa Rosa Junior College, and she enjoyed it so much she decided to take two this year. She didn't have a spare minute for R & R, as Mitch put it, not between commuting to Santa Rosa, attending classes, studying, writing papers, and working twenty hours a week at Java Joe's. When she did get a weekend off, she often drove out to Jenner and stayed with Granny until Sunday morning, when she'd drive back to attend CCC with Mom, Mitch, and Christopher.

With dismay, but no protest, Mitch had given up his old church. Dawn knew he was glad Mom had finally found a church where she felt comfortable. Christopher couldn't have been happier now that he could spend even more time with his friend Tim Eckhard. People had welcomed the family with open arms, even Georgia Steward, who came and shook Mitch's hand and gave Mom a quick hug. She greeted Dawn with cool courtesy.

Kim always made a point of telling Dawn when Jason planned to come home. Dawn didn't attend services on those Sundays. It wasn't until Thanksgiving and Dawn's suggestion that she and Granny go back to Jenner Saturday afternoon that Mom spoke up about it.

"You can't avoid Jason forever, Dawn."

When Christmas came around, Mom, Mitch, and Granny ganged up on her and insisted she attend church with the family. She said she would if she could drive her own car.

Jason sat in the third row with his mother. Dawn and her family sat in the middle on the same side. She tried to concentrate on what Pastor Daniel said, but her eyes kept drifting to Jason. He'd cut his hair, had grown a little taller, broader. As soon as the service ended, Dawn stood and made her way toward the exit. Kim stopped her, a perplexed expression on her face when Dawn made a quick excuse, gave her a quick hug, and headed for the door, where Pastor Daniel stood shaking hands.

"Great sermon, Pastor Daniel." When he offered his hand, she took it. He gripped her hand firmly and asked why she seemed in such a hurry to get out the door. She didn't dissemble. "You know why. Jason's here." He gave her a sad smile and let go.

She didn't stop until she was safely inside her car, key in the ignition. Jason stood at the door with his mother. When he looked toward her, she started her car, backed out, and put it quickly into gear. She glanced in her rearview mirror one last time before she pulled out onto the street and headed home. Jason stood with all their old friends, home from college.

Her telephone was ringing when she walked into the house. She put her purse on her desk and sat on the bed as her answering machine picked up with her recorded message. "This is Dawn.

Sorry I missed your call. Please leave a message at the sound of the beep." No one spoke. Her heart pounded harder the longer the silence stretched. The answering machine clicked. She breathed again. The phone rang again. The machine picked up. Again, the long silence.

You have nothing to offer Jason.

She hadn't forgotten what Georgia Steward said or the truth of most of it. She *didn't* have anything to offer Jason.

The phone rang again. Sobbing, she put her hands over her ears.

A few days later, Dawn drove Granny home to Jenner by the Sea. "That young man you used to date, Jason what's-his-name . . . ?"

"Steward."

"He was at church on Christmas."

Dawn focused on the road.

Granny studied her. "When you got up and headed out, he never took his eyes off you. I think he was trying to catch up with you, but people kept getting in the way."

"He has a lot of friends." Her voice came out with a soft catch in it. She adjusted her sunglasses.

"So do you, Dawn." Granny spoke quietly and didn't ask about Jason again.

❄ ❄ ❄

1989

Mom and Mitch gave her the gift of another mission trip to Mexico. Since she had the equivalent of four years of Spanish classes under her belt, Pastor Daniel lined her up with another church that planned to put on a vacation Bible school in Tijuana. He also thought the preparatory meetings held on Thursday evenings rather than five in the morning on Wednesdays would be an added benefit to her. "Your parents said you're burning your candle at both ends."

The work in Mexico felt like a vacation after her grueling school and work schedule at home. And though she loved the children, she knew by the end of Easter week she was not meant to be a teacher. When she shared that conviction, Granny talked about her nursing days.

❄ ❄ ❄

Fall enrollment at Santa Rosa Junior College rolled around, and Dawn signed up for human anatomy. By midterm, she decided to work toward a bachelor of science degree in nursing. Mom didn't seem surprised by the idea, saying Granny would be pleased to know Dawn intended to follow in her footsteps. Mitch said Dawn could always do real estate later if nursing didn't pan out, to which Dawn replied she hoped to finish at the junior college and transfer to a four-year college by the end of the following year. Mom seemed a little taken aback by that announcement. "You'll be going off to college."

Mitch leaned down and kissed her. "You'll still have Christopher around. And me." He straightened. "With your grades, Dawn, you can go anywhere you want. Why not consider UC Berkeley? It's not too far from home."

UCB was a great school, but Dawn knew the competition would devour her. She'd considered UC Santa Cruz, but it had the reputation as a party school. UC Davis was too close, UC San Diego too far away. Her counselor had graduated from Cal Poly, and she spoke highly of it. Dawn researched a dozen colleges, all good, some too expensive. Something had nudged her toward Cal Poly. Maybe it was the location—half a day from home, close to the coast. When people asked why there, her inclination was to ask, "Why not?" She couldn't really explain.

1990

All Dawn's old friends came home from college that summer, except Sharon, who had found a job in Santa Rosa and moved into an apartment near the Coddingtown Mall. Dawn caught up with their news after Sunday services. Most had lined up summer jobs at the downtown mall or various businesses in Healdsburg or Windsor. Kim called a few days after coming home from Pepperdine. "We're going to get together every Wednesday evening. It'll be better than old times."

"Who all is coming?"

"Everyone but Jason. He's off doing some kind of training this summer."

"I'll come when I can." Rather than drive back and forth twice a day to Healdsburg, she had quit the job at Java Joe's and worked at a coffee shop near the junior college, saving time and gas money.

All the old gang turned up at the Archer house the next Wednesday evening, eager to hang out with old friends. Kim and

Tom had become engaged. Amy King had lost twenty-five pounds and added blonde streaks to her brown hair. Steven Dial had shot up six inches and now towered over Dawn.

Kim's mom stood in the front doorway and announced she was going to have a ladies' night out with friends from church. "Coffee's ready, and there's hot water for any who prefer tea. Lots of cookies. Popcorn for those of you who are worried about your weight, which seems to be just about everyone these days." She waggled her fingers at Kim. "You're in charge. If it turns into a wild party, it'll be your head on the block, not mine. Good night, children." She closed the door behind her.

Everyone lounged around the living room talking about old times. Two hours passed before they got around to talking about what Bible book to study over summer. Tom Barrett suggested Song of Solomon and earned a round of guffaws and teasing remarks, while Kim reminded him, in hushed tones, they would be going through premarital counseling and could discuss *all that* some other time.

"Oh, yeah." Tom groaned loudly. "Like I'm going to feel so at ease talking about sex with your father."

Kim blushed crimson. "I hadn't thought about that."

The unattached of the bunch voted Song of Solomon down and suggested Proverbs. "It's practical." Pam grinned. "And God knows, we need practical advice on how to live the Christian life in the midst of a pagan culture."

"As long as we skip chapter 31." Kim smirked at Tom, and she added in an aside to Dawn and Pam, "Last thing I need right now is hearing what *I* have to do to be the perfect wife."

Grinning, Tom slung an arm around her shoulders and hugged her close. "Come on now, babe. Aren't you the one who's been telling me all Scripture is inspired by God and profitable for teaching, for reproof, for correction, for training . . ." He let out a yelp. "She pinched me!"

While the others laughed, Steven paged through his Bible. "We don't have time to finish all this."

Amy reached into a bowl of popcorn. "How about Philippians? Only four chapters and lots of encouraging words." They put it to a quick vote and settled it.

Lying in bed that night, Dawn thought about all the steps she had taken over the past three years to grow closer to the Lord. Even though she knew she didn't have a future with Jason, she still harbored a dream of being a wife and mother, God willing. She hadn't considered God would have a definition for the perfect wife. Pushing the covers aside, she turned on the desk light and opened her Bible. She felt depressed after reading Proverbs 31. How could any woman be all those things? Of course, it had taken the woman time. Her children were old enough to call their mother blessed, and her husband had gained enough standing in the community to be respected as a leader, and she managed servants.

Dawn covered her face. *Lord, I've worked so hard to become better, to become someone who could be a proper helpmate to a godly man. I know I was all wrong in the way I pursued Jason. Is it too much to hope that even so, You might have a husband and children in store for me someday?*

I love you. The answer came from the depths of her. Nothing was ever wasted, not even the damage she had done. Hadn't shame and guilt sent her down a new path?

I'll never be perfect, Lord. I'll never be good enough for someone like Jason.

My grace is sufficient for you, for power is perfected in weakness.

Slipping the leather journal Oma had given her from the top drawer, Dawn wrote: *How to Be a Good Wife.* But as she wrote, she searched for traits that would please God rather than a man.

❄ ❄ ❄

Pam called and asked Dawn if she'd like to get together. "We could do a little shopping and then go to Bakers Square for pie." Dawn knew something was up. Pam hated to shop. She suggested possible days and times, and they set a date to meet at the entrance of Ross Dress for Less.

Spotting her friend coming across the parking lot, Dawn laughed. Pam looked like she had an appointment for a root canal rather than an afternoon of shopping. "What are we looking for, Pam?"

"I don't know. You're the one who always loved to shop." Pam shrugged and stood outside the store. "I need your help. You always look like a fashion model, so put-together. I sort of agreed to a date with Steven."

"What sort of date?" Dawn knew they'd gone to their high school prom together as friends, but she hadn't noticed anything more between them.

"Dinner."

"Sounds serious."

"Oh, shut up. I wish I'd never . . ."

Dawn took her by the arm and pulled her through the front doors. "Did he say where you're going?"

"How would I know? I mean, he could've meant he was taking me to Taco Bell. Something casual, I guess." She looked around, her expression one of panic.

"You could've asked him where he plans to take you."

"I did! All he'd say is it would take us an hour to get there."

"Well, then it's not Taco Bell. Someplace nice, probably. No jeans. No T-shirt."

Pam rolled her eyes. "Just shoot me now."

Dawn laughed. "Relax. This is going to be fun!" She started pulling things off racks. "Start with these. The dressing room is back there." She pointed. "I'm going to keep looking. I'll be there before you have the first outfit on."

Holding half a dozen garments on hangers, Pam looked baffled. "What outfit?"

"This skirt, this top. Now go!"

After a few changes, Pam grumbled. One hand behind her head and the other on her hip, she struck a pose. "How about this one?"

"Not bad, but not all that great either. Take it off. Try these."
She hung more garment possibilities on the hook and took the
discards. After an hour, Pam had had enough of being a model
and pleaded for an end to the torture. Dawn pointed. "The black
skirt and tunic with the red belt. It looks great on you. What about
shoes?"

"Shoes?" Pam sounded horrified.

Ignoring further protest, Dawn thrust the favored garments into
her friend's arms, grabbed the others, and handed them over to the
attendant on the way out of the dressing rooms. Dawn ushered Pam
to the racks of shoes. She pointed out several pairs that would look
nice. Pam found reasons not to try them on—too high, too red, too
fancy, "You have got to be kidding me. No way!" When Pam picked
up a pair of purple sneakers, Dawn grabbed them and shoved them
back on the shelf. Pam reached for them again, and Dawn slapped
her hand. They both laughed like little girls and finally settled on a
pair of black slip-ons with two-inch heels.

"Boring, but serviceable." Dawn shook her head in dismay.
"Do you have new nylons?"

Pam seemed to shrink. "I'll get them on the way home. I
promise!"

They went to Bakers Square and sat in a booth by the front
windows. Pam ordered apple pie à la mode, Dawn, caramel pecan
silk supreme. They lingered and talked about college. Pam attended
Arizona State and had declared a physical education major.

"How many applications have you sent out?"

Dawn debated whether to say anything. "One."

"One? You know what they say about putting all your eggs in
one basket. Which college?"

"Cal Poly."

"Why there? I thought it was an engineering college."

"High rep for technology and sciences. I'll be in the nursing
program."

"Is that where Jason went?"

"Jason?" Dawn's heart turned over.

"Jason Steward." Pam gave her a wry smile. "Don't pretend you've forgotten him."

"No, but I thought he went to UCLA."

"He applied, but didn't qualify for a scholarship."

"Oh." Pinched by guilt, Dawn winced.

Pam frowned. "I can't remember where he went. He doesn't come home very often." She shrugged. "San Diego, maybe." She moved on to other subjects.

Jason Steward. Dawn's mind drifted into a vortex of bittersweet memories. Sending up a quick prayer, she asked God's blessing on him and let him go.

❄ ❄ ❄

Mom and Mitch sat Dawn down and told her they intended to pay for her last two years of college. The first two years hadn't cost them anything, and they'd set aside money that would enable her to concentrate on school instead of having to work a part-time job. When she argued, Mitch turned adamant. "You've done nothing but study and work the last three years, Dawn. You have no life."

"I go to church. I go to the college group."

"Two hours a week."

"Everyone works. You work; Mom works."

"You're nineteen. You should have a little time to enjoy life."

Mitch handed her a checkbook and told her how much would be deposited each month—enough for tuition, books, and a studio apartment. He also handed over a credit card and gave her a limit, plenty for living expenses like food and gas. She'd even have enough to pay for car insurance.

Stunned, Dawn felt the tears coming. "You don't have to do this, Mitch."

Mitch's mouth tipped. "I'm not, Pita. It's all your mother's doing."

Mom shook her head. "Don't, Mitch."

He ignored her. "She's been banking her commissions since we married just so she could give you this gift. If you say no, I swear I'll turn you over my knee."

"Mom . . . I . . ."

Mom shrugged. "I didn't get to give you a car."

Dawn's smile trembled. "This is a whole lot more than a car."

"It hurts to see you work so hard to . . ." Mom stood abruptly and went to the kitchen counter, where she picked up some papers. "You'll need to find a place soon. I have a list of apartment complexes that offer furnished studios." She put them on the table. "The ones closest to campus are highlighted. You'll have to stay in a hotel while you're looking. I have a list of those as well." She stood, hands gripping the back of a chair. "You're going to be on your own." Her eyes filled.

"She'll be coming home for vacations." Mitch put his arm around Dawn's shoulders. "Won't you?"

It sounded more a command than a question. "Yes." She looked at her mother. "And you'll come down, too, I hope."

Dawn drove to San Luis Obispo the beginning of August. She listened to the radio on the drive, music interspersed with news reports of the Iraqi invasion of Kuwait, and the first U.S. troops being deployed to Saudi Arabia. Mitch had told her many high-ranking U.S. military officers were veterans of Vietnam. This war would be swift and decisive. Dawn thought of the uncle she had never met who died in Vietnam, and she turned off the radio.

The skies were clear that afternoon and cloudy the next morning when she arose. She left her things at Motel 6 and headed out to find a furnished studio apartment close to campus for a price she was willing to pay. She didn't want to blow through her mother's gift like found money, but use it wisely.

After three days, she signed a rental agreement with Bishop Peak Apartments. Her studio had a kitchenette with a small table and two chairs. The living room and bedroom were divided by an accordion partition. On one side was a sofa, one chair, a coffee table, and a hanging lamp, and on the other a full-size bed with two simple side tables and two cheap lamps. After her designer-decorated bedroom in Alexander Valley, it seemed drab, but she reminded herself of Mexico and felt thankful.

As soon as the phone service had been turned on, she called Mom with the new number. Then she called Granny and talked about the trip down, the hunt for an apartment, what she had seen of the town. "I'm going to try one of the churches tomorrow."

"You sound lonely, honey."

"A little, I guess. I'll get used to being on my own."

Over the next few days, Dawn took long walks around campus, familiarizing herself with its main buildings, the library, the dining complex. Hills dotted with oaks rose around campus with Bishop Peak in the distance. Sitting on a bench, Dawn watched others pass by. Was she really hearing God's voice about Cal Poly? Or had she come three hundred miles from home on some sort of delusion?

Once Dawn knew her way around the campus, she took drives to the Pacific beaches, coastal dunes, ridges, forests, and nearby lakes. She spent an afternoon at the mission, wandering through the garden with its fountain and statue of Father Junípero Serra and sitting in the chapel praying God would lead her in the days ahead.

She met with Mrs. Townsend, a college counselor, who helped her plan out schedules to earn her degree as quickly as possible. Mrs. Townsend looked dubious. "If you find what we've laid out too ambitious, you can drop a course."

Classes started, and the first weeks felt like a grueling marathon of lectures, reading, studying. A throng of students moved from building to building. Dawn felt overwhelmed by the numbers. SRJC had nearly as many students, but somehow it had felt smaller to her, less intense.

She hated studying in her drab apartment and started going to the Robert Kennedy Library instead. She preferred the smell of books, the soft sound of footsteps and hushed voices, to the silence in her studio or someone partying nearby. She felt more at home in the stacks than in her flat.

Around lunchtime one day in the library, her stomach growled, reminding her she hadn't eaten since breakfast. Glancing at her wristwatch, she saw she had less than an hour before chemistry class. She didn't have time to run to the dining complex and stand in line for a full meal. The eggs and toast she'd eaten for breakfast wouldn't carry her through the whole day.

Gathering her notes, textbook, and purse, she headed for the library café. Better a cup of coffee and pastry than nothing.

She'd just finished a blueberry scone and half her coffee when Jason Steward walked in. Dawn's heart dropped into the pit of her stomach.

She stared, trying to calm the tumble of emotions. Jason was even more handsome than she remembered. Short hair suited him. He looked tan and fit, taller and broader through the shoulders. He was with two other young men and a pretty girl with shoulder-length dark hair and a bright, sunny smile. Was she his girlfriend? A sharp stab of pain went through her heart. She thought she'd gotten over him.

As the four made their selections, paid, got their coffee, and sat across the room, Dawn drank in the sight of him. He talked easily, laughing at something one of the boys said. He pulled out the chair for the girl. He sat with his back to Dawn, but one of his friends noticed her and smiled. She'd seen that same smile on a dozen other male faces in the last few weeks. It usually predicated an attempt to start a conversation or ask her out. Dawn averted her eyes so he wouldn't be encouraged.

A few seconds later, she glanced over again and found Jason half turned in his chair, staring at her. Surprise didn't begin to describe the expression on his face. A flood of feelings swept over Dawn. Her smile felt stiff, her insides like Jell-O. When Jason scraped his chair back, she went hot and cold all over. He said something to the others and rose. The girl looked past him to Dawn.

Breathing in slowly, trying to slow her rapid-fire heartbeat, Dawn watched Jason cross the room. She offered a tremulous smile. He didn't seem happy to see her. He stood at her table, hands gripping the back of the chair. "What are you doing here?"

Why did he sound angry? He'd been the one to initiate their breakup. "I'm having coffee."

"I don't mean that. I mean here, on campus."

"I'm a student."

"A student?" He frowned.

"I'm in the nursing program."

Emotion flickered, and then his mouth flattened. "You could've gone anywhere." His hazel eyes cooled.

His last telephone message came back to her so clearly. She remembered pressing the button and hearing his voice. *"I love you, Dawn. I'll love you forever."* Pain lanced through her. She'd listened to that message over and over, for days, weeks, before she finally surrendered to God and erased it. *Jesus, where is Your purpose in this?* If she'd known Jason was attending Cal Poly, she never would have applied. She didn't know what to say to him now, so she resorted to the mundane. "It's good to see you again, Jason." She spoke as though they had been mere acquaintances, not lovers.

"Really." He sounded doubtful.

She blinked, wishing her heart would slow down. "How are you?"

"Fine." He mocked her. "I'm doing great." He nodded toward his friends at the other table, the girl watching their exchange. He didn't ask Dawn if she wanted to be introduced. The dark-haired girl gave her a curious smile. Jason moved enough to block her from view. Dawn could feel his animosity.

"It took me a long time to get over you, Dawn. I don't even know why I'm talking to you."

What could she say to that? She'd never gotten over him, never would. She hadn't realized that fully until now. *Oh, Lord, why?* Lowering her eyes, she put her hands around the cooling cup of coffee. She didn't know what to say.

"You're wearing the bracelet I gave you."

She glanced at the gold chain with the delicate heart and glistening pearl. "I've never taken it off."

He looked as though she'd punched him in the stomach. "I don't get it."

"Get what?"

"I called, Dawn. You never called back. I left you a message. I never heard a word from you. Not one. You want to explain?"

"You know why, Jason."

"Yeah, right." He sneered. "Why don't you enlighten me?"

She hadn't planned on a public confession, but she didn't feel like being a silent martyr. "We went too far, Jason. It was always going to be all or nothing with us. And it was all sin three years ago." Her eyes burned. "I . . ." She had to swallow before she could confess more. "I wanted to get right with God."

Jason studied her face and then turned his back and walked away. Suffocating with pain, Dawn watched him sit with his friends. Was he telling them who she was, what they had once been to each other, what he thought of her now? The dark-haired girl leaned back and looked at her again. One of the guys looked, too, scraped his chair back, and got up until Jason said something that made him sit down again.

Why was she still sitting here, torturing herself with regret and shame? She couldn't change the past. She couldn't undo what she had done. She had no control over what Jason thought about her now.

Gathering her things, Dawn threw away the cup and crumpled napkin and left the café. Her throat burned with tears as she hurried down the steps and along the walkway away from the library.

Oh, God, I must've misunderstood. Why did I come here? This is the last place I should be. Oh, Lord, the look on his face . . . I thought I was over him. She brushed tears away and kept walking. *You are my first love, Jesus, my forever love. But it hurts, Lord. I wish You had arms to hold me.*

She headed for her chemistry class.

41

DAWN CONTINUED STUDYING in the library every afternoon, but didn't go back to the café. She got up early every morning and sat at her nook window, with the sun coming in, and read her Bible. Sometimes she felt she was walking in the valley of the shadow of death, her heart trembling and broken. She feared running into Jason. She couldn't bear to see the coldness in his eyes.

Studying held off the pain. She'd pushed herself through class after class for three years. She would do it again. Surely God had a purpose in all this. She prayed constantly. Sometimes she talked aloud to Him when she sat alone in her apartment. *What do You want me to do with the rest of my life?* She could never be the Proverbs 31 wife. Maybe God intended her for the mission field. There must be dozens of organizations who needed nurses. Maybe she'd serve on an Indian reservation or in Africa or the Far East. *Someplace far away, Lord, at the ends of the earth.*

Every night, she dreamed of Jason. Every morning, she woke up and cried. She begged God to stop the dreams.

Day after day, she set her mind on attending classes, taking notes, completing assignments to the best of her ability. God had a plan for her. She would trust God to work it all out.

She thought of Oma and how she had said she had made plans of her own and then found God had made better ones for her. She searched for God's promises and wrote them in the leather-bound journal Oma had given her.

I have loved you, my people, with an everlasting love. With unfailing love I have drawn you to myself. . . . I know the plans I have for you . . . plans for good and not for disaster, to give you a future and a hope.

I want to believe You, Lord. Help me believe.

Eventually, she found a church similar to CCC and finally felt at home, comforted among the flock of believers, less vulnerable than when she was by herself battling loneliness and loss. The second week she attended, she spotted Jason in the third row. She would have left if the service hadn't already started.

God, why are You doing this to me?

When the pastor called for prayer, Jason didn't just bow his head; he hunched over. Dawn felt grateful. She'd stolen his innocence, but at least she hadn't destroyed his faith. When the congregation rose to sing, Jason stood taller than the others around him. He looked like a soldier, shoulders back, head up. Throat tight, Dawn mouthed the praise songs, unable to make a sound.

The service ended. She thought about heading quickly for the door, but Jason rose and started down the aisle. Afraid he'd see her, she kept her head turned away as he made his way toward the doors. Departing parishioners greeted him, drawing him into conversation. She leaned down as though to get her purse as he passed by and then sat up and watched him go out the door.

The sanctuary emptied. The praise band stowed their instruments. Dawn rose. She'd try another church next Sunday. Or maybe she'd just stay home and read her Bible.

Monday, Dawn dragged herself out of bed and did her morning Bible reading. She barely made it to her anatomy class and had to struggle to keep her eyes open. She downed a cup of coffee before she went to her nursing history course, then went to the dining complex for a slice of pizza at BackStage. She had two hours before her next class, enough time to study in the library.

After an hour, she felt drained. She massaged her forehead, wishing the coffee had helped the headache. She'd lived in San Luis Obispo two whole months; it felt like ten years. She didn't know if she could stay here. Maybe she should transfer. Maybe it had been a mistake coming here, even though she had felt certain God had been directing her. She hadn't expected more pain, more sleepless nights, more confusion. If she transferred, she wouldn't face the risk of seeing Jason every day. She might have a chance to see what God wanted her to do.

Someone pulled out a chair and sat opposite her. She didn't feel like sharing her space. Gathering her notes, she tucked them quickly into a folder. She leaned over for her backpack.

"I've been trying to find you."

Her heart lurched to a stop and then raced.

Jason folded his arms on the table. "How are you doing?"

Why now, Lord? I don't know what You want from me anymore. She gave Jason a bleak smile. "I'm managing." All the old attraction swam through her blood as he looked her over.

Standing, she lifted her backpack onto the table and began putting her books away.

"You look tired, Dawn."

"I haven't been sleeping very well."

"Neither have I." He leaned forward, keeping his voice low. "Do you want to go somewhere? talk?"

She recognized the glint in his eyes and went hot all over. She remembered all too well how it had been between them. Reason enough to withdraw. *Now.* "I have a chemistry class."

"I joined the Army."

"Very funny, Jason."

Jason caught hold of her arm and pulled her to a stop. "I joined the Army, Dawn." When she pulled back, his hand slid away. "They're paying for my education. When I finish, I'll be on active service for six years."

Dawn went cold with guilt. "And it's my fault." She thought of Iraq and Kuwait and the young men being deployed. Mitch had told her things would heat up before it was over. What would that mean for Jason? Would he finish college and end up shipped off to a war? All because she'd distracted him from his studies and he couldn't get a scholarship? Georgia Steward had every right to hate her. "I'm sorry, Jason." An apology would never be enough. Her eyes blurred with tears. "I'm so sorry." She stepped back. "I *was* the worst thing that ever happened to you." She turned away.

Jason caught hold of her again. "Will you just wait a minute?"

She wrenched free. "You had everything planned out before I messed things up. You'd be at Berkeley on scholarship right now if we hadn't . . ." Unable to say more, she spun from him and wove quickly into the throng of students, half-running.

❄ ❄ ❄

Chemistry class passed in a blur. She took notes, trying to make sense of things, but she kept thinking about Jason's announcement. The Army! He'd wanted to be an engineer or a Christian business-man—or maybe even a pastor. Now he'd be a soldier building bridges or roads into some godforsaken battle zone. What a mess she'd made!

Dawn emerged from class and saw Jason leaning against the wall. Pushing away, he caught up with her. "We need to talk."

"I think your first instincts three years ago were right on, Jason. We need to let things go."

"Please, Dawn." He took her hand and pressed it flat against his chest. She felt his heart pounding hard and fast. He leaned closer. "I could barely catch my breath when I saw you sitting in the café. It's not over, Dawn. It's never going to be over between us."

Her body filled with sensations. Unthinking, she stepped forward and slid her arms around his waist. As she pressed herself against him, she heard him suck in his breath. He put his arms around her and let it out again, slowly. "I love you, Dawn. I'll love you forever." Dawn felt the heat of his hand press against the small of her back. His breath was ragged. "Are you finished with classes for the day?"

"Yes."

"Let's find someplace to be alone and talk. I have a couple of roommates. What about you?" When he stepped back, she watched his eyes go dark the same way they had every time she came to the trailer while his mother had been away working. That look had intoxicated her then. It still sent curling heat into the pit of her stomach and down her legs.

"I live alone." She could feel the heat coming off him at that, or was it her?

"It's been too long, Dawn." Jason took her hand. "Let's go."

The Spirit within Dawn warned her. Alert to Him after three years of walking close, she listened and obeyed. "No." She pulled her hand free and didn't move from where they stood. "We can't be alone, not with our history." And not with the way she was feeling right then. If they were alone and he touched her, she'd forget all about what God wanted of her. Three years had obviously changed Jason. She had to find out how much.

He didn't pretend not to understand. Running his hands down her arms, he gave her a slow smile that melted her insides. "Okay. We'll set rules. Kissing, but no petting, no—"

Dawn shook her head. "I'm not strong enough, Jason, and I'm not willing to go down that road again."

Jason let out a shuddering breath. "Okay." He took her hand and wove his fingers through hers. "Make a suggestion."

"Someplace public, so we'll have to behave ourselves."

He laughed. "Then I guess it's going to be the Dexter Lawn." When he smiled at her this time, he looked like the Jason she remembered.

EVERY MORNING, DAWN and Jason met on the Dexter Lawn after he finished ROTC classes. They met on the walkways between classes and at the dining complex for lunch. They talked on the telephone every night until they couldn't keep their eyes open.

Jason introduced her to his friends: Dod Henson, Jack Kohl, and Alice Jeffries, the pretty, dark-haired girl who turned out to be Dod's girl. None were Christians and they seemed surprised to find out Jason was. "When did that happen?" Dod wanted to know, and Jason said a long time ago, but he just hadn't been walking with the Lord lately. He'd been ticked at God and hadn't felt like talking to Him. He laughed when he said it, grimacing in self-mockery. They all went into town and talked over Chinese food or hamburgers. On Saturdays, Dawn and Jason studied in the library. On Sunday mornings, they went to church together.

A month passed like a Santana wind, and Jason wanted to do something special to celebrate their "anniversary." Dawn suggested a Sunday afternoon picnic on the beach and brought homemade fried chicken, potato salad, and fresh-baked cookies. They ate at a table, with the wind blowing cold off the ocean, and stowed the leftovers in the backseat of his white Honda. Throwing a blanket over his shoulder, Jason took her hand and said he wanted to walk awhile. He found a cove shielded from the wind and spread the blanket so they could sit and watch the waves.

Dawn talked about the sermon they'd heard that morning and raised questions. Jason's answers seemed more seasoned with life than they had when he was seventeen. Shivering, Dawn wrapped her arms around her raised knees and told Jason about the day she'd seen him sitting near the front of the church. "You came in late. I watched you pray."

Jason stretched on his back, arms behind his head. "That was the first time I'd been to church since moving down here."

Dawn stared at him in surprise. "Kim said you were in church every time you came home."

"Yeah," he drawled. "Because Mom insisted." He frowned. "Is that why you weren't there? Because I was?"

She looked out at the ocean. Seagulls dipped and floated on the wind. "It hurt to see you."

Jason's hand curved around her hip. "I didn't feel much like seeing Pastor Daniel after that surprise fishing trip he and Mom pulled on me."

"What'd Pastor Daniel say to you that weekend?"

Jason grimaced. "That a man protects those he loves, and I was putting you at risk. I won't go into the gory details, but Daniel told me what *I* thought of as protection wasn't what God had in mind. I knew he was right, which was the problem, of course. I just didn't want to hear it. I figured you'd be upset when I wasn't there, but—"

"Your mom was there."

"Well, I know, but I'm sure you and she didn't have much to talk about. "

"Oh, your mom had a few things to say."

"What?" He exploded to his feet and raked his hands through his hair. "I asked you what the two of you talked about, and you said nothing! Now you're telling me she said something to you? Did she say something that made you build such a wall between us?"

Dawn had had three years to think over what Georgia Steward had said that day. "She told me the truth."

"I'll bet she did." His eyes darkened. "Her version of it." He swore.

"Sit down, Jason. Please."

He did, body tense, jaw clenching, fists against the sand. "Like my mother has any right to cast stones. She had me out of wed-lock, remember?"

"Yes, so who better to recognize the danger we were putting ourselves in? Your mom spoke God's truth, Jason. And the Lord used her words to open my eyes to what *He* wanted. I see that as a great kindness. We both owe Pastor Daniel and your mother a debt of gratitude."

"You think so? What about the pain they caused?"

"Pain builds character, and *they* didn't cause it. *We* did that to ourselves. I knew what I was doing that night at Jenner. I wanted you. That's all I cared about. Not how I went about getting you or what the price might be. Sin always has consequences. When I look back now, I see God's mercy in the way it all turned out."

Jason's eyes softened. "You're not the girl you were, Dawn."

"I hope not."

"God got hold of you." Jason pulled her down on top of him. "But I want to hold you, too." He dug his fingers into her hair and kissed her the way he used to when they were alone in his bedroom. "You still taste like heaven." Rolling her onto her back, he kissed her again. "Will you marry me?"

Dawn smiled and brushed some sand off his sweater. "I think you already know the answer. Of course I will."

Joy and then determination filled his face. "We'll get married during Christmas break."

She laughed. "Thanksgiving is only ten days away."

"I know, and I wasn't planning to go home until now."

"You mean it!"

"Yes. I mean it." He stood, pulling her up with him. "Now we'll go home together, in my car. I'm calling my mother tonight, so she'll have fair warning. And then I'm calling Pastor Daniel and finding out what day he has open for a wedding." He shook out the blanket. "You'd better call your folks before they hear from someone else."

Dawn tried to catch her breath. "They'll probably suggest we wait until we graduate."

"That's not for another two years—or maybe even three. I don't think either one of us can wait that long." Jason stopped folding the blanket. "Say something." He frowned. "You don't want to wait, do you?"

"No." Joy bubbled up inside her. God had given her the desire of her heart. She laughed. "No, Jason, I don't want to wait." She threw herself into his arms.

❄ ❄ ❄

Jason said his mother didn't have a lot to say about them getting married. Pastor Daniel said he'd check his calendar and they could talk when Jason and Dawn came home for Thanksgiving. Expecting resistance, Jason rehearsed arguments on the long drive north. Despite her fears, Dawn counseled him to listen and not storm in the front door of the trailer half-cocked for a gunfight. "Your mom and Pastor Daniel love you, Jason. They want the best for you."

He glanced at her. "This is about *us*, Dawn, not *me*." He frowned. "You haven't said much about your folks' reaction. If Mitch and your mom say wait, are you going to listen?"

"I'm going to hear them out without interrupting." She shoved her hands under her thighs. "This isn't about what makes *us* happy, Jason. It's about God. Let's try to focus on what will make *Him* happy. Okay? You told me a long time ago the Lord knows better than any of us."

Jason cast an apologetic smile. "I guess I needed the reminder."

When he dropped her off, Mitch and Mom came out to welcome them. Eleven-year-old Christopher darted out and hugged Dawn, telling her how much he'd missed her and she was getting married and did that mean Jason would move in with them for the summer and why didn't Jason come in and see the city he'd built with his LEGOs. They all laughed. Jason was clearly relieved by the warm greeting.

Mom threw cold water on both of them with an announcement. "Jason, you and your mom are having Thanksgiving dinner with us." She looked at Dawn. "And Granny's coming, too, of course. She called me right after you called her about your engagement."

Dawn winced inwardly. No wonder her mother had been so quiet when Dawn called with the news she and Jason wanted to get married.

❋ ❋ ❋

Dawn answered the door when Jason and his mom arrived. Georgia Steward's smile was tense as Dawn ushered them into the house. As his mother walked ahead, Jason stole a kiss from Dawn. Mitch and Mom greeted them in the family room, offering sparkling cider and appetizers. Mitch made a toast. Granny chattered happily, eager to help plan the nuptials. "We'll have to work fast if we're going to pull everything together before Christmas. Dawn will need a wedding gown. We'll have to find a photographer, order flowers and engraved invitations."

Pensive and silent, Mom went into the kitchen. Georgia followed, asking if she could help.

Jason took Dawn's hand. "Can we take a walk in the garden?"

Out of view of the windows, Jason took her in his arms and kissed her. "You look like a deer in the headlights."

"A gown, wedding invitations, photographer, flowers . . ."

"I didn't stop to ask what kind of wedding you want. Something big and white, I guess."

"I think Granny is dreaming about all that because she and Papa didn't have it. And she didn't get to put on a big wedding for my mom, either."

"What do you want?"

"*You!*"

"You've got me." He kissed her again, pressing her to him. He raised his mouth, then whispered against her ear. "Maybe we should save everyone the trouble and elope."

Conversation didn't lull around the dinner table. Even Georgia seemed loquacious when Mitch asked about her business. Booming, she said. She'd hired two more maids over the past two months and was on the lookout for another. Christopher barely spoke, too busy stuffing himself with turkey and dressing. Mom said she and Georgia would work out some of the details regarding the wedding. "We just have to know what you two have in mind."

"Something simple." Dawn's smile wobbled. "Close friends and family."

"What about flowers?" Georgia lifted her glass of sparkling cider to sip and peered at her over the rim.

"Poinsettias." They could be left in the church to decorate through Christmas.

Georgia set her glass down carefully. "What about your bouquet?"

"Gardenias smell wonderful," Granny volunteered. "And roses . . . or white orchids . . ."

"I want to carry five long-stemmed white roses."

Granny looked surprised and then disheartened. "That's not a bridal bouquet, Dawn."

"Maybe not." Dawn leaned over and kissed Granny's cheek to take away any sting of disappointment. "But it's what I want."

❄ ❄ ❄

Pastor Daniel sat behind his desk when Jason ushered Dawn into the office Friday morning. They held hands as they sat on the couch in front of him. "You two act like you're facing a firing squad instead of coming in to talk about a wedding."

Jason sat straight and tall, poised for a fight. "Don't try to shoot us down. We want to get married as soon as possible."

It occurred to Dawn what Pastor Daniel might think about hasty wedding plans. "I'm not pregnant, Pastor Daniel."

Jason shot her a glance. His hand tightened around hers as he faced their pastor again. "And we're not sleeping together either, nor will we until we're married."

Pastor Daniel blushed. "Wow! Last time we talked, Jason, I must've come across as judge and jury. I hope you'll both forgive me."

Dawn smiled. "We do. You were right. I'm thankful that God gave us enough time to realize that for ourselves. Not to mention a second chance." She turned her smile on Jason.

Jason's hand loosened. "You said something about a premarital Bible study." He had said on the way home he thought Pastor Daniel or his mother might come up with some sort of delaying tactic.

Pastor Daniel lifted two workbooks and put them on the front of his desk. "These are for you two to take back to Cal Poly." Leaning forward, he folded his hands on the desk. "There's lots of Scripture to read and things to ponder together. The intent is for you to be forewarned so you'll be able to work through problems that will come up in the course of your marriage, not just in the first year, but in the years to come."

Pastor Daniel smiled warmly at Dawn. "I've watched your relationship with Jesus grow over the last three years." His expression turned grim when he shifted his focus to Jason. "I'm not so sure about you. Still wandering in the wilderness?"

"Not anymore. I'm back in church and I plan to stay." Jason let go of Dawn's hand and leaned forward to take the workbooks. "Thanks, Daniel." Smiling, he relaxed on the sofa.

"I hoped it would all work out this way."

"Did you?" Jason sounded dubious.

"What do you say we take a bike ride tomorrow? Talk a little more."

Jason agreed.

Leaning back in his chair, Pastor Daniel gave them a smug smile. "You'll be the first couple to meet and marry in our church. December is a nice month for a wedding."

Dawn laughed. "What about Kim and Tom?"

Pastor Daniel chuckled. "Ah, but they're not getting married until June. We'll tie your knot on December 21."

❄   ❄   ❄

When Dawn got home, a light blinked on her answering machine. She pressed the button, thinking it might be Kim or Pam or one of her other friends. Instead, she heard Georgia Steward's invitation to the trailer for coffee Saturday afternoon at three. "We have a few things to settle between us, Dawn." Her voice sounded cool and detached. "If three isn't convenient, please call so we can set another time."

Dawn sank onto her bed. What would Jason's mother say to her this time? Was she afraid this marriage would ruin his chances of getting through college? that Dawn might get in the way again? that she might be pregnant?

Dawn wanted to call and make some excuse not to go. How could she face Georgia again, after all that had been said the last time? *God, help me. What do I do?*

Reason took hold. Georgia Steward would be her mother-in-law in a few weeks. She deserved respect and consideration. Georgia might not like her, but for Jason's sake they needed to make some kind of peace. Dawn didn't want to become a stumbling block between mother and son. She prayed about it all afternoon.

Jason called that night. When he didn't mention his mother's invitation, Dawn knew Georgia hadn't told him. That did not bode well.

Jason said he had a great idea for their honeymoon. They'd

have only a few days before they needed to come back for a family Christmas. "It won't be the Ritz, but I think you'll like it." He wanted it to be a surprise.

"I'll love it, wherever it is."

Unable to sleep, Dawn sat at her desk, reading her Bible until well after midnight.

She covered her face and prayed for Georgia's heart to soften toward her. When she finally went to bed, she dreamed she wore a scarlet wedding dress, and Georgia, dressed in black, wept in the front row.

43

DAWN'S INSIDES QUIVERED as she parked her Sable behind Georgia's van. Mrs. Edwards peered through her living room curtains. Georgia opened the door, leaned out to wave to her neighbor, and then beckoned Dawn inside. Blushing, Dawn went up the steps onto the small porch. One glance over her shoulder confirmed Mrs. Edwards still waited with bated breath to witness the outcome of this meeting between Georgia and the girl who had seduced Jason.

A small potted plant sat on the table where Dawn and Jason used to spread their books out before going into his bedroom. Georgia moved tensely about the kitchen. Dawn pressed her damp palms on her dark skirt.

"Do you like coffee, Dawn, or would you prefer tea?"

"Whatever you're having will be fine, ma'am."

Georgia gave a sharp laugh. "*Ma'am* makes me feel like a nasty old woman. Call me Georgia. I'm a coffee drinker. Do you like cream or sugar?"

"Nothing, thank you."

Georgia carried a wooden tray with saucers and cups of coffee and a plate of homemade chocolate chip cookies into the living room and set it on the low table. "Sit down. You're making me nervous." She waved her hand toward the sofa. "We both know we have to have this conversation. We might as well get it over with, don't you think?"

Dawn took her coffee. The cup rattled in the saucer. Mortified, she set them on the table before she could spill coffee all over the beige rug.

Georgia cleared her throat softly. "This is difficult for both of us, Dawn. I wanted to talk with you alone and try to clear up a few things." Georgia closed her eyes for a moment and released a slow breath before she looked at Dawn again. "I said awful things to you the last time you were here." She turned her face away. "Afterward, I knew I'd jeopardized my relationship with my son. You had the power to make Jason hate me."

"I didn't tell him anything about that day."

"Oh, honey, I know you didn't. He asked me after the two of you broke up if I'd ever spoken to you. I asked if you'd said I had—implying, of course, I hadn't. He said you'd pulled out of school and wouldn't return his calls."

Georgia gripped her saucer and stared into the cup for a moment. "When Jason said you two should stop seeing each other for a while, he meant a few weeks. But you backed out of his life entirely. I watched him suffer. I heard him sobbing one night. A few days later, he put his fist through the wall. And I watched you suffer, too."

"I couldn't . . ." Dawn pressed her trembling lips together and tried again. "I knew if we saw each other, we'd go right back—"

Georgia held up her hand. "I'm not finished, Dawn. Please, let me finish." She drew in a breath, her mouth working. When she regained control, she spoke quietly. "I watched you. I listened to everything people said about you. For three years. You sat in church and soaked in every word Daniel said. I heard how well you were doing in independent study—high grades, taking college courses while you finished high school. You went on mission trips. Daniel said he'd never seen God work in a person's life the way the Lord worked in yours. You fixed your eyes on Jesus and never looked away. But while I watched your faith grow, I saw Jason struggling. When I heard you'd transferred to Cal Poly, I prayed harder than I ever had in my life."

Dawn hung her head. She could imagine how hard Georgia Steward had prayed. She must have assumed the girl who'd caused her son so much grief had gone after him again.

Georgia's eyes glistened. "Jason thanked me the other day. When I asked him what for, he said you told him I'd been kind to you." She smiled bleakly. "He apologized for assuming I'd said the same things to you that I'd been saying *about* you for weeks before that last fiasco." She shook her head. "And I know everything you've done, even forgiving me, has been out of love for my son." Her voice broke.

Dawn realized she wasn't the only one consumed by guilt. "You weren't wrong about me."

"Oh, I was very wrong. I couldn't have been more wrong. When I looked at you, I saw myself at fifteen—arrogant, selfish, defiant. I wanted what I wanted when I wanted it. I didn't care what anyone thought. *You* listened. *You* repented. When I got pregnant, my world fell apart. My boyfriend dumped me and moved on to a new girl. My parents kicked me out. I was living on the streets when Jason was born. It took five years to crawl up out of the gutter life I'd made for myself. I don't even want to remember the things I did to put bread on our table. And then, feeling holier-than-thou, I had the audacity to ambush you. I dug a hole and tried to bury you under my hurt and bitterness. Everything I said to you was all about the girl I'd been. I didn't even see you."

Dawn let out a shuddering breath. She'd prayed so hard about this meeting and now felt the warmth of God's answer filling her. "But don't you see? I *was* all the things you said, Georgia."

When Georgia opened her mouth, Dawn raised her hand. "Let *me* finish. If you'd been gentle, I might not have listened. It took you speaking the truth the way you did to get through to me. I'm grateful that you did. God used your words to draw me to Himself, and that's when the Lord started working. Maybe if someone had spoken to you the way you spoke to me, things would have turned out differently for you too." She'd been afraid she wouldn't be able to say a word when she walked through the front door, but words flowed naturally and with a love she hadn't known she possessed for Jason's mother.

Georgia let out a long breath. "Just to be clear: I couldn't be more pleased you're marrying my son."

"Me, too."

They laughed together.

"Well. All that being said . . ." Georgia leaned forward and lifted the plate. "Have a cookie. And then let's talk about how I can help put on a beautiful wedding."

❄ ❄ ❄

From the day Dawn told her family she and Jason were getting married, Granny had pressured Dawn to go shopping for a white wedding dress. Dawn didn't feel entitled to wear a white gown, but she didn't want to hurt Granny by explaining why not. She didn't know what to do until her mother offered the pale pink gown and veil she'd worn when she married Mitch. "I think it'll fit you." Her mother seemed shy about it. "If you want it."

"I do." She'd felt her mother stiffen slightly when she hugged her. Sometimes Dawn wondered why her mother seemed so uncomfortable with physical affection, unless it came from Christopher or Mitch.

On the morning of the wedding, deaconesses were on hand to decorate the church with the poinsettias Georgia had delivered, and by eleven, the place was packed with well-wishers. Dawn saw Jason's gaze fixed on her as Mitch walked her down the aisle. She gave white roses to Granny and Mom. When Pastor Daniel pronounced them man and wife, the congregants erupted in

applause and cheers. On the way back up the aisle, Dawn paused and gave Georgia a white rose and kissed her cheek. She had two left, one to throw and one to keep.

While pictures were being taken, deacons rearranged chairs and set up tables. Caterers covered everything with linens and spread platters with enough fancy sandwiches and salads to feed an army. A three-tiered wedding cake stood on a central table. The stack of beautifully wrapped packages grew on two back tables. After the receiving line, Jason and Dawn sat at the head table and nibbled at lunch. They cut the cake, carefully feeding each other small bites, and then danced to the music of the professional band Mitch had hired.

Jason held Dawn close as they waltzed, his warm breath sending shivers down her spine. "Can we go now?" he whispered against her ear. His hand spread on the small of her back. "We've cut the cake and had our dance."

She laughed softly. "The reception is supposed to last another hour."

Mitch cut in. "Dad's turn." Grinning broadly at Jason, he took Dawn in his arms. "You look like you can't wait to get her out of here, but you won't want to drive your Honda anywhere until you run it through a car wash."

Jason grimaced. "I'm going to—"

"Do nothing." Mitch chuckled. "Carolyn will give you the keys to my Bonneville."

"Thanks, Mitch." Jason stepped forward. "Can I have my wife back now?"

"Not so fast. You have duties to perform. Dance with your mother and mother-in-law first. And I've been informed Dawn still has to throw her rose to a gaggle of single girls. And you have to toss her garter to that pack of wolves you call friends. Then Pita's all yours for the rest of your life, buddy boy."

Laughing, Dawn punched him.

It was a long, dark drive and well after ten before they reached Fort Bragg and signed into the Harbor Lite Lodge as Mr. and Mrs. Jason Steward. The suite was larger than Dawn's studio apartment.

Someone had already lit the fire in the small Franklin stove. She opened the sliding-glass door and went out on the small balcony overlooking the Noyo River. A light rain sprinkled, and fog curled around the security lights on the docks below.

Jason slid his hands around her waist and drew her back against him. "Finally. We're alone." He kissed the curve of her neck, sending warm tendrils through her body. "And married."

❆　❆　❆

After spending two nights and two days in their suite, with only brief outings for meals, Dawn and Jason returned to Alexander Valley for the family Christmas celebration. "Wait until you see!" Christopher bounded ahead of them to her bedroom and threw the door open. All the wedding presents had been stacked, waiting to be unwrapped. Dawn gaped.

Jason dumped their two small suitcases inside the door and stared. "Holy cow!"

Mom peered in. "Welcome home, you two." Her eyes shone. "It seems you both have a lot of friends who wanted to help you set up housekeeping."

Mitch, standing right behind her, nudged her into the room. "Don't panic. Once everything is opened, pick what you need and leave the rest here for later."

Granny asked Dawn and Jason to come out to Jenner for a few days after Christmas, but Jason said they needed to go home to San Luis Obispo. He had to move his stuff into Dawn's apartment, and they needed to get settled in before classes started.

Dawn knew another reason Jason didn't want to go to Jenner. She waited until they were alone that night to ask his forgiveness for what she brought about in the downstairs apartment.

"You weren't alone, you know." Jason touched her cheek. "I stayed overnight *hoping* you'd come downstairs. I could have stopped things if I'd wanted, Dawn. It wasn't all your idea." He drew her close and kissed her.

❋ ❋ ❋

1991

It didn't take long for Jason and Dawn to decide they had to study somewhere other than in the apartment. With two small desks and the nook table, they didn't have room to spread their books and reports. They made other adjustments as well. Dawn liked to do her Bible study before the sun came up pink-yellow over the hills. Jason, a night owl, studied Scripture at night.

They walked to campus together. They ate lunch together, and they spent every spare minute studying at the library. Dawn cooked and did laundry on Saturdays. Sunday, they went to the early service and then took long walks, went to the beach, talked over Chinese food, and hung out with Dod Henson and Alice Jeffries, their closest friends on campus. Sometimes Jack Kohl joined them, if he had a new girlfriend.

They talked of nothing but the war in Iraq, the need to protect the oil fields and Persian Gulf, the hope for success with the air campaign and bombing of leadership targets in Baghdad. Coalition ground forces drove on Iraqi forces in Kuwait. After four days, Iraqi forces agreed to a cease-fire and retreated from Kuwait. The push to reach Baghdad halted. Jason and Dod sneered over U.N. objectives being met. Even when Iraq agreed to a permanent cease-fire, they saw trouble ahead. "Saddam Hussein fancies himself the second Nebuchadnezzar. He's not done. They've just given him time to coil for another strike."

44

LIFE FELT REGIMENTED, but comfortable and with frequent moments of delight. The only dark cloud was approaching summer break. Jason would be leaving for two months, undergoing military training at Fort Lewis, Washington. Dawn knew she had to keep busy or be miserable while he was gone. Still intent upon finishing college as quickly as possible, she registered for a summer session psychology class.

The week before finals, Dawn had difficulty sleeping. One morning she rose while it was still dark and quietly slid the partition between the living room and bedroom closed. Turning on the swag lamp over the kitchen nook table, she opened her Bible and workbook. She and Jason had been married five months, and she still hadn't finished all the sections. She'd been taking her time, praying over the questions, and examining herself, asking God to reveal areas of her life that needed change.

As the warmth of the sun spilled in the window, she heard a soft click. Startled, she glanced toward the bedroom. Jason stood there holding a camera. "Perfect." Grinning, he set it on the coffee table.

"You took a picture?" She was still in her robe and slippers, her hair loose and wild.

Leaning down, he hemmed her in with his hands planted on the table. He nuzzled her neck. "I love the way the sun lights up your hair in the morning. You look like an angel studying God's directives for the day." Straightening, he put his hands on her shoulders. "And I wanted something more natural than a wedding picture to keep me company while I'm at Fort Lewis."

❄ ❄ ❄

The first thing Dawn saw when she walked into the apartment after her last final exam was Jason's physical training uniform hooked on the closet trim, ready to be worn. She burst into tears. They'd been married only five months, and he'd be gone tomorrow morning. He'd spend a month in cadet troop leadership training and then be off to airborne school right after that. "Two months," she muttered. "Two months!"

He said the camp was designed to develop leadership skills, teamwork, water safety, land navigation, fire support, weapons use, and tactical and physical training. Portions of it sounded ominous and dangerous to her, but he dismissed her worries. Thankfully, the war in Iraq had ended in March. Lord willing, Jason would not see actual combat during his military service. Dawn didn't know how she would cope with that.

Jason had told her he first started thinking about ROTC after her grandfather had regaled him with World War II stories. After their breakup, Jason started thinking more about the military. He'd sought out Mitch and asked questions about the Vietnam War and his military experience. Mitch had told him the military had a lot to offer and the country always needed good men trained and ready. His school counselor told him to talk to the ROTC recruiting officer at Cal Poly. When he learned the Army would give him the financial aid he needed to get through college in exchange for six years of his life, Jason decided it was a generous offer. Without discussing it with his mother or Pastor Daniel, he entered the program freshman year.

Dawn dumped her backpack on the bed. Jason admitted he hadn't consulted God about that decision, but whether he had or had not wasn't an issue now. God was sovereign. Man might plan, but God would prevail. She believed that with all her heart. She just hadn't realized how much military life might suit Jason—or how much it might demand of her.

Jason took her in his arms. "I'm not gone yet."

"You'll be jumping out of airplanes, Jason."

"Yeah."

He sounded excited about it. She pushed away and looked at him. He looked excited, too. "You can't wait, can you?"

"I'm not going to lie to you."

"I know." She'd overheard him talking with Dod and Jack. In truth, all three were looking forward to the training, like it was some kind of grand adventure!

Letting out her breath, she withdrew. "I'm just being ridiculous." Would she rather he was miserable and wishing he didn't have to follow through on his obligations to the military? When she reached for the duffel bag, he grabbed it and slung it onto the bed. She started packing for him. "I'll be all right. I'll keep busy."

"I'll call you every chance I get."

Jason called to let her know he'd arrived safely at Fort Lewis. After less than a minute, she heard another man asking to use the phone. After that, she waited in vain to hear from him. His second call came before he headed into airborne training, though Dawn still couldn't understand why an engineer needed to know how to jump out of an airplane. She didn't waste time asking. They talked for fifteen minutes before he had to hang up so someone else could make a call.

To keep from being depressed, Dawn poured herself into her psychology class. While going through lecture notes on symptoms of abuse, she thought about her mother for some odd reason. Dawn realized she knew very little about her mother's past, other than what Granny had told her.

What had kept Mom away from church for so many years? Why did she withdraw from any show of affection, unless it came from Mitch or Christopher? Granny took a step toward her, and Mom retreated. What caused the tension between them? When Dawn thought more about it, she realized her mother had always had difficulty with relationships, especially if they were casual. She served, but didn't mingle; she watched from a distance, but didn't attempt to participate. Dawn had this mental picture of her mother peering over a protective wall while keeping the gate to the outside world locked.

What might have caused that? Could it have something to do with the Haight-Ashbury years? Dawn didn't know much about that time in her mother's life. Granny said the past was best forgotten, and Mom never talked about it. Anytime anyone mentioned the turbulent sixties, Mom became very quiet.

Maybe she should ask. . . .

Dawn tried to during one of her weekly calls home. As usual, Mom stayed on the phone less than five minutes, leaving it to Christopher to report the family's news. Dawn didn't even get close to broaching the subject with her.

Dawn asked Granny what Mom had been like as a little girl. "Beautiful." Granny sounded wistful. "Quiet. There weren't any other little girls her age on our road, but she always seemed content playing by herself."

"Did she ever seem nervous or exhibit any odd behavior?"

Granny chuckled. "The trouble with studying psychology is you begin to imagine symptoms of all kinds of neuroses in everyone you know. Your mother was a perfectly normal child, just a little quieter than most."

"So Mom never had nightmares or sucked her thumb . . . ?"

"Oh, there was a while when she used to sneak into Charlie's room and sleep with him or on the floor beside his bed. It didn't last long. I put a stop to it as soon as I knew."

"And she was fine with that, no crying or arguments?"

Silence for a moment. "She started sleeping in her closet. But really, Dawn, you're making way too much of it."

"I know, Granny. I'm just curious. That's all."

"We started leaving a night-light on in the bathroom. She seemed fine after that. Or maybe it was Oma."

"Oma?"

"She came to live with us about that time." Her tone turned brisk. "Either way, your mom stayed in her own bed after that."

On impulse, Dawn called her mother that evening and asked if she remembered having nightmares as a child.

"Why do you ask?"

"I'm taking psychology."

"Oh. Well. I suppose all children have bad dreams. Don't they?"

"Granny said you used to sneak in and sleep with Uncle Charlie."

"Did she?"

"And when she put a stop to it, you slept in your closet."

Silence.

"Mom?"

"What started this line of questioning?"

Dawn winced. Mom might as well have said *interrogation*. "I'm taking psychology, and the lectures have been on child abuse."

"I was never beaten, May Flo—" She stopped. "Dawn." She spoke the correction quietly.

"We'll have to talk about my name someday." Dawn tried to keep her tone light. When her mother didn't respond, she apologized for asking such personal questions. "I was just curious."

Her mother's reticence only served to make *her* more so.

❄ ❄ ❄

Dawn sat at the nook table, flipping through her class notes. Slapping her binder closed, she stared out the window. She'd studied enough. She didn't want to think about psychology or come up with any more theories on why her mother was the way she was. She'd never know anything more about her than she did now. It wasn't her business anyway.

She knew what the problem was: she had too much time on her hands. She needed something to do other than go to class, study, and hang around the apartment, waiting for Jason to call. She had to stop counting the days until he'd come home. She looked at the bare white walls, the worn beige couch, the drab chipboard coffee table sitting on the beige rug. Life without Jason was as colorless as the apartment.

The place needed cheering up. It needed *color*!

Grabbing her keys and purse, Dawn left the apartment. She drove downtown and bought half a dozen women's magazines. She spotted notices on the coffee shop bulletin board: garage sales popped up like weeds every Friday afternoon. She'd always thought it might be fun to visit a few, see what treasures she might find among the piles of junk. On the way back to the apartment, Dawn stopped by a hardware store and picked out paint color strips.

"Walls have to be back to white before you leave," Mr. Cooper, the apartment manager told her when she explained what she'd like to do. "Otherwise, you forfeit your security deposit."

After psychology class, Dawn went to the library and looked for books on interior design. She jotted down ideas, then went back to the apartment to take measurements and map out furnishings. She tore pages from magazines.

Early Saturday morning, Dawn drove south to Santa Maria, hoping to be the first arrival at the *Huge Neighborhood Garage Sale: furnishings, fine linens, china* . . . She wasn't. Already a crowd wandered the cul-de-sac, picking through racks of cloth-ing, looking over electronic gadgets, tools, toys, and totally useless knickknacks. Dawn bargained for two matching crested chairs with burgundy upholstery and got them for twenty dollars. She fitted them carefully into the backseat of the Sable and continued her search. She bought two Talavera plates for five dollars; an old, worn, imitation Persian rug in jewel tones for twenty-five; and a glass bowl full of seashells for a buck.

Still on the hunt, Dawn wandered, looking for anything that caught her eye. She became engrossed with a shoe box full of maps and another of postcards. She bought three framed posters of rock groups. On her way back to the car, she bargained for two large sky-blue blankets and a somewhat-faded yellow and blue French provincial tablecloth with deep pink peonies and daisies.

Mr. Cooper saw her pull up and laughed. "When the dog's away, the cat will play. Need some help unloading all that junk?"

She laughed, excited about getting to work on decorating. "Yes, please." She started pulling the rolled carpet through the back window. "And I'll have you know these are *treasures*."

Over the next week, Dawn painted the living room wall butter yellow, folded and pinned one blue blanket around the body of the sofa and the other around the two large cushions, unrolled the Persian rug, tucking it beneath the sofa, and set the oval-backed chairs in opposite corners, the coffee table in the middle. Making do without a sewing machine, Dawn folded and pinned colorful cloth covers over cheap pillows and arranged them on the sofa.

Removing the rock concert pictures, she used two of the frames to mount maps of Monterey and Washington, D.C. As the center-piece of wall art, she created a colorful collage of old postcards from national parks across the country. She hung the two Talavera plates in the kitchen, put a yellow valance over the nook window, and spread the Provence tablecloth. Last touches included the glass bowl of seashells on the coffee table, the new issue of *VIA* from the California Automobile Association, and a bouquet of yellow roses in a lime green Fiesta water pitcher.

Arms akimbo, she admired the room. Eclectic, she decided, already imagining other things she could do to make the room more interesting. A potted palm in the corner would be nice, and some nice coverings for the ugly end tables. Changing the lamp shades . . .

She stopped the train of thoughts running through her head. The living room looked warm and cozy. Now she needed to read another chapter in her psychology text and review her notes. She still had five more days for decorating before Jason came home.

Flipping through her notes, she became distracted. She had a great idea for adding a little wow factor to the bedroom.

❄   ❄   ❄

Dawn spotted Jason in his uniform coming down the steps of the small jet disgorging its twenty passengers. She wanted to hurtle herself into his arms, but had already been warned the military frowned on public displays of affection. Apparently, Jason forgot. When she got her breath back, she noticed Dod Henson and Jack Kohl approaching and called out a greeting as Jason took her hand.

They all waited at the conveyor belt that would deposit passenger luggage.

Jason brushed his other hand against her cheek. "What've you been doing while I've been away?"

"Keeping busy."

"How's your psychology class going?"

"Fascinating, but I've discovered another passion."

"What's that?"

She gave him an impish smile. "Wait and see."

When he stepped through the door of the apartment, he stared. "Wow! Did you call in a decorator?"

"Nope. I did it all by myself. I spent less than two hundred dollars on the whole place. What do you think?"

"Classy." He looked closer at the maps on the wall. "Where did you come up with all these ideas?"

"Women's magazines, garage sales . . ."

He stepped around the partition. "I'm impressed." He stared at the ceiling medallion where she'd tucked and hot-glued mosquito netting that draped the top half of the bed. He turned to grin at her. "Reminds me of a pasha's tent. Do you have harem girls in the closet?"

"There's only room for one girl in this apartment, Jason." She stepped close and unfastened the top button on his camouflage shirt. She looked up at him as she unbuttoned the next and the next. "And don't even think about adding another to your life."

Jason swept her up in his arms and tossed her into the middle of the bed. "Not unless we have a daughter."

45

1992

When she finally started student nursing, Dawn was distressed
to discover that working in a hospital wasn't anything like taking
nursing classes. She could make beds and cheer the patients. She
could do sponge baths and plump pillows. She could take vitals
and fill out charts. But she felt queasy every time she watched a
procedure. When called to help change dressings, she sucked in her
breath every time the patient did. The sight of more than a table-
spoon of blood made yellow and black spots dance before her eyes.

It wasn't her calling. That was the problem. She watched the
other nursing students and knew they loved what they were doing,
while she dreaded every minute. She felt tense and uncomfortable
the moment she stepped into the hospital, afraid she wouldn't be
up to whatever emergency she'd face.

Jason tried to cheer her up. "You should've majored in art and
interior design."

Too late now. Mom and Mitch, Christopher, and Granny came
down together for Dawn's graduation. Georgia arrived a day ahead,

thought the apartment "stunning," and accepted the invitation to sleep on the sofa rather than pay for a motel room.

The rest agreed with Georgia. "I think you missed your calling, Pita."

Great. Just what she needed to hear.

Jason sat proudly in the audience as Dawn received honors for her academic work. He needed another year to finish his engineering degree, especially now that he'd decided to add on a master's.

Christopher begged Dawn and Jason to come home for the summer. Everyone else joined in. Georgia said Kim and Tom were coming home. "She's pregnant."

Dawn couldn't wait for the day when she and Jason could start a family.

Granny patted Jason's arm. "You haven't been out to Jenner since before Papa died." Dawn felt heat flood her face and lowered her head, hoping no one noticed. Granny rushed on. "You two can stay in the downstairs apartment as long as you like, take drives along the coast, walk on the beach. Spend a week . . . or a month."

Mom looked at Dawn. "It'd be nice if you'd spend a few weeks with us, too."

"Don't forget you have a mother, Jason."

Under the table, Jason's hand slid to Dawn's thigh. "Nice to be in such demand." He gave her a teasing smile. "We wouldn't have to pay rent for two months."

❄ ❄ ❄

Dawn and Jason spent the first two weeks with Georgia. Dawn felt odd the first night, sleeping in Jason's old bed with Georgia just across the narrow hall. Both tense, they spoke in whispers and barely touched.

After their stay with Georgia, they moved to Alexander Valley to spend time with Mom, Mitch, and Christopher. Christoper jabbered all through the first dinner and left shortly afterward for an overnight at a friend's house. Dawn insisted on doing the dishes.

When the phone rang, Mom answered. Dawn could tell by her shuttered expression Granny was on the other end of the line.

"They just got here. . . . I don't know. They haven't said anything. They were over at Georgia's for two weeks." She listened for a moment, shoulders drooping. "They have friends to see and things to do. . . . Yes. I know." She looked at Dawn and mouthed, *Granny wants to talk to you.*

Dawn dried her hands and took the phone. Mom went into the family room, where Mitch and Jason were watching a golf tournament. Mitch said something, and Mom sat next to him. He draped an arm around her and she leaned into his side.

Granny wanted to know how soon Dawn and Jason were coming to Jenner. Feeling guilty, Dawn said they wouldn't come for three weeks, at least. So long? Granny didn't try to cover her disappointment. "I'd like to spend as much time with Mom and Mitch and Christopher as I can, Granny."

"Oh. Well. Of course, I understand." Her tone hinted the opposite. "There are three of them to visit with and only one of me."

Dawn winced with guilt. "We could come out for a visit on Saturday."

"I'll fix a nice lunch."

When Dawn told Jason, Mitch gave her an odd look. Mom kept her focus on the television.

Later that night, Jason slipped his arm around her as they lay in bed. "What's with your mom and grandmother?"

"I'm not sure, but I think I'm the bone of contention."

"How so?"

"Mom came home from Haight-Ashbury pregnant. Granny had to give up her nursing career to take care of me."

"Somehow I don't think she minded." He ran a finger over her brow. "Where was your mom while your grandmother was taking care of you?"

"Going to school, working. I think she was trying to piece her life back together."

"She picked a good man to help her."

"Mitch picked *her*. As far as I know, my mother never even went on a date until he rode into town on his motorcycle. He was Uncle Charlie's best friend. He told me once he's been in love with Mom since high school."

"Sounds like someone else I know." Jason leaned down and kissed her.

When he raised his head, she ran her fingers through his short hair. "Mitch is the only person Mom allows close." She sighed. "Mothers and daughters should be close, too. I know Mom and Granny love each other, but they can't talk. I'm not sure who put up the wall first or why. I just wish I knew how to tear it down."

They curled together like two spoons in a drawer. Jason wrapped his arm around her. "Ask God to do it for you."

❋ ❋ ❋

1993

Everyone came for Jason's graduation. Jason wore a black cap and gown to receive his bachelor's and master's diplomas. Later that same day, he wore his Army uniform with red trim and socks to designate he was an engineer. Dawn had never seen him more handsome.

The past year had been difficult, but she knew harder days were to come.

While Dawn sat silent, Jason told everyone what was coming. He had orders to Fort Sill, Oklahoma, where he'd go through three months of basic infantry training. After that, he'd train with the corps of engineers at Fort Leonard Wood in Missouri. Then he could apply for Airborne, Ranger, or Special Forces training.

Granny jumped in and pressed Dawn with advice to quit her nursing job at the clinic and stay at Jenner until Jason had a duty station.

Mom spoke quietly. "That could be months away."

Granny looked annoyed. "It's not easy chasing all over the country. I've done it." She turned to Dawn. "You move into a room somewhere and wait until he has a weekend off. You'll be lonely and depressed."

Jason frowned as though that side of things hadn't even occurred to him until Granny brought it up.

Mom interrupted. "Dawn should decide."

"I wasn't saying she shouldn't. I just think Dawn would be better off spending time with family *now*."

Dawn jumped in before things could get worse. "I've already decided what I'm going to do."

Jason looked at her in surprise. "You have?"

"Yes." She smiled at him, trying to project more confidence than she felt. "Where you go, I go." She glanced around the table, at Mitch, Mom, Christopher, Granny, and Georgia. "I love all of you very much, but Jason is my husband."

"But . . . ," Granny stammered.

"If I have to live in a tent, Granny, it's all right by me. I belong with Jason."

A few seconds of silence could feel like an eternity.

"Okay then." Jason's eyes shone. He took her hand and kissed it.

Granny's shoulders slumped. "Thank God there's no war."

"What, Hildie?" Mitch grinned down the table. "Dawn might strap on a rifle and follow him into battle?"

Everyone laughed, even Granny, though not as brightly. "I shouldn't be surprised. Dawn is my granddaughter." She told the gathering she'd almost enlisted in the nursing corps during World War II, but Trip made her ineligible.

"How'd he do that?" Christopher wanted to know.

"He got me pregnant!"

More laughter resounded around the table. Georgia winked at Dawn. "Now, there's a welcome idea."

❄ ❄ ❄

Dawn put in her two-week notice at the clinic. They offered a bonus if she would stay until they could find a replacement. After discussing it with Jason, Dawn agreed to stay on staff for a month. Jason had his Honda serviced, packed, and headed for Oklahoma, leaving Dawn to decide what to take, sell, or give away before following him to Fort Sill.

Until Jason walked out the door, Dawn had no qualms about the decisions they had made. After he left, she lay awake at night, filled with anxiety. What had ever given her the idea she could drive cross-country alone? What if the car overheated or broke down? What if she ran out of gas on some long stretch across Arizona or New Mexico? Where would she stay when she arrived in Lawton, Oklahoma?

Burying her face in her hands, Dawn prayed. Her mind wandered to Abraham and Sarah. God had told Abraham to go forth from his country, his relatives, and his father's house to the land God would show him. And he'd gone without question, just like Jason. Maybe she should have been like Sarah and gone with him rather than stay behind and follow later.

Lord, help me not to be afraid.

Oma came to mind. She'd never been afraid of anything, had left home at fifteen and gone out alone into the world to make her own way. Oma had lived in Montreaux and then moved to France and on to England. She boarded a ship, crossed the Atlantic, and started all over again in Montreal, Canada. When she married, her husband went off to the wheat fields to work, leaving her behind to run a boardinghouse and then travel by herself with a babe in arms to join her husband. Then she gave birth to Granny in a cabin out in the middle of nowhere—no hospital, no doctor, not even a midwife to help her. Later, with three children, she packed and came with her husband to California, where they lived in a tent before finally having a place of their own.

Fear lost its grip when Dawn thought about her great-grandmother. Granny had always said Oma was hard, but Dawn hadn't found her that way during that week in Merced. Crusty on the outside, perhaps, but she'd revealed a softness inside that had made Dawn wish she'd spent more time with her, gotten to know her better. Still, she had assurance Oma's blood ran in her veins.

God didn't give His children a heart of timidity, but of power and love and discipline. She would get maps, lay out her route, and take the journey one day at a time. What sense did it make to worry about tomorrow?

❄ ❄ ❄

Dawn talked with her mother before setting off. She half hoped Mom would volunteer to come with her. Instead, she talked about Oma. "She loved to take long drives and explore. She would've loved the kind of trip you're going on."

Doodling on a notepad, Dawn tossed out another hint. "It's a little daunting driving so far without any company."

"I know. I did it once."

"You had a friend with you."

"Half-comatose from drugs and alcohol."

"Oh."

"You don't have to go alone, Dawn. You could ask Granny."

Dawn's heart sank, and she rubbed her forehead. "I think I should go alone. I might as well grow up now and not put it off."

"You're growing up quite nicely, May Flower Dawn."

The softly spoken compliment brought tears to Dawn's eyes. "Do you really think so, Mom?" She felt like a baby, wanting to wail.

"Yes. I do. I'm proud of you."

Dawn almost blurted out that she wanted her mother to come with her. She wanted time alone with her so they could talk. She wanted to get to know her mother before they were separated by half a continent. "I'm a little nervous about the trip."

"Understandable, but you won't be alone, Dawn. You're never alone. God is with you. He goes ahead and He watches your back. He walks with you and dwells inside you. Just keep listening to Him."

"I'm glad you finally started believing in God."

"I've believed in Jesus for twenty-four years, Dawn. It's people I never learned to trust. I'll be praying for you. So will Georgia and a host of others. Granny, too. You know that. If you wouldn't mind, I'd like you to call me, let me know how far you make it each day. You don't have to talk long."

"Jason insisted I check in with someone every day."

"Good for Jason."

When they hung up, Dawn finished packing the last few things and went to bed, hoping for a good night's sleep before she set off the next morning. But her mind wouldn't shut down.

Twenty-four years. Isn't that what her mother had said? That would make it right around the time she had gotten pregnant. Maybe it had been the hardship and accidental pregnancy that had driven her mother to her knees. A desperate surrender.

Dawn yearned for the open affection Mom gave Christopher. But at least now her mother felt pride in her. They could talk more. Their best days as mother and daughter had been during the worst time in Dawn's life. Mom had known she grieved over Jason. When she came to Dawn's bedroom that dark night of despair, and Dawn confessed, Mom never spoke a word of condemnation or disappointment. What Mom said helped Dawn change course: *Examine yourself; take what is true and do what's right. And when others hurt you, forgive.*

Maybe someday they'd be able to sit down and really talk. Maybe someday they could go back to the beginning and go deep and rise up out of the pain of the past, together.

46

Dawn set out early Saturday morning, a disposable camera close at hand. She drove north to Atascadero, cut across to Shandon, and then took the road southeast toward the Central Valley. Orchards covered the area around Blackwells Corner. She pulled in at James Dean's Last Stop and browsed shelves of candy, dried fruit, jars of preserves and salsas, Indian art, and fifties memorabilia. After buying trail mix and a few souvenir postcards, she got back on the road. She passed rows of pink, red, and white rosebushes near Wasco before joining Highway 99 south.

She stopped at a roadside café on the other side of Bakersfield for lunch and studied the map while she ate. Later in the afternoon, she stretched her legs by walking through a Route 66 museum. Heat kept her in the car after that. Finally, as night approached, she could see a dome of light on the horizon. Las Vegas. She drove the Strip and found the hotel where she'd made a reservation.

Tossing her duffel bag on the green paisley spread, she picked up the telephone and punched the number for an open line.

Mom answered on the second ring and sounded relieved when she heard it was Dawn. "Everything go okay today?"

Dawn summarized what she'd seen in less than a minute.

"Are you in a decent place?"

"Clean, good lock, close to the Tropicana. I'm going to walk over there for dinner."

"I'm sorry. I didn't mean to delay you."

Dawn realized how abrupt she must sound. "I didn't mean to . . ." Why was it so much easier to talk to Granny than her mother?

"You go have a nice dinner, Dawn. I'll talk to you in a few days. Call me collect."

After a very reasonably priced buffet dinner, she returned to the hotel and wrote to Jason.

> *I wish I could sketch like Aunt Rikki. . . . I bought a copy of On the Road by Jack Kerouac. Maybe it will boost my enthusiasm for this trip. . . .*

She spent half the next day at Hoover Dam and then drove nonstop to Hurricane, Utah, checked into a hotel, and ate at a small diner next door before calling Granny. She hadn't talked more than five minutes when Granny started worrying about long-distance charges. When she mentioned it again a minute later, Dawn surrendered.

She left early the next morning to see Zion National Park. Mom wanted to hear all about it, but Dawn was too tired to talk long and wanted to get a letter off to Jason before she went to bed.

> *This will be a short letter, my love. I miss you so much! I wish you were making this trip with me. I'm trying not to rush. I know if I do, I'll just end up sitting alone in an apartment and crying all day. . . .*

The farther she drove, the lonelier she felt. She tried not to think how many more days it would take to reach Lawton, Oklahoma. Jason would be living in the barracks for three months. They'd see each other only on weekends.

She thought about her mother trying to keep her on the telephone and Granny trying to hurry her off. It seemed such a turnaround, now that she thought more about it. That night she checked in with Granny first and then called Mom.

"Jason called this afternoon. He gave me the names of two apartment complexes he wants you to check out when you get to Lawton. Both are near the base."

Dawn jotted down the information.

"Did you make it to the Grand Canyon?"

Dawn flopped back on the bed. "I'm about ten minutes away from the south rim. Japanese tourists got there ahead of me." She laughed. "They all had cameras. I had to wait an hour to get close to the rail." Mom kept asking questions and Dawn kept answering.

"Are you planning to stay over tomorrow, see a little more?"

"I don't think so. I want to keep going. I hope to make it to Monument Valley." Dawn heard Mitch talking in the background. "Does he need the phone?" She hadn't talked to her mother this long on a telephone ever.

"No. He just wants to know if you're checking oil and tire pressure and making sure you have plenty of gas before you make those long hauls across the desert."

"Tell him yes. I'm being very conscientious."

The next day seemed to last forever. Monument Valley was an endless expanse. Worried she might overheat the car, she turned off her air-conditioning and opened the window.

Granny let her talk for five minutes that night, then told Dawn she should get a good night's sleep. Dawn hung up and wrote another long letter to Jason.

❄ ❄ ❄

Dawn saw the sign for the turnoff to Mesa Verde National Park and calculated how long it would take to go in, see the ruins and museum, and drive out. *Forget it!* She headed for Durango. She'd had enough of traveling alone. Even if she and Jason couldn't live together, she still wanted to be as close to him as possible. It might cheer him up to know she was ready and waiting when he did get liberty.

Canceling reservations in Pagosa Springs and Albuquerque, Dawn headed for Amarillo, Texas. Other than stopping now and then to use a restroom, check her oil and tire pressure, fill the tank with gas, and have a fast meal, she didn't see anything that held as much interest for her as Jason Steward in Lawton, Oklahoma.

The following afternoon, exhausted, Dawn arrived, checked into a Best Western, and called her mother. "I made it."

"I wondered how long you'd last before you decided to make a run for Lawton. Will you be able to see Jason?"

"Probably not, but at least I'm close to him. When he calls you, give him this number."

Dawn let a hot shower massage her aching muscles. She put on sweatpants and one of Jason's T-shirts and fell asleep on top of the bedspread. Bleary-eyed, she looked at the time and realized she had slept five hours. The sun was going down.

Her motel room phone rang.

"You're *here*?" Jason lowered his voice. "How close?"

"Five minutes from the gate."

He laughed softly. "Didn't see Mesa Verde?"

"Waved as I drove on by."

"Durango?"

"Drove through."

"What happened to seeing some of the country?"

"I'm only interested in one natural wonder. You."

❄ ❄ ❄

Jason's old Honda was parked in the hotel lot when Dawn returned from moving their things into the apartment she'd found. He came out of the office, looking annoyed. She rolled down her window and called out to him. "Hey, handsome!" Grinning broadly, he headed straight for her like an airplane landing on a carrier. He opened her car door. She got out and threw herself into his arms. "I found us an apartment. I moved our stuff in this afternoon. All white and beige . . ."

"Don't waste time or money fixing the place up. Okay? I'm only going to be here two more months and then Missouri."

She closed her eyes. Another long, lonely drive lay ahead of her, but she wouldn't allow herself to think of that now. This was the path Jason had chosen. God had brought them back together so she could walk it with him. When her stomach growled loudly, she grimaced. "I'm so hungry, my stomach is about to digest my lungs."

"We'd better feed you then."

Dawn packed and checked out the next morning. Jason followed in his old Honda and pulled into the space beside her. "Nice complex." He liked the apartment, though after a barracks, he said even the hotel room had been Shangri-la. While Dawn pulled sheets and pillowcases from a box and made up the queen bed, Jason talked about his training, the guys he'd met in the barracks, his instructors. Dawn stowed pots and pans while Jason set up their computer on the nook table.

"We're all moved in." Jason thunked his booted feet on the coffee table and draped his arms over the back of the couch.

Dawn looked at the nook table covered with computer components and printer and wires snaking everywhere. "Not very homey."

"Functional. And we can use the coffee table for dining." He smirked at her when she stared pointedly at his boots. "Or go out."

She sat beside him, tucking herself under his arm. "We need groceries." She looked through the glass doors to the naked patio.

Their home needed color and spots of interest. Two patio chairs and a little table with a potted plant would perk up the outside. A couple of pillows, a simple cabinet to cover all the computer wires, a framed picture, and . . .

Jason gripped her head like a basketball. "I can hear your wheels turning."

❄   ❄   ❄

Monday morning, Dawn awakened alone, puffy-eyed from crying herself to sleep the night before. Jason had stayed as long as he could before heading back to base, but watching him walk out the door left an empty, aching feeling inside her. It would be five days before she saw him again. She remembered what Granny had said about sitting around all day, waiting and feeling lonely and wondering when she'd see her husband.

Standing at the kitchen counter, Dawn ate her eggs and glared at the nook. She had no place to write notes and study her Bible, and the computer was an eyesore. The apartment felt like a beige tomb. She shoved her Bible, journal, and spiral notebook into a backpack and headed out to Cameron University, only a few blocks away.

The college library felt more like home. She found a quiet table where she could read. She felt less lonely with others nearby, comfortable with the studious silence. After an hour, she looked through books on interior design. She made quick sketches and jotted down ideas. The *Lawton Constitution* and *Anadarko Daily News* had a list of upcoming garage sales.

Dawn drove to the base to fill out the paperwork for her ID, then went on a self-guided base tour of grave sites of famous Indians warriors—Geronimo and Kiowa Chief Satanta and Comanche Chief Quanah Parker.

She stopped at a large home improvement center on the way back to the apartment and bought a computer table kit, screwdriver, and small hammer. The store put on workshops for basic carpentry and home repairs. Unfortunately, most were on Saturdays. She asked if they had anything during the week; the clerk said no, but showed her a wall display of how-to books.

Jason called that night. "What did you do today?"

"Explored Lawton and the base. The wind sure blows here." She told him about the Indian Wars, the Chiricahua Apaches. "Did you know Geronimo is buried on Fort Sill?"

Lying alone in bed that night, Dawn stared at the ceiling. During the day, she could keep busy and not feel so alone. When the night rolled in around her, the wind whistling outside, the loneliness blew in and stayed. She imagined Jason lying on his bunk in a barracks full of other soldiers. Bunching up Jason's pillow, she hugged it close.

Seven weeks later, she packed up and followed Jason again.

Dear Granny,

Jason and I are now settled in on-base housing at "Fort Lost in the Woods," Missouri. Jason has been told he'll be here for "a while," though that can mean anything from a few weeks to a few years in the Army. Wherever Jason is needed, we'll go.

Driving on snowy roads is an experience. I wouldn't want to drive cross-country this time of year! There'd have to be a good reason! We are looking forward to a white Christmas, though we will miss you and the rest of our family.

We looked for apartments in Devil's Elbow, Hooker,

Gospel Ridge (don't you just love those names!) but decided to choose on-base housing. A two-bedroom, one-bathroom unit opened up. Our little house shares a wall with Ricardo and Alicia Martinez and little Lalo, their adorable two-year-old. Alicia had him outside making snow angels.

Jason sold his old Honda, and we used the money to buy a secondhand bedroom set, an "antique" round oak table with claw feet, and two chairs. We also bought a new sofa and television, which we will pay off quickly now that I have a part-time job at the FLW hospital. . . .

1994

Dawn checked the calendar again, trying not to get her hopes up. When they moved into this little house a year ago, Jason had taken her birth control pills out of the medicine cabinet, looked her square in the eye, and with a grin, tossed them into the bathroom wastebasket. She'd been ecstatic, and she'd expected to get pregnant right away. After six months, she tried not to obsess. They'd thought she might be pregnant once, but the test had come up negative. But each day for the past two weeks, her hopes had been slowly building again. It was time to tell Jason.

Jason came home for lunch, as he did every day. Dawn never got over how handsome he was in his Army combat uniform. He left his hat on the hall table, kissed her, and frowned. "You look awfully pale."

"I'm fine. Just . . . have something on my mind, that's all." She smoothed mayonnaise onto one slice of bread and mustard on another, laid on two thick slices of bologna, tomato, purple onion, lettuce.

Jason sat waiting. "Well?"

"I wondered if you could run an errand for me on your way home tonight." She put Jason's sandwich on a plate and put it in the refrigerator.

Laughing, he got up and retrieved it. "I guess I'd better, because you're obviously not thinking straight. What is it?"

"Well, I thought we might want to take another pregnancy test."

"Really? Okay. Will do. We'll know tonight." He set his plate on the table and made another sandwich for her. "Wait until my mother hears."

"Don't say anything to anyone, Jason." Both sides of the family would be ecstatic. Georgia and Granny had been campaigning for a grandchild since Jason graduated and received his commission. Dawn thought they should wait until Jason received orders for his duty station.

Jason turned her around and kissed her. When she relaxed in his arms, he held her closer, his hands moving up and down her back, then resting on her hips. When he drew back, he gave her a purely male smile. "Doesn't change how we feel."

"Did you think it would?"

"It occurred to me." He put his arm around her. "Maybe you should quit working."

"Let's talk about that when we have a firm answer."

Jason came home with a small plastic bag from the pharmacy. She took it into the bathroom. When she came out, Jason sat on the edge of the bed, head bowed, hands clasped between his knees. She waited until he raised his head.

"Well?" He stared at her intently.

"Which way do you want it to go, Jason?"

He frowned. "Whichever way God wants it." He tucked her hair back. "We can always keep trying."

"You make it sound like work." She ran her hands over his chest. "I guess it is time you took a vacation."

It took him a few seconds to catch her meaning. Then he laughed, lifted her in his arms, and swung her around.

❄ ❄ ❄

Mom didn't shriek like Granny. "I'm happy if you're happy, May Flower Dawn." Dawn knew when her mother used her full name, she felt more deeply than she let on.

"I am happy, Mom. I'm so happy I could burst!"

"We've been thinking about flying out to see you. Would that be all right?"

"Of course!"

"We'll fly into Branson as soon as Christopher is out of school. Second week of June. We'd love to have you and Jason meet us there. We'll put you up in a nice hotel, eat out, and see some shows. You wouldn't have to do a thing."

Dawn chuckled. "Oh. I get it. You don't want to stay in guest housing."

"Oh, we'll come up to Fort Leonard Wood for a few days. You've written about all you've done with the house. I'd like to see it. If that's all right."

"Mom! Of course! Any chance you could bring Granny with you? She's been wanting to come, but she's never been on an airplane before." Nearing eighty, she was afraid to come alone. "We could help pay for her plane ticket."

A momentary silence. "No, that's fine, Dawn. We can take care of her ticket. I'm sure Granny would love to come along. Do you want to call and tell her? Or shall I?"

Dawn heard the subtle change in her mother's voice, then realized she had hurt her feelings. "I'll leave it up to you, Mom. I'm sorry. I shouldn't have asked."

"No. I should have thought of it first." Voices in the background. "Christopher wants to talk to you." Mom was gone, and Dawn's little brother took her place. Although Dawn had to remind herself that he wasn't "little" anymore; he'd just turned fifteen. And he'd been taller than she was the last time she'd seen him.

He talked nonstop for five minutes, excited about soccer, excited about summer, excited about coming to see her and Jason.

"I want to see the Indian caves. . . ." Dawn heard Mom say something to him. "Mom said to tell you she'll call Granny as soon as
we're off the phone."

Granny called an hour later, excited but nervous about flying,
eager to see Dawn and Jason. "I hope we'll have a little one-on-one
time together, honey. I've missed you so much."

One-on-one time meant cutting Mom out.

"I always end up hurting one of them," Dawn told Jason over
dinner.

"You probably won't get any time alone with your mother."

"No." Dawn cleared dishes. "I won't." She had only herself
to blame for that.

❄ ❄ ❄

Granny, Mom, Mitch, and Christopher visited for only four days.
It was nerve-racking trying to make sure she had time with Granny
and Mom. She never had to worry about how to entertain Mitch
and Christopher. They took off to see the Indian caves or talked
Jason into going bowling "so the girls can talk."

Granny talked. Mom didn't get the chance to say much of
anything.

Mom went out for long walks every afternoon. She always
retreated when she felt uncomfortable. Dawn wondered if she
did it so Granny could have more time with Dawn. If so, Granny
didn't return the favor. Even when the three of them sat together,
the men off somewhere, Granny dominated the conversation,
asking questions or reminiscing about Dawn as a baby, a toddler,
a child.

Dawn was certain that they loved each other. They just didn't
know how to talk to each other. There was a lot of unfinished business between them. And she was a big part of it.

She hadn't realized how stressful it would be having Mom and
Granny together for four days. Not that anything untoward had
been said. Jason had to get up early, and he found it hard to keep

his eyes open after nine o'clock. Mitch would suggest it was time to head back to the Ramada Inn. Mom would then ask Granny if she was ready to go. It became a ritual, leaving it up to Granny to decide.

If there had been an extra bed in the second room instead of the new crib, Dawn would have asked Mom to spend the night. With Granny, Mitch, and Christopher back at the Ramada Inn, maybe she and Mom could've talked more.

Her mother never said much, but what she said counted.

❉ ❉ ❉

Over the next few days, Dawn couldn't shake the feeling something was wrong. Granny called to thank her for the wonderful time. Now that Granny had been on an airplane, she might make the next trip on her own. "Your mom can drive me to the airport."

Mom called, but didn't talk long. Christopher talked for half an hour. He hadn't cared all that much about the bright lights and entertainment in Branson, but he'd loved hanging out with Jason and hiking with Dad. They'd explored the bluffs above the Big Piney.

Dawn went to bed shortly after dinner. Jason followed. "Are you okay, honey?"

"Just tired." Lying on her side, she went over her prayer list. She didn't make it halfway through before sleep pulled her down.

She stood knee-deep in murky swamp water, surrounded by cypress trees with low-hanging Spanish moss. Something moved close by, rippling the water and making her heart quicken with fear. She moved carefully forward toward a savanna with solid ground and grassland undulating like a golden sea. The thick mud pulled at her feet. She managed another step. Gasping, she went deeper, the dark water around her rib cage. Her body felt like a heavy weight. Something slick slithered between her legs. Grasping hold of a cypress root, she kicked free. A broad, diamond-shaped head appeared, black eyes staring at her. The huge snake coiled around her middle. She groaned as the pain grew worse. She couldn't get her breath.

A hand moved across her face. "Dawn." Jason caressed her cheek. "Wake up, honey. You're having a bad dream."

She stared into the darkness; her heart still pounded. "Hold me, Jason."

Jason tucked her into him. Wide-awake now, she felt it again. No dream this time. Her abdomen cramped. Searing pain spread downward. "Jason . . ."

Jason turned on the light. When she pushed the covers off, he sucked in his breath. "Don't move! I'm calling 911."

❉ ❉ ❉

Dawn awakened in a hospital room, white ceiling overhead, white curtain blocking her view, an IV drip hanging beside the bed. A monitor beeped. Somewhere close by, Jason talked in a low voice, tone questioning. A stranger answered. ". . . lost a lot of blood. . . . couple more hours in recovery. . . . taking precautions. . . . Try not to worry. . . ."

Jason stepped around the curtain. He looked haggard and pale, but his expression filled with relief when he met her eyes. "You're awake. Are you in pain?"

"No." But she felt so tired she didn't think she could move.

He took her hand and kissed it. "You're going to be all right."

She knew what that meant. She couldn't see him through her tears. "Our baby, Jason," she sobbed. "I lost our baby."

Jason slipped his arms around her, and he held her close, his voice raspy. "I almost lost you."

The nurse came in and added something to the IV. "She'll sleep now."

Dawn fought to keep her eyes open. "You should go home, Jason."

"I'm staying."

She awakened on the gurney as they moved through the

hospital corridor to another room. Two orderlies lifted her gently onto a bed. Jason stepped around one of them and took her hand again. A nurse tucked warm covers around her, checked her vitals and the IV.

Rousing again later, she saw Jason in a chair beside her bed. He slept with his head on his crossed arms. Running her hand over the short-cropped hair, she thanked God she had a husband who loved her enough to stay so long at her side. He woke and leaned over her. "Do you need anything?"

"No." Just him.

He sat down again and took her hand, rubbing it against his cheek. He needed a shave.

"You must be AWOL."

"I called Cap." Jason put his hand on her forehead. "Good. No fever." He let out a deep breath. He looked older than his twenty-six years. "Try to go back to sleep. Everything's going to be okay."

Okay? Without their baby?

Once, at fifteen, she had feared she might be pregnant. Now, Dawn wondered if she and Jason would ever have children. God willing, someday. She would hold on to that hope.

❋ ❋ ❋

Alicia came over to visit. Watching Lalo play made Dawn feel her loss more acutely. She grieved even more when she went to the commissary and saw young mothers with babies. Unwilling to burden Jason with her emotional state, she called Granny, who told her it wasn't unusual to have a miscarriage and not to let it get her down. Then she talked about how wonderful it would be when Dawn had babies, how she'd forget all about the pain of losing this one.

On the phone, Mom listened while Dawn talked. Dawn had to ask her to say something. "I turned away from the Lord, Dawn, and I learned my lesson. I turned back because He was the only One who understood. He became my comfort."

Dawn hadn't opened her Bible in a week. "Why did you turn away?"

"I was afraid of Him."

Dawn had learned to wait until Mom was ready to speak. Mom wasn't uncomfortable with silence the way Granny was.

"I didn't think God loved me. I thought everything that happened to me was punishment because I couldn't measure up."

"But now you know that's not true. Don't you?"

"Do you?"

Dawn cried then. She'd been asking herself for weeks what she had done wrong. "Oh, Mom . . ." Shoulders heaving, she sobbed into the telephone.

"I learned God loves me. Even when I felt down for the count, May Flower Dawn. He loves you that way, too. He'll lift you up. Just hold out your hands and give your sorrow to Him."

48

1996

Jason got orders for Fort Bragg, North Carolina. Dawn admonished herself for being surprised. After three years at Fort Leonard Wood, she forgot Jason could be transferred anytime and anywhere the Army wanted. She'd just put in roses. She wouldn't be around when they bloomed.

The inspecting officer came through. All the walls would have to be repainted white. She had known the rules, but the thought of her hard work being undone depressed her.

Jason hired two privates to paint the interior walls on their off-duty hours. They needed the extra money. Dawn needed their help. The Army movers arrived. Dawn supervised. She had all the boxes labeled and kept an inventory list in her purse. As soon as the moving van left, Jason and Dawn threw two suitcases into the trunk of the Sable and headed out.

Jason had leave before reporting in at Fort Bragg. So they took the scenic route, wanting to see more of the country on the way. They spent nights in St. Louis, Nashville, and Chattanooga. After

the flatlands and wind of Fort Sill and the low hills and bluffs
of Fort Leonard Wood, Dawn drank in the beauty of the Great
Smoky Mountains. They took their time driving the Blue Ridge
Parkway, stopping at overlooks, snapping pictures of one another,
and staying two nights in a bed-and-breakfast. Fall had come with
a burst of reds, oranges, and yellows among the myriad evergreens.

❄ ❄ ❄

Fort Bragg wasn't like little Fort Lost in the Woods. It had over
170,000 inhabitants, schools, churches, hospitals, golf courses,
bowling alleys, and theaters. It even had a mall! While Jason
worked, Dawn drove around, getting acclimated to her new
surroundings. When the Sable broke down, Jason decided it was
time to sell it and buy another car. Dawn spotted a van and said it
would come in handy when she started going to garage and estate
sales. Jason took it for a test drive, had a mechanic look it over, and
made an offer. After a few months, with things so spread out, Jason
decided they both needed transportation and bought a used GMC
Jimmy. Dawn teased him about his "cheap jeep."

Their new house was twice the size of the last.

Uninspired, she made a replica of their last master bedroom,
turned another into an office, and left the door of the last bedroom
closed. The living room looked bare and uninteresting. She needed
to find one piece of *something* to inspire her, so she drove eighty
miles up to Raleigh to see an art sale. Within the first hour, she
found what she needed to fire her imagination: an oil-painted
reproduction of John William Waterhouse's *Knight*. The handsome
young man in full armor sat on a stone wall, his sword set aside, a
beautiful red-haired lady kneeling at his feet with her hand over his
and an expression of adoration.

"You like that, huh?" The vendor, an old man with thinning
gray hair and one arm missing, said he had worked twenty years for
a museum in New York, painting reproductions of various masters.

"It's gorgeous." She could see the whole living room coming together around it.

He wanted three hundred dollars for the painting. Dawn's heart sank. He might as well have asked for a million. Dawn smiled with regret, told him it was worth that and more. Unfortunately a knight's wife couldn't afford it.

She searched for two more hours and came up empty-handed. She had to get home so she'd be in time to fix dinner.

"Milady," the old vendor called to her as she came abreast of his booth. "I still have it."

Surprised, she walked over. "No offers at all?"

"Oh, I had offers, but none that made me want to hand it over. I took a lot of time on this one. It's special." The old man propped it up so she had to look at it again. "Is your husband as handsome as the knight?"

Dawn studied the painting and smiled. "As handsome as that knight is, mine is more so. Thanks for letting me look at it again. I know you'll find the right buyer." She started to walk away.

He called after her. "Where would you hang it if you could afford it?"

She turned and looked at him. "In the living room, of course, where everyone would see it first thing when they walked in. And I'd tell everyone who did the reproduction, if he gave me his card."

"Well, that's a whole lot better than having it hang in a guest room." He wagged his fingers at her. "Give me whatever you've got before I change my mind. Okay, okay. Calm down. You're welcome. I'll even wrap it for you."

Dawn drove home, singing praise songs. She couldn't wait to get started!

Jason noticed the painting when he walked in the door. He stood in the living room staring at it. Dawn slipped her arm through his. "Romantic, isn't it?"

He grinned at her. "I can hardly wait to see what you do with the rest of the place."

A laugh bubbled out of her. "A man's home should be his castle. Don't you think?"

He pulled her close. "It's good to hear you laugh again, Dawn."

They both knew why she hadn't.

❄ ❄ ❄

1997

They'd been stationed at Fort Bragg six months when Dawn took a home pregnancy test. She hadn't mentioned the morning sickness. She didn't want to get Jason's hopes up or worry him. When she checked the test results, joy flooded her. Fear quickly followed. She saw it in Jason's eyes, too, when she told him the news.

He pulled her close. "If you are pregnant, you're quitting work. We're not taking any chances."

She'd already decided that. Two ladies from her Wednesday Bible study had offered to pay her to help decorate their houses, so they could easily do without her part-time nursing income.

Jason held her hand tightly in the examining room as the nurse practitioner moved the monitor over Dawn's abdomen. They both heard the baby's heartbeat at the same time. Jason frowned. "It's so fast." The nurse and Dawn smiled and assured him it should be.

Jason wanted to call their families that night, but Dawn asked him to wait. He asked why. "I don't know, Jason. I just . . . I don't know." She couldn't dispel the feeling something might go wrong.

At five months, Jason insisted. "You're fine. You haven't been sick for two months. The baby is growing. So are you!"

Dawn gave in.

Georgia and Granny were ecstatic. So were Christopher and Mitch. When Mom came on the phone, Dawn poured out her fears. Mom didn't dismiss them. "I'll pray for you, May Flower Dawn." Dawn knew it wasn't a platitude.

Granny called every few days to check on her. Dawn called Mom and did most of the talking.

At six months, Dawn sensed something wrong. The flutters had stopped. Rather than wait for her scheduled checkup, she called the doctor. Jason went with her. The stethoscope felt ice-cold on her abdomen. The doctor moved it several times, listening intently. His expression became increasingly grim. Jason stroked her shoulders. "It's going to be okay," he said again and again, like a litany of prayer.

When the doctor straightened, Dawn held her breath. "I'm sorry." He looked at Jason first, then Dawn. "There's no heartbeat."

Jason stood silent, his hands gripping her shoulders. He looked down at her, love and tears spilling from his eyes. "It's going to be okay, Dawn."

She sobbed. They both knew nothing was okay.

The doctor admitted Dawn to the hospital and induced labor. Dawn gave birth to a perfectly formed little boy who weighed just under two pounds.

It would take longer to get over the loss this time.

❄ ❄ ❄

Jason took Dawn home to California for Christmas. They spent the first few nights with Georgia, Christmas Eve and Day with Mom, Mitch, and Christopher, home on break from his first year at Stanford.

Granny came in from Jenner, but kept pressing them to come out and stay with her on the coast. Approaching her eighty-first birthday, she had aged. Her hair was almost completely gray now, and she bore signs of osteoporosis. Mom, who had turned fifty last spring, still wore long, colorful tiered skirts and tunics with leather belts. Her hair had streaks of silver. Mom still didn't ask for Granny's help, and Granny no longer offered. Dawn could see the rift had widened. Granny talked to Dawn and spared some attention for Jason, Mitch, and Christopher. Mom listened from the kitchen.

No one talked about the baby, though Dawn knew her stillborn son was on everyone's mind. Christopher sat beside her on the couch and took her hand. He had grown six inches since she last saw him. He called her his little-big sister now. He had Mitch's dark red hair and their mother's blue eyes. "You're turning into a hunk, Chris."

Mitch laughed. "He's got girls calling him all the time. The phone hasn't stopped ringing since he got home last week."

Christopher blushed to the roots of his hair.

"Good for you. You've always been good at making friends." Dawn tried to keep things light. It was Christmas, after all. Had all gone well, she would have had a newborn in her arms.

And a child shall be born to you . . .

Jason agreed to go to Jenner. They spent the last four days with Granny. Dawn and Jason walked on the beach every afternoon. They sat on the sand and watched the waves. On the last night, he went to bed before she did. Granny broached the subject everyone else had avoided. "You'll have a baby, Dawn. I know it. I feel it!"

Dawn cried and blew her nose. She felt like Hannah in the Old Testament, begging God for a child. "It's up to God, Granny. I have to accept that it may not be His will for me."

"Nonsense. You have time, honey. You're young. Keep trying."

Dawn knew trying wasn't the answer. God was. And she was going to trust Him with her future, no matter how difficult it might be right now.

On the long flight home, Dawn dreamed she sat on the beach north of Goat Rock. The wind blew warmer than usual, sun sparkling off turquoise and green waves. Dawn felt the wind in her hair, the sun on her face. Granny and Mom sat nearby, talking together as they never had before. A little girl with long blonde hair pranced along the edge of the waves. Water splashed up like white flashing lights around the child's knees. She flapped her arms like a bird learning to fly. Now and then, she stooped and picked up a sea-washed rock, a bit of driftwood, a seagull feather, then raced up the beach to show off her treasures. Dawn got up and went down to join the child. She danced with her in the frothy, foaming waves. She felt happy. She felt free.

Dawn awakened in the darkness, the hum of jet engines

soothing. Jason slept, his knees wedged against the seat in front of him. She saw the moon outside the airplane window and city lights below. She felt at peace for the first time since losing the baby, hope rising inside her like a sunrise.

Jason awakened and took her hand. "Are you okay?"

"Yes." More than okay. "I had a wonderful dream, Jason." She told him all about it.

"Sounds like a promise."

"It was."

❊   ❊   ❊

1998

Dawn painted the spare bedroom a pale pink. She added furnishings: a crib; a white dresser; a gliding rocker; a plush, pale blue area rug. She hung an embroidered alphabet sampler she found at a garage sale.

As each month passed, Jason seemed less certain. He brought up adoption. She said, yes, that was something they might consider. Eventually. His suggestion didn't diminish her faith. The dream would come to pass. In God's perfect timing—not hers, not Jason's.

"You know I can get transferred at any time, Dawn."

"I know."

"You're putting a lot of time in that bedroom." The house didn't belong to them. "We may have to move. What then?"

"We'll take the furniture. I'll start over."

Jason's six-year commitment to the Army was coming to an end, too. By next year he would need to make a decision about his future. They talked about what Jason could do as a civilian. The opportunities seemed endless.

"If I stay in the Army, I'd only have fourteen more years before I could retire. I'd still be young enough to start another career." She asked if that's what he wanted, if he believed that was what God wanted him to do. Jason said yes.

"We may still get transferred, Dawn. There's no guarantee we're going to stay here."

Dawn knew what really worried Jason, what worried him all the time. He feared she might be crushed if she didn't become pregnant again soon. She told him God was sovereign. God was trustworthy. Whatever happened, they could trust God with the outcome. Even so, she kept the door to the baby's room closed, so he wouldn't have the constant reminder. She held God's promise close to her heart.

Even after a year, Dawn didn't lose hope.

When two passed, then three, the ache grew, but her faith didn't diminish.

Dolores, one of Dawn's Bible study ladies, called. She sounded on the verge of hysteria. "Are you watching your television?"

"No. Why?"

"Two airliners just crashed into the twin towers of the World Trade Center!"

Dawn sat frozen in front of the television for the rest of the day. She watched the World Trade Center buildings crumble in a cloud of dust and debris over and over. She listened to minute-by-minute reports on how terrorists had hijacked two airliners out of Boston, another hijacked jetliner crashed into the Pentagon, and a fourth went down in a Pennsylvania field after passengers on board the aircraft called family members on cell phones and learned how the other airliners had been used. They fought back, or the fourth plane might have gone into the White House. No one knew yet how many had died. Fifty thousand people worked in and around the World Trade Center.

The front door opened. Dawn jumped up. "Jason!" She flew into his arms.

He held her close for a minute, rubbing his chin on the top of her head. "How long have you been watching the news?"

"All day. Jason, what does this mean for us?"

"We're at war. That's what it means."

"Will you have to go?"

"We'll have to find out who we're fighting and where, first."

Airports shut down. President George Bush flew into New York and stood at ground zero speaking to the rescue workers. He assured them the nation was on bended knee in prayer. When some cried out because they couldn't hear, Bush said *he* could hear *them*, everyone could hear them, and those who had knocked down the buildings "will hear all of us soon!"

People chanted, "USA, USA . . ."

President Bush called out, "God bless America," a hope all would cling to in the coming days.

Dawn spent her days reading newspaper stories about heroes: a man who stayed behind to help another man in a wheelchair—both died when the buildings crumbled; firefighters and police officers who worked tirelessly searching for survivors; cadaver dogs and their handlers searching the rubble. The Salvation Army responded to the tragedy. New Yorkers pulled together.

War loomed, but against what country?

Jason was deployed to New York to work with civil engineers. The mammoth job of clearing a city block began. Jason would be gone for months, maybe more if terrorists found other ways to blow up more Americans. Every newscaster speculated on what terrorists might do next—poison water systems, unleash deadly viruses, tote backpack-size atomic bombs.

People flooded into the churches for the first few weeks. Crowds dwindled after three months.

Jason came home to Fort Bragg on weekend leave, burning with anger against Osama bin Laden, who had denied responsibility for the attacks, though the U.S. government still considered him the prime suspect.

Exhausted, he slept twenty-four hours straight, leaving only half a day before he had to go back. "Why didn't you wake me up?" Dawn said she'd come to him next time. Jason ordered her to stay home. He didn't want her in New York. He wasn't sure he wanted her at Fort Bragg. What better target for another attack than one of the biggest military bases in the world? He wanted her to go home. She said no. They argued. She cried after he left.

Jason returned to Fort Bragg after three months away. He and Dawn flew home for Christmas again. CCC was packed with new people. "You should have seen it after 9/11," Mitch told them. Chris asked a dozen questions. Jason made it clear he didn't want to talk about what he'd seen at ground zero. Granny worried about war and what part Jason would have to play in it. Dawn still prayed diplomacy would work. Mitch and Jason talked behind closed doors. Mom and Dawn had tea and didn't talk at all.

❄ ❄ ❄

2002

When Dawn and Jason returned to Fort Bragg, Jason bought a new laptop computer and a Rosetta Stone program on Arabic. "If I get sent anywhere, it'll be the Middle East."

Everyone knew it was only a matter of time before the Army started deploying troops. America couldn't ignore the murder of three thousand citizens. It was a miracle there hadn't been tens of thousands. But three thousand was more than the number of lives lost at Pearl Harbor, and the country couldn't let it go.

Dawn knew the waiting had come to an end when Jason came home and said he had orders to Fort Dix, New Jersey. Dawn packed and followed. She rented a two-bedroom, one-bathroom bungalow off base. She didn't paint the walls. Every hour with Jason was too precious to waste.

❊   ❊   ❊

2003

The first U.S. troops were deployed to the Persian Gulf region on
January 1. On March 17, President Bush issued an ultimatum to
Saddam Hussein, giving him forty-eight hours to leave the country
or face war. On March 19, the deadline passed, and Operation
Iraqi Freedom began. By April, they took Baghdad and toppled
Saddam Hussein's statue to Iraqi and American cheers.

The hunt for weapons of mass destruction intensified. Hussein
had used chemical weapons on the Kurds. Had he buried bombs
in the desert the same way he had buried airplanes? Had they been
sold and scattered to neighboring countries? Or had it all been an
empty boast by a mad dictator?

May rolled around, and Jason received orders for deployment
to Iraq. Dawn wept. They made love the way they had when they
were first married—hungry, with abandon. They said everything
they wanted to say to one another, knowing they might never have
another opportunity.

"It's up to God." He held her close. "There's a time for peace,
and there's a time for war. Remember Nehemiah. He ordered the
people to keep their weapons close at hand while they worked. The
biggest job we're going to face in Iraq is rebuilding the country,
giving the Iraqi people the protection and resources they need
to hold on to the freedom they've never had before. I'll have my
weapon strapped to me, Dawn. We're trained to watch each other's
back."

Jason wanted no public displays of affection when she saw him
off. She had to be brave and tearless for his sake. He kissed her.
"Write to me." He spoke roughly, his hands gripping her head. He
kissed her again. "I'll e-mail you when I can."

She took his hand in both of hers before he walked away. "May
the Lord bless you and keep you, Jason. He goes ahead of you. He
stands at your side. He dwells within you. He is your rear guard."
And though she saw tears in his hazel eyes, she smiled at him and

said the rest. "This isn't our home, Jason. Heaven is. And there, nothing can ever part us."

❄ ❄ ❄

Two months later, at the end of July, Dawn sent her sixtieth e-mail, knowing it might be days before Jason could read it.

> God is good, Jason. He always keeps His promises. Our baby is due on Valentine's Day. The doctor won't know the baby's gender for a few more months, but I told him God already promised us a little girl. She's going to have blonde hair, and she's going to run on the beach, collect rocks and seashells and bird feathers, and dance at the edge of the sea. . . .

Jason e-mailed whenever he could.

> Hey, Mama, I miss you so much I ache. I started a Bible study with three men in my unit. We're rebuilding a hospital. We're reading Nehemiah. Thought it appropriate. We do a lot of praying as we work.
>   . . . went into one of Saddam Hussein's palaces. Marble floors, mosaics, pillars, fountains—the guy had it. Figured he was the next Nebuchadnezzar. Must have forgotten the end of the story—the king on his hands and knees eating grass like an animal. God said pride comes before a fall.
>   I wish I could see you getting as round as a pumpkin, big as a house, weighing in at 185 with my baby inside you. . . .

Dawn wrote letters every day. She wanted Jason to have something at mail call, not just on his computer.

> Hello, my love.
>   I went for my checkup this morning and heard our daughter's heartbeat. I may not weigh 185 pounds yet, but

everything is fine. I walk two miles every evening (yes, dear, before it gets dark). Since everyone works, this is the best time to meet people.

Only Maura Kerwin and LaShaye Abbot have come for tea. Neither is ready to commit to a Bible study. Maura's husband (Mick) just got shipped over. LaShaye is pregnant for the third time in four years. They're still paying hospital bills for the last baby. Rory told her to get an abortion. I got weepy and told them about our lost babies. LaShaye left.

I keep remembering the prayer Mom gave me when you and I weren't seeing each other. "God, grant me the serenity to accept the things I can't change, the courage to change the things I can, and the wisdom to know the difference. Thy will, not mine, be done." I've been saying it a lot lately. . . .

❄ ❄ ❄

A suicide bomber blew himself up in the middle of a market this morning. He took innocent women and children with him. All in the name of his god! These people need to hear the gospel, and we're forbidden to evangelize. I'll probably get busted, but I'm not going to be silent when given an opportunity to talk about the difference between Allah and Jesus. Only Christ can make men free! The enemy of our souls wants to keep these people captive. . . .

LaShaye didn't come for tea. So I dropped by. She couldn't even look at me. I told her I love her and I'm praying for her. If she ever wants to talk, my door is open. She closed hers, and I haven't seen her since. Maura came. She and LaShaye were friends long before I came on the scene. Maura took her to the clinic.

I pray. I still take my walks.

Picture attached. Notice the nice little bulge under my new sweater!

Thanks for the photo! You look beautiful. But so thin! You look like you're losing weight instead of gaining. Are you eating enough? Maybe you shouldn't be walking so much. . . .

I don't have to look like a pumpkin or a house to be healthy, Jason. I'm eating constantly. I don't know why I'm not gaining a lot of weight. Must be my metabolism. The doctor said walking is good for me. Don't worry—I'm not overdoing it.

Good news! LaShaye came over. We talked for hours! She and Rory are struggling. I found a crisis pregnancy center in the area. They have a postabortion class. I said I'd take her and sit with her if that would help. I'm praying LaShaye and Rory can work things out. They have enough grief between them without discarding their marriage.

I have another checkup tomorrow. I know everything is fine, Jason. I've been feeling our little girl move for a couple weeks now. Only four months to go before I meet her face-to-face.

50

DAWN GULPED DOWN sobs as she headed home from her prenatal appointment. The doctor had put her through a battery of tests over the last two weeks and insisted that she see a specialist besides. He gave her the results this morning. "We have a problem. . . ." She had sat stunned and silent as he talked in quiet, grim tones, hands folded on his desk. "I advise you not to wait, Dawn. I know it's going to be difficult for you, especially with your history, but the alternative is—"

"You don't need to say any more!" Dawn had stood abruptly, slinging her bag over her shoulder with shaking hands.

"Please sit down, Mrs. Steward. We need to discuss this. The longer you wait, the more—"

"I understand everything you've said, Doctor. I was a nurse." And she wouldn't do it! She'd rather die than do it.

She yanked the door open and walked out.

Two other pregnant mothers sat in the waiting room. Dawn managed to get out the door before the tears came. She sat in her car until she thought she had regained enough control to drive home. Now she couldn't even see the road. Swiping tears away, she pulled onto the shoulder, jammed on her parking brake, and put on her emergency lights. Gripping the wheel, she screamed. "Why, Lord? Why? *I don't understand!*"

Cars flew past. Sobbing, Dawn ran her hands over the slight bulge in her belly. A police officer tapped on her window. She hadn't even noticed the cruiser pull in behind her. She let her window down and fumbled through her shoulder bag for her license. She found the car registration in the glove compartment. He glanced at them and handed them back. Leaning down, he looked at her. "Anything wrong, ma'am?"

"I've just had some very bad news." She gulped down sobs. "I'm sorry. I just thought it'd be safer for everyone if I sat here for a little while. Is that okay?" She wiped her cheeks.

"I noticed the Fort Dix base sticker on your car."

"My husband's in Iraq."

"Sit until you're ready, ma'am." The officer walked back to his cruiser. She glanced in the rearview mirror. He talked into his radio. She thought he'd drive away, but he didn't. Regaining some control over her emotions, Dawn took the brake off, put on her blinker, and pulled out onto the highway again. The police cruiser pulled out right behind her. He stayed with her all the way to off-base housing, gave her a salute, and kept going.

Dawn raised her hand in thanks. *God puts angels all around us. Some in uniform.*

Dumping her keys on the coffee table, Dawn sank onto the couch. She felt her baby move and ran her hand over her abdomen. "What am I going to tell your daddy, sweetie?" She hadn't mentioned the tests to Jason. Why worry him? He needed to keep his mind on what was happening around him, not on her and the baby. Now, she didn't dare tell him.

Lord, help me. Please help me.

Someone knocked on the door. Dawn didn't answer. They knocked again. She waited before going to the front door. Peering through the peephole, she watched LaShaye walk down the path

to the sidewalk where Maura stood waiting. They both talked for
a few minutes, then went their separate ways.

Dawn went into the bathroom, turned on the shower, and
undressed while she waited for the water to get warm. Stepping in,
she closed the glass door and let the water rain down on her.

*Lord, You breathed out the universe. You made the stars in the
heavens, the earth, everything. Nothing is too difficult for You! You
made me Your vessel. Your Holy Spirit lives within me. You opened
my womb so I could carry this child. You showed her to me. I saw my
daughter on the beach, dancing, flapping her arms like a little bird.
She is strong. She is full of the life You gave her. Oh, God, You are
merciful! Please. Be merciful.*

She didn't stop praying or get out of the shower until the warm
water gave out.

❄ ❄ ❄

Dawn fixed a square meal and sat alone in the dining room. She
needed to eat, whether she felt like it or not. She and the baby
needed nourishment. The telephone rang.

I'm not ready to talk, Lord, not to anyone but You.

The answering machine picked up. "It's Granny, sweetheart.
Just thinking about you and wanted to talk. You said something
about joining the choir. You're probably at church. Call back when
you have a minute. I love you."

Church. She'd forgotten about the choir. Those sweet old ladies
would take one look at her and want to know what was wrong.
They'd have all kinds of wisdom to share.

She'd already made her decision. No matter what the doctor
said, she would have this baby. She'd face everything else later.

She had to e-mail Jason. If a day passed and she didn't, he
would wonder why. He always checked dates. Did he look at the
times, too? It was getting late. She put her dish and utensils in
the dishwasher, then went to the computer.

What was she going to say to him? She didn't like keeping

secrets from her husband, but she couldn't write about what she'd been told today.

Hands resting on the keyboard, she tried to think. She double-clicked the e-mail icon; nothing from Jason today, but several others, including one from her brother. Christopher wrote like he talked. He was taking classes part-time toward a master's degree. He had a job at a trendy, expensive restaurant.

> Hardest part of the job is warding off advances from cougars. Even when I turn them down, they leave nice tips. I'll have enough saved to go to London this summer.

Leaning on her elbows, Dawn rubbed her temples.

I will trust in You, Lord, no matter what happens. I believe the dream You gave me on the airplane about our little girl. I believe, Father! Oh, God, help my unbelief.

Dawn clicked *New Mail* and typed *Ja* and Jason's address filled the send-to line. Subject? *How do I love thee? Let me count the ways.* Words flowed out of her as she recounted the first time she'd seen Jason in the high school corridor, then being dragged by Christopher to CCC VBS and working with Jason. His faith and dedication to God had awed her. She had felt blessed every time he told her he loved her. When they broke up, she set her heart and mind upon becoming like the wife in Proverbs 31, a woman of character, substance, faith, and purpose—for God and for whomever He might have in store for her, never dreaming He would give the two of them a second chance. She reminisced about their wedding day and the intense joy he'd given her on their wedding night and every time he'd made love to her since.

> I just miss you so much, Jason. I wish I could curl up with your arms around me. I wish . . .

Weeping, Dawn got up without sending the message. She puttered, fluffing pillows, wandering through the house, trying to step back, trying to think more clearly and not allow her emotions to rule. After an hour, she went back and reread what she had written. He would know something was wrong. She deleted everything and started again.

> I saw the doctor again today. Our daughter is strong and healthy. I can feel her moving inside me right now as I write this note. Maybe she's waving hello to her daddy. Your wife and daughter have both had a big day today. I'm exhausted. I'm going to make this short and head for bed.
>
> I love you so much, Jason. I pray constantly that God will command angels to guard you. Remember Elisha and how he opened Gehazi's eyes so he could see the fiery chariots all around? The Lord is with you. He hears our prayers. I'll love you forever, Jason.
>
> Always yours,
> Dawn

❊ ❊ ❊

Dawn dreamed about Granny and Mom. They argued over something, but Dawn couldn't hear what. They turned their backs to one another, both weeping. Dawn wanted to call out to them, but she'd lost her voice.

She awakened as the sun came in the window. It had snowed the night before, and everything lay beneath a cover of white. She sat at the dining room table, where she could see everything, and opened her Bible. She couldn't get Granny and Mom out of her mind. She felt an intense longing for both of them. She wasn't Moses, but wouldn't it be nice to have her mother holding up one arm and Granny holding up the other as Dawn beseeched God for victory in the battle she now faced? But another picture came to mind. Granny pulling one way and Mom the other.

❋ ❋ ❋

2004

Dawn had made excuses not to fly home for the holidays. Just before Thanksgiving, she'd passed the six-month mark in her pregnancy and breathed easier. The baby had an excellent chance of survival now, even if she should come early. But Dawn still prayed every day for a full-term, healthy delivery for their daughter.

Mom had said she'd fly to Newark when Dawn got closer to delivery. And then, just as she always did, Dawn had said it would be nice to have Granny come, too.

Why did she have to choose between them?

As Christmas came and went, she found herself wishing she were at home. Now, January rolled around. She'd have a birthday soon. *What do I do, Lord?* Dawn covered her face. *Lord, I want to go home!*

She couldn't fly now. It was too risky to fly at seven and a half months. She could drive. Four thousand miles alone, in winter? Jason would have a fit!

Jason didn't have to know.

Dawn shrugged into her heavy parka and went out for a walk. It was midmorning. Blank spaces on the street showed where cars had been during the snowfall last night. Everyone had gone to work by now. Maura worked at a co-op preschool. LaShaye never stepped outside her door. *Okay, Lord, if I'm supposed to drive home to California, Maura and LaShaye will be home and both will want to talk with me.*

She'd just passed LaShaye's when the front door opened. "Dawn! Wait a minute!" LaShaye hurried down the path to the sidewalk. "You look awful. Is Jason all right?"

"He's fine."

She took Dawn by the arm. "Come inside out of the cold. I'll fix some tea. Tell me what's going on." The phone was ringing when they walked in. Maura wanted to come over.

An hour later, they all sat crying in LaShaye's kitchen. LaShaye gripped Dawn's arm. "What are you going to do?"

"I'm going home to California. I want to be with my family. I'm going to need Mom and Granny's help. The hard part is going to be getting them to work things out between them so they can."

Maura held out her hands. "What can we do?"

Dawn took hold. "I have to call the landlord, then call the base to store our furniture. Or sell some of it. I don't know which."

"If you're driving across the country, you should have your car serviced," LaShaye said. "Rory can do that for you."

Between the three of them, they worked out the details. Dawn held out her hands. Maura and LaShaye each took one. "It's been a pleasure, ladies." She blinked back tears. "I didn't have as long as I wanted with you."

LaShaye squeezed tight. "Maybe we ought to pray."

Dawn thanked God for these friends. "Yes. Please." She felt a quiver of apprehension at the journey ahead of her. "And don't stop."

Dawn made all her calls the next morning. She didn't think the landlord would return the security deposit, but when he heard the reasons, he brought the check over that afternoon. She bought a new laptop so she could continue e-mailing Jason every day on the long drive home. She studied routes on MapQuest. She decided against the straight route across the country. She didn't want to go through Colorado and deal with heavy snows. Better to go south.

Maura came over when the movers arrived. Everything would be stored until Jason returned from Iraq. Suitcases packed, Dawn spent the night with Maura.

"How long do you think it'll take, Dawn?"

"I don't know. I'll have to take it one day at a time." She would need to get out and walk around every hour or risk thrombophlebitis and edema. Main highways had rest stops. She planned to use them. "I'll drive until I need rest."

"The weather's bad all across the country. You couldn't have picked a worse time to travel."

"I don't have a lot of choice. I can't wait."

"You should have someone with you."

"I will. I'll have Jesus. He'll get me home."

She got up early the next morning, showered, dressed, and left a note on the kitchen counter beside the coffeepot.

Dear Maura,

 Thanks for everything. I'll be in touch. May the Lord bless you and yours.

        Love, Dawn

For the first time in days, it didn't snow.

51

DAWN KNEW, EVEN before she had driven the short distance to Baltimore, the trip would test her physical and emotional endurance. She took one hour at a time, trying not to think how many miles she had to go. Each afternoon, after checking into a hotel and having dinner, she hooked up the laptop.

She wrote regular e-mails to Jason, as though still in New Jersey. She wrote about the baby, tidbits of good news she found in whatever newspapers she picked up in hotel lobbies, anything that might keep his spirits bolstered, and not hint she was driving cross-country alone, nearly eight months pregnant, in January. Once the e-mail was sent and the others answered, she unhooked and packed away the computer, watched television weather reports, and went to bed. After a week on the road, she awakened with night sweats and back pain. She lay in the darkness praying God would give her strength and peace of mind. She had a long, long way to go.

Christian music stations kept her spirits up throughout the day. When she made it to Oklahoma City, she felt more at home. She thought of the friends she and Jason had made, all scattered now like seeds in the wind. Some had settled in other U.S. bases, others in Germany; many had gone to Iraq. A few hadn't made it home.

After a good night's rest, she pushed on to Amarillo, Texas.

The baby moved vigorously, reminding her of why she was on this trip. Dawn draped her arm over her expanding abdomen. She wanted desperately to call home, but knew if she did, Mom and Mitch would be frantic. They worried enough already. "Be good, little one. Hang in there! You need to grow a little more. You need to be strong for Mommy."

It took three days to drive from Amarillo to Flagstaff, Arizona. Pushing harder, Dawn made it all the way to Barstow the next day, but got no farther than Buttonwillow the day after. *One more day,* she told herself. *God, help me.* One more day and she could rest.

Dawn dreamed she stood on a stone arch over a black chasm. Granny stood on solid ground on one side and Mom on the other. The bridge began crumbling beneath Dawn's feet. Granny and Mom both reached out and caught hold. Both called for the other to let go. Dawn begged them to stop! Please stop! Gripped by pain, she cried out. Her child broke free of her body and dropped into the darkness below.

❄ ❄ ❄

Exhausted, Dawn pulled in next to Georgia Steward's trailer and parked. Rain pounded on the roof of the car and slicked over the windshield. Mrs. Edwards peered through her living room curtains. Dawn barely had strength to get out of the car. She hadn't walked often enough today, and her legs felt swollen and stiff. The baby had turned and now pressed down heavily inside her. Gripping the rail, Dawn climbed the few steps and knocked on the door.

"Dawn!" After a split second of shock, Georgia stepped outside and hugged her. "You've been on my mind for days. I called, but couldn't get through. Your mom said she talked to you the other day and everything was fine."

Dawn leaned on Georgia as they went inside. She had kept to

her schedule of calling Granny and Mom. She apologized for not calling Georgia. "I'm sorry. I've been driving for days. . . ."

"You *drove?*"

"I couldn't fly. I was past seven months." Dawn sank gratefully onto the sofa and let out a deep sigh of relief.

"Honey, you look pale as a ghost." Georgia lifted Dawn's feet onto the couch. "Your ankles are swollen. Lie back." She tucked a pillow under Dawn's feet and put a blanket over her. "Are you hungry? thirsty?"

Dawn smiled weakly. "Both." She hadn't stopped for dinner, too eager to finish the long journey and rest. "But don't go to a lot of trouble, please."

Georgia opened the refrigerator. "Now I know why God had me praying for you."

Covered with the blue fleece, Dawn listened to the rain pounding the metal roof of Georgia's trailer. She could barely keep her eyes open. Georgia brushed her forehead. "You're perspiring." Her mother-in-law leaned over her, brow furrowed with worry.

"Night sweats."

"And fever, too. I'll find some Tylenol. Can you sit up and eat?"

Struggling into a sitting position, Dawn gave a weary laugh. "My center of gravity is off." The baby moved strongly. "Our little Steward is protesting." Dawn took Georgia's hand and held it against the side of her abdomen. "I think that's her foot."

Georgia sat beside her. Heads together, they waited for the baby to stretch again. They didn't have to wait long, and this time the baby kicked. Georgia laughed. "A soccer player like her mama." She patted Dawn's swollen abdomen. "We should call your mom. Let her know you got here."

"No one knew I was coming."

"No one?"

"I didn't want everyone fretting the entire time I drove."

"What about Jason?"

Dawn shook her head, but the question served to remind her.

"I need to get the laptop out of the car and e-mail him, or he'll wonder what happened to me."

Georgia looked troubled. "What's going on?"

Dawn fought tears. She shook her head and looked away, struggling with her rising emotions. She had done nothing but ponder her circumstances and plead with God for days. She didn't have the strength to talk about what was wrong. Now now. Not tonight. Swallowing her tears, Dawn met Georgia's worried gaze. "Don't call anyone. I'll explain everything in the morning."

❄ ❄ ❄

Pushing the covers off, Dawn was thankful the swelling in her ankles had gone down. Her stomach growled. Georgia had left a blue velour robe on the end of the bed. Pulling it on, Dawn opened the door. The rain had stopped. Daylight streamed in the living room window. Georgia set aside her book and got up from her easy chair. "You look better. How do you feel?"

"Rested. Can I take a shower?"

"After dinner."

"Dinner?" She noticed the table had already been set.

"You've slept eighteen hours." Slipping on mitts, Georgia opened the oven and took out a casserole dish. "I hope you like lasagna."

"Love it." She pushed her fingers back through her hair.

Georgia set it on a trivet in the center of the table. She opened the refrigerator and took out a tossed green salad and small carafe of dressing. "Milk or water?"

"Milk." The baby needed protein.

Georgia said the blessing and filled Dawn's salad bowl. She scooped lasagna onto Dawn's plate. "We should call your family doctor and get you in for an appointment. You're still awfully pale. And so thin."

"I need to work things out with Granny and Mom first."

"They're both in for a shock when they find out you're here."

Georgia served herself a smaller portion. "Are you ready to tell me what's going on?"

Dawn had had days to plan her words, but found them stilted and tremulous now. Georgia didn't utter a word or eat a bite. Dawn didn't have much appetite either by the time she finished. But she had a good reason to eat at least half of what Georgia had served her, and she intended to do so, even if it took an hour.

"I don't believe it, Dawn." Georgia's mouth wobbled. "God wouldn't do that to you." She pressed her lips together. "Jason should have some say about this. You can't leave him in the dark."

"Jason needs to know when to duck. He doesn't need to be worrying about us."

"You and the baby are not distractions. You're his family!"

Georgia's fierceness frightened Dawn. "Georgia. I'm begging you. Don't tell him! He worries about me and the baby enough already." Her eyes filled. There was a time to be gentle and a time to be blunt, even if it bordered on cruelty. "I don't want Jason coming home in a body bag."

Georgia closed her eyes in anguish.

"Pray. That's what I need you to do, Georgia. That's why I came to you first. I have to get Granny and Mom to work together and help me through this. I have to get them in one place. And they've never been able to talk. I have to be the bridge this time, not the wall between them."

❄ ❄ ❄

Dawn called Mitch at his office. She told him everything and what she wanted to do. "I have to spend time with them both, alone. Can you help that to happen?"

He cleared his throat before speaking. "You sure you don't want to have your grandmother come to our place?"

"Granny will do better in her own territory. I'm going to call her and have her call Mom to invite her out there. Don't tell Mom anything yet, okay?"

"I'm not sure how your mom will do. I don't think either one of them realizes how they've pitted themselves against each other."

"God got me home, Mitch. He'll get us through all the rest."

"What about Chris?"

"You can tell him after Mom leaves for Jenner." She wiped tears from her cheeks. "Tell him I'll see him in a few days and we can talk then. And . . ." She had to swallow and draw a slow breath before she could go on. "Pray. Pray hard."

"I am. Right now and every minute from here on out." He made a hoarse sound. "Pita?" He spoke gruffly. "I've always loved you like you were my own flesh and blood."

"I know. Dad."

❊ ❊ ❊

Dawn called Granny. "I want to spend a few days with you and Mom at Jenner."

"When do you plan to come home? spring? The baby will be—"

"I'm here, Granny."

"Here? Where? Alexander Valley?"

"I'm staying with Georgia right now. Mom doesn't know I'm home yet."

"Why didn't you come out and stay with me?"

"I wanted to see my mother-in-law, too. And I was pretty tired when I got here."

"Well, come now. We can visit for a few days and then call your mom."

She needed to make things clear. "I'm not coming out until Mom's there. I don't want her feelings hurt."

"I would never hurt your mother's feelings."

"You'd never hurt her intentionally, Granny, and neither would I; but we both do it all the time, and it has to stop."

"What's happened, Dawn? Something's wrong. Tell me."

"When the three of us are together, Granny, we're all going to talk."

"I'll call your mother as soon as we're off the phone."

"Let me know when she gets to Jenner. Then I'll come."

Georgia sat on the sofa, waiting. When Dawn sat down, Georgia took her hand. "So?"

"I don't know where to start, Georgia. I'm not a psychologist. I don't know what's going to happen at Jenner."

Georgia enfolded her in her arms and leaned back into the sofa so Dawn's head rested against her shoulder. "God didn't bring you home to let you down, honey. And I'm going to pray for a miracle."

Dawn closed her eyes. "We need one."

Jenner by the Sea

January 2004

52

HILDEMARA PICKED UP the phone and punched in Carolyn's number. Her son-in-law answered. "Mitch, I don't know if you've heard, but Dawn's home. She's staying with Georgia Steward."

"I know. She called me at the office a little while ago. I'll get Carolyn." He put her on hold. His abruptness surprised her.

Hildie chewed her lip. She pulled out a chair at the kitchen nook table and sat staring out at the Russian River. It was running high, as it often did this time of year. Hildie hunched deeper into her terry-cloth bathrobe.

Winters had always been too long out here on the coast, but bearable as long as Trip had been with her. Then, even if the roads closed and phone and power lines went down, Hildie hadn't been alone. She and Trip joked about "roughing it" without lights, heat, television, or stove, like it was a grand adventure.

The sense of adventure died with Trip. While Hildie was still reeling from Trip's death, Carolyn suggested Hildie sell the house and move into town. It had seemed utterly insensitive. Give up the Jenner house? after all the work Trip had put into it? He'd spent five years—and more money than they'd paid for the place—improving it and bringing it up to his standards. Throwing it all away seemed disloyal. She said as much to Carolyn, and her daughter didn't mention moving again until a few months ago, after Hildie had taken a fall.

This year, winter had become a black hole sucking Hildie down into a vortex of despair. The last time Carolyn came out "for a visit," she broached the subject of moving again. Hildie told her *no*. When Carolyn tried to keep talking about it, Hildie ignored her and turned on the television. Carolyn didn't say anything for a long time. Hildie felt guilty and uncomfortable with the silence, but she didn't know any other way to get her point across. Sure, she was almost eighty-seven, but so what? She still had all her faculties. She didn't need to be put away. "All right, Mom," Carolyn said after fifteen minutes. "Have it your way." She left two residential care facility brochures sitting like cemetery contracts on the coffee table.

Unease filled Hildemara. Had Carolyn called Dawn and enlisted her help in getting old Granny to give up her home and move? Why else would her granddaughter fly to California when she was eight months pregnant and then insist the three of them get together at Jenner and talk? Hildemara felt her anger boiling.

"Mom?" Carolyn sounded breathless. "Are you all right?"

"Why wouldn't I be all right?"

"You never call unless something's wrong."

Was that true? When had she last called Carolyn? two weeks? a month? "Nothing is wrong. Not unless you said something to Dawn about trying to move me into an old folks' home. She's *here*."

"At Jenner?" Carolyn sounded shocked.

"No. Not Jenner. In town. She's staying with Georgia. She called a few minutes ago. She wants you to come to Jenner so the three of us can talk."

"I don't understand. Is it the baby?"

"She said she's fine."

"This isn't about Jason, is it? If she's with Georgia—"

"She sounded fine. She wouldn't be fine if anything had

happened to Jason. Just pack and get out here. Dawn said she wouldn't come to Jenner until you arrive. I don't know what that's all about." Hildie could hear Mitch saying something in the background.

"The roads are terrible, Mom. Mitch can come out and bring you back here. I could pick up Dawn."

"Didn't you hear what I said? We need to meet *here*, at *Jenner*." Hildie knew she sounded angry and impatient, but she didn't want Carolyn wasting any more time.

"It can't always be the way you want it."

Hildie hated that phrase. Mama used to say it. "It's not my way. It's Dawn's way."

Carolyn sighed. "I'll be on the road in half an hour."

"I'll call Dawn and let her know." Hildie hung up, flipped through her address book, and punched in Jason's old number. Georgia answered and said Dawn was sleeping and could she take a message. "Tell Dawn her mom is on her way out here. Jason is all right, isn't he?"

"Jason's fine. He e-mailed Dawn yesterday."

"Thank God." Hildie felt some relief, but then had to ask, "And the baby?"

"Dawn is as big as a house. Hang on a second. She's awake." Hildie heard muffled voices, then Georgia again. "Dawn will head out to Jenner in an hour."

"Tell her to be careful. The weather is mean."

As soon as Hildie got off the telephone, she opened the wooden accordion doors into the small bedroom off the kitchen. She had bought a pretty blue and white Laura Ashley comforter and curtains in the hope Carolyn might come out and spend a weekend now and then. No such luck. Dawn could sleep in here and use the nice, new, plush pink towels and pretty seashell soaps. Carolyn could sleep downstairs. Hildie switched on the lamp before leaving the room. The glow could be seen outside through the lacy sheer curtains. She liked the house to look like a Thomas Kinkade painting.

She debated turning on the downstairs thermostat, then

decided to wait until after Carolyn arrived. Propane was expensive, and the delivery truck had gotten stuck on a nearby ranch, delaying the refilling of her tank.

How could she be so tired after doing so little? She sat in her recliner and put her feet up. Oh, for heaven's sake! She was still wearing her fuzzy slippers and bathrobe! Maybe she *was* entering her dotage.

Slamming the recliner, she headed for the bathroom and turned on the electric wall heater. She put on her shower cap and washed, rinsed, and stepped out of the tub in under five minutes. Toweling dry before the heater, she pulled on her white silk Cuddl Duds leggings, a long-sleeved T-shirt, and the red velour pantsuit Carolyn had given her for Christmas. She brushed tangles from her gray hair. Carolyn had treated her to a perm three months ago. Wash-and-wear hair, her friend Marsha called it. They'd been neighbors until Marsha's daughter flew out, packed her up, and took her back to Colorado Springs. No old folks' home for Marsha. Her daughter *insisted* she move in with her family. Hildie tossed the brush in the drawer and banged it shut.

Standing in the living room, Hildie looked at the Russian River flowing wide and muddy, swollen and treacherous, from heavy rains. Rain hit the window like pebbles tossed against the glass. Surf pounded in the distance. She hadn't been to the beach since Trip's heart condition worsened. "My wings are clipped," he'd said. So were hers. She hadn't wanted to leave him alone, and he'd been irritated by his limitations. No more fishing in the surf. No more volunteer work at the visitors' center. No long walks up the hill for the panoramic view of the coastline.

Now, the closest Hildie came to the beach was the wide spot on the curve of Highway 1 where she parked her Buick Regal and used Trip's binoculars to watch the sea lions on the other side of the river. Her big outing these days was walking down the hill to the post office in a trailer next door to the Jenner Gift Shop. And going to the Guerneville Safeway store every two weeks for groceries.

How long could she manage that steep walk? She didn't like to go when the road was wet and slick. How long before she would have to give up driving?

It galled her that Carolyn was right. She *was* getting too old to live alone.

The last time she had seen Dr. Kirk, he'd told her she had a strong heart and she'd probably live to be a hundred. Considering how difficult it was for her to get around now, the prospect had been annoying.

She picked up the information Carolyn had left and looked at the glossy photos. If she moved into one of those facilities, would she see more or less of Carolyn? Since Trip had died, Carolyn had called once a week. Duty calls, right up there with the groceries Carolyn brought every two weeks, not that Hildie needed them. With professional attendants keeping watch, her daughter wouldn't need to check on her.

What Hildie needed and wanted was a relationship with her daughter. After so many years, it was just wishing for the moon. She'd never known how to bridge the gap to Carolyn any more than she'd ever been able to make a bridge to Mama.

Depressed, Hildie tossed the brochures on the coffee table. *So be it, Lord. If Carolyn wants to put me away, I'll let her.* Maybe it'd be the one thing she did that finally made her daughter happy.

❋　❋　❋

Carolyn hung up the telephone and turned to Mitch. His gaze slid away from hers. He poured himself a cup of coffee. "I can take care of everything here, Carolyn. You don't have to worry about anything."

"Have you talked to Dawn?"

"Briefly."

"What's going on, Mitch?"

"She wants you to meet her out at Jenner."

"*Why?*"

He set his cup down and took her in his arms. "She's been away from home a long time, Carolyn. She wants time alone with the two women she loves most in the world."

"Why now? Why out there?" Pushing away from him, she headed for the master bedroom. He said her name, dumped his coffee, and followed. She felt him watching her as she took her small duffel bag from the closet and threw it on the bed. When had Dawn arrived? today? yesterday? Why had she gone to Georgia instead of coming home? Was something wrong? Carolyn packed two tunic sweaters and two pairs of leggings that coordinated with her tiered skirt. Jenner would be cold. She added socks, cashmere scarves, and a flannel nightgown. What else did she need? She went into the bathroom for her toothbrush, toothpaste, brush, and deodorant, stuffing them into a cosmetics bag.

Mitch stood in the doorway, watching her. "You'd better take a raincoat and umbrella. It's pouring." He didn't say anything else, and she worried even more. He looked grim, hands shoved in his pockets.

He took her duffel bag and walked her to the garage. "Take the Suburban." She didn't argue. She took the keys from the hook and tossed her coat and umbrella onto the passenger seat. Before she could slip in and get away, Mitch turned her around. "She loves you, you know."

"I know, Mitch, but given a choice, she always goes to someone else."

Mitch held her shoulders firmly, not letting her turn away. "Don't make her choose, Carolyn. Love the two of them the way Jesus loves you."

"I do."

"Maybe you should stop stuffing your feelings. Talk to them."

"What would that do, other than make things worse?"

"You won't know unless you try." Mitch gave her a tender, lopsided smile. "No kiss?" She went into his arms and held on tight. She burrowed her face against his chest until she had control of her emotions. "I love you, Carolyn. I wouldn't let you go out there if I didn't think it was important. Call me."

"The phones might go out. You know how it is."

"Stay put when you get to Jenner. Don't come back until it's over." Mitch shut the door as she settled into the driver's seat. He raised his hand as though in blessing.

Carolyn had been watching the news and knew not to take East Side Road. Wohler Bridge was underwater. She took the freeway south and headed west on River Road. Wind-whipped eucalyptus trees cast debris on the road, filling the air with their pungent scent. She slowed, driving cautiously through flooded areas. She drove between hills covered with oak and pine, wound through groves of towering redwoods, root-locked against wind and rising water. Madrones dressed in red bark and green leaves hugged steep hillsides draped with fern boas.

Carolyn pulled into the Safeway parking lot in Guerneville, threw on her raincoat, and ran for the front door. Mom probably hadn't been able to get to the grocery store since the storm hit, and now she would have company for who knew how long. She quickly filled a cart with milk, vegetables, meat, and cookies. Shelves were emptying fast. "Everyone's picking up supplies for the next storm." The checker weighed broccoli and slid it across to the bagger. "Good thing, too. I hear another one is coming in this afternoon."

On the road again, Carolyn slowed through low areas where runoff had collected. Mitch was right. The Jag never would have made it. The river raged to her left, swollen and boiling with debris. The houses along the bank were flooded. How long before the road was closed?

As she headed up Willig Drive, she had to stop and drag part of an old apple tree off the road. Drenched, she climbed back into the Suburban and drove the last hundred yards. The old redwood on the corner of Mom's property had dropped piles of small branches. Carolyn pulled around its massive trunk and parked parallel to the house.

The gate was locked. Carolyn dumped her duffel bag and rang the bell, then returned to the car to unload the groceries. She set down the first three plastic bags and went back for the rest.

Shivering, she rang the bell again. Maybe Georgia had dropped Dawn off already, and she and Mom were too busy talking to hear the bell.

The door slammed. "All right! I'm coming!" The latch clicked and the heavy gate swung open. Mom held an umbrella. She looked at the bags of groceries. "I didn't tell you to bring anything."

"I just picked up a few things on the way through Guerneville."

"It looks like you shopped for a week!"

"Could we discuss this inside? I'm soaked and freezing."

Her mother took two bags and headed for the back door, leaving Carolyn to bring everything else after she closed the gate and latched it. "Is Dawn here yet?"

"No." Mom shook off the umbrella at the back door. "I don't know what I'm going to do with all these groceries, Carolyn. I don't have a big Deepfreeze like you do, you know."

Carolyn's frustration rose like a tide. She let it crest and recede as she put the laden bags on the counter. When would she learn her mother wanted nothing from her? "I'll take care of it." She wondered if her mother ate the home-cooked, packaged meals she brought out every two weeks. Probably not.

"Dawn will be in the blue room. Take your things downstairs."

Carolyn hadn't even been in the house two minutes and already felt unwelcome. "Okay." She went back into the cold rain. It was warmer than the kitchen.

The apartment was as chilly as a meat locker. Carolyn's breath puffed steam as she dumped her bag on the end of the queen-size bed with its chintz spread. At least it had an electric blanket. She could hear Mom tromping around upstairs in the kitchen, probably unloading the bags. Carolyn hurried upstairs. Mom looked annoyed. "Potatoes, carrots, turnips, rutabagas, celery, onions, canned tomatoes . . . Let me guess. You want to make stone soup."

Carolyn nudged her aside and took out round steak. "It's good for a cold, rainy day like this, don't you think?"

"And a lot of work, but you go right ahead if that's what you want. What does it matter that it's *my* house and I might have other plans."

"Did you?"

"That's not the point. I was getting around to it." Her mother sat at the kitchen nook table. "Go ahead." She waved her hand and looked out the window. "I'm just a little out of sorts today."

"What time did Dawn say she was coming?"

"She'll be here any minute."

Carolyn put the milk, eggs, bacon, and cheese into the refrigerator. "What's this all about, Mom?" She rummaged in a drawer for a potato peeler and paring knife.

"I thought you knew."

"Me?" Carolyn felt confused. "You called me."

Her mother looked disgruntled. "Are you sure you haven't said anything to her about pressuring me to move?"

"I'm not pressuring you. And no, I haven't discussed it with Dawn."

Carolyn let the silence settle as she rinsed potatoes and carrots. How long before her mother realized she couldn't stay out here alone, miles from a grocery store and medical care? She'd lost power for five days last winter! Mitch had to fight with the Coastal Commission to put in a generator. Not that she'd ever thanked him.

Carolyn dumped peels into the coffee can under the sink. The meat browned in an iron skillet while she diced vegetables. Her mother hadn't said a word in thirty minutes. Carolyn wanted to suggest her mother think about moving in with her and Mitch. They had plenty of room. Mom could have the never-used maid's quarters. The apartment had a nice bedroom, private bathroom, sitting room, and kitchenette. Her mother wouldn't even have to eat at the same table with them if she didn't want to. But Carolyn knew better. Her mother would make some lame excuse about not wanting to be a burden. If May Flower Dawn wasn't there, Mom had no interest in being there either.

Still, she needed to make amends. Carolyn sat at the nook table. "I never meant to hurt your feelings, Mom. I worry about you out here all by yourself." She didn't want to remind her of the fall that had left her limping for weeks.

Her mother looked like a little girl lost. "Do you?"

"Yes. Especially this time of the year. If this rain keeps up, the roads will close. What if something happened?"

"I haven't fallen again." Hildie looked toward the back door. "I hope Dawn gets here soon."

Dawn. Mom's only concern.

Carolyn let the hurt slide like water off a gull's back and admonished herself for wishing Mom could make a little space in her heart for her. Life didn't always work out the way you wished. At least she had Mitch and Christopher. "I forgot to call Mitch. My cell phone won't work out here. Do you mind if I use your phone?"

"Go ahead."

Carolyn lifted the receiver. Nothing. She checked the cord, just to be sure it hadn't been unplugged accidentally. "Too late. The phone lines are down."

"Here comes a car. Do you think it could be Dawn?" Mom headed for the door, flipping on the porch light before going out with her umbrella.

Carolyn shoved the chair back and followed. Mom had left her standing in the rain for five minutes, but now opened the gate and stood waiting with the umbrella as May Flower Dawn drove up the hill. Carolyn stood under the gate overhang as her daughter parked.

Mom didn't wait for Dawn to get out of the car before going out and making sure she was protected from the rain. Carolyn could barely catch a glimpse of her daughter as she maneuvered herself out of the front seat. "Well, look at you!" Mom laughed. They hugged. They chattered.

Carolyn shivered, rain dripping down the back of her neck. Wrapping her arms around herself to ward off the chill, she waited for them to remember her.

Not surprisingly, it was Dawn who did. She stepped out of her grandmother's embrace and came to Carolyn. "I'm so glad you came."

"Why wouldn't I?" Carolyn smiled, feeling teary at the sight of her daughter. "You're looking in full bloom." Dawn and Jason had waited a long time for this baby. It was a time for joy. When Dawn threw her arms around her, she gave a soft gasp.

Dawn held tight. "I've been dreaming about this for days."

Carolyn lifted a tentative hand to her daughter's back, disturbed by the embrace. It wasn't their usual way. "Of coming home to Jenner?"

Dawn drew back and gave a wobbly smile. "Of having a few days alone with you and Granny. I . . ." She wiped rain from her face—or was she crying? "I'm just so *happy!*"

"Well, that's good, honey, but you're getting wet." Carolyn's mother looped her arm around Dawn and herded her through the gate. "Let's get you inside where it's warm." She glanced over her shoulder. "Are you coming?"

Carolyn supposed that was as warm an invitation as she would get.

❄ ❄ ❄

Dawn smelled something wonderful when she walked in the back door. "Stone soup!" She hadn't had it in over a year.

Granny chuckled, hazel eyes bright with joy. "You'd better be hungry. Your mother made enough to feed an army." She took Dawn's bag. "You're sleeping in the blue room, honey. I don't want you having to go out in the rain, and those stairs can be awfully slick. We can't have any accidents." She set the bag inside the bedroom, then drew Dawn into the living room. "Why did you rent a car? Someone could have met you at the airport." Granny sat in her recliner.

Dawn eased her body onto the faded blue sofa. "It's not a rental. It's my car."

Mom sat in one of the swivel chairs near the fireplace. "You drove?"

"Yep." Dawn tried to make light of it.

"All the way across country in winter?" Granny stared at her. "In your condition?"

Dawn felt the tears coming. "I wanted to come home." She bowed her head and ran her hand over her swollen belly. "Don't ask me why. I know it was crazy. I just packed and came." She raised her head and smiled at her mom first, then Granny. "I want to have my baby here."

Granny frowned. "In Jenner?"

Dawn giggled. "No, Granny. In California, in Healdsburg or Santa Rosa. I want to be close to family and friends." She wasn't ready to talk about everything, not five minutes after she'd arrived, maybe not tonight or tomorrow morning either. "I didn't want to be alone."

"Well, that makes perfect sense." Granny leaned back, making herself comfortable. "When the baby is born, you can come out here and stay until Jason comes home. Then you can fly back to New Jersey to meet him." Granny, taking over again. Mom didn't argue. Dawn sensed the hurt she tried to hide and gave her an apologetic smile. "I hope you can get your money back for the airline tickets, Mom. It was important I be with both of you."

"Well, of course, it is." Granny nodded. "Your mom understands. This is where you belong."

Granny meant with her, at Jenner. Dawn saw that's the way her mother understood it, too, and spoke quietly. "I don't want to be in between anymore."

Granny frowned. "What do you mean 'in between'?"

"Between you and Mom." Dawn glanced from one to the other. "We three have a lot to talk about."

Granny's expression soured. "I should've known. Dawn drives all the way across country in the winter, and you say you don't know a thing about it." Granny glared at Mom. "I suppose you want me to believe you didn't tell her you've been after me to sell and move."

"I didn't."

"I don't believe you!"

Mom hunched her shoulders and looked away, fixing her gaze somewhere outside the window. How many times had Dawn seen this happen before? Anytime an argument arose between her and Granny, Mom pulled inside herself like a turtle in its shell. The only one who had ever been able to coax her out was Mitch, and he kept Mom's confidences.

"Mom didn't say anything to me, Granny. This is the first I've heard of any discussion of you leaving Jenner."

"You don't have to pretend, Dawn." Rain blasted the window, even as the storm in Granny's eyes grew.

"Are you going to accuse me of lying, too?"

"It's all right, Dawn. Don't put yourself in the middle. I think I'll see about dinner." Mom got up slowly and went into the kitchen, closing the door behind herself.

Dawn hurt inside. This wasn't the beginning she wanted. She looked at Granny sadly. "I wouldn't lie to you and neither would Mom." She held out her hand. Granny took it. "But now that you've brought it up, it might be time to think about moving." She squeezed Granny's hand before she let go and pushed herself up. She didn't want Mom hiding in the kitchen.

"Just leave her alone." Granny gave a weary sigh. "She'll come back when she's ready."

"I need to use the bathroom." Dawn rubbed the small of her back. "I hope you'll apologize when she comes back." *God, You got me all the way across the country. Please get me through this, too!*

When she came out of the bathroom, Mom sat at the kitchen nook table, face in her hands. Granny still sat in the corner recliner in the living room. Dawn felt the tears rise again; she hadn't been here fifteen minutes and she was right back in the middle. Granny's head lifted as Dawn stepped toward the living room. "Come on in and sit down, Dawn."

"Why don't you come in here, Granny? I'll fix some tea."

Granny glowered at both of them. "I don't want to talk about moving."

"Why not?"

"Look around." Granny's shoulders slumped. "And I'm not talking about the million-dollar view. I'm talking about—" she waved her hand like a white flag—"everything."

Dawn understood. "I have to pare down every time Jason and I move, Granny. I pick what means the most and sell or give away the rest."

"Well, it all means something to me, honey. There's a story behind everything in this house. You know how much Papa loved this place. It was his last big project." Granny's eyes grew moist as she looked at Mom. "It might not mean anything to you, Carolyn, but Dawn understands."

Mom didn't even try to defend herself.

"I understand, Granny, but Papa wouldn't want you living here alone." She didn't let Granny's look of hurt silence her. "If you wait too long, someone else will have to make all the decisions—what to keep, what to throw away."

Granny got up. "Well, that would be fine with me. When I'm dead, I won't care anymore." She dumped her tea in the sink. "Have it your way, Carolyn. If you're that set on getting me out of this house, go on down to the garage and get started sorting." She slammed her mug on the counter. "I'm going to turn on the TV and see how bad this storm is going to be." Granny went into the living room.

Dawn sighed. "I'm sorry, Mom. I was trying to help."

Mom shrugged. "It's not your fault. It is overwhelming."

Dawn smiled at her. "What was that you used to say? First things first."

"One day at a time."

"Granny loves you, Mom."

Mom made a soft sound of doubt, got up, and put her mug carefully on the counter. "I think I'll take advantage of the moment." She took her jacket by the door and went out.

Dawn went into the living room. Granny tipped her recliner up and peered around her. "Your mother isn't leaving, is she?"

"Would you care if she did?"

"Of course, I'd care." She started to push herself up from the chair.

"It's all right, Granny. She's going to the garage."

"Why?"

"You told her to get started, didn't you?"

Granny sank back in her chair. "I didn't mean *now*." She frowned. "It's freezing out there. It'll be dark soon."

"She's not going anywhere, Granny. I think she just needs to be alone for a while."

"She's always preferred her own company."

Dawn sat on the couch. Sonoma County was on the national news. "Another storm coming in tonight . . ." Aerial film crews showed the Russian River at flood level. The vineyards around Wohler Bridge were underwater. So were the ones near the Korbel Winery. The roads had closed. The river had risen high enough to close the Safeway in Guerneville.

53

SHIVERING, CAROLYN STOOD in the garage, surveying the massive project ahead of her. Dad's white Buick Regal still took up half the garage. Mom had forgotten to take the keys out of the ignition. Carolyn backed the car out of the garage and parked it behind Dawn's car.

Shelves lined the walls. One section displayed canned vegetables and soups; jars of peanut butter, jelly, and jam; cans of tuna; and boxes of macaroni and cheese. Another rack of shelves held small appliances in their original boxes and enough Costco plastic-wrapped boxes of Kleenex, toilet paper, and paper towels to last a year. Carolyn set a kerosene lamp near the door. They might need it. Cabinets lined the back wall: one held shelves of vases in all shapes and sizes; another Korbel champagne, Johnnie Walker Scotch, bottles of Mondavi cabernet sauvignon, Wente Brothers zinfandel and chardonnay, all dusty. *The devil prowls like a lion.* After more than thirty years of sobriety, Carolyn felt the sharp urge to drown her sorrows.

She still attended AA meetings, but Cornerstone Christian

Church filled another gap in her life. It had started with Pastor Daniel's compassion the day Dad died. Then Georgia openly shared her life on the streets before God got ahold of her. Others with less-than-pristine pasts rejoiced over restored lives and made others, still struggling, welcome. Carolyn made friends, though she never let anyone as close as Chel, with whom she had shared all her secrets, even the one she had never told Mitch.

Why was she thinking about all that now?

Carolyn looked over Dad's tools, mounted neatly above his worktable, all rusting in the sea air. She counted five boxes tucked in the rafters. She set up the ladder, pulled her tiered skirt up between her legs and tucked it into her leather belt, and climbed. Brushing away cobwebs, she brought them down one by one. She was warm by the time she lined the boxes on the cement floor. Mom had labeled each: *Family Pictures, Clothing, Trip, China/ FRAGILE,* and *Mama.*

Carolyn pulled open the top flaps of the box marked *Mama* and drew out a hand-crocheted granny-square afghan. It reeked of damp and mold, holes eaten away by mice or rats. She folded it into the garbage can, annoyed that Oma's labor of love had been stuffed in a box to rot. Next was a shoe box. Carolyn uttered a soft gasp when she found Oma's leather journal on top of bundles of thin, folded airmail letters with Swiss stamps. She took out the journal and carefully opened it. A picture slipped out and fell on the floor: Oma sitting on a chair holding a baby, a little boy beside her, and a tall, blond, very handsome man in a dark suit standing behind them. He was holding a little brown-haired girl and had his other hand on Oma's shoulder. Carolyn picked up the picture and turned it over. *Winnipeg, 1919.*

"Mom?" Dawn stood in the doorway, bundled in a down coat. "Please come back inside."

"I was just going through a few boxes." She tucked the picture back into Oma's journal and glanced around. "It is going to be a big job."

"Not one you can finish tonight. Granny fixed corn bread. The table is set for dinner. We can bring in a few boxes and go through them later, if you'd like." She examined one of them. "Might be kind of fun."

Carolyn put Oma's journal on top of the shoe box and stacked them on the box labeled *Family Pictures*. May Flower Dawn lifted the box marked *Trip*. They carried the two boxes into the house and put them in the living room. "It'll just take me a minute to get the others." When she'd stacked the other boxes in the middle of the living room, she washed her hands in the kitchen sink before sitting down with May Flower Dawn and her mother, who gave the blessing.

Carolyn put her napkin on her lap. "I found Oma's journal."

"My inheritance." Her mother snorted, scooping stone soup into bowls. "She gave Rikka a few pieces of jewelry. She'd already given Bernie her car. Cloe earns a stipend for handling the college trust Mama set up. I got her recipe book and a box of letters, written in German." She set a bowl in front of Dawn and filled another for Carolyn.

Dawn took a spoonful of soup and smiled. "Yummy." She glanced across at Carolyn. "It's not just a collection of recipes, Granny. When we visited her, Oma gave it to me to read one night. She told me she only wrote important things that made a difference in her life: tips on how to keep a house, yes, and some recipes, but also quotes from people she met, important dates like when you were born and the circumstances, ranch schedules, a funny poem a boy wrote about Summer Bedlam, her thoughts on life. It's wonderful. It defines her. I'd love to read it again." She looked at Carolyn. "She sent me a journal after that visit. Remember?"

"You sent her a diploma." Carolyn smiled, pleased to know that week had meant something to May Flower Dawn, that those few days in Merced had left her daughter with fond memories of Oma.

"The journal she sent me is leather and has my name engraved in gold. *May Flower Dawn.* I have it with me. I think of Oma every time I open it. I followed Oma's lead. I didn't write a lot of teenage nonsense in it. I wrote goals, favorite Scriptures, meaningful dates, places Jason and I have lived, dreams . . ." She smiled wistfully. "I wish I'd known Oma better. Oma's journal meant more to her than jewelry, a car, or money, Granny. She gave you the best of herself."

Carolyn's mother looked surprised—and a little perplexed.

The lights flickered and went out, enclosing them in complete darkness. "Wow." Dawn's voice sounded louder in the inky wrapping. "I can't see my hand in front of my face."

Carolyn hated the darkness. "I forgot the kerosene lantern in the garage. Where's a flashlight?"

"In one of the kitchen drawers, under the dish cabinets—middle I think—but the batteries are probably dead."

Carolyn fumbled around in the darkness, opening drawers and feeling through contents.

"Just wait a minute, Carolyn. Or did you forget you and Mitch put in a generator? There it goes." A distant whir sounded, and then noise.

Dawn laughed. "No muffler on that baby."

The lights came on. Relieved, Carolyn returned to her seat. Her mother sat calmly, hands folded on the table. "I don't think I ever thanked you, did I?"

"No. You didn't. But then we didn't ask your permission either." If they couldn't get her to move, they'd make sure she had heat and power. Four thousand dollars, not to mention the money spent on a lawyer who took over the fight with the Coastal Commission, and not one word of thanks until now.

❊ ❊ ❊

After clearing and washing the dishes, Carolyn joined her daughter and mother in the living room. She hesitated on the threshold when she saw them on the couch, May Flower Dawn holding her granny's hand on her abdomen. They spoke in whispers. Biting her lip, Carolyn stepped back. She felt like an intruder. Mom glanced up and frowned. "Why are you standing there? Come feel the baby moving."

Carolyn treaded carefully around the stacked boxes and knelt in front of them. Dawn took her hand and placed it on her abdomen. Carolyn didn't feel anything. Dawn sighed. "Little Miss must have fallen asleep again." Carolyn rose and sat in the yellow swivel rocker.

Her mother pushed herself up and settled into her recliner. "This is nice, having the two of you here, together."

Dawn grinned. "Three girls on a sleepover." She winced in pain and shifted on the couch until she looked more comfortable. Carolyn remembered the final month of pregnancy when her babies had pressed against her rib cage and bore down on her pelvis. The last month was the hardest.

Dawn yawned. She looked so tired.

"Why don't you go to bed, May Flower Dawn?"

"It's only eight, Carolyn."

"She looks exhausted, Mom."

"I'm not ready for bed yet." Dawn gave them both a tired smile. "I want to sit and visit."

"You can lie down and visit." Carolyn got up and lifted Dawn's legs onto the couch. "Your ankles are swollen." Dawn murmured a weary thank-you and said not to worry. Carolyn tucked a needlepoint pillow under her head and draped a soft, white knitted blanket over her. She brushed a wayward strand of blonde hair back from her daughter's face. She was perspiring. "Do you have a fever?"

Dawn took her hand. "Relax, Mom. It's a lot of work carrying around an extra thirty pounds."

Carolyn took her seat and watched Dawn fall asleep. She snored softly. "I guess she is tired." After a few minutes, she fidgeted in her chair. She felt night fold tight around them, the glass their only barrier against it. "I guess we could go through the boxes."

"I don't want to go through those boxes." Her mother shook her head. "Not tonight. Besides, Dawn would probably get a kick out of it." She rubbed her leg as though it ached. "You stood in the doorway just now. Why do you do that?"

"Do what?"

"Stand outside a door, peer around corners, listen in."

Carolyn felt the words like a slap. "Like a sneaky little mouse, you mean. Like I'm planning to steal a bit of cheese?"

Mom looked shocked. "No." She shook her head. "Like you don't belong. Like you're waiting for an invitation."

"I was told to stay out."

"Who told you that?"

Why not tell the truth? Mom never spared her feelings. "You did. You said you never wanted me anywhere near you."

"That's a lie!" Her eyes darkened in anger.

Carolyn pressed her lips together. She should have known better than to say anything.

"I suppose Oma told you that!"

Heat flooded Carolyn. "You always blame Oma for everything, but I remember you yelling right into my face, 'Get out of here. . . . Get away from me.' Not Oma."

"When did I ever do such a thing?"

"It's the earliest memory I have."

Mom's expression changed, as though remembering. "When you brought me a bouquet of flowers . . ."

"Wildflowers. You didn't want them."

"You dropped them. They scattered all over the floor. I picked them up. Oma brought me a vase."

Picked them up? Put them in a vase? "I never went into your room after that."

Mom looked stricken. "I was sick, Carolyn. Don't you remember how sick I was?"

Carolyn didn't want to go back and visit that time. She wanted to close the trapdoor that had sprung open. She didn't want to look down into the darkness and see what lay hidden there.

"I had tuberculosis. No one but Dad and Oma were allowed in my room, and they had to take precautions. Do you remember any of that?"

"It doesn't matter."

"It does matter."

"It was a long time ago."

"I *loved* you, Carolyn."

Loved. Past tense. Why talk about the past? Why bring it up at all? Chel told her once that just because you were family didn't mean you got along. Her father hadn't liked her. "You just live with it and move on," Chel said. "Don't waste energy trying to make them love you."

Chel. Why was she thinking about Rachel Altman now? Why were her words ringing in Carolyn's head after all these years? Twice in the last few hours.

Carolyn tried to close that door on the past, but memories kept flooding in. She remembered sitting in the tall grass, plucking petals from a daisy. *She loves me; she loves me not; she loves me; she loves me not . . .*

Oma loved her.

Mom and Dad loved Charlie.

Charlie. Oh, Charlie. The pain came up quick, squeezing her heart.

"What are you thinking about, Carolyn?"

"Charlie." She spoke without thinking. Did the mention of her brother still bring Mom pain? "Sorry."

Mom appeared calm, pensive. "What about Charlie?"

"He told me you got sick after I was born."

"Not right away. I let myself get run-down. I knew better. I'd had TB before."

"When?"

"Your father and I were courting. I thought you knew all this."

"I guess I don't know anything."

"I spent months in Arroyo del Valle Sanatorium. I got better, but the disease is always there, hiding, waiting. When I got sick again after you were born, I thought I was going to die. Oma came so I could come home. Die at home, I thought. I didn't want to leave your dad in debt. So Oma moved in and . . . took over everything." She smiled sadly. "That may be what gave me the incentive to get well—watching Oma take over my family."

The rain pounded harder, like fists on the roof. "Oma loved me, Mom."

"Yes. And you loved her. Exclusively. You never came to me. You always went to Oma. That's why I told her to go home."

"So I wouldn't have anyone?"

Mom looked crushed. "You were *my* little girl, not Oma's."

Carolyn's fingers curled around the seat cushion. She remembered Dad shaking her and telling her to stop crying or else. "I felt so alone."

"You had *me*."

When had that ever been true? "No. I didn't."

"Yes, you did!"

Carolyn refused to let it pass this time. "We moved out to the new property! You and Dad worked all the time on the house and gardens."

"Not all the time."

"You told me to stay out from underfoot, to go off somewhere and play. I'd wait for Charlie, but when he got home from school, he always grabbed his bicycle and took off."

"You were right there with me. You picked flowers. You made mud cookies. You flattened down a little private place in the mustard flowers where you played with your rag doll."

That wasn't the way Carolyn remembered it. She didn't want to tell Mom what she did remember. "I think I'll go to bed." She got up.

"Carolyn. Please. Can't we talk about this a little more? I didn't know you—"

"I'll see you in the morning."

"It'll be cold downstairs." Mom tried to push herself out of the chair. "I haven't opened the heating vent to the downstairs yet. It'll take half an hour to warm up the apartment."

"Save the energy. I'll be under the covers anyway."

Carolyn struggled into her jacket at the back door. She had to get out of the house, away from her mother, away from the past that shoved its way up like a demon coming from Hades.

The cold hit Carolyn in the face. Rain pelted her. She held the rail as she hurried downstairs. The screen door stuck. She yanked twice before it creaked open. She flicked the light switch and stood in the sitting room, heart pounding. A whoosh of cold air hit her. It warmed quickly. Mom had opened the vent. Wrapping her arms around herself, Carolyn turned her face into it.

She heard muted voices. Dawn must have awakened. Carolyn thought about going upstairs again, but that might put a damper on their conversation. Mom and Dawn had always been able to talk. Carolyn knew there was more to Dawn's cross-country trip than she'd said. She didn't look well at all. Maybe she'd tell her grandmother what she couldn't tell her mother.

Carolyn turned on the electric blanket before going into the bathroom. She brushed her teeth, then sat on the side of the bed, brushed and braided her hair. Changing quickly into her pajamas, she pulled on a pair of Mitch's athletic socks and slipped quickly between the warming sheets. Shivering violently, she snuggled down deep into the covers, waiting for the warmth to soak in, while above her, Mom and Dawn went on talking.

Carolyn felt her throat close. Hadn't it always been this way? How could it be any other way when her daughter had spent the first six years of her life completely dependent on Mom? Carolyn didn't want to be bitter. She owed Mom gratitude for taking care of Dawn. If not her mother, it would have been some indifferent babysitter earning minimum wage in an overcrowded day care center.

Footsteps crossed the room above her—two pairs this time, one toward the master bedroom, the other toward the refurbished front bedroom. After that, she listened to the storm rattle the windows.

Closing her eyes, Carolyn listened to the surf and wind and rain. She dreamed she was a child again, walking in a forest of mustard flowers. Bees hummed around her, but she wasn't frightened of them. She came to a barbed-wire fence and climbed through. Her dress caught and tore. She stood behind a white house watching a man in overalls walk among two rows of white boxes on wooden pedestals. He removed a lid, setting it aside, and then carefully and slowly lifted out a wooden frame filled in with honeycomb. Breaking off a piece, he turned and smiled at her. "Come on over, honeybee. I won't hurt you."

Carolyn awakened abruptly, heart pounding. It took a few minutes for the dream to recede. Shivering, she turned the electric blanket to ten and pulled the covers over her head.

54

DAWN AWAKENED WHEN the Black Forest cuckoo clock struck three. She curled onto her side, listening to the rain coming down like the cadence of a marching band. She and Granny had talked after Mom went to bed. Granny wanted to know about Jason, and she wondered what Dawn had done with her latest house. Dawn wanted to talk about Granny's future. After some resistance, Granny gave in.

"You know your mother wanted me to move right after Papa died. It was just too soon to make any changes. And I've been fine here by myself." She let out her breath. "At least until this past year."

"What happened?"

"Last winter the power went out for five days. If your mom could've gotten out here, I would've started packing. As soon as the weather improved, your mom and Mitch went to all the trouble of putting in that generator. They had to hire a lawyer. Heaven knows how much they spent on the whole project. It wouldn't have been much of a thank-you if I'd said 'Oh, by the way, I'm ready to move now.' And besides, it can be very nice out here most of the year."

Dawn grinned. "And you always said Oma was stubborn."

Granny put her head back. "I didn't think I was being stubborn. But I guess that's how it looked. Then after my fall a few months back, your mother brought up the idea again."

"But you're ready to move now. Aren't you?"

"As ready as I'm ever going to be." Granny glowered. "But I want a place of my own, not a room in some senior care facility."

"You don't want to live with anyone, Granny?"

"I don't want to live with *strangers*."

Dawn caught something in Granny's tone that gave her hope. "What about moving in with Mom and Mitch?"

Granny gave a derisive laugh. "That's not going to happen."

"Why not?"

"It just won't, that's all. And don't go asking your mother about it. You'll just put her in an awkward position." Granny had changed the subject after that.

Sleepless, Dawn pulled the covers over her shoulders and snuggled down into the flannel sheets. *Lord, they never really talk to each other, do they? They love each other, but they don't see love is shared.*

Dawn ran her hand over her belly. Her daughter would be arriving soon. She wanted it to be a time of joy, a chance to come together and celebrate. Dawn didn't want them at odds with one another, seeing one another through past hurts. The stakes were too high for that now.

Love one another, You said, Lord. Help me show them how.

❄ ❄ ❄

Hildie awakened early. The house creaked like a ship adrift in rough seas; the rain still pounded. She had a flashlight on her side table and pointed it at her clock. Six fifteen. Trip had always been first up and started the coffee. Oh, how she missed that man! Trip had been the only man she ever loved.

If she wasn't careful, she could sink into despair over her losses. She still missed her son, Charlie. She missed Carolyn, too, aching for what might have been. It was too late now. And she would never stop missing Mama—or wishing they had somehow made peace before the end. Dawn had been the light that pulled her up out of the darkness after Charlie was killed and Carolyn came home like a starving waif. Feeling needed, Hildie stepped in, wanting to help. Dawn had been God's blessing.

Hildie pushed the covers off, tucked her feet into her fuzzy slippers, pulled on her robe, and went into the bathroom. When she finished her morning ablutions, she turned on the lamp in the living room and went into the kitchen to set up the coffeemaker, decaf.

A few minutes later, the back door opened. "I heard you get up." Carolyn came in, hair in a French braid, and wearing another sweater over her long hippy skirt and leggings, blue this time, the exact shade of her eyes. Trip's eyes.

Hildie apologized. She hadn't meant to awaken anyone. In truth, she was glad of the company. "Did you sleep all right?"

"Okay." She poured herself a cup of coffee.

"Do you realize how long it's been since you stayed overnight out here?"

"Christmas, before Dad died." Carolyn sat at the table.

"I want a house, Carolyn, not an apartment or a room."

Carolyn raised her brows in surprise. "Like the one you and Dad built for Oma?"

Wouldn't it be nice to have a little house on Carolyn and Mitch's property? Close enough to be a part of their lives, but not so close she'd be in their way. A dream for her, probably a nightmare for Carolyn. She'd better set her daughter's mind at ease. "There's a nice trailer park in Windsor, seniors only, right around the corner from the church." Why was Carolyn frowning like that?

"Well, we can look there if you like."

"What's wrong with that idea?"

"I just can't see you in a trailer park, Mom."

No doubt, she'd like it better if her mother were under lock and key with guardians to keep an eye on her. "We had wonderful trips in our trailer."

"Yes. I guess we did."

"You guess?"

"It was a travel trailer. Not something to live in."

"Well, I'm not talking about moving into a travel trailer. I'm talking about one of those double-wides."

"Okay. Don't get upset." Carolyn sipped her coffee. "Did Dawn tell you why she drove out here?"

"She told both of us."

"Did she give you any other reason why she wanted to do something as foolish as drive cross-country in winter when she's about to have a baby?"

"Being with family isn't foolish, Carolyn. It's a good enough reason, if you ask me." She had thanked God countless times Carolyn came home when she did. They might never have known what happened to her otherwise, though at times she wondered if she knew much of anything about her daughter.

"I hope so."

"I wouldn't worry too much." Carolyn had always been overly sensitive. "A girl usually wants her husband or mother around when her time comes." A shadow flickered across her daughter's face, and Hildie felt a twinge of remorse. She had sent Carolyn to Boots. Hildie had cried buckets over that decision, but she and Trip knew it was the only way to protect Carolyn from all the gossip. They'd both been depressed for ages after she left. They'd lost Charlie in Vietnam. They'd no sooner gotten their daughter back than they had to send her away. It had hurt even more believing she would give up their only grandchild for adoption.

When Boots told them Carolyn wanted to keep the baby, Hildie had been overjoyed. Boots said she'd love to have Carolyn live with her, but Hildie wanted her daughter back. She wanted to hold her grandchild. She told Trip she wanted to quit nursing and stay home. They didn't need the money, and Carolyn would need help. They sat down and laid out a plan to help their daughter recover from the lost years in Haight-Ashbury. They wouldn't ask questions. They'd leave the past behind them. And Carolyn had done so well. She'd finished college and excelled in the real estate office.

Hildie thought they'd go on as they were. It had been a shock when Carolyn said she wanted to move out. Hildie had seen something in her eyes. Her daughter couldn't wait to get away from them. And, oh, the pain, when she had to give up Dawn.

"The sun's coming up," Carolyn said. "Not that we can see much of it through the clouds."

"More rain through today and tomorrow." Hildie sipped her lukewarm coffee. "I'm a little worried we'll run out of propane. The truck is supposed to try again on Monday."

Carolyn got up. "'Through waves and clouds and storms, He gently clears the way.' Let's hope the roads are open on Monday." She took the carafe from the coffeemaker. "Would you like your coffee warmed up?"

"One cup is about all I can handle these days."

Carolyn replenished her own. "Didn't Dad buy presto logs?"

"They're under the garage."

"I'll bring some up, just in case." She sat again. "I should take a look at what's under there anyway."

"Why don't you wear a pair of my pants so you don't ruin your nice skirt? Take a look in my closet." While Carolyn went to see about the pants, Hildie took out eggs and bacon. Carolyn came into the kitchen wearing a pair of red polyester slacks that hit midcalf. What a difference four inches in height could make. Hildie laughed. "High-water pants."

"Clam-diggers." Carolyn laughed with her.

Dawn opened the accordion door. Hair mussed, bleary-eyed, and pale, she wore a pair of white athletic socks and Trip's old navy blue terry-cloth bathrobe. Her blue eyes still looked shadowed with exhaustion. Carolyn greeted her before getting her jacket and going out the door.

"Where are you going, Mom? Aren't you having breakfast with us?"

"I'm going to check under the garage, bring up some presto logs for a fire."

Hildie turned bacon in the frying pan. "Forget the presto logs for now, Carolyn. Just open the safe downstairs and bring up whatever's inside." She told her the combination. "If I'm going to be downsizing, a good place to start is some of the jewelry I've been keeping locked up and never wear."

Carolyn went out into the rain. Dawn eased into a chair, rested her elbow on the window, and looked out at the glutted Russian River.

Hildie studied her granddaughter. It was such a pleasure having Dawn under her roof again. "It is a beautiful view, even in flood season, isn't it, honey?"

Silent, Dawn rubbed her back in an abstracted manner.

"You okay, honey?" In the morning light, Hildie noticed even more clearly the signs that something was wrong. Other than her swollen abdomen, the girl was skin and bones. Was she just worried, anxious about Jason and the baby they'd both hoped and prayed for, for so long?

"Hmmm? Oh." Dawn smiled, still distracted. "Just tired."

"Thinking about Jason?"

"I think about Jason all the time, Granny. I miss him so much, especially now. But God is using him where he is. Two guys in his unit have become Christians."

"You picked a good man, Dawn."

"I won't be able to e-mail him until I get back to town. He'll be worried. I should've thought of that."

"Georgia will let him know you're fine."

"Jason didn't know I was coming home."

Hildie found that information disturbing. "I should've come into town instead of having you drive all the way out here. We could have been warm as toast in Alexander Valley. And you could've kept in touch with your husband."

"I wanted to be out here."

"At least someone besides me loves the place."

"I didn't want any interruptions."

Troubled, Hildie looked at her, but before she could ask what was going on, Carolyn came back in the door with a stack of papers and a box covered with flowery contact paper. "Set it over there on the counter, Carolyn. We'll go through everything after breakfast."

❄ ❄ ❄

Carolyn watched May Flower Dawn pick at her food. Her blue eyes didn't have any sparkle, and her cheeks were pale. "Didn't you sleep at all last night, Dawn?"

"I couldn't shut off my mind."

Her mother offered more toast. "She's been thinking about Jason."

"Not surprising." Carolyn took a piece and buttered it. "The whole church is praying for him. So are we." Carolyn noticed Dawn grimace. "Are you having contractions?"

Dawn rubbed her sides. "She's running out of room in there."

Carolyn folded her hands and watched her daughter closely. "You're sure the baby is a girl?"

"She would've had a sonogram, Carolyn. Of course, she knows."

"I knew long before that, Granny. I had a dream about her. She was running and playing along the edge of the surf at Goat Rock Beach." She smiled at Carolyn. "And you and Granny were sitting together on the sand, talking like good friends."

A nice dream. Carolyn cleared dishes. She scraped Dawn's cold scrambled eggs into the garbage while imagining talking with her mother like that. When had there ever been a time when she hadn't needed to be careful about every word she said?

Her mother set the pile of papers and box on the table. "Let's see what we've got here." While Carolyn washed dishes, her mother and Dawn sat at the table, going through papers. "Deed to the house, car and life insurance policies, Social Security cards, wedding and death certificates, living trust, burial arrangements, list of bank accounts . . ." She fanned the papers, pausing over one. "Oma's naturalization papers. I forgot I had them. She was so proud when she passed the test."

Mom set the certificate aside. "Oma said we were the *real* American citizens. Those born to it didn't appreciate it. She made us all study as if we had to take the test too, to earn the right to call ourselves Americans. She thought that until Trip went to war and then Charlie . . ." She picked up an envelope yellowed by age. "The letter from Charlie's commanding officer . . ." She held it for a moment and set it aside unopened.

Carolyn dried her hands and picked it up. While her mom opened the box filled with smaller boxes, Carolyn opened the letter and read.

> . . . offer my heartfelt condolences on the death of your son. . . . excellent young man . . . well-respected by everyone who served with him. . . . could always count on him . . . brave . . . a pleasure to know him. . . . will never forget . . .

Mom lifted out a black velvet box and snapped it open. "Papa gave me these pearls on our twenty-fifth wedding anniversary." She took them out and handed them to Dawn.

"They're beautiful."

"You keep them."

"I can't, Granny. They should go to Mom."

Carolyn folded the letter back into the yellowed envelope and put it on the table. "Granny wants you to have the pearls."

"You and Mitch gave me pearls for my sixteenth birthday. Remember?"

Carolyn's mother looked hurt. "I'm not slighting your mother, Dawn. Mitch gave her better pearls than these for Christmas two years ago and a bracelet and earrings to go with them."

Dawn fingered the necklace. "They're lovely." Her eyes grew moist. "Save them for my daughter."

Her mother closed the box and opened another. Unfolding a lace-trimmed embroidered handkerchief, she showed off a gold, pearl, and jade brooch. "I gave this to Oma on her eightieth birthday. You . . ." Her voice faltered. "You were gone. Anyway, Oma would want you to have it."

Touched, Carolyn accepted the box. "I don't remember ever seeing Oma wear this."

"She didn't. Not once. I doubt she ever took it out of the box." Mom pointed. "That's real, not cheap costume jewelry. I wanted to give her something special, something she would never buy for herself."

Carolyn understood all too well. "Like the cashmere shawl I gave you for Christmas a few years ago? or the pendant I gave you for Mother's Day?"

Mom's eyes widened. "They're too special to use for every day."

Carolyn searched her face. "I thought you didn't like them."

"Of course I like them. They're the nicest gifts I've ever received."

Dawn interrupted. "Maybe Oma felt the same way about the brooch, Granny."

Mom shook her head. "I thought she'd love it, but she said I'd wasted my money."

Seeing the sheen of tears in her mother's eyes, Carolyn took the brooch out of the box. "This is exquisite, Mom. Maybe she was afraid to wear it." She pinned the brooch to her sweater. "It's beautiful. I'll cherish it. Thank you."

Eyes glistening, Mom gave her a wobbly smile. "You're welcome."

Dawn's blue eyes shone. "Perfect." She propped her chin in the heels of her hands. "This is exactly what I prayed for all across the country."

"What?" Carolyn's mother looked blank.

"That we three could just sit and talk about things that shaped our lives and our relationships."

Carolyn had spent years sidestepping questions, pushing memories back, training herself to live in the present. Dredging up the past wasn't her idea of an answer to prayer. She felt her mom's glance and didn't meet it.

Dawn rose. "Why don't we go through the boxes from the garage?" She went into the living room, not waiting for them to follow. "They should be full of memorabilia."

Carolyn's mother studied her. "You don't seem particularly enthused."

Carolyn hadn't moved from her seat. "Are you?"

Her mom pushed her chair back, but didn't get up. "Maybe we *should* talk about the past, Carolyn. God knows, you've been weighed down by it for years. And so have I."

Was that how she saw it? "There are some things I don't want Dawn to know."

"Do you think anything could change how much Dawn loves you?"

"What about you?"

"Me?" Her mom searched her face, comprehension seeping into her eyes. "I'm your mother." She shook her head. "I wonder if we know one another at all."

"Are you two coming?" Dawn called from the living room.

Dawn had already opened a box and pulled out a navy blue dress with white cuffs, faded red buttons, and a red belt. "Wow! This looks like old Hollywood, Granny."

"Your great-aunt Cloe designed and made that for me when I went away to nursing school."

"You'd get a small fortune for it on eBay now. Clotilde Waltert Renny first design . . ."

"Hardly the first."

Carolyn opened the *Pictures* box and found all the pictures that had once hung inside the front door of the Paxtown home: Charlie in his football uniform, in his cap and gown, with his Army buddies; his Army portrait with the ribbons mounted below. A dozen pictures of Charlie, all framed beautifully. Not one of her. Carolyn rocked back on her heels.

"What's wrong?" Carolyn's mother looked from her to the box. "What did you find?"

"Pictures of Charlie."

Dawn lowered an ashes-of-roses dressing gown. "Are you okay, Mom?"

The hurt rose, squeezing tight around her heart. "I'd better get the presto logs. Just in case the generator goes out."

❄ ❄ ❄

Dawn put the dressing gown aside and pulled over the box her mother had opened. "Pictures of Uncle Charlie." She took out a high school graduation picture. "I remember these. They were on the wall in the Paxtown house." Every picture was of Charlie, a few of Granny and Papa with him.

"Our memorial wall."

Granny used to tell her stories about her uncle: how well he played football, baseball, basketball; how popular he had been, how handsome. Mitch had added to her uncle's legend by telling stories about their teenage angst and antics, things Granny and Papa wouldn't have known. "Did he and my mom get along?"

"More than got along, honey. She idolized him. They were polar opposites. He always watched out for her. Charlie was outgoing. Your mom was shy. He had lots of friends. She was a loner. Charlie was like my brother, Bernie. Everyone was so taken with him they never noticed his little sister."

"Mitch told me he had a crush on Mom in high school. He wanted to ask her out, but never got up the nerve. That's why he came back to Paxtown—to look her up." Dawn set Uncle Charlie's picture on the coffee table. "Did you ever meet Mom's friend, Rachel Altman?"

Granny tilted her head. "So she told you about her."

"A little."

"Carolyn brought her home once, just before Charlie went to Vietnam. They were both still attending Berkeley at the time. Rachel came from wealth. She rented a house. That's when things started to go downhill. They dropped out and disappeared. We didn't hear from your mother for two years, and then one day, I came home and there she was sitting by the front door."

Dawn sat on the couch and curled her legs up under her. "Were you angry with her?"

"Angry?"

"She was gone so long. It must have been awful for you and Papa."

"You can't even imagine how awful." Granny sounded distressed. "Don't ask her about those days. She was worrying just now in the kitchen, thinking it would make a difference in how you feel about her. She doesn't want to talk about it. We tried a few times to open the subject, but learned to leave well enough alone."

Dawn wasn't convinced. "Maybe if she talks about it, it won't haunt her so much."

"She put it all behind her and moved on with her life."

"I'd like to know who my father was."

Dismayed, Granny shook her head. "Did you ever think she might not know? And asking would just make her feel worse about it."

"I love her, Granny. No matter what she tells me, that's not going to change."

"So do I. That's why I don't ask." Granny's mouth worked, as though she fought tears. "Just leave things alone. I lost her once; I don't want—"

The back door clicked open. Mom came in with a box of presto logs and set them beside the fireplace. She gave Dawn a questioning glance. "Is something wrong?"

Dawn shook her head and couldn't think of what to say.

Mom looked at both of them and headed for the back door again.

Dawn struggled to her feet. Pain stabbed into her side. Sucking in her breath, she went outside and leaned over the rail above the stairs. "Mom, wait."

Mom glanced at her, expression bleak.

"You don't have to leave."

Her mouth curved in disbelief. "You should go back inside and stay warm. You don't want to catch cold. " She went down the steps and disappeared around the corner.

55

CAROLYN STEPPED INSIDE the storage area under the garage and pulled the string attached to a swaying overhead light. She hefted another box of presto logs and set it near the door. She'd take it up in a little while. She wasn't in any hurry to go back upstairs and walk into another private conversation.

She could use an AA meeting right now. She felt at home among others who had struggled with life. She felt Jesus' presence there. He'd come to redeem sinners, hadn't He? He'd raised her up from out of the mire and planted her feet on His sacred ground. Sometimes, she forgot the past entirely, until something or someone reminded her again.

Carolyn breathed in slowly and exhaled. She had other things to think about . . . and no time to feel sorry for herself.

Most of the stuff under the house would have to be hauled away, like the red vinyl and chrome kitchen stools from the Paxtown house. Why had Mom and Dad hung on to them all these years? The metal frames had rusted and the seats cracked. Dad's fishing poles, net, creel, and box of flies hung on one wall, along with his brown chest-waders, two pairs of hiking boots, and an old backpack. An old AM/FM radio sat between stacks of *National Geographics* bound in bundles of twelve. Dad said they'd be worth something, someday. Water-damaged and worthless now, the whole collection would have to be lugged up to the road and taken to the dump. She wondered what Dad would say if he knew the entire collection was now available on CD-ROM.

Removing a canvas cover, Carolyn found a fertilizer spreader and push mower. The Jenner house didn't have a lawn. She opened a coffinlike chest and stepped back from the stench of molding blankets and towels. Not even a rat or mouse would make a nest in there. She found Charlie's old Lionel train, complete with engine, cars, caboose, tracks and railroad signs, station house and town buildings. Christopher would have enjoyed setting this up when he was a little boy. Had Dad forgotten about it or left it in storage because it hurt too much to be reminded of Charlie?

Another box held Charlie's high school yearbooks. She sat in the red Adirondack chair she'd given Dad for his sixtieth birthday and opened the 1962 *Amadon* yearbook. Leafing through the pages, she found his senior picture, hair neat and short. She found Mitch's picture. She loved his smile. She found other pictures of Charlie and Mitch: kneeling in the front row of the varsity football team, helmets on their knees; standing with other members of the basketball team; Charlie, head back as he laughed while hanging out on the senior lawn with friends. Friends had scrawled notes everywhere.

"I still miss you, Charlie," Carolyn whispered and closed the book. Her brother had always had a contagious laugh. Had he lived, he'd be married with grown children and grandchildren by now.

She put her head back against the chair and closed her eyes. Her heart still ached. Being cooped up and feeling like a third wheel didn't help. Mom and May Flower Dawn were close. That was good.

God, grant me the serenity to accept the things I cannot change.

She couldn't undo the past. She couldn't reclaim what had never belonged to her.

God, grant me the courage to change the things I can.

Maybe it was time to talk about the past . . . if she could do so with love. As much as she wanted to say it didn't matter, it still had the power to torment her. She'd come out to the beach a hundred times and written her sins in the sand, watching them wash away. But the guilt and shame always came back to haunt her.

"God won't take you where His love won't protect you," Boots had told her. "You lived through it. You're a survivor. The past doesn't have any power over you anymore."

Only the power she gave it.

Boots knew about the circumstances of her pregnancy. Carolyn had told her about her life in Haight-Ashbury and Rachel Altman. She'd even confessed her relationship with Ash—sordid, abusive, heart- and soul-crushing. But she'd never told her about the bee-keeper who lived next door and what she'd done with him.

God, grant me the wisdom . . . Your will, not mine be done.

Your will, Lord. Not Mom's or mine or even May Flower Dawn's.

Calm again, she stacked the yearbooks on top of the box of presto logs and headed back upstairs.

Mom sat in her recliner, reading a magazine. She glanced up as Carolyn came in the back door. "It must be freezing down there."

"Cold and damp, but not too bad." Dawn was asleep on the couch, the white afghan tucked around her. Carolyn set the box of presto logs on top of the other one and put the yearbooks on the coffee table. "She's awfully pale."

Mom put the magazine away. "She is, isn't she? And so thin."

"Did she tell you what made her drive across the country?"

"Just what she told us already. Pregnant women get strange urges. Maybe we're like salmon. We want to return to the stream where we were born."

"Then she should've headed for LA." Carolyn saw Mom wince and wished she hadn't said it. "I found Charlie's high school yearbooks."

Pain flickered across Mom's face. "I haven't looked at them in years. I won't have any room for them when I move."

When she moved, not *if.* "I'd like to keep them, if it's all right with you."

"Of course. You probably want some of the pictures in that box, too. I have my favorites hanging in the bedroom. I'll take those with me."

The lights flickered. Carolyn opened a box of presto logs. "I need to break a couple of these so we have kindling, and I'd better do it now before we lose power." Mom told her where to find Dad's hatchet and suggested taking one of the grocery bags under the sink to carry the pieces.

Carolyn chopped two logs into thick, pancake-size chunks; tucked a few old newspapers in the bag; and went back inside. Just as she closed the door behind herself, the lights went out and the heater shut down.

"Well, there it goes." Mom sighed. "At least we still have some daylight, but the house is going to get cold. There won't be heat downstairs. Why don't you bring your things up? Dawn can sleep with me in my bed and you can have that room. We'll keep the fire going and leave the bedroom doors ajar."

Carolyn rearranged several boxes. "First things first, Mom. We've got fuel; now we need to figure out how to cook."

"There's a Coleman stove under Dad's workbench."

Carolyn went out to find it.

❄ ❄ ❄

Dawn awakened to rain splattering the windows and a crackling fire. Granny sat quietly reading Oma's journal. "Where's Mom?" Dawn pushed herself up slowly, rubbing at her side.

"Out in the garage." Granny put the journal aside.

It was growing darker by the minute. "How long have I been asleep?"

"A couple of hours. You must have needed it." Granny studied her. "How do you feel now?"

"Groggy. Hungry."

"Your mom is trying to find the Coleman stove. We'll need it if we're going to cook. The generator went off. I'm out of propane. No light, no heat, no stove."

Dawn heard her mother come in the back door and move around in the kitchen before entering the living room. She sank wearily into the chair closest to the fire. "Finally found it under the garage. It was with Dad's fishing poles."

"Logical place for it." Granny nodded. "Did you see a down sleeping bag?"

"Yep, but it's mildewed."

"More stuff for the dump," Granny muttered.

"I'll use Dawn's bedding, Mom."

Granny took the flashlight and went into the master bedroom. She came back with a pile of clothes. She dropped a dark green sweatshirt and pants onto Mom's lap and a navy blue set beside Dawn. "Dad's. I meant to offer these things to Mitch and Christopher, but I kept forgetting. Take off those dirty pants, Carolyn, and put on the sweats. You must be frozen through."

Mom laughed. "After all the trips in and out of the garage and up and down those stairs, I'm nice and toasty."

"Well, you won't be for long."

Mom went to change. Dawn pulled on the extra layer. Papa's sweatpants pooled around her feet. She laughed. At least they fit her waistline. "Don't I look fetching?"

Granny chuckled. She went back into the bedroom and returned with thick pairs of Papa's socks. She insisted on warming the stone soup. "It's my house. I'm supposed to be the hostess." They ate in the living room, Mom sitting cross-legged on the rug in front of the fireplace, Dawn and Granny in the two yellow swivel chairs on either side of her.

Dawn relished the closeness. This was a first—the three of them sitting and talking, like three buddies at a sleepover. "I'm glad the roads are closed and the power is off."

Granny shook her head. "Being cut off from the world is the last thing a lady in your condition should want."

"This is fun, don't you think? The three of us sitting around the fire, enjoying one another's company." Deeper conversations could happen under these circumstances. She wouldn't push yet. *God, You do it. Strip away their resistance. Open their hearts. Get them talking.*

Granny tucked her hands inside Papa's old sweatshirt. "It's why Papa and I moved out here. We hoped this would become a gathering place for the whole family. Maybe I should keep the place, for you and Jason and your children to enjoy."

Mom looked at her with dismay. She set her empty bowl aside and pulled her legs up against her chest, gazing into the fire. Dawn didn't have to guess what she was thinking, and she decided it was time to make a few things clear. "Jason intends to stay in the military, Granny. He could be transferred anywhere anytime."

"Just a thought." Granny sighed. "Things don't always turn out the way we hope."

"I noticed you were reading Oma's journal again. Did she ever come up here, Granny?"

"She drove up once to see the place, stayed for two days, and went back to Merced. We invited her to live with us, but Mama said there wasn't anything in Jenner that mattered to her." She pinched lint off the sweatpants.

Dawn felt her hurt, but saw no reason for it. "I doubt she meant you and Papa didn't matter, Granny."

"Well, what else could she mean?"

Mom glanced at her. "Oma liked meeting people."

"There are people here."

"She liked exploring in her car."

"She had to give it up soon after that."

"And she wasn't happy about it. She started taking walks around the neighborhood, then started riding the city bus. She said it took a while to feel comfortable riding around town with strangers, but she got to know the drivers and some of the regular passengers. She rode the bus to the community college and took classes there. She was enrolled in another American history course when she passed away."

Granny leaned back, taking in that news. "I didn't know that." She sat quietly, contemplating what Mom had told her. "Oma always valued education. College for Bernie, trade school for Chloe, art classes for Rikka. She was disappointed when I chose nurses' training."

"Why?" Dawn curled her legs into the chair and pulled Papa's sweatshirt over her knees.

"She thought I was training to be a servant. Oma wanted me to go to the University of California."

Mom glanced up. "Her father made her quit school. Oma told me she would have loved to have gone to a university and I should take advantage of the opportunity."

Granny gave a soft laugh. "She said she'd pay my way if I'd go to the school she had picked out for me. I enrolled in nurses' training anyway. It was the first time I bucked her about anything." Her smile turned sardonic. "It makes sense she set up that fund for girls wanting to go to college. And it never occurred to me that might be the reason Mama didn't want to live up here."

"Did Oma ever earn a degree?"

Granny shrugged. "I don't know. She would've told you, Carolyn."

Mom smiled. "Dawn gave her the only diploma she ever received. I think Oma just liked learning new things. She took art history once so she and Aunt Rikki would have things to talk about."

"Did she ever take biology?" Granny asked.

"She took anatomy, physiology, and biology by correspondence course while living at the cottage. When she moved to Merced, she took chemistry. She said she could've used your help with that one."

Granny frowned. "Why didn't she ever tell me?"

"She tried. She invited you over for tea every day. You always had other things to do."

Granny sat with her lips parted, a deep frown furrowing her brow. Dawn remembered that when Oma died, Granny had grieved deeply. Was it because things had been left unsettled between them?

Granny crossed her arms, hugging herself. "I've been reading her journal. I'd hoped it might share some of her feelings. But it's just recipes, housekeeping information, boardinghouse rules, farm schedules—"

"You haven't read all of it yet, Granny."

"I'm sure it's unrealistic to think she'd have written anything about me, when she could never be bothered to talk to me. Or to say she loved me. She never said that to me, not once in my entire life."

Mom turned to her. "Maybe we have something in common."

"Don't you dare sit there and say Oma never told you she loved you. I heard her say it to you all the time! Every day when I was sick in bed, I'd hear her say it. 'I love you, Carolyn. I love you. I love you.'" Granny's voice broke.

"I didn't mean Oma." Mom turned her face toward the warmth of the fire.

Granny looked as though Mom had slapped her. Her eyes shone with tears as she stared at Mom.

Dawn wanted to weep for both of them. "Oma loved you, Granny."

Granny hadn't taken her eyes off Mom. "I'd like to believe she did, but she never said it. Not to me."

"Not everyone knows how to say it, Granny. They show it. Did Oma tell anyone she loved them? Uncle Bernie? Aunt Chloe?"

"She never said it to anyone, not even my father."

Mom frowned. "She loved him, didn't she?"

"So much so, I worried she'd grieve herself to death after he died. She'd go out into the orchard and scream and pound the earth. . . ." Her eyes filled. "I never understood her."

"Oma wrote about love in her journal, Granny." Dawn got up and retrieved the worn leather book from the side table. She turned pages. "Here. From 1 Corinthians 13. 'Love is patient, love is kind and is not jealous; love does not brag and is not arrogant. . . .'"

She turned more pages until she found what she was looking for near the end. "'We try to do a little better than the previous generation and find out in the end we've made the same mistakes without intending. Instead of striving to love as God first loved us, we let past hurts and grievances rule. Ignorance is no excuse.'" She looked up. "It's right here in her handwriting."

Dawn sat down. "Oma told me she only wrote important thoughts in her journal, things that helped her in life." She turned more pages. "Here's more about love. 'I know how Abraham felt when he placed Isaac on the altar. I know that pain. But what did Isaac feel lying there, bound, his father holding the knife? afraid? abandoned? expendable? Or did he, too, understand God would rescue him? God tested Abraham, and He showed Isaac what it meant to trust God. Will my Isaac ever understand that what I do, I do for love?'"

Dawn looked pointedly at Granny. "Who do you suppose Oma's Isaac was?"

"Bernie or Papa. Perhaps. How would I know?"

Mom's face filled with compassion. She met Dawn's eyes, but spoke to Granny. "I think it was you, Mom."

Granny closed her eyes and shook her head, as though the idea was too painful to consider. "We'll never really know, will we?"

56

CAROLYN LAY AWAKE on the couch after Mom and Dawn went to bed. She imagined them curled up together, sharing warmth under the covers. Why couldn't she get warm? She got up and dragged the blankets with her as she sat closer to the fire. She kept thinking about what Oma had written about Abraham and Isaac. That kind of love seemed a mystery. She understood Jacob better. Like Jacob, she had worked to earn the one she loved—May Flower Dawn— and felt cheated in the end. She also identified with Leah, the least loved, always second best.

God caused all things to work together for the good for those who love Him, and she did. Would she have learned to center her life on Jesus if she'd gotten everything she wanted? She might have poured all of her love and hope onto her daughter. God had seen that that wouldn't happen. Even Mitch, the love of her life, came in second to Jesus.

Why this sudden, deep, inexplicable desire to understand her mother, and have her understand as well? After all these years . . . Carolyn had learned, slowly, to let other people in. She opened the door of her heart to Mitch first, then allowed him free access to all her rooms. Christopher had never had to struggle with that.

She wondered if her mother had been knocking all these years, and she'd been too afraid to look through the peephole, let alone open the door. Oma once told her not to waste time on regrets, but to grasp opportunities. She remembered something else Oma had said, something that had made no sense to her at the time. "Your mother will take good care of May Flower Dawn. She never really had the chance to take care of you."

Carolyn looked up when she saw a movement in the shadows. Mom came out in her thick bathrobe and fuzzy pink slippers. "Are you cold?"

Carolyn forced a smile. "I shouldn't be. You should go back to bed. Keep warm."

"Maybe you caught cold working out in the garage. I can get you another blanket out of the closet."

"I'm fine, Mom. Really."

Her mother eased herself into the yellow swivel chair. "I've been thinking . . ." She folded her hands in her lap. "It's easier to talk about lesser sorrows, but we're silent about the ones that break our hearts and change everything."

Carolyn wanted to apologize. "Charlie." Maybe she should've left that box of pictures in the garage. She should've left the year-books under the house.

"I wasn't thinking about Charlie. I've been thinking about you, Carolyn." She looked uncertain. "It was hard for me to turn you over to Oma. I don't think you have any idea how much I love you. I do, you know. I always have."

Carolyn couldn't catch her breath. When she did, she put her head against her knees and cried.

❄ ❄ ❄

Dawn awakened when Granny got out of bed. She didn't move or speak as Granny quietly left the room. Dawn heard Granny speaking softly. Then Mom started to cry. Easing out from under the covers, Dawn wrapped Papa's old robe around herself and approached the door.

Finally, Lord.

She pressed her fingers against her trembling lips.

Mom didn't say anything.

God, please, help her speak. I don't mean to be selfish, but I need them to work things out.

"Carolyn?" Granny spoke softly, tentatively. "Why are you crying?"

Dawn covered her face and prayed.

❄ ❄ ❄

Carolyn turned her head and gave her mother a watery smile. "I didn't think you even liked me."

"Can you tell me why you thought that?"

Her mother looked so bleak, so concerned, Carolyn decided it was time to unlock the door and open it a little. "A lot of reasons."

"You said I yelled at you to get out of my bedroom. Is that why?"

"Yes, but I understand that now." It wasn't what her mother had done as much as what she hadn't. "You never allowed me to sit close to you. You never held me on your lap or kissed me."

"I couldn't, Carolyn. The TB."

"You couldn't wait to get your hands on May Flower Dawn, Mom. You held and kissed her all the time."

"I wasn't sick anymore then."

Carolyn smiled sadly. "You weren't sick when we moved to the property."

Mom bowed her head. "Maybe it became a habit with us." She raised her head. "I wanted to hold you, Carolyn, but by then you didn't want anyone but Oma to hold you. I sent her home so I could win you back, but instead, you withdrew. You didn't seem to want me; you didn't seem to want friends. You never showed interest until you met Rachel Altman."

Carolyn's heart started to pound the way it did in AA meetings when she knew God was nudging her to share. She looked into the fire. She could remain silent and let Mom believe what she did, or she could risk everything and tell the truth. The tension inside her built until she thought her heart would explode if she didn't say something. "I had one friend."

"Who?"

She could say Suzie, the girl who moved away. Mom might remember her. "Dock." His name came out before she thought better of it.

"Dock?"

Her mother didn't even remember him. It seemed so strange she wouldn't when Dock had dominated so much of Carolyn's child-hood. "Hickory, dickory, dock." He didn't chase mice up a clock. He offered cheese and crackers to a little girl, then drew her slowly into his lair.

❄   ❄   ❄

It was a moment before Hildie remembered him, but when she did, she went cold. "You don't mean Lee Dockery, do you?" She could picture the beekeeper next door, his disturbing smile, the way he never looked her in the eye. He'd been polite, but some-thing about him had made Hildie's skin crawl. They'd told the children to steer clear of him.

She studied her daughter. Carolyn sat hunched, arms locked around her knees, face turned away. Was she trembling? "How did you meet him?"

"Charlie took me over to his house. Before you and Dad told us to stay away."

Hildie pressed a hand against her stomach, trying to ignore the uneasy feelings stirring inside her. The man had mysteriously vanished around the same time Carolyn started having nightmares. Hildie had worried that there might be a connection, but Trip had assured her there couldn't be. *No. Please, God, no.* "Did you go back to see him?

"Yes."

"Often?"

"Yes." Carolyn pulled her knees in tighter to her chest and kept her head down. "At first, I sat by the fence and just watched him take honeycombs from the hives. He'd talk to me. He told me all about his bees. He gave me pieces of honeycomb. It dripped all over me once, and I started crying because I thought Daddy would be mad and he'd give me another spanking. Dock said I could come inside his house and wash off. He let me take a bath while he washed my clothes. He told me how lonely he was all by himself."

Hildie closed her eyes tightly. *Oh, God, oh, God! Why couldn't my little girl come to me?*

"I went back the next day and the next. He'd give me crackers and honey . . ."

Hildie clenched her hands. Her daughter had always loved baths. Hildie remembered being so tired by the end of the day; she'd wash Carolyn quickly, efficiently, like a nurse with a patient. Just get the job done. "Don't dawdle, Carolyn," she'd say. "It's time for bed." Hildie had been so tired, afraid she would get sick again. She needed to get some rest.

"Dock put the lid down on the toilet and talked to me while I was in the tub. He'd tell me stories." She closed her eyes tightly. "Later . . ."

The fire cracked. The rain drummed on the roof. A pulse beat in Hildie's head.

"What happened later?"

"He washed me."

Hildie fought rage and sorrow. What had she been doing that had been so important she hadn't noticed her daughter missing? Was she tending the vegetable garden? planting walnut trees? hanging up laundry? Busy, always busy with something! There had always been something to do. Charlie had been off on his bike visiting friends. She'd assumed her quiet, timid little girl was close by, picking flowers, making mud pies, watching butterflies. How could she have been so blind?

"We played games."

Hildie bit her lip. She and Trip had moved to the country so their children would be safe, so they'd have plenty of fresh air and sunshine. She felt sick with premonition, but had to know. "What sort of games, Carolyn?"

"Secret games, he called them. Touching games." Carolyn spoke so softly.

Hildie gave a soft sob and pressed her hands over her mouth. Carolyn glanced up sharply, eyes wide. She looked down quickly, putting her arms over her head. "I'm sorry. I shouldn't have told you. I'm sorry. I'm sorry." Her body shook.

When Carolyn tried to get up, Hildie reached out and pulled her back against her legs, pinning her there, arms wrapped around her. Sobbing, she rested her head on Carolyn's until she could speak. "It's not your fault, honey. It's mine." She felt a shudder go through Carolyn and held on tighter. "It's my fault, sweetheart. I'm so sorry."

Carolyn started to cry again, body relaxing, giving in. Hildie didn't let go of her. She stroked her hair and kissed the top of her head. She hadn't been there when her little girl needed her, and she might never be able to forgive herself for that. But she could try to comfort the woman in her arms now.

Carolyn wiped her face with her sleeve. "I knew I wasn't supposed to go there, Mom, but he was nice to me. He held me and kissed me and said he loved me." She gulped down a sob. "I was stupid. I was so stupid!"

"You weren't stupid. You were a *child*."

"He didn't hurt me until the last time. And then there was blood, a lot of blood, and he cried. I was so scared. And he wouldn't let me go until I promised . . . He said we'd both be in big trouble if I told anyone what we'd been playing. At first, he told me not to come back. Then he came to my window that night and said he loved me. He wanted me to be his little girl. He said he was going to look for a safe place for us. I'd know when he found it because he'd leave some honey at the front door. I don't think I dreamed it all. It was so real."

Horror filled Hildie. That man would have kidnapped Carolyn. She and Trip never would've found her. *Oh, God, thank You.* She hadn't been looking out for her daughter. But God had.

"That's why you crept into Charlie's room and slept with him."

"Yes, and when you told me to stop, I'd hide in my closet." She shuddered and moved away slightly so they could face one another. "I heard you and Dad talking about Dock. I was afraid you'd figured out what I'd done and I would be in trouble. But you never did."

Hildie wanted to reach out again and pull her daughter close. She wanted to brush her hair the way she had when Carolyn was a toddler. She ached for the time lost, hating the disease that had made her push her daughter away in the first place. She couldn't bear the thought of her precious little girl living in fear, having nightmares about the monster next door, allowing only Oma inside the walls she built to protect herself. Had Mama known? Surely she would have said something!

Hildie's arms ached to simply hold her. But it was important to keep talking, to get it all out in the open. "Lee Dockery was killed in an accident, Carolyn."

"When?" Carolyn looked up at her, face pale and strained.

"A few weeks after your nightmares started. No one disappears without a reason. Dad knew something had happened to him. He went over to see if he'd had a heart attack or something. He went into the house and found everything in order."

Hildie leaned forward, clasping her hands tensely, uncertain how her daughter would take what she had to tell her. "Lee Dockery's place stood vacant until the bank repossessed the property and sold it at auction. A year after the new family moved in, a couple of boys found Lee Dockery's truck in a ravine down in Niles Canyon. Apparently, he'd swerved off the road and gone over the edge where it wouldn't have been seen from the road."

"Was Dock in the car?"

What was left of him, after the animals had gotten to his body and time had stripped his flesh. "Yes, he was. So were his bees." They'd built a hive inside the cab of his truck.

Carolyn let out a long breath and closed her eyes. Her face looked serene. "All those years, I thought he'd come and take me away."

"He would have, Carolyn. God protected you."

"I know."

"Did Charlie know about Dock?"

"No."

It hurt to ask, but she had to know. "Did you tell Oma?"

"No. The only person I ever told about Dock was Chel. And I was drunk at the time."

❄ ❄ ❄

Dawn winced at the growing pain. Gripping the edge of the dresser, she pulled herself up. It eased a little. She sat on the edge of the bed. She felt warm, but the chill made her breath visible. Her daughter kicked twice. Smiling, Dawn ran her hand over her belly. "Sorry I woke you up." She took a pillow and put it at the end of the bed, then stretched out on her side so she could listen to Mom and Granny talk. She stroked her belly slowly, rhythmically. "They're going to love you, sweetie."

The sound of their voices filled her with hope for the future. "No tug-of-war this time."

57

"CAN WE TALK about what happened in Berkeley, Carolyn? Please."

Carolyn braced her back against the other chair. Her mother hadn't blamed her for what happened. She'd blamed Dock. Maybe it was time to get everything out in the open. Haight-Ashbury and all the rest.

"I wanted to end the war, Mom. I wanted to save Charlie. I didn't care about school. It seemed pointless to attend classes when my brother was risking his life every minute of the day. So I quit and went on protest marches. When I wasn't doing that, I drank to forget. All I could think about was trying to get Charlie out of Vietnam. And I failed. When Charlie died, I just lost it."

"You were gone before you knew about Charlie."

"No, I wasn't."

"Yes. You were. We called the day after the officers came to the house, and your phone was disconnected. We drove to Berkeley. Your neighbors said they hadn't seen either of you in a while. The landlord was there. He said the place was trashed."

"Oma called the day the soldiers came to the house. I knew

what that meant. I remember screaming and Chel giving me some-thing. The next thing I remember is Chel driving me across the Bay Bridge, Janis Joplin screaming on the radio, Chel screaming along with her." She closed her eyes so she wouldn't have to see Mom's face when she said the rest. "I woke up in a strange house, in a strange bed, with a guy I'd never seen before. It got worse after that."

Carolyn pressed the heels of her hands against her eyes. "I used to dream about Charlie all the time." She gulped down tears. "I'd see him in a rice paddy. I'd see him burning in napalm. I'd see him—" She stopped, appalled, realizing what her words must be doing to her mother. She took her hands away. "I'm sorry."

"Don't stop, honey." Her mother spoke in a soft, choked voice. "Tell me the rest."

"I stayed stoned and drunk, trying to deal with his death."

"You looked so frail when you came home."

Carolyn remembered all too well. She'd been starving slowly, living on garbage. And then a young vet gave her a chocolate bar and kept her warm. A young woman gave her hope and a ticket home. "I lived in Golden Gate Park for a while. I don't remember how long. I had to get out of that house and away from Ash."

"What house? And who is Ash?"

"We lived in a big house on Clement Street. He moved in while Chel and I were in New York, celebrating rock and roll at Woodstock." She spoke wryly, then went on. "She was messed up on drugs. I didn't know if she'd come out of it. Her mind cleared in Wyoming. When we got back, we found this beautiful stranger sitting in the living room. He used to wear white robes like Jesus and spoke in poetry. A fake guru, speaking bull, seduc-ing everyone. Everyone was stoned all the time and sleeping with whoever. Chel was the one with the money. Ash took her over the minute she walked in the door, or he thought he did. Chel always knew what was what. She knew Ash for what he was long before I did. When she got tired of him, he turned to me. All I saw was the beautiful mask, not the devil behind it. I thought I loved him. Lee Dockery was a lot kinder." She saw the anguish in her mother's face. "I'm sorry, Mom. Maybe you don't want to hear about this."

"I need to know what happened to my daughter. Don't you think it's time?"

"I guess." Carolyn rubbed her face.

"I always wondered, but I was afraid to ask. Did Chel live in the park with you?"

"No. She overdosed on heroin. A few weeks before, we went out for a long walk in the park. She gave me her father's telephone number and said if anything happened to her, I was to call him. It scared me. I watched over her for days. The one day I didn't . . ." Her voice broke.

"I'm so sorry, honey."

"I found her sprawled across her bed. Ash was furious. He told me to lie if the paramedics asked for her name."

"Why?"

"Why do you suppose? The money would keep being deposited as long as her father thought she was alive. When the ambulance came, I waited outside. Before they took her body away, I gave them her full name. I called her father. And then I just walked away. I didn't look back. I didn't care where I went or what happened to me after that."

Carolyn raked her fingers into her hair and held her head. "I begged, Mom. I slept on benches and under bushes. I ate out of trash bins and slept in a few. I wanted to die, but I didn't have the courage to drown myself in the ocean." She gave a mocking laugh. "It was cold." Sighing, she leaned back against the front of the swivel rocker. "One night I was sitting on the beach and thinking about how nice it would be to have it all over. And then I heard a guitar playing. I saw a young man wearing an Army jacket. I thought it was Charlie, at first." Her eyes swam with tears. "Of course, it couldn't be, but I followed him anyway. He'd made a camp in the park. He had a fire and an old sleeping bag. I was so hungry. He gave me a chocolate bar. He was a veteran. He hadn't just bought the jacket from a surplus store; he'd served in Vietnam. I told him about Charlie. He told me about friends he'd lost in the war."

She drew her knees up against her chest again, hugging them close. "He shared his sleeping bag. He kept me warm. I got up and wandered off. When I couldn't find my way back, I slept on the grass. I woke up at dawn." Tears came and spilled down her cheeks. "It was May, and little white flowers grew in the grass like stars had dropped from heaven. I felt someone touch me. He sat right there on the grass with me."

"The young veteran?"

"No." She shook her head, chewing her lip a moment before she had the courage to say it aloud. She never had before. "I know you won't believe me. You'll think I was drunk or stoned. But I hadn't had anything since leaving Ash." She couldn't see Mom through her tears.

"I'll believe anything you tell me, Carolyn."

Carolyn drew a shuddering breath and prayed she would. "I saw Jesus." She let the memory fill her. "He said it was time to go home. I thought He meant I was going to die. I wasn't afraid. When I sat up, He was gone." She had sat for hours, praying He would come back and take her with Him. "A young woman came and set up a picnic for her two children. She called her little boy Charlie." Her voice wavered.

Her mother put a hand over her mouth.

Carolyn kept going. "It was like watching me and Charlie play together. She invited me to sit with her; she offered me a sandwich. I was so hungry. We talked. I told her about Charlie; she told me about her husband. He was MIA in Vietnam. She called her kids and loaded all of us in a van and took me to the bus station. She bought my ticket home. Her name was Mary."

Carolyn felt the weight lifting as she talked. "She gave me her telephone number and said if you didn't want me, she'd come and get me. I lost the slip of paper on the way home. I've thanked God a thousand times for her over the years, Mom. When the planes landed at Travis Air Force Base in 1973, and all those POWs came off, I cried and prayed Mary's husband stood among them. But I'll never know for sure if he did."

Mom wiped tears from her cheeks, but didn't say anything. She didn't seem shocked or disgusted. Carolyn wondered if she could keep going and decided it was worth the risk. "You asked me why I didn't believe you loved me. When I came home, you and Dad were ashamed of me. I could see it in your faces. When you found out I was pregnant, that was the last straw."

"No, Carolyn. It was a shock, that's all."

"You and Dad asked Rev. Elias to talk to me. He told me not to come back to church."

"What?" Mom spoke weakly, eyes wide.

"He didn't believe I was truly repentant. He said enough to convince me I wasn't good enough to set foot inside any church. When I came home, Dad made a point of asking me if I'd taken everything Rev. Elias said to heart. I did. Then you and Dad told me you were sending me to Los Angeles to live with Boots. You couldn't wait to be rid of me."

"No. *No!*" Mom looked furious, tears streaming down her white cheeks. "We asked Rev. Elias to talk to you because we thought he'd give you wise counsel. For heaven's sake, if we'd known what he said to you, we would've left the church! Why didn't Oma tell me about this?"

"Oma didn't know, Mom. I never told anyone."

"Then she must have guessed, because she left the church right after you did."

"I assumed you and Dad felt the same way he did."

"Of course not! If your father had known, he would've raised holy hell. We sent you away to protect you, not get rid of you." She took a handkerchief from her pocket and blew her nose. "I sent you to Boots. She was my best friend! I knew she'd love you and take good care of you." Her mouth wobbled, tears still streaming. "I wouldn't have entrusted you to anyone else."

Carolyn wanted to believe her, but evidence stood in the way.

"The day I walked into the house, I saw a wall of pictures, all of Charlie."

"We wanted to honor his memory."

"I looked around the house when you and Dad went to work. There wasn't a single picture of me anywhere. Not one."

Her mother clenched the crumpled, damp handkerchief in her lap and looked straight into her eyes. "I put them away a few months after you disappeared. We loved you, Carolyn. We agonized over you. The truth is we grieved more over you than Charlie. We knew what happened to him. He was killed in the line of duty. Don't forget your father was a police officer. He worked in forensics. He dealt with homicides. He had nightmares when he came home from the war. He had worse ones when you disappeared. I put your pictures away because he died a little more inside every time he looked at one. I couldn't bear to lose everyone I loved."

Carolyn's heart hurt. She pressed her hands against her chest, wanting to make it go away. She had spent so many years hiding the pain, not asking why things had been the way they were, afraid the answers might hurt even more.

Mom's eyes warmed, and she gestured toward her bedroom. "I cherish your pictures. Your wedding portrait is on my dresser, your senior picture on my wall, where I can see both of them every night before I go to sleep. All the rest are in an album over there in the cabinet." Her mouth trembled. "I love you. How could I not? You're my own flesh and blood."

Carolyn searched her mother's face and saw raw pain. "How would I know? I haven't stepped foot in your bedroom since I was three years old." She never opened any cabinets except those in the kitchen. She gave a broken laugh. "Oh, Mom . . . we've both been so good at hiding what we feel."

"I just told you I love you, Carolyn. Do you believe me?"

Carolyn looked into her eyes, eyes the same color as Oma's. "Yes." She felt all the tension drain from her body. She smiled. "And in case you don't know it, I love you, too."

❄ ❄ ❄

Dawn was thankful Mom and Granny weren't arguing anymore. She shifted her body, trying to get more comfortable. She could feel the pressure of tiny arms and legs stretching inside her. Taking two pillows and the comforter from the bed, she sat near the door. She covered herself with the comforter, scooted down, and tucked the pillows under her knees. The solid carpeted floor felt better than the soft bed.

Let the words keep flowing, Lord. Dawn knew others were praying for them, too. Georgia and the women of CCC, Pastor Daniel, Mitch, all the people who loved Mom and Granny. Her eyes grew heavy, but she forced herself to stay awake. It gave her joy and hope to hear them talking openly with one another. She probably shouldn't be eavesdropping, but she had been praying for this for so long that she felt she had to hear it to believe it.

Her mom was talking again. "I used to be afraid to love anyone. Charlie died. Then Chel. Oma. Dad. I don't even want to think about losing Mitch."

"Your dad and I rooted for him."

"Mitch told me he was going to marry me that first time he came over for dinner."

"And not for your cooking, I'll bet," Granny teased.

Dawn's mother laughed. "Thanks a lot."

"We knew he had a crush on you when he was a boy. It was hard to miss when he came over all the time."

"To see Charlie."

"And you. It is frightening to lose someone you love. I loved your dad every bit as much as you love Mitch . . . and the way Mama must have loved Papa. We all die sometime. Someday you'll lose me, too, you know."

"Yes, but I'd rather not think about that."

"At least we'll be speaking to one another."

Dawn put her hands over her face and tried not to cry. Some

things might never be worked out. Granny might never believe Oma had loved her.

Granny spoke. "I'm sorry about Rev. Elias, Carolyn. God forgive him. And I'm sorry you didn't understand why we sent you to Boots."

"It was the best thing you could have done for me. She recognized a dry drunk when she saw one and took me to my first AA meeting. She had a band of friends who were full of hope and experience and didn't mind sharing. They all thought I should give up my baby. Boots wanted me to keep May Flower Dawn and stay with her."

"You'll never know how happy Dad and I were when you decided to come home."

"I didn't know I could until you sent that car seat. And then Dad laid down all the rules, and you quit your job so you could take care of May Flower Dawn. . . ."

"We wanted to help you get back on your feet."

"I know."

"I didn't want you staying with Boots."

Dawn heard the tension building in Granny's voice, as though quick words could ward off something she didn't want to hear. But Mom wasn't going to let her get away with it this time. She spoke gently. "I loved Boots, but I didn't want to depend on her. I'd lived off Chel for too long."

"I wanted to help, Carolyn."

"I know."

"You wouldn't have made it on your own." Granny sounded defensive.

"Georgia did."

"Because she didn't have any choice. Her parents kicked her out. We wanted to help."

"Yes. You helped yourself to May Flower Dawn."

Dawn sat up and held her breath. She'd known for years she was the cause of much of their contention. She'd grown up in the middle. Granny had stepped in when needed, then held on. For a long time, Dawn had helped Granny win the tug-of-war. It wasn't until she had sex downstairs with Jason that she understood how guilt and shame could imprison a person, keep her silent, keep her distant. Like Mom.

When Georgia held up the mirror before Dawn's face, and Jason suggested they stop seeing one another, it had been her mother who came in and sat silently on the end of Dawn's bed, empathizing with her pain. It had been Mom's careful words that planted the seeds to let go and let God work, to follow the Lord and not her own deceitful heart and flesh. Mom had understood what Granny couldn't.

And now, Dawn had come home to create a bridge between them, one built on truth and love. She needed them to mend their relationship. She prayed fervently they wouldn't allow Satan to rebuild his stronghold. *Please, God, not now. Not ever again.*

"I'll take the blame for everything else, Carolyn, but don't you dare accuse me of stealing your daughter. That's not fair!"

"You didn't steal her." Mom spoke tenderly. "I placed her in your arms."

"I was helping!"

"Yes, but you didn't leave room for me."

"Of course I did!"

Dawn wept at Granny's pain and defensive tone. *God, help her see the truth!*

"When? I came home aching to nurse her, and you'd already given her a bottle. You wouldn't even let me hold her. You'd tell me she'd been fussy and you'd just put her down and I shouldn't wake her. I worked on Saturdays. You took her to church every Sunday. I never had time with her."

Granny cried, but insisted, "It wasn't my fault Dawn bonded to me. I was the one with her all the time."

"But I wanted to be. You even changed her name."

"Because people thought she was named after the Pilgrims' ship."

"Because you and Dad thought it was a hippy name. Dawn told me. It wasn't a suitable name for an Arundel."

Granny blew her nose. "I suppose I did cut you out."

"I saw how much you loved her, Mom. I was jealous, but I was grateful, too. You and Dad didn't give me a handout. You gave me a hand up. When I finally got on my feet, I tried to win Dawn back. When I married Mitch and we moved to Alexander Valley, I thought I might have a chance."

"And we followed you." Granny sniffled. "I would've lived next door if Trip would've allowed it."

"Dawn told me she hated me for making you cry, and I gave up. Dad reminded me you wanted to help. Looking back now, I think he saw how much we were both hurting."

"My mother 'helped,' too," Granny said bleakly, "and I never really forgave her. It still hurts. Can you forgive me?"

Dawn heard movement and turned so she could see into the living room. Mom knelt in front of Granny. "I forgave you a long time ago."

Granny laid a hand against Mom's cheek. "But it still hurts."

"Yes, but maybe we'll heal now. I saw as a child, but now I see through a woman's eyes. I'm glad it was you and not some stranger in a day care center."

Granny cupped Mom's face and kissed her. "I'm glad it was Oma and not Mrs. Haversal."

Dawn got up carefully. She braced herself against the dresser until the pain eased. Stooping cautiously, she gathered the pillows and comforter and put them back on the bed. She slipped beneath the covers and thanked God for answering her prayers.

She knew her biological father, though nameless, had been a kind, young vet suffering post-traumatic stress like her mother. She knew why Mom named her May Flower Dawn. And Mom and Granny were finally talking. Love would win this time.

CAROLYN GOT UP first, stoked the fire and added two presto logs, then went into the kitchen to start the Coleman and get some water boiling for coffee. She heard a loud, ominous crack from somewhere outside. The house shuddered. Another loud boom, and the house jumped on its foundations. The kitchen picture window cracked. Carolyn clambered away.

"What happened?" Her mother came rushing in, gray hair sticking out in all directions, her robe half-on. "What crashed?" She tied the sash around her waist and opened the back door.

"Wait! Mom, don't go out there." Carolyn pulled her back.

The redwood tree had fallen on the garage. Two-by-fours protruded in all directions. The deck tilted.

"My car!"

"I parked it on the road yesterday so I could sort things in the garage. It should be okay."

"Oh. Good." Her mother started to giggle. "We're going to have a lot less to sort through now."

Carolyn took her by the arm. "Let's go sit in the living room."

"Why? Because the kitchen seems to be tilting?"

"It's not. Is it?" Carolyn's insides quivered as her gaze darted around the room.

As they headed for the living room, her mother glanced out the door again. "At least we won't have to worry about firewood. We have a mountain of it."

Carolyn sat near the fire. "I can't believe Dawn slept through that!"

Mom sat across from her. "Thank goodness that's the only tree in front of the house."

"As long as the house doesn't slide down the hill."

"Well, aren't you the optimist." Mom gave her a humorless smile. "Dad said this house is built on rock."

"Did he mean granite . . . or Jesus?"

"Let's hope he meant both." They sat in companionable silence. "I wonder what all that redwood is worth," Mom mused. "Maybe enough to pay for a new garage." She shook her head. "I'll tell you one thing. I'm more than ready to get out of here now."

Carolyn chortled. "I would hope so."

Dawn came out of the bedroom, bleary-eyed. "What's all the noise?"

They told her while she made herself comfortable on the couch, the white afghan around her shoulders again. "Can we get out?"

"I don't know." Carolyn studied her. "Do we need to?"

Dawn smiled. "No."

Carolyn brushed aside a niggling worry. "I'm going to take a look around, anyway."

The gate was stuck, but she managed to shove it open after several tries. The unearthed roots of the redwood tree stood seven to eight feet high, and they had pulled up most of the road. A steady flow of rainwater raced down the hill, undercutting the cracked macadam. She went back inside. "I have four-wheel drive. We can drive up the hill and around."

"No, we can't," her mother informed her. "That road has been closed for the last week. There's a big crack down the middle of it."

"We're nice and cozy and all together," Dawn said, perfectly calm. "Let's not worry about it. Let's just talk."

"Granny and I talked most of the night."

"I know. I'm afraid I was eavesdropping. I heard everything."

Heat spilled into Carolyn's cheeks. What "everything" did she mean?

Dawn hugged the blanket closer. "The young veteran who played the guitar was my father, wasn't he?"

So her daughter had heard everything. Carolyn desperately wanted Dawn to understand. "Biologically. But I never thought of him as your father. To me, you were always a gift from God."

Dawn smiled. "I know, Mom. That's why you named me May Flower Dawn."

"Oh!" Carolyn's mother spoke with sudden comprehension. "You said it was May and the flowers were blooming in the grass, and the Lord appeared to you at dawn." Mom's eyes grew moist. "No wonder you were so hurt when I changed it." Her mouth softened. "You couldn't have chosen a better name, Carolyn."

Dawn grinned. "You could've called me Epiphany."

Carolyn laughed as the tension dissolved. "I almost did."

Mom spoke slowly, in wonder, eyes glowing. "May . . . Flower . . . Dawn."

❄ ❄ ❄

After a breakfast of cereal, they went through the other boxes. Dawn felt odd and edgy. She wanted things settled. Now. She didn't have time to wait anymore.

"Now that you don't have a garage, Granny, are you going to park your car in front of an American bungalow in Santa Rosa or a pretty Tuscany villa in Windsor?" She had something else in mind, but her mom would have to bring it up.

"Windsor's closer to Alexander Valley."

Dawn looked pointedly at her mother and raised her brows.

Dawn's mother frowned slightly and sat back on her heels. Then she turned to Granny. "Do you want to live with me and Mitch?"

Granny gaped. "Well, I didn't think you'd want me too close."

"We have maid's quarters we've never used. There's a living room, bedroom with full bath, and a little kitchen."

Granny just stared at her.

"You don't have to live with us. I just thought maybe you'd think about it. I wanted to ask you after Dad died, but you wouldn't even discuss it. You insisted you wanted your independence."

"Then it's your own fault for believing every stupid thing I say!" Granny burst into tears. But she was smiling. "And I thought Marsha had all the luck!"

Mom said they could remove the furnishings, and Granny could bring whatever she wanted, within reason. "Not that old faded couch, please. Let's get a new one."

Dawn felt everything recede in a gray cloud of pain and pressure. Then silence.

"Dawn?" Mom spoke. She and Granny were both staring at her. "What's wrong?"

"I wanted to wait—" Something popped inside her, like a balloon. She gasped as she felt a pool of warm slickness spreading beneath her. "Oh!" Drawing in her breath sharply, she struggled to lift herself off the couch. The moisture went down her legs, soaking through Papa's old sweats and spilling onto his thick socks. "Oh, *no!*"

❄   ❄   ❄

Carolyn tried not to panic while she helped Dawn lie down in the bedroom.

Her mother stood close, speaking with authority. There was an eighty-six-year-old nurse in the house, and she'd just gone on duty. "Raise up, honey. Okay. Carolyn? Get the wastebasket." She peeled off Dawn's sodden sweats and panties and dumped them into the can.

Dawn wept. "I'm so sorry, Granny. I ruined your couch."

"Didn't you just hear your mother say it was ready for the junk-yard? She wasn't going to let me keep it."

"Your nice sheets . . ."

"Oh, hush!"

Carolyn wanted to scream. A couch? Sheets? They had other things to worry about! The baby was coming *early*. The telephone didn't work. The roads were closed. A giant redwood had just upchucked its massive root system all over the road and turned the garage into a pile of giant splinters!

"Another contraction?" Carolyn's mother picked up her wrist-watch and checked Dawn's pulse.

Dawn groaned low and spoke through clenched teeth. "I thought first babies took a long time. . . ."

"Not always. Take a big breath and blow it out. Rest as much as you can, honey."

In less than a minute, another contraction came. Dawn looked at Carolyn. "Mom. You brought the Suburban."

"Yes, but Granny said we can't drive out of here."

"No." Dawn panted. "But you have GPS and OnStar, don't you?"

"Yes!" Carolyn rushed out. Rummaging through her purse, she found her keys and ran for the door.

❄ ❄ ❄

Hildie wiped Dawn's forehead. The poor girl was burning up. Though it had been decades since Hildie had assisted at a child-birth, she could still recognize a serious situation when she saw it. "Is there anything else I should know about your condition, sweet-heart? You haven't looked well ever since you arrived. Do you want to tell me what's going on?"

Dawn met her eyes briefly, then glanced away. "Hodgkin's lymphoma. It's why I came home. Well, partly why." Dawn grabbed her hand. "Don't you dare cry. Not now. And don't say anything to Mom. Please, Granny. I was going to talk to both of you at the same time, but I wanted you two to work things out first." Another contraction came, harder than the last. "God won't take this baby. He won't."

Hildie stroked Dawn's hair back and told her to ride on top of the pain, like a surfer on a wave. "When did you find out?"

Dawn panted, beads of perspiration on her face. "October. The doctor wanted me to start chemo." Tears streamed from her eyes into her hair. "They told me they could limit the dose to protect the baby, but I just couldn't take that chance. Not after waiting so long for her."

"Why didn't you tell us? Your mom and Mitch would have flown out to be with you—or to bring you back here. We could have helped you."

The back door opened. "Don't tell her! Please. Not yet. Let me—"

"Shhh." Hildie wiped her cheeks quickly. "Don't worry. Concentrate on having your daughter."

Carolyn came back into the bedroom. "I got through. They're calling it in." She came around the bed and took Dawn's hand. "How're you doing?"

Dawn gave her a tremulous smile. "Fine, Mom."

"There's a rescue helicopter at Santa Rosa Memorial, but it's going to take a while." Carolyn squeezed Dawn's hand. "It stopped raining a few minutes ago. God's clearing the way. They'll have to land on the road down by the Jenner Inn and hike up."

Another contraction had Dawn crying out and pushing down. Hildie put her hand on Dawn's abdomen again, timing the contraction. "What about the tree? Can they get by it?"

"I wish I had a chain saw!" Carolyn didn't take her eyes off Dawn.

Trip had bought one, but Hildie wasn't about to tell Carolyn where to find it. She didn't even want to think about the damage her daughter could do to herself with one of those things. "Bring the Coleman stove into the bathroom. Get a big pot, fill it with water, and get it boiling. There should be string in one of the kitchen drawers, and bring my sharp paring knife. And tongs."

Dawn giggled. "Granny sounds like my nursing instructor at San Luis Obispo. Bossy!"

"Thank God!" Smiling, Carolyn rushed out again. She set everything up. "I put some of your new towels on a kitchen chair in front of the fire. They'll be warm enough for the baby."

"Not too close, I hope," Granny muttered. "The last thing we need right now is a fire."

They all laughed a little wildly.

Five minutes later, they knew the baby wasn't going to wait for the helicopter.

"Wash your hands carefully, Carolyn, but hurry up about it." Hildie knew she didn't have the physical strength to finish the job. Dawn's body shook through transition. Her granddaughter had no break now, one contraction rolling right over into another, crushing her with pain.

Now that she knew it wasn't just childbirth racking Dawn's frail body, Hildie had to will herself not to weep. All her knowledge and training kicked into overdrive, but her legs had begun to ache so much she could barely stand. "I need that vanity chair, Carolyn."

Carolyn set it where she pointed.

"Stand there. You're going to deliver your granddaughter."

"What?"

"I'm going to tell you what to do. Don't argue or say you can't. You can."

Carolyn obeyed. Hildie put her hand on Dawn's arm and talked them both through it. She told Dawn to let nature take its course. "Don't hold back. Push!" She gave Carolyn instructions and watched her do exactly as told. Dawn's daughter broke into the world, red-faced and screaming.

Carolyn laughed joyously. "She's beautiful, Dawn. She's perfect, just like you were."

"Put the baby on Dawn's abdomen. Tie the cord, Carolyn. That's it. You can cut it now. I'll get the towels."

The *womp-womp* of a helicopter went over the house.

Hildie took the warm towels draped over the chair in front of the fireplace and brought them back to her girls. "Early bird or not, her lungs are in great condition." Dawn and Carolyn laughed in relief. Carolyn wrapped the baby and placed her in Dawn's arms.

Dawn drew the soft toweling down and gazed into her daughter's face. Smiling, she kissed her. "Your name is Faith." She looked up at her mother and sorrow mingled with joy. "Sit here close to me, Mom. You, too, Granny. I have to tell you something."

Hildie already knew. When Dawn finished, Carolyn was white. "No." Hildie reached for her hand and held it tightly, her own heart breaking.

"I didn't want it to be true either, Mom. But we can't hide from the truth. You and Granny will need to work together. Jason's life isn't his own. You'll be Faith's guardian, Mom. Granny, you're going to help her. So will Georgia. God is going to give back all the years the locusts ate, Mom."

"May Flower Dawn." Carolyn crumbled, head against Dawn's side.

Dawn put her hand on her mother's head as though offering a blessing. "You're stronger than anyone I know. Keep Faith, Mom." She smiled at Hildie. "Promise me you'll share."

❄ ❄ ❄

When the paramedics arrived, they worked quickly, efficiently. They said they had room for only one more in the helicopter. Hildie almost said she'd go, but stopped herself. "You go." She cupped Carolyn's face. "You're her mother."

"Mitch and I will come out and get you as soon as we can."

Hildie kissed Dawn and the baby. "I'll see you both soon." She tucked a strand of golden hair away from Dawn's cheek. "You hold on to faith, honey. Don't you dare give up."

When they left, Hildie went back inside. She sat in her recliner and cried. Then she prayed. She kept praying until dusk came. She forgot to stoke the fire, and it went out. She took the blanket off the couch and bundled up in it. She had weathered other winters without fire or light. She could weather this one. The darkness fit her despair.

She awakened to someone calling her name. She saw a flash of light. The back door opened, and the beam caught and blinded her. "Who . . . ?"

"Sorry it took so long to get out here, Hildie." *Mitch.* "I had to come around through Sebastopol and Bodega. The river's gone down enough to come across from Bridgehaven."

Her son-in-law had come to her rescue. God had already sent him to rescue her daughter years ago.

"You want to pack a few things?"

"I think I should, don't you?" She was still in her pajamas.

Mitch helped her around the tree roots and buckled road. He'd driven the Jaguar. It roared to life. He told her Dawn and the baby were both doing well. The baby weighed almost six pounds. Hildie asked him if he knew the reason May Flower Dawn had driven across country in the dead of winter.

"Yes. I know. The only one who doesn't know yet is Jason, and I've got a few friends in high places moving heaven and earth to get him home."

Hildie didn't learn until later how many had been praying for the restorative miracle that had taken place at Jenner—and went on praying Dawn wouldn't be called home. Not yet.

Epilogue

Six years later

CAROLYN PUT HER shoulder bag and two tote bags into the compartment beside her seat in the mammoth Lufthansa 747 aircraft. Mitch had made the arrangements and, as usual, spared no expense to make sure she was comfortable. Her husband had put her, Faith, and Georgia in business class for the long flight to Frankfurt. Faith, blonde hair in pigtails, sat on the big leather seat, jean-clad legs straight out, feet dangling, Puppy Brown hugged in a protective embrace. She looked so much like May Flower Dawn at six years of age, it pierced Carolyn's heart. She buckled Faith's seat belt before her own and brushed her knuckles down her grand-daughter's satiny cheek. "Excited to see Daddy, sweetheart?"

Faith nodded. Carolyn leaned forward and looked across the aisle. "How's GeeGee doing over there?"

Georgia sat across the aisle, face pale and strained. She gave a nervous smile. "I'm fine." She looked anything but fine, but Carolyn understood all too well. Learning Jason had been seriously wounded in Afghanistan and flown to Landstuhl had them all on their knees.

They'd gotten the news two weeks ago that Jason had been

wounded, but didn't know until a few days later the extent of his injuries and where he had been transferred. Eventually, Jason would end up in the States, but how long before that happened? weeks? a month? two? Just as he'd done in the days following Faith's birth, Mitch had moved mountains to get family members together during this time of crisis. He had gotten Jason home from Iraq within five days of Faith's birth at Jenner. May Flower Dawn had spent a week in the hospital after Faith was born. Tests confirmed what she already knew: she didn't have much time. The doctor ordered palliative radiation to control the pain. Dawn came home, and hospice was called in. Christopher withdrew from classes at Stanford and came home to spend as much time with his big sister as possible.

Everyone had worried about Jason. He'd been strong through Dawn's last weeks, but grieved hard when she died. He lost weight, couldn't sleep, wouldn't talk. Pastor Daniel took him away for a few days, and Jason seemed better when they returned, less lost and broken. He held Faith close. When called back to duty, he went with God before him and as his rear guard.

Carolyn looked at the beautiful little girl sitting in the big, cushy leather seat next to her. If not for this adorable little munchkin, they all would have fallen to pieces.

"Champagne, madame?" A pretty, dark-haired flight attendant carried a tray of tulip glasses filled with juice or champagne. Georgia took orange juice.

Faith looked eagerly at Carolyn. "Can I have some juice, Grammy?" Carolyn said yes and declined anything for herself. She felt a little queasy with nerves. The last time she'd traveled any distance on her own was driving Chel across country after Woodstock, and that didn't offer the best of memories. Dawn would have told her not to worry. God would be flying with them. She smiled as she imagined Jesus in uniform, sitting in the cockpit.

Faith squealed in delight and spread her arms. "GeeGee, we're flying!" Georgia closed her eyes and gripped the arms of her seat. After what seemed a surprisingly short amount of time, the bell pinged and the captain announced the 747 had reached its cruising altitude and everyone was free to move around the cabin. Dinner was served. Carolyn took Faith to the bathroom, then strapped her back into her seat, covered her with a blanket, and read her favorite book to her, *Horton Hears a Who!* Faith fell asleep halfway through the third reading. Georgia had lowered her seat and finally looked peaceful.

Carolyn took out her wireless laptop. While she waited for it to boot up, she thought of how many times she'd used the computer over the past few years to connect with Jason on the other side of the world, Faith perched in her lap. When he came on the screen, she'd point. "There's your daddy. Say hello, sweetheart."

Jason would grin. "How's my little girl?" Carolyn hadn't wanted Jason to miss anything. She'd posted movies of Faith rolling over, sitting up, crawling. Faith had been walking by the time he came home from Iraq. Jason made the most of what little time he had with his daughter. Eighteen months after returning from Iraq, he was deployed again.

Georgia went to pieces when Jason was called up for a third tour of duty, this time in Afghanistan. "They'll keep sending him," Mitch told Carolyn. With so few men, the military had no choice but to reuse the ones they had. "As long as there's war in the Middle East, he'll be going in and coming back." It didn't look like it would end anytime soon.

Every night, Faith said the same prayer. "God, please bless Daddy and bring him home safe and soon. Help GeeGee not to worry so much. God bless Grammy Caro, Bumpa Mitch, Granny H, and Uncle Chris. In Jesus' name, amen."

Then word came that Jason had been wounded and was being airlifted to a hospital in Germany. He wouldn't be sent back into a war zone again. His war-won disabilities would bring him a Purple Heart and commendation, but also very likely an early out from the military. Jason had hoped to serve his full twenty years before returning to civilian life.

Mitch came on the screen. "Hey, darlin'. I miss you two already."

"Thank you for putting us in business class, Mitch. It's luxurious." They talked for a few minutes, and then he let Carolyn's mother take his seat. Even Mom had grown accustomed to sitting in front of a computer and carrying on a conversation via webcam.

"How's our munchkin, honey? Behaving?"

"Momentarily. She's asleep. So is Georgia. They both conked out right after dinner, which was served on white tablecloths with china and silver. Can you believe it?"

"We had pizza on paper plates." Mom winked, so Carolyn knew she was needling Mitch again. Carolyn could hear Mitch laughing and speaking in the background. "Oh, shut up." Mom sighed. "He wants me to tell you I almost lost my dentures. Not to worry though. Your man is taking good care of me."

"Don't forget to use your walker, Mom."

"Now don't you start!"

Mitch leaned down so Carolyn could see both their faces. "Don't worry about us. We get along just fine. If your mother misbehaves, I'll send her to her room." He gave Mom's cheek a brisk kiss. "My turn." Mitch helped Mom off the chair, then sat in front of the monitor. "Someone will be waiting for you at the airport. I arranged a ride to the train station."

Mom leaned down. "I put something in your suitcase, honey. If you have time . . . well, you'll understand. Give Jason a big hug from his granny-in-law."

"The whole church is praying, Carolyn."

Carolyn slept easily after that.

As the train flew down the tracks toward Landstuhl, Carolyn felt Faith pressed close beside her, Puppy Brown still tucked under her arm. He'd fallen from Faith's seat while she slept on the plane. They'd been so busy gathering their things, they had forgotten him. Fortunately, one of the flight attendants spotted the well-worn, well-loved stuffed animal tangled in the blue blanket and caught up with them in the Jetway. Faith had held him at arm's length and told him not to get lost again.

Carolyn kissed Faith on the top of her head. "Your great-great-grandfather came from this country, Faith. He grew up somewhere near Hamburg." Carolyn imagined Oma making her way through Europe to England and eventually boarding a ship to cross the Atlantic, then marrying a German boarder who rented a room in her house. Under other circumstances, they could have been on a heritage trip with Mom and May Flower Dawn.

She and Mitch had talked about Mom's coming, but she refused. "No, no. You need to get to Jason as soon as you can, and I'd hold you back. If I were younger, maybe, but not now. I'm not up to it."

In truth, Carolyn had been relieved. Even with a wheelchair, the trip would have been too grueling for Mom, who had just turned ninety-three. She had a hard enough time getting from her rooms to the dining room table these days. Carolyn and Faith often served tea in Granny's "parlor" rather than have Granny make the long walk to the kitchen.

Carolyn dreaded the time when she wouldn't have Mom with her. The last six years had been precious, a time of finally getting to know each other. God had given them back the years the locusts had eaten, just as Dawn had prayed He would.

When they reached the *Schloss Hotel*, they checked in, went upstairs, dumped their luggage, and then took a cab to the hospital. Georgia had to provide Jason's full name, serial number, and doctor's name at the reception desk. The nurse gave them directions to intensive care. Only one person could go into the room at a time.

Carolyn sat in the waiting room with Faith. "Am I going to see Daddy, Grammy?"

"I hope so, sweetheart. That's why we've come so far."

When Georgia came out, Carolyn knew things weren't good. Her smile wobbled as she took Faith on her lap and said Daddy was sleeping and it might be a while before he'd wake up.

Carolyn went in next. Jason looked like death, with tubes and IVs and everywhere machines beeping and blinking, his head swathed in white. His left leg had been amputated above the knee, his right set in a cast. His left arm was bandaged from wrist to shoulder. Carolyn took Jason's right hand and leaned down. "It's Carolyn, Jason. Faith is here with us. Everyone sends their love. They're all praying. You hold on, soldier. You come back to us." She kissed his brow. "You have Faith, Jason. She needs her daddy."

When Carolyn came out, Georgia stood, holding Faith's hand. The nurse had said she could stay as long as she wanted, and it would be good if she talked to her son. She leaned down and kissed Faith. "Don't wait around here, Carolyn. She needs to go to bed. I'll be fine."

After dinner in the hospital cafeteria and looking in on Jason once more, Carolyn took Faith back to the hotel. She tucked her granddaughter into bed and read *Horton Hears a Who!* again.

"Grammy? Is Daddy going to die?"

Carolyn didn't want to lie. "I don't know, sweetheart."

"Does he still want to be with Mommy?"

Children never missed anything. "Mommy would want him to stay here until you're all grown-up." She held her granddaughter close, and they prayed Daddy would wake up soon and get better.

Georgia didn't come back to the hotel that night.

Getting ready the next morning, Carolyn found the bundle of letters from Oma's friend Rosie Brechtwald tucked under her clothes.

When Carolyn and Faith arrived at the hospital, Georgia was just coming out of Jason's room in intensive care. Tears streamed down her cheeks.

❄ ❄ ❄

"He's going to be okay!" Carolyn cried as she shared the news with Mitch and her mother. Mom leaned down behind Mitch and asked for medical details. "He came out of the coma last night. They're moving him into another room tomorrow morning. That's all I know."

"How's Georgia holding up?"

"She's exhausted, but a lot better than she was." Carolyn ran her hand over her granddaughter's head. Faith grinned around her straw and then went back to drinking her milk. People milled around the hospital cafeteria. "Faith got to see Jason this morning. He's pretty weak right now, but he smiled." She winked at Faith. "A big smile when he saw his little girl."

Mitch asked questions, and Carolyn told him as much as she knew. "He'll be sent back to the States for rehabilitation. Texas, I think." Carolyn spotted Georgia entering the cafeteria and waved her over. "Georgia just came in. She's smiling. There must be more good news."

Georgia leaned in to say hi to Mitch and Hildie, then asked Faith if she wanted to talk with Daddy. He was asking for her. Georgia took Faith by the hand, and Carolyn said she'd follow in a minute.

"Mitch, I've been thinking about going to Switzerland in a few days, as soon as we know everything is fine with Jason. I'd like to see Oma's hometown. Would that be all right with you?"

Mitch nodded. "Mom told me about the letters. Maybe you can even find someone from your grandmother's friend's family to give them to."

"I don't know if *Hotel Edelweiss* is still there, but I'll see what I can find. Georgia will keep Faith here. We bought a few games and crayons and a coloring book to keep her occupied. She's been good as gold. Jason told her she's going to grow up to be as beautiful as her mommy. He's been carrying a picture of May Flower Dawn he took when they were first married and living in San Luis Obispo. Faith thought she was an angel with a halo of light. Jason told Faith her mommy always read her Bible in the morning as the sun was coming up. I told Jason I want a copy of that picture. It would make a wonderful portrait."

Mom leaned closer so Carolyn could see her on the screen. "Take lots of pictures, honey. I'd love to see where Oma grew up."

❄ ❄ ❄

Carolyn searched the Internet and booked one night at the *Hotel Schweizerhof* in Zurich. The grand old hotel was expensive, but it was right across the street from the train station. Now that her plans were falling into place, she felt like a child facing the first day of school. She laughed silently at herself. Oma had gone around the world by the age of twenty-three! It seemed ludicrous to hesitate in the face of any challenge with Oma's blood running through her veins. "You have to take life by the horns," Oma said once.

Oma had certainly done that. Oma had told her about the fake Count and Countess Saintonge who ran the housekeeping school in Bern, about Herr Derry Weib and Chef Warner Brennholtz at the *Hotel Germania* in Interlaken. She had talked about Lady Daisy Stockhard and her spinster daughter, Miss Millicent, always on the hunt for a suitable husband. It had surprised Carolyn to find out Mom hadn't heard any of those stories.

She got up early, packed, and kissed Faith on the forehead. Georgia walked her to the door. "I don't know how to thank you and Mitch for flying me over here, Carolyn."

Carolyn hugged her. "Jason's our son, too. I'll call tonight so you can tell me how our boy is doing."

She caught the early train to Zurich. The scenery was glorious, the passengers friendly. *Hotel Schweizerhof* couldn't have been more convenient. She checked in and asked where she might do some shopping. Her winter coat kept her warm in Sonoma County, California, but she knew after walking from the train station that it wouldn't suffice in the Alpine country of Switzerland. And she'd need boots instead of walking shoes.

She hunted from store to store until she found a coat and boots at reasonable prices. After a late lunch in Old Town, she headed back toward *Hotel Schweizerhof.* She spotted the ornately beautiful

Swiss National Museum, but it was too late in the day to visit. She went inside the Central Station and had dinner in a café where she could watch travelers come and go.

She called Georgia that evening.

"Jason was in a lot of pain today. Faith and I went out for a long walk." Georgia laughed. "I needed to wear her out before we went back to the hospital." Faith had crawled up into bed with Jason while Georgia was in the bathroom. "The nurse found her asleep next to her father, with Puppy Brown tucked under her chin. When she started to move her, Jason told her to leave her there."

Before calling it a night, Carolyn e-mailed Mitch.

> Hotel Schweizerhof is a grand, glorious old hotel right across from the train station where I dined this evening. I'm having dessert now—a bar of Lindt white chocolate with almonds, which was delivered, free of charge, to my room. Tell Mom I'll bring her some. Off to Steffisburg tomorrow.

❄ ❄ ❄

Carolyn caught the morning train to Thun. Resting her chin in her hand, she gazed out the window at one picture-perfect Christmas scene after another passing by. Small bursts of color, painted or natural, splashed against the white. The Alps rose like mighty sentinels on guard.

The two-hour train ride passed quickly, and she found herself standing once again in the crisp Swiss air, her breath steaming like a dragon's. The station manager spoke English. Yes, *Hotel Edelweiss* was still in business, though it didn't take in as many guests as it once had. He knew the family very well. "Ilse Bieler and I went to school together." He made two calls. A room was available. A taxi was on its way.

While she waited, snow fell like goose down after a pillow fight. The driver took her along a small river, across a bridge, and along the main street of what had been Oma's childhood hometown. A

white church with a thick bell tower stood at the end before the road curved right. He drove up the hill overlooking Steffisburg and parked in front of a two-story Bernese-style house. A small sign with *Hotel Edelweiss* painted in red had been bolted to the dark wood of the house.

As Carolyn walked up the steps, a woman wearing ski pants and a heavy blue and red sweater opened the door. She had dark hair and brown eyes and looked to be in her late thirties, around the same age May Flower Dawn would be, had she lived. Carolyn felt a sudden welling sense of loss. She introduced herself. "Ludwig Gasel called earlier. He said you have a room."

"Come in, please. I'm Ilse Bieler. My family owns the hotel." The woman stepped back, leaving the doorway open.

Carolyn liked the cozy feel of the stained wood walls, red sofa and chairs, multicolored woven carpet, and fire ablaze and crackling. Ilse Bieler showed her to a room upstairs with a view of the church steeple among the trees. "We have coffee and cookies downstairs," Ilse told her, then closed the door as she went out. Carolyn quickly unpacked and went downstairs. She hadn't come all this way to hide in her room. Ilse Bieler offered coffee. "What brings you to Steffisburg?"

"My grandmother grew up here. I was curious to see if any family members might still be here. She had a special friend who lived here at the *Hotel Edelweiss*."

"Really? What was your grandmother's name?"

"Schneider."

"A common name. Do you know anything about them?"

"Oma said her father was a tailor and her mother a dressmaker. She had an older brother, Hermann. I don't know what happened to him. Her mother died young. And she had a younger sister, too. Her name was Elise."

"Elise." Ilse lifted her shoulders. "Also a common name."

The telephone rang and Ilse excused herself. She spoke German for several minutes and hung up. "The church may have information on your grandmother's family." Ilse suggested Carolyn check

the public records as well, and she told her how to find the building where they were stored. "And you'll meet my grandmother later. She's napping right now. But she knows everyone in town."

The church records gave the date of her great-grandparents' wedding as well as her grandmother's baptism. The town records office yielded drawers of family information that went back to the seventeen hundreds! Overwhelmed, Carolyn said thank you and left. Maybe she would just take lots of pictures around town and then return to Landstuhl. She headed up the hill to *Hotel Edelweiss*.

Ilse introduced her to her grandmother, Etta, a lovely, gray-haired lady around the age of Carolyn's own mother. She switched from German to English and back again with enviable ease, while Ilse served cabbage soup, sausages and vegetables, fried potatoes and onion salad.

Ilse asked Carolyn if she'd found any information about her family at the church or records office.

"A few important dates at the church, and I practically ran out of the records office when I saw how much they had. I could spend the rest of my life going through all of it." She shrugged. "My mother wanted me to take lots of pictures. I think that's what I'll do."

Etta passed the plate of sausages around again. Carolyn told her they were delicious.

"An old family recipe," Etta said with a smile. She cocked her head and studied Carolyn. "You mentioned that your grandmother had a friend here at *Hotel Edelweiss*. Do you know her name?"

"Yes. Rosie Brechtwald. Have you heard of her?"

Etta gasped. "Rosie Brechtwald was my mother! My granddaughter is named after her—Ilse Rose. My mother wrote letters to a friend who ended up in America, but her name was Waltert. Is that your grandmother?"

"Yes! Marta Schneider Waltert. I have your mother's letters with me." Carolyn went to her room, retrieved the bundle, and returned downstairs.

Etta looked delighted. "I grew up on stories of your *oma*. My mother used to read her letters aloud to us. They wrote back and forth for over fifty years! When Mama died, I wrote to Marta, but the letter came back. I would like to hear the end of the story."

"I'd like to hear the beginning and the middle." Carolyn smiled. "I have a hundred questions."

"Do you still have Marta's letters, Mama?" Ilse glanced at Carolyn. "She never throws anything away."

"I'll look in the family trunk after dinner is finished."

❄ ❄ ❄

Etta Bieler brought a box into the living room and set it on the coffee table in front of the fireplace. She took out bundles of letters, tied with faded ribbons. "My mother learned about organization from her father. When he died, she took over this little hotel. She kept perfect files." The letters had been kept in chronological order.

When Carolyn started looking through Oma's letters, her heart sank. "They're written in German." Why hadn't she thought of that? All of Rosie's letters to Oma had been in German.

"Ah, but look in the bottom of the box." Carolyn removed the rest of the letters and found a thick sheaf of papers under them. Etta's eyes twinkled. "My children found the story of their grandmother's friend so fascinating, I encouraged them to translate the letters when they were studying English in school. They enjoyed the practice, and we all enjoyed reading through them again. I remember them very well. Marta's father made her leave school. He sent her to Bern to become a servant." She chuckled. "But your *oma* had bigger dreams than being someone's maid. She wanted to learn French and English so she could have a hotel like this one. Mama said what Marta set out to do, Marta *did*."

"She never had a hotel."

"No, but she owned a boardinghouse in Montreal. That's where she met her husband. They moved to the Canadian wheat fields and, later, to California. It's all in the letters. I think the only thing she didn't plan was meeting your *opa*. We all loved that romantic story. Marta didn't think she would ever marry; then she met handsome Niclas, graduate of Berlin University, also an immigrant. Marta taught him to speak English."

Ilse yawned and said she needed to get to bed. She had to get up early and have breakfast ready for some guests who wanted to go out cross-country skiing. Carolyn apologized for keeping them up so late. "Would you mind if I took these upstairs to read?"

Etta had already begun opening Rosie's letters. "They're yours to keep. Our family enjoyed them, but you must have them. They're part of your family history."

"I can't wait to read them. There is so much I'd like to know about my grandparents. Maybe she wrote about her sister, Elise, too. She sometimes mentioned her to me—even used to tell me I looked like her. But she'd never tell me anything more than that."

Etta looked troubled. "My mother told me the story. It's in the early letters—references to it, not details. You may not want to know."

"I think it's important I do."

"Mama said Elise was very beautiful. I'm sure you do look like her. She was very quiet and painfully shy. She stayed in the shop with her mother while Marta was sent out to work. Mama didn't say much about what went on in your grandmother's family, just that Marta did not have an easy life. Her father sent her to Bern."

"To housekeeping school."

"*Ja*, but Mama said Marta wanted more than that. She went to Interlaken."

"And worked at the *Hotel Germania*."

"That's when her father sent Elise to work for a wealthy family in Thun. It turned out very badly."

Carolyn saw how Etta hesitated. "How badly?"

"The master of the house and his son abused her." She lowered her eyes and Carolyn understood. "Marta took her sister out of that house and brought her home, but Elise was already pregnant. No one knew yet, but the girl never went out after she was brought home. She stayed inside the house. Everyone assumed she was taking care of her mother, who was very ill with consumption. Marta confided in my mother that she feared for Elise. Apparently the girl was very dependent on her mother, whom Marta felt coddled her all too much. Then when her mother died, Elise disappeared. Everyone went searching for her. It was my mother who found Marta's sister by the river. She had frozen to death. And she was heavy with child."

Carolyn closed her eyes. Oma had kept secrets, too. Her sister's rape, an unwed pregnancy, suicide.

Etta went on with the rest of what her mother had told her about a plain girl wounded by a father who didn't love her, but used her as a source of income for the family while her mother languished with consumption and her exquisitely beautiful and delicate sister remained hidden away like Rapunzel inside a tower. When Marta went away to work, her father had demanded a portion of her wages, and Marta capitulated until Rosie Brechtwald had written the truth. "Mama knew Marta would never come back after her mother and sister died."

Carolyn ached for Oma.

"I'm sorry. Perhaps I should not have told you."

"I'm glad you did. It explains so much." No wonder Oma had been so determined to make sure her own children could stand on their own two feet. Cloistered by fear, weakened by a needy mother's coddling, Elise had been unprepared for the world. In the end, she gave up her life without a fight.

How many times had Carolyn considered doing the same thing? Once she had almost walked into the sea. God had used a man wounded by war to draw her back. He'd used an unexpected pregnancy to give her reason to keep on living, to work hard, to accept consequences and blessings along the way. But she had kept silent, too, keeping the pain locked in and pressed down.

"You look like Elise. She was my little sister, and she was very, very pretty, just like you," Oma once said, but wouldn't explain. Yet, Oma hadn't treated Carolyn the same way she had treated Mom. Oma had held her close, told her repeatedly she loved her,

encouraged her to step out in faith. Oma had learned that with-holding love might make a daughter strong, but also left deep wounds. On both sides.

❄ ❄ ❄

Carolyn read the letters translated by Etta's children and tucked them into the corresponding originals written by Oma in German. She read until her eyes blurred.

I am in England. Papa sent a wire telling me to come home. He said nothing about either Elise or Mama, and I knew he would expect me to spend the rest of my life in the shop. . . .

Cousin Felda said it was you who found Elise. I dream of her every night. . . .

Later, Oma moved away from London to "better air" and lived and worked in the "fine Tudor home" of Lady Daisy Stockhard, who loved high tea every afternoon at four o'clock. When one of the other servants left to get married, Oma replaced her as Lady Daisy's companion.

She is a most unusual lady. I have never known anyone to discuss so many interesting topics. She doesn't treat her servants like slaves, but is genuinely interested in our lives. She had me sit with her in church last Sunday.

Her daughter is never happy with anything, not even her mother. She is off on another hunt for a husband, and when she's gone, everyone in the house breathes easier, even Lady Stockhard.

Oma wrote of the long voyage to Canada:

I had days when I would have jumped overboard to end my misery if I could have climbed the stairs to reach the deck. They have packed us like cattle in a barn. The woman in the bunk next to me moans day and night. I know how she feels, but sometimes think about putting a pillow over her head, if I had a pillow. I can laugh about it now that I am on terra firma again.

And in Canada, she found so much more than she was looking for.

Dear Rosie,
I am married!
I never thought anyone would want me, and certainly never a man like Niclas Bernhard Waltert. . . . I thought I was happy when I bought my boardinghouse, but I have never been as truly happy as this. It makes me afraid sometimes. . . .

Carolyn understood the feeling of unworthiness all too well. She continued reading. Oma's letters changed. Disappointment set in when Niclas lost his job at the railroad and decided to become a farmer. Oma couldn't understand how a man of learning would want to work the land.

Dearest Rosie,
Niclas has left me and gone off to work on a wheat farm in Manitoba. He went away three weeks ago and I

have not heard from him since. I begin to understand how
Elise felt when she walked out into the snow. . . .

I would have given anything for an education, but
Papa said schooling was wasted on a girl. And Niclas,
who has the knowledge to be a professor, wants to throw it all
away and live out in the middle of nowhere tilling soil and
planting wheat. He wants me to sell the boardinghouse. He
wants me to go on this "adventure" with him. I would kill
him if I didn't love him so much. . . .

Opa had gone alone, and Oma's letters showed how much she
suffered for her decision.

Why must I give up everything I have worked so hard to
gain to follow a man whose dream will impoverish us? But
how can I not? Life is barren without Niclas. I will have
his child soon. . . .

Carolyn read of life on a wheat farm miles from the nearest
town, winters when the temperature dropped well below zero, a
landlord who cared nothing about their plight and cheated them
out of their share of the profits. She wrote lovingly of Bernhard,
and she worried about the new baby coming.

Several months passed before Oma wrote another letter, and
it held the first mention of Hildemara Rose.

I fear for this little one. I understand now how Mama's
heart broke every time she held Elise. She was small and
frail, too. . . .

Pray for your namesake, Rosie. One breath from heaven could blow her away, but God forbid I go too far in protecting her and bring her up to be weak like Elise.

Opa and Oma left the farm and went to Winnipeg. Opa went back to work for the railroad. Another child came.

Our third child, Clotilde Anna, arrived a month after Niclas went back to work. She is as robust as Bernhard, and every bit as loud in her demands.

Soon, Opa began to talk about farming again. This time he was dreaming of California.

The man will not be happy until he has his way. And I am tired of fighting with him.

Life in California was difficult. First the family lived in a tent by an irrigation ditch, then in a structure not much better on a farm owned by . . .

. . . Mrs. Miller, who orders us around like serfs while she and her daughter, Miss Charlotte, sit on their behinds and listen to radio programs in the big house. The wind and rain blow through ours, and she expects us to pay for "improvements." The children have constant colds. I fear most for Hildemara Rose. She has Mama's constitution. . . .

Oma reported on the achievements of Bernhard and Clotilde and Rikka in a matter-of-fact way, but her eldest daughter perplexed her and seemed a constant worry.

What must I do to make my girl strong? Niclas tells me to be gentle with her, to love her for the child she is. But he doesn't understand what happens to a child who cannot stand up for herself. I can't give in and become like Mama, coddling and protecting her. . . . I would rather she hate me than end up like Elise.

And then the day came when Hildemara got the courage to speak up. Carolyn could hardly imagine the scene as Oma's letter described it.

After all this time, my girl speaks up to me and what do I do? I slap her across the face. I did it without even thinking. I had said something hurtful to Niclas, and he left the table, and Hildemara Rose exposed my shame. . . .

I could see the hurt in her eyes. I wanted to shake her. I wanted to tell her she had every right to scream at me. She doesn't have to sit there and take it! She would have turned the other cheek if I'd raised my hand to her again.

I have not cried so much in years, Rosie. Not since Mama and Elise died.

Carolyn lay back and closed her eyes. She'd never seen Oma cry, never guessed the depth of pain she carried. Oma had gone to her grave in silence, still wounded. Carolyn realized how alike they were, and Mom, too. *How many other unhealthy coping tools have we passed down, Lord? Show us, so we can turn swords into plowshares.* Wiping tears away, she thanked God again for May Flower Dawn. God had used her and other prayer warriors to bring the walls between generations tumbling down. *I miss her, Lord. I had so little time with her.*

And she felt His answer. *You have time and eternity.*

Then Hildemara further asserted herself by choosing to go to nursing school, against Oma's wishes. But when she graduated at the head of her class, Oma's pride was evident.

> *She is not a timid child anymore. My girl knows her place in the world. I am so proud of her, Rosie.*

Opa got cancer.

> *I had no choice but to ask Hildemara to give up her life and come home. He needs a nurse. He worsens by the day and I can't bear to see him in such pain. She is a great comfort to us both.*

Oma grieved over Opa's passing, then began to worry about Hildemara Rose again. She didn't return to Merritt Hospital, where she had been working before Oma asked her to come home and take care of Papa. Carolyn knew a crisis was on the horizon, and in the next letter, it had happened.

> *A young man came to Niclas's funeral. I had never seen him before, and Hildemara had never mentioned him. But I knew when I saw them together, they love each other. She had it in her head that she had to stay and take care*

of me. As if I cannot take care of myself! I said enough yesterday to make her pack and leave. I appreciate all she's done, but enough is enough.

I offered to drive her to the bus station this morning, hoping for a chance to explain myself a little better. But she had already asked her brother to take her.

She was hurt and angry, once again misunderstanding my intentions. When will she understand how much I love her? How easy it would have been to let her stay and be my comfort! But at what cost to her? Elise was Mama's comfort and suffered for it. So did Mama in the end, though she didn't live with the fullness of it. No matter how much it hurts, I must be strong for Hildemara Rose's sake.

When Hildemara became sick with tuberculosis, Oma lived in fear of her dying.

I went to Arroyo del Valle to see Hildemara Rose. She had Mama's pallor and the deep shadows under her eyes. I could see no life in them when I first arrived. It terrified me. . . . I called her a coward. Though it broke my heart, I mocked and belittled her. Thank God she got good and mad. Her eyes spit fire at me and I wanted to laugh with joy.

Better she hate me for a while than give up on life and be put in an early grave. She was trying to get up when I walked away. . . .

Carolyn blinked back tears as she read Oma's description of Charlie's birth. *Oh, Charlie. I still miss you so much it hurts.* Oma was concerned even then about the breach between herself and Mom.

Hildemara Rose and I get along, but there is a wall between us. I know I built it. I doubt she's forgiven me for my harsh words at the sanatorium, and I will not apologize for them. I may have to prod her again. I'll do whatever I must to keep her spirits up. Oh, but it hurts me so to do it. I wonder if she will ever understand me.

No, Oma, I don't think she ever did. At least not yet.

Years later, Oma wrote about the gold, jade, and pearl brooch. Carolyn fingered it as she read.

I was so stunned and touched by Hildemara's gift, I said something stupid. I could see the hurt in her eyes. It's become a bad habit, saying hurtful things to her. I reached out, but she'd already turned away, and I had no voice to call her back. I take out the brooch every day and look at it. My girl has a fine, generous heart. . . .

Oma had tried to reach out to Mom in those later years, and Mom shrank back. Mom and Oma never had someone who pulled them together the way May Flower Dawn had done for Carolyn and Mom. She had built a bridge so the same mistake wouldn't be carried into the next generation.

Sometimes seeds fell on rock, but they still found a way to grow, to press up toward the sun, to cling to life no matter what. Oma had done that. She had left a legacy. *Endure whatever life dishes out.*

Learn all you can. Count your blessings. Never give up. Keep growing in the Lord.

One week with Oma had changed May Flower Dawn. Oma said once her great-granddaughter had a teachable spirit.

Dawn had been the best of all the women in their family. She had Oma's drive and ambition, not for possessions, but to become the woman God intended her to be. She had become a nurse like her grandmother, caring for others. Carolyn often wondered what qualities she might have passed along to Dawn, and she realized her daughter had been broken, too, and humbled. But God had not crushed the tender reed.

❄ ❄ ❄

Carolyn came down for breakfast and found the other guests already on their way out. Etta set a basket of fresh rolls on the sideboard as Carolyn poured herself a cup of coffee. "I was up most of the night reading the letters. I've certainly learned a lot about my grandparents . . . and my mother. Thank you so much for giving them to me."

Etta smiled. "I grew up on stories of Marta's adventures. Your *oma* was a remarkable woman. I would love to have met her."

The telephone rang. Etta held it out. "It's for you."

Georgia. "Jason is being transferred to Brooke Army Medical Center in San Antonio. He'll be flown to the States in a few days. We're ready to go home anytime you are."

Carolyn Skyped Mitch and gave him the good news, then asked, "Is Mom already in bed?"

"No, she fell asleep on the couch while we were watching the news." He chuckled. "I'm in my office and I can hear her snoring."

"Can you get her? I have something important to tell her."

It took several minutes before Mom appeared in front of the monitor. "Mitch said you wanted to talk to me."

"I'm at *Hotel Edelweiss* with Rosie Brechtwald's daughter. Oma loved you, Mom. She was proud of you."

"I know."

"No, Mom, you don't know. But I have proof, lots of it, and it's all in Oma's handwriting. Rosie Brechtwald saved all of Oma's letters. Her daughter gave them to me. You'll be able to read them when I get home."

"Did you take lots of pictures?" Mom's voice had a tremor.

"Yes, Mom. At least a hundred."

"When you and Faith get home, we'll have tea and cookies and make an album together."

"Sounds wonderful."

They would talk about things they had kept hidden, shine light on the shadows, cast out any remaining doubts.

"I love you, Mom. I'll see you soon."

"I love you, too, honey. I always have."

❄ ❄ ❄

Love one another, Jesus said. Sometimes it took a lifetime to learn how. Sometimes it took hitting rock bottom to make someone reach up and grasp hold and be lifted from the mire to stand on a firm foundation.

Sometimes a child had to show them how to love, and another child, left behind, had to remind them to take one step at a time.

Faith. How appropriately Dawn had named her child. Every time Carolyn said it, she remembered what May Flower Dawn had dreamed. So did Mom. So did Jason. So did every member of the family. *Keep faith. Nurture it. Let it grow. Watch what can happen when you do.*

God would light the way. Faith would keep them on the right path.

A Note from the Author

Dear Reader,

    Since I became a Christian, my stories have begun with struggles I'm having in my own faith walk, or issues that I haven't worked out. That's how this two-book series started. I wanted to explore what caused the rift between my grandma and my mom during the last years of my grandmother's life. Was it a simple misunderstanding that they never had time to work out? or something deeper that had grown over the years?

    Many of the events of this story were inspired by family history that I researched and events I read about in my mother's journals or experienced in my own life. You may have guessed that Carolyn is my alter ego. But only some of my life is interwoven through hers. Mom did have tuberculosis when I was a little girl, and Grandma did move in to help while Mom recuperated at home. When Mom was well enough, we moved to a piece of property where they built their own home from the foundation up. I still love the scent of sawdust. But unlike the Arundels, our family was close.

Francine as a little girl with her dog Dusty

We had sit-down dinners and lingered around the table, talking. In many ways, growing up in the fifties and early sixties in California was like living in Camelot. I had an idyllic childhood, despite the serious things happening—the "Red Scare," the Cuban Missile Crisis, and Kennedy's assassination. My dad, along with other neighbors, built a bomb shelter. (Last I heard, people have converted them into wine cellars.)

Francine as a high school student

Like Carolyn, I've known my husband, Rick, since we were children. My brother, Everett King, served in the armed forces like Trip, Charlie, and Jason. He was in Army intelligence and was wounded and captured during the Tet Offensive of '68. By the grace of God, he escaped. It was his story in the hometown paper that brought Rick back into my life. Rick was serving in the Marine Corps and stationed in Vietnam at the same time my brother was. Rick's mom sent him a newspaper clipping about my brother being MIA and, later, one about his escape. Rick wrote to me and said I was lucky to have my brother back alive. We started a correspondence, dated when he returned, and married a year after he came home.

Rick got an early out for Vietnam service and went back to college, first to Chabot junior college and then to UC Berkeley, where he graduated with a degree in American history. However, aviation was in his blood, and he started his own business— Rivers Aviation Services. We had three small children by then, and all of us spent time together at the office. Our children played in the packing materials, hiding in the Styrofoam peanuts, thinking we didn't know where they were. They grew up helping out and learning what it means to work hard and build something together.

Francine and Rick's engagement photo

Like Carolyn, I lost faith in God for a time and then (much later than she) cried out to Him. Carolyn suffered more insecurities and hardships, but many of us have to "hit bottom" before we acknowledge our need for Jesus as Savior *and* Lord. Rescue is never enough. We still have to walk through the rest of our lives. Trusting God has a plan and purpose for each of us frees us to move forward, knowing— in Christ—we have great potential.

Though this saga often focuses on mother-daughter relationships, the men in both books play important roles, too. I never knew my grandfather, though I like to imagine he was like Niclas. He died of liver cancer before I was born. He was Mom's first private patient. Mom once told me he sang German hymns in the orchard when he was working. Trip reminds me of my father, who served as a captain in the U.S. Army during World War II and was a medic during the second wave on D-day. He had dreamed of being a doctor, but gave it up to be a police officer and, eventually, coroner and public administrator of Alameda County. He never shared details of the war. (Neither did Rick's father, who spent three and a half years in Los Baños, an infamous Japanese prison camp in the Philippines.)

Mitch is very much like my husband, Rick. He loves me despite my faults. We've grown up together and encourage one another in our faith. He's given me the freedom to do what God has called me to and is my biggest encourager and supporter (literally—for years while I didn't make a cent off my writing). And Jason has similari-

Francine (far right) with her mother and grandmother

ties to our son-in-law, Rich, a hardworking young man of faith who joined the military to offer our daughter, Shannon, a better life. After four years on the other side of the country, he left the Air Force and entered the private sector. We are blessed to have them living in the same town (blessed also that our sons and their spouses and children are all close by). Rich is my "tech support," and Shannon manages my Web site.

During the past three years of working on Marta's Legacy, I have come away with a heart full of wonderful memories and valuable lessons hard-won by Grandma and Mom, but passed down lovingly to me. I am grateful. Neither ever felt she measured up, but that did not stop them from encouraging me. May Flower Dawn begins as a self-centered child and grows into a grace-filled, wise woman. Her journey is one every woman hopes to witness in her daughter, as I am witnessing in mine.

Our experiences may be different. The times in which we have grown up may be poles apart. Yet I know I share the same longings of my grandmother, mother, and daughter. I want to be loved and accepted as I am. I want purpose. As I grow older and look back over my life, I want to leave a legacy of faith in Jesus Christ. Like Marta, I want my children and grandchildren to stand firm in faith no matter what the world throws at them. I want them to know that while they wait for heaven, God has a good purpose for them right here in this chaotic world filled with lost souls longing for the kind of love, acceptance, and purpose they will find only in Christ Jesus.

And, like Marta, I dream we will all one day be together with our Lord, having cast off the imperfection of human nature, transformed into Christlike children of the King of kings.

Proverbs 3:5-6
Francine Rivers

Discussion Guide

1. Both Hildie and Trip miss some obvious signs that something traumatic has happened to Carolyn. What are they? Later, in chapter 4, when Hildie and Trip argue about Hildie's going back to work, Trip says, "A little girl shouldn't be alone so much. Things could happen." Discuss the irony in that statement. What is it about their family dynamics that makes Carolyn vulnerable to a predator like Dock?

2. Do you think Hildie's character changes from book 1 to book 2? If so, how does she change and why? Did you like her more or less in this book?

3. Carolyn runs away—literally and figuratively—after getting the news of her brother's tragic death. Is that a realistic response? Why or why not? Have you ever wished you could run away from a painful reality? How did you deal with it? Have you ever been in the place of Carolyn's parents and grandmother—not knowing the whereabouts of someone you love? What was that like? What advice would you give someone who is facing such a situation?

4. When Carolyn meets Mary in Golden Gate Park, Mary says she felt an impulse to make extra sandwiches that morning, even though she had no idea why. Have you ever felt God nudging you to do something you didn't understand? Did you follow through on that impulse? Why or why not?

5. After Carolyn comes home following her two-year disappearance, neither Hildie nor Trip presses her for details about what happened. Do you think that is wise? How does this both help and hurt Carolyn? In your own life, how can you balance being nosy with being concerned for those you love?

6. When Carolyn graduates from college and pays off her debt to her parents, Trip and Hildie give the money back to her. Were you surprised by Trip and Hildie's action? Why or why not? Why is it hard for Carolyn to accept their gift? Have you ever given or received an unexpected, extravagant gift? What was the motivation behind it? What was the response?

7. For many years, Carolyn finds more appealing fellowship and support in AA than she does in the church. Why is that? What does that say about AA? about the church? What finally changes Carolyn's view of Christians? Do you know anyone who has a negative view of the church? What could you say or do to encourage that person to give the church another chance? What other influences does God bring into Carolyn's life to show her the truth of His love for her?

8. Near the end of the story, Hildie reflects that God sent Mitch to rescue her, just as he had rescued Carolyn years earlier. In what ways does Mitch "rescue" Carolyn? How might her life have been different if she had never married? if she had married someone less understanding and supportive?

9. Marta's choice not to move to Jenner by the Sea with Hildie and Trip seems to finally make the gap between mother and daughter so wide it can't be crossed. Why does Hildie think

Marta doesn't want to move in with them? What does Marta really want? Why are they unable to discuss it rationally?

10. In chapter 30, when Dawn and Carolyn go to visit Marta for a week, Marta says that "making things easier on your children is sometimes the worst thing you can do." Do you agree or disagree? How do you see this illustrated in the story? in your own life?

11. How does Marta change over the course of the two books? What changes her the most? In what ways is she still the same?

12. When Dawn confesses to her mother that she slept with Jason, Carolyn's response is gracious and nonjudgmental. How do Carolyn's own experiences play into her response to Dawn? How would you respond to such a confession from your son or daughter? How would you like to respond?

13. How does Dawn's experience of the church after she sleeps with Jason differ from Carolyn's experience after returning from Haight-Ashbury? Why is it different? How does Paster Daniel's gracious response affect Dawn's future and her walk with Christ? Have you ever been in a position to counsel someone who has made a mistake they think cannot be forgiven? What did (or would) you say?

14. Near the end of the story, Dawn makes an important decision that affects the life of her unborn child. How might her struggle with miscarriage and infertility have affected her decision? What would you have done in Dawn's place? Discuss her choice not to talk about it with either her husband or her family. Was that the right way to handle it? Why or why not? How do you think Jason felt when he learned what had happened?

15. In chapter 55, Dawn reads this excerpt from Marta's journal: "We try to do a little better than the previous generation and find out in the end we've made the same mistakes without intending." How do you see this illustrated in the story? How

have you seen negative behaviors easily turn into a habit in your own life, as Hildie mentions in chapter 56?

16. When the three generations (Hildemara, Carolyn, and May Flower Dawn) finally sit down to talk, they discuss many of their "family secrets." Discuss the revelations and the effect of finally getting them out into the open. Are you satisfied with what they talk about and how it goes? In what way do you wish it had been handled differently? Are the responses realistic and/or what you expected?

17. At one point, Marta tells Dawn that people either weigh you down or give you wings. How do some of the characters in this saga give people wings? What can you do in your own relationships to give those you love wings instead of weighing them down?

18. While Scripture makes it clear that children are not held responsible for their parents' sins (see Ezekiel 18:20), it's also true that destructive patterns tend to continue in families and have a negative impact on successive generations (see Exodus 20:5). Over the span of these two novels, what relationship patterns are repeated between mothers and daughters? between grandmothers and granddaughters? In what ways are the patterns finally broken? Is the resolution realistic? What relationship patterns—either negative or positive—have occurred in your family? If the patterns are negative, what have you done or what could you do to break them?

19. Are there secrets in your family—either from generations past or from the present? To whom would you like to talk about these secrets? What kind of response do you think you would get? What response would you hope for?

20. This novel contains many relationships, conversations, rifts, and moments of reconciliation. Take a few minutes to list some of your favorite scenes and tell why you were especially touched or challenged by them.

About the Author

New York Times best-selling author Francine Rivers began her literary career at the University of Nevada, Reno, where she graduated with a bachelor of arts degree in English and journalism. From 1976 to 1985, she had a successful writing career in the general market, and her books were highly acclaimed by readers and reviewers. Although raised in a religious home, Francine did not truly encounter Christ until later in life, when she was already a wife, a mother of three, and an established romance novelist.

Shortly after becoming a born-again Christian in 1986, Francine wrote *Redeeming Love* as her statement of faith. First published by Bantam Books, and then rereleased by Multnomah Publishers in the mid-1990s, this retelling of the biblical story of Gomer and Hosea, set during the time of the California Gold Rush, is now considered by many to be a classic work of Christian fiction. *Redeeming Love* continues to be one of CBA's top-selling titles, and it has held a spot on the Christian best-seller list for nearly a decade.

Since *Redeeming Love*, Francine has published numerous novels with Christian themes—all best sellers—and she has continued to win both industry acclaim and reader loyalty around the globe. Her Christian novels have been awarded or nominated for numerous honors, including the RITA Award, the Christy Award, the ECPA Gold Medallion, and the Holt Medallion in Honor of Outstanding Literary Talent. In 1997, after winning her third RITA Award for inspirational fiction, Francine was inducted into the Romance Writers of America Hall of Fame. Francine's novels have been translated into more than twenty different languages, and she enjoys best-seller status in many foreign countries, including Germany, the Netherlands, and South Africa.

Francine and her husband, Rick, live in northern California and enjoy time spent with their three grown children and taking every opportunity to spoil their grandchildren. Francine uses her writing to draw closer to the Lord, and she desires that through her work she might worship and praise Jesus for all He has done and is doing in her life.

Visit her Web site at www.francinerivers.com.

BOOKS BY BELOVED AUTHOR
FRANCINE RIVERS

The Mark of the Lion series
(available individually or as a boxed set)
A Voice in the Wind
An Echo in the Darkness
As Sure as the Dawn

A Lineage of Grace series
(available individually or in an anthology)
Unveiled
Unashamed
Unshaken
Unspoken
Unafraid

Sons of Encouragement series
The Priest
The Warrior
The Prince
The Prophet
The Scribe

Marta's Legacy series
Her Mother's Hope
Her Daughter's Dream

Children's Titles
The Shoe Box
Bible Stories for Growing Kids
(coauthored with Shannon
Rivers Coibion)

Stand-alone Titles
Redeeming Love
The Atonement Child
The Scarlet Thread
The Last Sin Eater
Leota's Garden
And the Shofar Blew
The Shoe Box (a Christmas novella)

www.francinerivers.com

CP0098

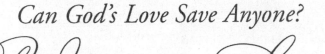
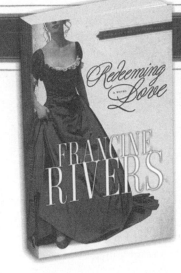